SHATTERED VOW

EVA CHASE

SHADOWBLOOD SOULS - BOOK 1

Shattered Vow

Book 1 in the Shadowblood Souls series

First Digital Edition, 2022

Cover design: Sanja Balan (Sanja's Covers)

Ebook ISBN: 978-1-990338-99-1

Paperback ISBN: 978-1-998752-00-3

BEFORE

Riva

When we said our goodbyes for the last time, the guys each held my gaze for a little longer than usual, as if they thought they could send some of their strength into me with their eyes.

The urge to hug all of them twined through my body, sharp as barbed wire when I resisted it. But I couldn't give in to the longing.

We never made a big production of parting ways at the end of the day, and we couldn't risk giving away that anything was unusual about this farewell. Not with the guardians watching: several in the gymnasium with us and others through the cameras mounted by the ceiling.

If we wanted to ensure that after tonight they could never separate us again, we had to be so careful. They had to believe that *we* believed we'd see each other in here tomorrow morning like always.

Who knew what they'd do to us if they realized what we were planning.

So far, the six of us had managed to act like everything was normal throughout today's training and socializing session. It helped that it'd been one of the easy days, basic testing rather than torment.

I'd raced Zian around the track twice as fast as any of the others could have run until our breaths came ragged.

Debated with Jacob about which of the knives would make the most effective long-distance projectile.

Plotted a hypothetical course across mapped terrain with Dominic's hesitant but thoughtful input.

Laughed at Andreas's banter while he decided to teach himself how to juggle, with only partial success.

Dropped onto the sofa next to Griffin during a break, when he put on the TV show only he knew was my secret favorite.

The other guys said the soap opera was corny with all the relationships that kept rearranging themselves after the characters' melodramatic outbursts, but Griffin pretended it was *his* favorite so that they'd heckle him instead of me. Because that was just how he was.

"You've got your tough-girl reputation to maintain, Riva," he'd told me once with one of his soft but brilliant smiles when I'd tried to say he didn't have to take the heat. "I'm allowed to be the sappy one."

But despite all our efforts, on the inside today's session didn't feel normal to me at all. The knowledge of what we were planning to do tonight weighed on my shoulders like a backpack full of bricks. Heavier bricks than any I'd actually carried before.

Our escape depended on me—on that toughness Griffin had talked about.

The weight became almost suffocating when I waved to the guys as the guardians escorted me and Griffin out first.

Andreas winked at me. "See you tomorrow, Tink." The silly nickname—born after we'd first watched *Peter Pan* as little kids and Drey had declared me as tiny as Tinkerbell —didn't do much to reassure me.

But then Zian mouthed the words that had become our mantra over the years as we'd prepared for this moment: *We are blood.*

With that phrase resonating through my body alongside my pulse, I walked out with my chin up.

Everything depended on me, but we were in it together. We were entwined by the strange powers that were ours alone and the eerie substance that ran through our veins.

The guardians always took Griffin and me first because our rooms were on the highest floor of the underground complex. In hushed conversations, the six of us had determined that Andreas and Dominic were one level below, and Jacob and Zian the level below that.

Beneath them were the training rooms we were leaving now. We had no idea how much farther down the facility might reach beyond that.

Sometimes I pictured it as a vast pit in the earth sinking down, down, down, all the way to the molten core some people called Hell. The image seemed fitting.

Hell seemed like exactly the word for the throbbing strain that would ripple through my body on the days they prodded my unearthly strength with their strange machines. For the sickening sight of the prop animals— and sometimes people—they tortured in front of me to gauge my reactions.

For the things they did to the guys in their own solo sessions that left them with anguish etched on their faces.

They probably thought they'd been *kind* to us today instead of just not totally horrific.

Even for a simple trip back to our rooms, the guardians always made sure to outnumber us. Four of them strode along in a ring around Griffin and me, the harsh artificial light glancing off their weird metal helmets and vests.

I sucked a little air in through my mouth, tasting and smelling it at the same time. The four today gave off pheromones with a faint tang of nervousness, but nothing extreme.

They weren't anywhere near as worried about what we could do as they probably should have been.

They didn't know I could now run even faster than I had in my race with Zian today. Or that the guy walking alongside me could not only pick up on other people's emotions but throw his own at them.

We'd learned to hide new talents as they emerged as much as we could during their brutal evaluations. And as long as our jailers didn't discover those talents in their tests, they wouldn't be guarding against them.

We marched up the blank white stairwell into a blank white hall to the blank white doors of what might as well have been prison cells. The guardians opened our doors across the hall from each other with a blue keycard.

Griffin raised his hand to my cheek and gave one of the silvery strands that'd slipped free from my braid a gentle tug. When we were little, he'd told me the pale streaks of hair falling over the slate-gray underneath looked like moonlight streaming through the night.

He smiled at me, a soft glint lighting in his sky-blue eyes. "Sleep well, Moonbeam."

"You too, Emo Boy," I retorted, and treasured the peal of his laugh as the door shut between us.

On the small table across from my bed, I found my dinner waiting: roast chicken leg, mashed potatoes, boiled carrots. I shoveled it down my throat without processing the flavor. It wasn't like there was a whole lot to miss anyway.

To pass the time afterward, I tapped the controls on the panel over the table to turn on the music channel I liked best. Lush melodies and thumping beats swept through the room.

Normally I'd have swayed along with them, maybe even gotten to my feet and let my whole body move with the music the way I never did when the guys could see me. I probably looked ridiculous when I danced, but I didn't care if I was on my own. It felt good.

It was one of the few specks of goodness I *could* cling on to in this place when I was alone.

But tonight I was too wound up to sink into the music. And if the guardians were watching from their cameras, my tension would become obvious the more I moved.

I couldn't let anything raise their suspicions.

Instead, I flopped down on my bed to simply listen.

My hand rose to the pendant that rested against my sternum.

Griffin had brought pewter necklaces back for all of us one of the first times he'd gone on a solo mission in the wider world, using the cash the guardians had given him. I couldn't imagine they'd intended it for that purpose, but for whatever reason, they'd let us keep the gifts.

Maybe that tiny act of generosity made them feel better about everything else they inflicted on us.

My fingers clicked apart the metal cat from the sculpted ball of yarn it was curled around and then snapped them back into place on their rolling joint.

Click. Snap. Click. Snap.

The rhythm settled my nerves just a little bit. I closed my eyes as if I were tired from today's workout, though I hadn't pushed myself anywhere close to my real limits.

One song bled into the next until the lights went out. In the darkness, I kept my eyes closed and pretended to sleep. But my thoughts only got louder.

What would it be like, out in the wider world without the guardians controlling our every movement, jabbing and zapping us if we resisted—or just because they felt like it?

I'd gotten a taste of freedom on my own missions, but those had always been alone. Alone, and knowing that if I disobeyed my orders, the guys I'd left behind here at the facility would pay for my defiance.

Once we were out there and free… could I let them all know how I felt about them? All the longings and hungers that were so much more secret than what TV shows I liked or how I danced?

Griffin knew, because Griffin could absorb emotions like I inhaled stress chemicals. We'd never talked about it openly, but sometimes when a flash of desire or a pang of affection hit me around the other guys, he'd catch my eye and give me a subtle nod, as if to tell me it was all right.

"We're blood, remember?" he'd assured me once, without ever saying exactly what he was talking about. "We're going to be here for each other in every way. It's *better* if no one's left out. The other guys will see it that way too."

Could he really be so sure about that? There were definitely times when I got into a friendly bickering match with Jacob and thought there was more than just passion for the debate flaring in his eyes. Or when I wrestled with Zian and his breath seemed to hitch at the exact same time mine did as our bodies collided.

When Dominic scooted just a little closer to me while we sat together in companionable silence. When Andreas's gaze lingered on my lips while he paid me a compliment I'd otherwise have taken as teasing.

But that didn't mean they'd be okay with me wanting *all* of them. If soap operas had taught me anything, it was how pissed off people could get when someone wanted to kiss more than one dude at the same time.

I shoved away the images my mind had conjured. We could figure out the rest once we had the space to do it, without guardians monitoring and dictating our every move.

After a while, the music shut off too. That meant it was really late. I willed myself not to tense up, to keep lying there in fake slumber.

The lock on my door beeped, and my pulse stuttered. As the door swung open, I sprang off the bed, claws springing from my fingertips instinctively with a rush of adrenaline.

The guardian in the dim hall outside stared at me with a befuddled expression. Just behind him, I made out Griffin's face, taut with strain.

It must have taken more energy than I could imagine for him to push so much emotion on the guardian that the man had felt compelled to unlock not just Griffin's room but mine as well.

Now, I took over.

Before Griffin's emotional control could slip, I sprang at the guardian.

One swipe of my hand knocked the helmet from the man's head. My other fist whipped at his temple at just the right angle and power to knock him out.

Our jailers had trained us well. The guardian slumped to the floor with a thud of his ass and a faint groan.

One down, who knew how many more to go.

I heaved the man into the room and tore up my sheet with swift jerks of my inhumanly strong arms. One strip, I wrapped around the man's mouth to gag him. With the others, I bound his wrists and ankles to the bedposts.

He wouldn't stay unconscious for long, and when he woke up, I didn't want him raising the alarm.

Griffin darted in after me and patted the man down. He grabbed the blue keycard and grimaced.

"He doesn't have any of the other cards," he said under his breath. Our friends needed green or red for the rooms on their respective floors.

I sucked in my breath with a hiss of frustration, but we'd known we might have that problem. Which was why we hadn't set the plan into motion until we'd been sure of where the main control room was.

"Come on," I said, and dashed out of my room.

No warning siren had gone off, which meant whoever was on security duty this late at night hadn't noticed the altercation yet. We'd never made any trouble for our jailers, not in years and years.

Now the complacency we'd encouraged was working in our favor.

I hustled down the hall, only holding myself back so Griffin could keep up. We ran up the stairs to the floor just below ground level.

The moment I peeked out into the next hall and saw it was empty, I hurtled straight to the door to the control room.

I threw myself at the door with my full unnatural speed, smacking it with the entire side of my body. It flew off its hinges into the room as if hit by an explosion.

I ricocheted off the door and lunged at the solitary woman who had just whirled around in front of the array of displays and buttons.

She didn't manage to get out more than a gasp. I punched her with the same force I'd used on the guardian downstairs, and she sagged across her chair like her bones had turned into beanbags.

Griffin caught up with me. We stared at the touchscreens together, my heart thumping fast with the sense of the seconds slipping away from us.

With a hitch of breath, he pointed. "There!"

One of the glass panes had an image on it that looked like a blueprint. I tapped at it and managed to flip through different floors.

Level 3. Dominic and Andreas had checked the numbers beside their doors and passed them on: 3-7 and 3-8.

I poked at the first, and a window popped up with various options. I jabbed again: *Unlock door.*

The screen requested fingerprint authorization. Swearing quietly, I hauled up the woman I'd toppled. Griffin leapt in to press her index finger against the circle on the screen.

The room flashed in the layout. *Lock disengaged.*

A jolt of exhilaration raced through my veins. We were really doing it.

I sped through the commands and the press of the woman's finger: one, two, three times more. All the rooms open.

Then I spun toward the doorway. We had to make sure the way was clear.

Well, *I* had to. Despite all our training, Griffin wasn't much of a fighter.

We charged up the last flight of stairs to the landing up top and slowed to slip out through the main door into the night. The cool, fresh air washed over us.

Griffin dragged in a deep breath and grinned. "No one nearby," he said, meaning no guardians whose emotions he would have picked up on.

Just in case, I scanned our surroundings, taking in the parking lot, the fields, the fence, and the forest beyond.

Everything was still. Peaceful, even, as ridiculous as that seemed.

Stars twinkled overhead. A piney scent laced the breeze. I wanted to gulp it down like lemonade after a long, sweaty workout.

Right now, the guys would be hurrying up the stairs to join us. Andreas had used his charm and his talent with memories to learn how to hotwire a car. Zian's X-ray vision had given us the code for the gate.

Everything was in place. Nothing could stop us now.

A grin crossed my face with a burst of pure joy. I caught Griffin's eyes, and the matching excitement shining from his face turned him so gorgeous the sight took my breath away.

This time, when a familiar impulse gripped me, I didn't will it away like I had every time before. I let the wave of elation propel me toward him, slipped my hand around the back of his neck, and pressed my lips to his.

An eager sound reverberated from Griffin's chest as he kissed me back. I could have gotten lost in him right then, forgotten everything but the feel of his body against mine.

Nothing had ever tasted sweeter than the collision of our mouths. It was like the perfect swell of melody in a song, resonating through every particle of my body and leaving me tingling.

This was what we could be. This was what we could *have*, once we were only ourselves, not anyone's belongings.

With the rush of giddiness came a starker, needier sensation clawing up through my chest. More. I wanted so much more than this.

But I hadn't completely lost my grip on reality. We weren't safe yet.

I forced myself to pull back, my gaze flicking over the terrain around us again—

And a boom echoed through the night.

Griffin's body spasmed, a dark splotch blooming on his chest alongside a puff of black smoke. As a cry I couldn't contain burst from my lips, his bright eyes glazed. His knees buckled.

I leapt to catch him before he could hit the ground. His body felt so limp and weak that a scream bubbled up from my lungs.

More blood gushed over my hands with the beating of his heart, alongside the dark mist that escaped our veins when we bled. I didn't know how to stop it.

Where was Dom? Where was—

The roar of engines rattled my eardrums, and my head whipped up, tears blurring my vision. Vehicles tore across the landscape all around me, sniper guns poking from windows and roofs.

I sprang up, claws slicing through the air, muscles braced. I wasn't sure what I was going to do, but I'd fight to the death to defend whatever life might be left in the boy at my feet.

Another shot rang out. Pain tore through my shoulder, slamming me backward.

Then a sharp zap of electricity blasted me. My nerves crackled and hissed like live wires; my mind reeled.

Footsteps thundered all around me. I lashed out with every ounce of strength I had left. Tears streamed down my cheeks, and the metallic flavor of my own blood seeped into my mouth from where I'd bitten my lip.

My fists and feet struck one form and then another—but another zap shocked me, shattering my control over my limbs. As I slumped over, the world beyond me hazed.

A horrible shout penetrated my growing stupor. "The others are secured!"

Rough hands grasped my arms and legs.

"It was a mistake to include a female with the rest," someone muttered.

Another voice chuckled as they hefted me off the ground. "Well, we're eliminating that factor now—and I hear we got a good price for her."

I groped for any remaining shred of control over my body, but everything went black.

ONE

Riva

It's been four years, eight days, and I don't know how many hours since I last saw my guys.

One of my current jailers cracks open the door to my room just wide enough to toss a bottle of water my way. The din of the growing crowd in the arena down the hall rises and then ebbs when he shuts the door again.

The bottle lands with a sloshy thump by my feet. I reach for it, the heavy shackles dragging at my wrists, and pop the cap immediately.

My throat is parched. Normally my keepers leave me with a few bottles on hand, but I finished my last one this morning, and the pricks didn't even bother to deliver a beverage with my dinner.

But obviously they expect me to be properly hydrated for this week's cage fight. Wouldn't want the star of the show giving a sub-optimal performance.

The lukewarm liquid slides down my throat, not half

as refreshing as I'd like it to be. When I've finished chugging, I toss the empty bottle back toward the closed door with a grimace.

I roll my shoulders and glance toward the workout area of my room, but I usually give my body a break the day of a match. I only did a light round of stretches and cardio on the mat this morning.

I need to preserve my energy—both to win the fight and to make sure I win it *my* way.

In the past several months, the boss who runs this place has been arranging increasingly volatile opponents. If I'm going to meet whatever unpredictable moves they'll throw into the mix, I have to be fresh and sharp.

My gaze veers to the TV mounted on the concrete wall, the only entertainment I'm given in my new prison. I don't get to pick the content. From breakfast time until lights out, it broadcasts a steady stream of different shows that I assume my keepers chose.

All I get to decide is how much I tune in.

I don't want to watch the gaggle of friends on the screen right now laughing and clinking glasses, even with the sound diluted by the voices filtering through the wall from the arena. The image makes my stomach twist with the thought of how much I've lost.

I close my eyes, and for a moment, Zian is here with me. His dark brown eyes glint fiercely as he cuffs me lightly in the ear. *You're going to take these assholes down, even if you're a shrimp.*

I haven't managed it yet, I say to my imagined version of him.

I picture Dominic standing nearby, watching us

with his usual pensive gaze. *You've done everything you can,* he says in that careful way of his as if he's measured out every word. *They haven't given you many options.*

They haven't. Except for the fights, I'm restricted to this room and these cuffs. I've seen enough guards march me to and from the arena to know the boss keeps a large force.

I could tear through five, maybe ten of them, sure—but then what? I'd end up riddled with bullets, with no chance at all of getting back to my guys.

Or worse, these bastards might report back to the facility that the property they sold is failing to meet expectations, and the guys would end up bleeding on my behalf too.

One of them has already died because of my failures.

The memory of Griffin's crumpled, bloody body flashes through my mind, and all my muscles tense against the prickle of tears. I don't want my keepers seeing the slightest vulnerability in me.

But not even the imagined figures in my head know what to say about my horrible mistake.

What if the other guys *aren't* still alive? What if—

My chest constricts. Without further thought, I flick out a claw and scratch it across the inside of my arm, just below the armpit, where dozens of matching scars crisscross my pale skin.

I've done this test before, so many times, but I need the visible confirmation.

A tiny trickle of blood spills out—and so does a wisp of black smoke. As I stare at it, my left hand drops to my upper thigh, where a tattoo marks my skin beneath my sweatpants.

The guys all had the same image etched in black in the same spot: a moon with a droplet dangling from its upper tip. The guardians pointed them out to us during our swimming lessons.

That tattoo shows that you all belong to the facility. You do your best for us, and we look after you.

Yeah, right. That worked out so well for us.

But the six of us are connected in other ways too.

I will even more memories of the guys to the front of my mind. Drey's broad grin. Jake's incisive gaze. Dom's steady voice. Zee's feral scent.

The tendril of smoke seeping from my arm trembles and then unfurls toward the wall in a thin but steady stream. One tiny piece of me relaxes.

We discovered this trick while messing around during one of our outdoor training sessions. The strangeness inside us seeks out its match if given a nudge.

We are blood.

As long as the smoke I bleed moves toward a target when prompted, I know the guys are still out there. Still someplace where I can find them.

If I ever get out of this shithole.

Pulsing bass draws my attention back to the TV. On the screen, characters bob and spin to the music at a house party.

I gaze at them for a few moments, but the sound doesn't stir even a fragment of the urge to join their dance. There's only one reason I move my body these days: to survive.

As the song fades out, the deadbolt rasps over again. Three guards walk in with guns and tasers at their hips. The empty water bottle crunches under a boot-clad foot.

I stand up, an ache of tension forming in my gut. The guards move briskly and silently to usher me out into the hall where more men are waiting, but when I inhale, whiffs of stress taint the air.

They're more anxious than usual—I might even catch a note of outright fear. But then, when the squad of guards came to escort me to last week's fight, I was keyed up and on edge because I'd realized yet another year had passed with me stuck in this place.

Another year apart from the guys who are my blood— the guys I love. Another year of failure.

That night, one of the guards pressed closer to me than I liked, and with my temper frayed, I elbowed him with more oomph than I intended. From the crack of bone when he slammed into the wall, I assume I broke his arm.

So I guess I can't blame them for feeling extra cautious tonight. I'll just blame them for everything else they put me through.

"Nice night, isn't it?" I say, glancing at the men around me for any hint of a reaction. Any clue that could help me, no matter how small. "Sounds like a good crowd out there. I bet the boss is *so* happy."

"Keep quiet, freak," one of them snaps.

The others ignore me, not even meeting my gaze. Their expressions look stern, impervious, but the prickle of fear in the air intensifies.

I *could* kill at least five of them before the others took

me down, and they all know that. None of them wants to find out if they'd be among the unlucky ones.

My attention moves on to rove across the hall, but I'm as familiar with the details of this corridor as I am with my room. That air vent is too small for me to fit. That steel door leads only to a windowless storage room.

If there was an easy escape route, I'd have found it years ago.

The furor of the crowd gets louder as we approach the arena. My pulse skitters, just for a second.

It does sound like a big one, and plenty worked up already, more so than usual. Just who am I going up against tonight?

In the back of my head, Jacob gives me a cool smile. The chiseled planes of his face look so much like Griffin's it's painful, but his voice is more forceful than his twin's ever was.

No matter what they throw at you, you've got this.

I summon the cool composure I first developed during rounds of sparring at the facility. For the next half hour, nothing matters except the fight.

The guards in front shove open the door to the arena. A blast of unmuffled sound smacks into me alongside a riot of scents.

More than a hundred people—mostly men, but a woman here and there too—are poised on the chairs all around the fighting ring. They've been talking, both in friendly conversation and in argument, and the moment they spot me, their excitement rises.

A few whoops of encouragement reach my ears, but plenty of scoffing and guffaws come too.

"Look at that little thing. How's she going to beat anyone?"

"He'll crush her like a twig."

"They've got to be kidding with this. Where's the real fighter?"

Those are the newbies in the audience—the ones who've never watched my previous matches. The ones who know hush them ineffectively, but they'll find out how wrong they are soon enough.

My five-foot-one, one-hundred-and-five-pound frame is what makes me such a big draw and earns my keepers so much money at the betting table. No one ever seems to get tired to the spectacle of me taking down an opponent twice my size.

I let the voices wash through me, unaffected by them or by the stink of sweat, stale beer, and adrenaline that permeates the arena. My focus is narrowing down to the raised platform ahead of me. I stare straight ahead as we walk to the ring.

Just as we reach the steps, an icy wave of dizziness washes over me. I have to lock my knees for a second so they don't wobble.

I grit my teeth in annoyance. Get a grip, Riva.

I can't let anything these people do get to me. I can't do anything but *win*.

A guard unlocks the door on one side of the metal cage that surrounds the ring and shoves me inside. Normally I'd keep my balance without a hitch, but tonight I stumble just a bit.

Another flicker of cold shoots through my nerves, fracturing my concentration. What is wrong with me?

A hulking man with scars zigzagging across his bare chest and arms postures at the other side of the cage, clad only in horrifyingly neon green training shorts. He spins the machete he's selected from the weapons he was offered and laughs like he doubts he'll even need to use it.

Only my opponents get the benefit of a weapon. It's to make the fight a little fairer for them, though they rarely see it that way at first.

I flex my fingers and turn toward the guards to have my cuffs unlocked through the bars. As they fall to the floor with a clank, I tuck my cat-and-yarn pendant under the neckline of my tight tank top.

It's a risk keeping it on at all, but I don't dare leave it back in my room. It's a miracle my keepers have let me hold on to this one thing from my past life to begin with.

I'm not giving them the chance to take it away too.

I turn back toward my opponent, and the referee blows his whistle for the match to begin. That's the only way he'll intervene until it's time to declare the winner.

The boss likes it best when the fight is to the death, ending with a throat slashed or a skull cracked against the bars. But while my keepers can force me to fight, they can't dictate how.

If I have any other choice, if I can simply knock the other fighter out to end the match, I'll do it, even if it's harder.

Across some two hundred opponents, all but eighteen have left this ring alive.

The hulking man with the machete takes a step—to the side, rather than right at me. He might be confident, but he isn't stupid.

We circle each other at opposite ends of the ring, studying each other's movements. He's big, but I know from experience that the bulk will slow him down, requiring broader motions while I can be swift and precise.

At least, normally I can be. A little of the dizziness lingers in the back of my head. My feet push through the air like they're wading through shallow water.

A twang of alarm goes off inside me that's beyond simple frustration. Something *really* isn't right. Across two hundred fights, I've never felt like this before.

I flick my claws free from my fingertips, willing my feral side to the surface. My ears tickle where I know the shells have turned pointed and lightly furred. Inhuman strength thrums through my limbs.

But it's not quite enough.

The man lunges at me. I should have picked up on the shift in his intentions in the wafts of pheromones he's giving off, but my senses have dulled.

I fling myself to the side on legs that now seem to be pushing through mud rather than water. Too slow.

The blade of the machete stabs close enough to split the skin of my shoulder. Blood streams down my arm while a puff of smoke gusts up.

Recognizing his advantage, my attacker charges again, snatching at my braid with one hand while he slashes with the other. I manage to duck both his grasping fingers and the swing of the knife and kick him in the gut hard enough to slam him backward on his ass.

With a startled grunt, he skids halfway across the ring.

More dizziness clouds my mind, and I hook my clawed fingers around the bars of the cage for balance. My gaze veers beyond the enclosure and catches on the most prominent of my keepers: the corpulent, balding boss with the heap of gold chains around his neck, sitting in his raised section of the stands at the far end of the arena.

He must be able to tell I'm faltering. He should look horrified—panicked at the thought of all the money he's going to lose if I fall.

Instead, a hint of a smirk curves his lips. He takes a casual puff of his cigar, lounging deeper into his seat.

As I whirl back toward my opponent, a sense of certainty clutches me.

He knows something's wrong, and he *wants* me to fall.

Abruptly, I remember the last-minute water bottle after the stretch of deprivation. He needed to be sure I'd drink it.

What was in the bottle besides water?

My jaw clenches with a flare of anger. After four years, he's decided I've outlived my usefulness. Because of the incident with the guard last week, or was it always going to end now?

I'll bet he's wagered all his money against me for this fight. Probably with extra for seeing me pummeled all the way into oblivion.

The hulk comes at me again, a little more cautiously than before but still menacing. He heaves himself to the side and snatches at my wrist to yank me toward him.

I duck again and roll across the floor. My breath starts to burn in my lungs.

What will happen to me even if I manage to win? Will the boss order the guards to kill me like a dog that needs to be put down?

He'll be pissed off that I didn't bend to his whims—and he won't trust me to stay in line now that I've realized he's willing to sabotage me like this. The ungrateful fuckhead.

My attacker hurtles into me and bashes me against the bars for a second before I squirm free. As I spring away under his arm, I rake my claws across his side. My legs sway under me, but his are steady as ever as he barrels toward me again.

I may as well already be dead. I'm never getting back to my guys like this—there's no fucking way.

Gritting my teeth against the rising anguish, I throw myself into the man's charge, low to the ground. His knees buckle under him, but he slashes the machete across my hip as I tumble away. Pain spikes down my thigh.

I've failed them again. That bloated asshole in his prime seat screwed me over. And all the pricks in the audience are watching my downfall and cheering it on.

Their voices ring in my ears. Feet stomp on the concrete floor.

My opponent rams his fist into the side of my skull.

More fury sears up inside me, sharper and hotter than my misery. The boss is up there grinning like he isn't killing five people instead of only one right now. My guys are waiting for me, and he's fucking *smirking*.

I swore I'd get them out of our prison, and all these bastards just roar in encouragement as my attacker catches my arm.

His hand tightens to yank me right into the poised machete, and all my pent-up emotion explodes from my chest.

Rage sears up my throat and bursts from my mouth in an ear-splitting shriek. It rattles my bones and reverberates through every particle of my being.

The scream goes on and on, drowning out the cheers and the stomping, ringing through my brain. A twisting, ripping agony wraps around me, lacing my mouth with the metallic flavor of blood, and—

Two

Riva

I blink, my eyelashes sticking together briefly before pulling apart, and find myself staring down at the floor of the fighting ring. I'm hunched over, my hands braced beneath me, fresh score marks streaking from my claws through the scuffed beige surface.

The most horrible smell I've ever encountered clogs my nose. Like raw meat tossed into a putrid public restroom.

My stomach lurches, sending a spurt of acid up my throat. I sputter and raise my head, and then I just stare, frozen in place.

The scene around me is just as deathly still.

The scene around me is *death*.

None of the horrors the guardians subjected me to prepared me for this.

Bodies lie sprawled all across the stands around the arena, but they look nothing like bodies should. My gaze jars at the twisted shapes formed by the limbs and torsos, splattered with blood where the skin has cracked.

It's like a giant stomped all over the crowd—and then stirred them a little more for good measure.

My eyes jerk to the nearest body—the corpse of my former opponent, stretched out on the floor just a few feet from where I'm crouched.

His mouth gapes in a vast, broken maw as if someone grasped his chin with one hand and his cheek with the other and slammed them in opposite directions, taking his jaw right off its hinges. Uprooted teeth dapple the puddle of blood beneath his head. His lifeless eyes bulge so violently they've almost popped from their sockets.

His limbs lie akimbo, snapped and bent in a half a dozen places to form far more joints than any arm or leg is meant to have. Jagged ends of bone gleam where the flesh has totally split.

His torso is a crater, the ribs collapsed inward. A dark stain marks his neon-green training shorts, seeping into a yellow-brown puddle beneath his ass that suggests he both pissed and shit himself.

As I take the wreckage in, more bile shoots up my throat. I lurch forward in a full-out vomit.

My half-digested dinner of spaghetti and meatballs—because the boss always wants me primed on carbs before a fight—splatters the floor. I jerk my hands back, my stomach still roiling, and push myself to my feet to study the wider arena again.

As my attention trails over the carnage beyond the cage, where dozens of bodies lie wrenched and deformed like the one next to me, I become distantly aware that my legs are holding me perfectly steady. My gut is churning, and my chest has constricted with horror, but the dizzy unsteadiness brought on by whatever the boss drugged me with has vanished.

The boss. My gaze shoots to his high seat, and I suck in a ragged breath that floods my lungs with more of the awful stink.

He's strewn buckled backwards over one of the chair arms, his spine bent so sharply his head could touch the backs of his knees. His eyeballs dangle from their sockets, his jaw torn right off and resting on the seat next to them. The one arm I can see is rippled as if it was wrung out like a wet towel.

What the hell—what the hell *happened* here?

The last few moments before I blacked out rush through my mind. My desperation and fury, the boss's smirk. My attacker's hand clamped around my arm, and the scream reverberating up my throat like a bolt of lightning.

Like some kind of power.

My arms stiffen at my sides. I pull them up to wrap them tightly around my chest.

I couldn't have done this... could I? I've never had any kind of vocal power before—I've never damaged a body through anything other than physical combat.

But I'm the only one left standing, with all but one of the corpses lying far beyond my physical reach while I'm trapped within the cage. And that scream...

The memory of it sends a shiver up my spine, one that feels like anticipation almost as much as revulsion. I shudder and hug myself tighter.

Only a monster could have done something like this. A much more terrifying and inhuman monster than I've ever been.

Than I'd ever want to be.

The bouncy melody of a pop song erupts from the stands and shatters my shellshocked daze. Flinching, I jerk into a defensive stance—and realize it's a ringtone.

Someone's phone survived the carnage.

There are so many people here. So many mangled corpses. It won't be long before someone on the outside realizes there's a problem and comes looking.

But for now, I'm all alone.

My heart leaps high enough to overtake my horror. This is my chance. No one is standing in my way.

I can get out of here—I can go back for my guys like I've wanted to for so long.

I have to move quickly. As soon as any of the boss's people find this bloodbath and realize I'm missing, they might warn the guardians that I'm on the loose. I'll lose any element of surprise.

And I'm going to need every possible advantage if I'm going to break the boys out of the facility on my own.

My jaw clenches, my focus narrowing with the same cool detachment I bring to a fight, shutting out every consideration other than the job I have to get done.

First, I have to find a way out of this cage.

The guard who escorted me to the door lies at the edge of the ring where he'd stood waiting. Glancing away from the horror etched on his distorted face, I stretch my arm through the bars toward his hip.

I barely manage to hook my fingers inside his jeans

pocket and snag the key ring. Breathing shallowly through my mouth, I push the key for the cage into the lock and twist it.

The door pops open. I'm free.

My limbs tense with the impulse to hurtle through the massacre to the exit, but I spot another object near the guard's fractured thigh: a pistol.

I prefer to work with my claws, but I can't deny that weapons would be an asset. Especially when I have no idea just how tightly secure the facility will be after our previous near escape.

The guys might not even be in that building anymore but moved to some place with additional protections.

I grab the gun and push myself onward through the deathly wreckage, scanning waists and hips and the items scattered in between, avoiding faces as well as I can.

There's another pistol, and a switchblade, and a thin knife that looks perfect for throwing, wedged beneath someone's contorted pelvis. My lips press flat as I yank it out.

It's all just meat now. Nothing worse than a butcher shop.

If I tell myself that enough times, maybe all of me will believe it.

I consider a fallen phone, but electronic devices are easily tracked. I do snatch up the least bloody wallets I spot—because I'm going to need money sooner rather than later—as well as a couple of lighters, a few pieces of jewelry that look pawnable when the cash runs out, and a voluminous purse with only a few scarlet flecks on the leather to shove my haul in.

Don't think about who this necklace or that bracelet once belonged to. Don't think about whether they were as immoral as the people who ran the cage matches or just someone who happened to get caught up with the wrong crowd at the worst possible time.

Don't think about how much they must have suffered, and who inflicted that suffering on them.

Jacob. Zian. Andreas. Dominic. All that matters is them. I'm finally coming for them.

By the time I've reached the exit, the one the audience arrives through that stands just beyond the boss's chair, I've added three more guns and another blade to my collection. One firearm for each of us, if the ammo lasts that long.

I don't know how many bullets they have in them, but I'm not lingering here to check.

My gaze flicks over to the boss's chair. To the thick gold chains looped around his purpling neck.

I bet they're worth plenty, but all of me recoils from the idea of taking anything of that man's with me.

I shove past the door into a wide but short hall that leads to a flight of stairs. Three more disfigured corpses sprawl on the floor here.

I don't want to think about the implications of that fact either. Or of the fact that the injuries I took in the fight aren't so much as stinging anymore.

With that sudden memory, I glance down at myself. The cut on my shoulder has sealed up, leaving only a ruddy line. The same with the one on my hip, visible through the slit carved in my sweatpants.

I've always healed quickly—we all did. The guardians

remarked on it more than once. But not *that* fast. How—?

That doesn't matter either. I don't have to think about it. All that matters is there's no one standing in my way when I race out into the night.

I find myself under a single dim security lamp at the edge of a parking lot packed with cars I don't know how to hotwire or drive. All the things the guardians taught us, and they never bothered with that particular skill, the pricks.

I sling the strap of the purse over my shoulder cross-body and tighten it until the bag rests firmly against my back. After scanning the area for movement and seeing none, I extend my claws and sever my skin just below the scratch I made earlier tonight.

Blood trickles down, and smoke wafts up. Up and, as I hold my memories of the guys firmly in my head, to my right.

Now I know where I'm going.

I set off at a swift lope, my braid swaying against my back. The concrete building that holds the arena stands between several decrepit industrial buildings on what appears to be the outskirts of a town—or maybe even a city. I mark the position of the nearest highway when headlights cruise by and keep a healthy distance from the few cars passing by this late.

The shabby warehouses give way to scruffy fields and then stretches of farmland with weathered wooden fences and the occasional darkened house standing at the end of a long drive. I keep the same pace whether I'm jogging through rows of corn or along the edges of pastures.

After several houses, I come across a bike leaning

against a post just down the drive. I yank it up and hop on.

Pumping the pedals, I can move so much faster, but I need some kind of firm path beneath the wheels. Thankfully the cars come even fewer between as the night creeps on.

I stick to desolate lanes when I can and sprint along the highway when I can't. Every now and then, I slow enough to squeeze more blood and smoke from my cut to confirm I'm still heading in the right direction.

It still feels too slow. I don't know how many hours of darkness I have left.

When I duck down in the ditch as a transport truck rumbles toward me, I decide to make a gamble. I drop the bike and dash over the shoulder at the last second to leap at the back of the truck.

Hooking my legs around the metal bar beneath the doors, I grasp one of the metal supports it's attached to. The truck keeps roaring forward with no sign that my intrusion has been noticed.

I prod a steady stream of smoke from my arm. It wavers through the ruddy glow from the lights on the back of the truck, pushing forward despite the rush of the wind.

We've sped past the fringes of another city, a couple of small towns, and a long stretch of forest before the dark wisp abruptly veers to my left instead of ahead.

With a hitch of my pulse, I spring from the truck. I roll over the grassy shoulder and stop with a smack of my side against a tree trunk.

It's only seconds before I'm on my feet and hurrying

onward again.

Hustling through the underbrush, I stumble on an overgrown dirt lane… where the tufts of weeds have been recently pressed flat by tire treads. My senses go on high alert.

I run onward, gulping down air both for oxygen to fuel my muscles and for any trace of pheromone-emitting humans nearby. The lane weaves through the woods, across a stretch of tall grass, and into a denser sprawl of forest.

I don't encounter anyone. But then, the guardians would mostly be concerned about their wards getting *out*, not about anyone coming *in*.

When I spot a fence up ahead around a bend in the lane, I slow, still sticking to the shadows at the edge of the road. Slinking closer, I ease farther into the shelter of the trees.

Then I come to a stop several feet from where the forest thins. The certainty rings through every inch of my body that this is the place.

I don't think it's the same facility where the guardians held us before, but that's not really surprising. Their security had been partly breached.

It's a similar setup, though: a clearing the size of a few football fields surrounded by forest, with a lone concrete structure not far from the gate, looking no larger than a bungalow. There's no way to tell just looking at it how deep and wide the building extends underground.

No cars are in sight. The guardians must have added some kind of underground parking garage to keep them out of unwanted hands.

The fence is taller, about twice my height, with barbed wire coiled all the way around its top. Cables that run between the metal posts just above the barbed wire give me pause.

Then it clicks.

The fence is electrified as well as barbed. The guardians want to tear into anyone who tries to breach it in every possible way.

I wet my lips. I don't have much time. Dawn is creeping closer with every thump of my heart.

It doesn't appear that anyone has sounded the alarm about my escape so far, or else if they have, the guardians aren't worried I'll already have made it here. I only spot a few armed sentries ambling across the field around the building.

Even if my nerves are screaming for me to race straight to my guys, I have to be smart about this. I'm not screwing up what's probably my last chance.

I prowl around the edges of the field until I've fully charted it. One pine stands close enough to the fence and tall enough that I plan to return to it later.

Before I can do that, I need as many of the guardians as possible diverted by other concerns.

I slink back around until I'm on the side of the facility opposite my pine. Digging through my stolen purse, I produce one of the lighters.

With a flick of the dial, I confirm the flame still works. Then I grasp a fallen branch covered in curling, dead leaves, set it against a crumbling log, and send it up in flames.

THREE

Jacob

I wake up too early, as always.

The room is pitch black. A faint burn still hums through my muscles from a workout that wasn't quite exhausting enough to knock me out all the way until morning.

They never are. I always find myself here in the dark, the firm mattress beneath me and the faint whir of the air filtration system overhead.

One more day I've made it to. Another day more than my brother got. Twenty-four more hours of useless existence under my belt.

The thoughts float through my head like shards of ice on a thawing river, freezing cold all the way through. I'm a void as endless as the total darkness of my cell.

Griffin would have told me to go easier on myself, to not let the past get to me. But Griffin is gone, and my awareness of the facts of my existence doesn't stir up my emotions anyway. It's simply the way it is.

Someone around here needs to see things clearly.

I close my eyes and focus on the rhythm of my breaths. Inhale. Exhale. Over and over. As repetitive as our days here are.

In an hour or two, the overhead light will blink on. A tray of breakfast will slide through the compartment on the door.

I will eat, and then I'll be tested, and then I'll eat again, and then I'll train. Then back to the cell for dinner. Then the lights go out.

Going through the motions, watching, waiting. Collecting all the little details that might someday add up to enough to make a difference.

I'm just thinking that when my chance arrives out of nowhere with the blare of a warning siren radiating through the walls.

I jerk upright on the bed, my heart thudding only a little harder than normal but my entire body gone rigid.

The alarm wails on and on through the darkness. Something's gone wrong.

The guardians have been disturbed, their plans shaken in some unexpected way.

It's an opening—it's exactly what we've needed.

At least, it will be if I can make use of it. This time, the first step in the tentative plan we've stitched together in fragments of conversation over the past few years depends on me, not my brother.

It should have been me all along. If it'd been me, maybe I'd have been the one who—

My mind snaps around the errant thought like a steel trap, shutting it away. I shove to my feet and step toward the door.

There, I tip my forehead against the cool metal surface, listening to the sounds from the hall with all my might. I don't have Zian's keen hearing or his ability to see through solid surfaces, but the people outside are making enough noise that I catch faint markers of their presence through the blare of the siren.

In the first moment I home in on the sounds, heavy footsteps are thundering down the hall by my door. By the time I register them, they've passed too quickly for me to reach out and catch hold.

I grit my teeth and strain my ears even more.

Is the situation bad enough that more of the facility's staff will come running, or has the opportunity already slipped through my fingers? This is the first time since we gathered all the pieces we needed for our plan that we've had our jailers at a potential disadvantage.

Who knows when it'll happen again.

As I listen, I press my fingers against the door as well, flexing my sense of my power from within my skull through my chest and arms. I need to be ready. And pulling this gambit off is going to take all my strength—all the strength the guardians have left me with.

Since we arrived at the new facility, we've all found our talents, even the ones we'd kept hidden, have been weighed down. Restrained. Something they're putting in the food or the air must be dulling us, taking the edge off the weapons inside us.

The guardians thought they could prevent us from

staging another rebellion. But they haven't blanked us out completely. No doubt they'd have to send us into a total stupor for that, and they want us alert enough to jump through their hoops and carry out their orders.

It's taken longer to pull a scheme together than it would have otherwise, but we've made the most of the diminished skills we still have.

Nothing else reaches my ears except the continuing screech of the alarm. The emptiness expands inside me again, tugging at me to give up, to lie down on the bed, to return to the void.

But I owe my brother. I owe it to him to make every last person who hurt him pay.

What else have I held on this long for?

So I stay there, the metal a firm pressure against my forehead and fingertips, energy twining through my veins.

And then I hear it: a muffled holler and the thudding of more footsteps.

The slightest smile curves my lips. I push my hands harder against the door, let the sounds form a picture of the man running down the hall, and hurl all my concentrated will at the figure outside.

My nerves lurch as my talent slams home. I can *feel* him now, caught in my power like a fly stuck in a spider's web.

He flails against it, one foot skidding on the tiled floor, his head thrashing from side to side. But all I need is one finger.

At my full strength, this would be easy. As it is, sweat beads on my forehead and trickles down the back of my neck with the effort of yanking him over to my door.

My jaw clamps so tight my teeth ache. Deeper twinges run through my shoulders and down my spine.

The guardian bangs against the other side of the door. My forehead furrows as I focus on keeping his body there while I drag his hand toward the keypad of the lock.

The mechanisms inside it have some kind of safeguard I haven't been able to override with my telekinetic ability, at least at my current dulled state. No more keycards— they were too easily stolen. So we had to steal the codes instead.

I've seen the outside of my door a thousand times. I fix the image of the keypad in my mind and jab the guardian's index finger at the sequence of six numbers Zian was able to watch them tap in through the wall of his own cell down the hall.

They kept us farther apart this time, but not quite far enough.

4-8-9-1-3-4. The lock beeps, and the sequence of multiple deadbolts rasps over.

My muscles tremble with the effort it's taking to maintain my hold. I yank the man to the side, heave open my door to the full blare of the alarm and flashing red lights, and lunge at him.

It takes all of a single heartbeat to slap my hands against the guardian's chin and the back of his skull beneath his stupid metal helmet. One more beat to wrench his head to the side hard enough to snap his neck.

For all the training we've done, all the tests of our strength and speed, all the practice with weapons and targets, I've never actually killed someone before. Animals, yes, when the guardians forced me, but never a human being.

For a second, staring down at him in the pulsing crimson light, I brace myself for a surge of emotion—any emotion.

The man crumples on the floor with a clank of his helmet, and I feel nothing but a muted sense of satisfaction. The job is done. He got what he deserved.

I don't think Griffin would approve of that reaction either, but I'm the one here, so we're doing things my way.

I'm not really done, though. I step away from the guardian and race down the hall to the room with Zian's number.

Seeing his own code was easy, but he didn't have any way of entering it. I poke the buttons with the other sequence of numerals he gave me.

He's waiting, no doubt as revved up by the alarm as I was. The second the lock disengages, I jerk myself to the side, which is a good thing, because the next instant Zee's brawny frame is barreling past it.

He skids to a halt on the tiles outside, looming over me as his chest heaves with panted breaths. Normally he's only a few inches taller than my six foot even, but his partial shift has given him more on top of that, his muscles bulging wider.

Tufts of fur ripple across his neck and shoulders, the same black as the short-cropped hair on his head but scruffier. Tips of fangs protrude over his lower lip.

He whirls around with a growl, scanning the hall. Tension flexes through his limbs. But when he whips his gaze back to me, a tremor runs through his body.

He contracts just slightly into the still intimidating but more human guy I grew up with, the fur and fangs vanishing.

"The others," he rasps, his dark brown eyes alight with wild intensity.

As I nod, I'm already moving. We dash together to the nearest stairwell, Zian charging a little ahead but reining in the full speed I know he's capable of.

We hurtle up the stairs to the next floor, where Andreas's cell is. He scooped a guardian's memory of tapping in the keycode right out of the prick's head.

Whatever guardians were stationed on this floor, they've already charged off to deal with the emergency. I punch in the code and throw open the door.

Andreas lopes out, his usual easygoing energy keyed up enough that he bobs on his feet when he comes to a stop in front of me. His dark gray eyes catch mine with a flicker of a ruddy glow totally separate from the flashing lights.

"Better get Dominic," he says, offering a tighter version of his usual grin.

At the same moment, a guardian strides out of a room just a few doors down. His head jerks toward us, and a shout bursts from his throat loud enough to compete with the siren.

His hand flies to his com unit, but Zee moves faster. The massive guy all but soars across the tiles and bodychecks the guardian into the wall with the full force of his beastly strength.

The man sags to the floor with a dent in his helmet

that turns the side of his head concave. Blood trickles out from beneath the metal to pool on the floor.

Zian stiffens, his teeth bared, his hands quivering at his sides. I freeze up, recognizing his struggle and not having a clue what the answer is, but Andreas is already loping to join him.

The leaner guy hooks his arm around Zian's burly one and nudges him toward the stairs. "Nice one, wolf-man. Can't get out of here without denting a few cans."

A halting chuckle that's half snarl erupts from Zee's chest, and he hurries with us to the next floor.

We had to rely on Andreas's skill to get Dominic's code too. It was a hell of a lot trickier than retrieving his own, since Drey has to see the person whose memories he's rifling through, and he can't pick and choose what he sees other than narrowing it down by other people present.

It was only a few months ago after over a year of trying that he finally caught enough small fragments to give us all the numbers.

We're just one level below the main one now, and a heavy thump reverberates through the ceiling. The flashing lights jitter—and a matching quaver of sensation echoes through my nerves.

I pause in the hall, scanning our surroundings while Andreas does the honors with Dominic's door. I can't identify the feeling that just came over me, but it's holding on, prickling into my skin. It isn't simple apprehension.

Dom darts out, his ever-present trench coat pulled tight around his slender frame and half of his dark auburn waves falling out of his sleep-rumpled ponytail to frame his tan face. As we set off toward the stairwell once more, my fingers curl toward my palms.

"There'll be more guardians upstairs, almost definitely," I say, pitching my voice to carry over the piercing wail. "We're going to have to mow through all of them."

Zian raises his fists, all traces of his momentary uncertainty vanished. "Not a problem."

Another odd flash tickles through my nerves. I frown. "And…"

Andreas glances back at me from where he's leaping up the stairs just ahead. "And what?"

"I don't know," I admit. "But just be ready. I think there's something else. Something… new."

FOUR

Riva

Another burst of flames licks up from a branch I've torched. I drop it on the heap of twigs I hastily pawed together and dash away.

Shouts ring out from within the compound. Guardians are charging over to the fence and through the gate to investigate the several fires I've already set, which are crackling and pluming smoke up toward the starry sky. The wavering orange light glints off the bars of the fence.

The fires might be enough on their own, but I want to bring as many of the staff as possible out of the facility. I don't know how long it'll take for me to get the guys out; I don't know what new security measures are in place.

The fewer bodies with guns standing between me and my goal, the easier it'll be.

I pull one of the pistols from my stolen purse and aim it at the treetops. I haven't gotten to practice my gunmanship in years, so the kick when I pull the trigger propels me backward with a jolt of surprise.

My aim is still true. The bullet smacks into a thin branch and cracks it at its base. It plummets to the ground, the crash of its landing punctuating the boom of the shot that split the air.

I don't want to waste bullets, but it'll work in my favor if the guardians think there's a whole army of hostiles out here. Darting in a semi-circle around the area where I lit the fires, I shoot five more times in quick succession, from spots farther apart than any one normal person could have traveled in that time.

Then the chamber clicks with a hollow sound. Empty.

I shove the pistol back in the purse in case we need it later once we can get more ammo, push the strap so the purse is pressed against my back again, and dash all the way around the compound to the pine I picked out earlier.

The gate stands open, but guardians are barging out through it—and I know without seeing it that at least a couple of them will hang back to stand guard. Trying to enter that way would send me straight into their midst.

But while they're all busy with the chaos I've created by the east end of the compound, no one's keeping watch over the southwest corner.

The tree comes into view up ahead. I sprint straight to it, flicking my claws from my fingertips, and leap at the trunk.

My arms wrap around it several feet above the ground, my fingers curling and claws digging in for a better hold. I brace my knees against the bark and scramble upward until I reach the branches. Then I start pushing off them to propel myself up faster.

As I near the top, the narrowing trunk sways with my weight. I swivel around it, take a split-second to confirm my distance from the fence, and then fling myself out into the air.

My braid whips out behind me. My back arches and legs splay to position myself in the perfect landing position.

I soar right over the barbed wire and electric cables and land with a soft thump in the grass far behind the aboveground structure.

A swift roll diffuses most of the impact of the landing. An instant later, I'm on my feet again and racing toward the building.

When I near the concrete wall, I slow to a prowl. Sticking close to the building, I slink along it and peer around the corner toward the lone entrance and the gate beyond it.

As I expected, two guardians have stationed themselves on either side of the gate, which is now closed while various other armored figures rush around beyond the fence near the growing blaze. As I hoped, even the two by the gate have their attention fixed on the forest rather than on the building behind them.

They think the threat is still out there. Suckers.

The door to the building stands half open, another guardian in the typical helmet and vest poised there as if waiting to see if her help will be needed too. I'm going to have to go through her—and fast enough to cut her off before she can sound a warning.

Her and anyone else who might be in the hall behind her.

My muscles coil. My jaw clenches. I don't have time to simply knock her out and truss her up for safekeeping like I did during our first escape.

She isn't a person. She's an obstacle between me and the men I need to set free.

She's one of the people who've treated *us* like objects to be tested and tormented for as long as any of us can remember. Why should I see her as more than an object herself?

I wait until her head turns away from me, tracking the continuing shouts from that end of the compound. Then I lunge.

I slam into her at an angle to send both of us tumbling into the hall, the door thudding shut in our wake. One clawed hand clamps over the start of a scream shooting from her mouth; the other slashes through her throat, hard enough to sever the artery.

Blood spurts up. Her body goes limp.

No one races to her rescue. I grasp at the first door within reach and shove the corpse into what looks like an equipment closet, swiveling her as I go so that her pants wipe away the worst of the blood on the floor.

Nothing to signal an intrusion to any other guardians who run by.

Now I'm alone in the hall. An alarm is shrieking, warning lights flashing red down the edge of the ceiling.

I can't let the clamor shake my focus. The control room has to be around here somewhere, most likely on this floor. They'd still keep it as far from the holding cells and the training rooms as possible, wouldn't they?

I lope down the short hallway, setting my feet as quietly as I can. One door opens to a meeting room with a boardroom-style table and chairs.

The next one gives me my jackpot.

Rows of monitors loom over consoles set up all around the square space. Warning messages blink on several of the screens.

To my surprise, the room is empty. Did I really freak out the guardians so much that they didn't leave anyone behind to monitor the facility from inside?

I grab one of the chairs and wedge it under the doorknob to hold off anyone else who might try to enter. My gaze darts over the controls.

There—the outer systems. It'll be good to have the gate fixed open when we make a run for it and the electricity in the fence turned off in case we have to take a more roundabout route.

The gate should wait until I have the guys with me, to give the guardians outside as little warning as possible. But I tap at the screen to turn off the flow of electricity through the cables.

That command doesn't require verification. Is that because someone with security access was using the controls recently enough that the system isn't asking for it again—or will the holding cells be a special case?

I'll have to try and see. I was counting on there being someone working in here for me to use.

But if I need a fingerprint for verification, I can always

drag that woman out of the storage closet—or her hand, anyway. Hopefully she's got clearance.

I hustle around the spread of consoles—and jar to a stop.

There's the display showing the holding cells. It looks just like the one from four years ago. Except... four of those cells are already lit up and blinking, yellow against the blue lines of the layout.

Lock disengaged.

And beneath the numbers for each of the cells, there's a five-letter label in all caps. JACOB. ZIAN-. ANDRE. DOMIN.

My guys. They're already out.

How—is *that* why the control room staff left? Did the guardians realize I was behind the chaos outside and run off to drag the guys someplace more secure?

Where are they now?

I scan the displays for any that might give me a clue of where to go. My eyes snag on one in the corner with what looks like a blueprint lit up with little glowing dots. A few of them are moving—

The doorknob rattles. Before I can do more than spin toward it, something rams into the door with enough force to send the chair flying and pop the hinges.

The door crashes to the floor. A big, brawny figure barges in and stalls in his tracks, staring at me.

It takes me a second to recognize him with the four years that've transformed him from a buff teen who still had a touch of softness to his features into a hardened, musclebound man. But that peachy brown skin, those angled cheekbones, and the dark brown eyes glued to me now—they're all my Zian, so familiar and even more stunning than I remembered.

He takes my breath away. My heart thumps faster.

My voice comes out in a hoarse whisper. "Zee?"

Zian looks startled and confused but also almost… upset? Nothing in his face reflects the surge of relief that I felt the moment I realized I'd already found one of the guys I came for.

Before I can figure out what to make of that or say anything else, two more familiar, gorgeous men burst into the room behind him.

"What's the hold-up?" one of them is demanding, and my heart leaps at Andreas's familiar jaunty tone, even if there's a terse note in it right now.

He jerks to a stop too, his tight curls swinging at his temples. The other man beside him goes completely rigid, as if the sharp angles of his face and his pale blond hair were carved out of marble.

Jacob. It's the first time I've seen him since Griffin died, and the echo of his twin shines through his face so vividly that I can't help flinching with that past pain. His gaze sears into mine, he raises his fists—

And then Andreas is pushing ahead of both of the others, his expression a little wild but his voice insistent. "Zee, grab her and bring her. Jake, come on, we need the gate."

Jacob nods with a sharp snap of his chin, tearing his attention away from me. He and Andreas leap to the controls, and Zian springs at me.

My thoughts are too muddled with a mix of joy and bewilderment for me to dodge him.

Why would I need to dodge him? We're blood.

He snatches me right off my feet as if I weigh nothing at all and tosses me partway over his broad shoulder, his bulging arm wrapping tight around my waist. The heat of his body radiates all across my skin, his musky smell filling my nose and sending a tingling through my veins alongside the hum of adrenaline.

I want to hug him, to sob in relief that I've found them, that this is happening, but at the same time nothing about their reactions makes sense.

Why did they look at me like that? Why haven't any of them said a word to me?

But I don't know what they've been through on their end getting this far into the escape. And we do need to get out of here as quickly as possible.

I bend against Zian's massive frame, making myself as easy a burden as possible.

"I have—" I start to say, but my offer of weapons is cut off by Andreas's crow of victory.

"We're out of here!"

All three of them dash from the room without another word. The last of my four, the one I'd just started to worry about, gapes at us from where he's been waiting in the hall.

"What—?" Dominic says, and Jacob interrupts him with a swipe of his hand through the air. He points toward the door.

Nothing else is spoken. The four men barrel out into the night with me in tow.

I'd insist on being put down, but I can't say for sure that I can run faster than Zian, especially when I haven't trained at long distances in the last four years. My guys seem to have a definite plan already, and making a fuss could throw the whole thing off.

But as we hurtle across the field and through the gate, Jacob hurling both of the guardians there into trees with a shove of his invisible power, my stomach knots.

Yells careen through the night. The guys charge off the road into the shelter of the forest.

Zian's arm stays tight around me, his grip almost hard enough to bruise. His scent has flooded my lungs, but it can't wash away my uneasiness.

Bobbing with his strides, I stare down at the expanse of his back in the navy tee he's wearing and try again. "Zee?"

He doesn't answer. Doesn't give the slightest indication he's even heard me.

I don't understand.

I didn't know what to expect from our reunion, but it wasn't this. And all my instincts are quivering with the growing certainty that there's something I'm missing.

FIVE

Riva

Twigs and dead leaves crackle under the guys' thumping feet. I can't see much except the darkened ground flying by below.

When I try to lift my head, I jostle even more awkwardly against Zian's shoulder, but I catch a glimpse of flashlights streaking through the trees behind us. The guardians are giving chase, shouting to each other as they follow us.

The guys have taken a smart approach by diving into the forest. We've all trained for moving swiftly over uneven terrain, them probably much more recently than me. The guardians can't outpace us with vehicles amid the trees, and the trunks shelter us from bullets unless our pursuers manage to get closer.

But where are we going from here?

I was so focused on getting the guys *out* of the facility, with frantic adrenaline driving me from the arena all the way here, that I haven't taken much time to consider what we'd do after I accomplished my initial goal. All I know is I want to get us away from our captors, someplace they'll never find us again.

Which means we're going to need to put more distance between them and us than we can accomplish on foot.

Zian hurtles steadily onward, his breaths brisk but even with the rise and fall of his chest against my thighs. He'll be pacing himself, though—restraining his strength so he doesn't outrun the other three guys.

I can only make out fragments of their forms in the darkness, but at least one of the others is panting now.

I bite my lip against the urge to demand to know what they're planning next. The quieter we are, the more chance the guardians will lose track of us during the limited night we have left.

There's muttered communication between two of the others, and Zian veers with them to the right without adding any comment of his own. He leaps straight over a log like its nothing more than a twig.

I concentrate on balancing my weight against him for as long as I can bear to shut off my thoughts. But eventually, I can't help raising my head for another glance behind us.

What I see makes my pulse stutter. The faintest of glows is hazing the sky beyond the treetops, making the branches stand out in silhouette against what's now not black but a dark blue.

Dawn has arrived, and it's only going to get brighter.

Beneath the treetops, the forest is still dark as night.

The guys must notice the emerging dawn, though, because they all push forward a little faster.

I can't hear any sound from our pursuers now, but glints of their flashlights still show in the distance. They've quieted down to focus on the chase.

If we dare to stop, they'll be on top of us in a matter of minutes.

All at once, we burst from the trees into a clear stretch of field. A sharply cool wind whips over me, licking across my back.

As the guys swerve farther to the right, my heart thumps faster with the sense of increased exposure. But in a few seconds, I understand why they've emerged from the cover of the woods.

We're dashing along the edge of a low cliff now—a cliff that looms over a four-lane highway. A couple of cars zoom by, but the road is mostly empty at this early hour. Headlights sear across the darkened landscape.

One of the guys sucks a breath through his teeth with a hiss. Another lets out a wordless sound of encouragement.

They're all ahead of Zian now, so I can't see them, but all at once, he starts running even faster. Then, with a heave of his chest, he launches us into open air.

A startled gasp breaks from my lips. He adjusts me against him as we plummet, cradling me closer to his chest. When we hit the ground with a smack, my body is tossed into his, cushioned by his brawn.

The impact is still hard enough to knock the breath from my lungs. His grasp loosens, and I squirm out of his arms to take in our surroundings.

We've landed on the flat bed of a moving truck, one that's roaring along the highway at what's got to be seventy miles an hour. The other guys have leapt on around us, Andreas swaying a little as he rights himself.

Dominic lifts the tarp that's covering the cargo of logs, which only covers one half of the truck bed, and motions for us to take cover under it. I scramble over, knowing we don't want the guardians seeing where we've gone if they make it to the cliff before the truck has zoomed out of view.

The moment we're inside our makeshift tent, I turn to face the guys. My gaze locks with Jacob's.

His handsome face hardens, a cold glint forming in his eyes. Without any warning, he throws himself at me.

The movement is so sudden and unexpected from a long-lost friend that my reflexes scatter and my muscles don't do much more than twitch before he's slamming me to the ground. My arms shoot up instinctively then, but his hand is already clamped around my throat and pressing in hard, cutting off my airway with a shock of pain.

Jacob glares down at me, his gaze pure ice now—icy hatred. Frigid enough that I shiver even as I squirm to shove him off.

Under normal circumstances, I could overpower him easily. But I'm tired from a night on the run, and he's got to weigh nearly twice as much as I do.

My wrists and ankles jar against the invisible hold of his telekinetic power. My thoughts are still too scrambled for me to come up with a coherent strategy to get him off me.

What the hell is going on? Why would Jake want to *hurt* me?

"So we got our freedom and you too," he says in a flat voice. "It's our lucky day. And now I get to—"

"Jake!" Andreas snaps, his tone sharp enough that Jacob's head jerks around, it's so unusual from the normally easy-going guy. "Get off her. We *need* her. She'll know things."

What is he talking about? I squirm more urgently against Jacob's hold, an ache digging into my lungs and my vision starting to waver.

But even with the choke hold he's got on me, the press of his muscle-hardened body against mine stirs a trace of old longings laced with horror.

I've wanted him this close to me—but not like this. Nothing like this.

"Drey is right." I recognize that quiet, even voice as Dominic's, though he's out of view.

Jacob swears, spittle hitting my cheeks. Then he shoves away from me as quickly as he sprang at me, as if he can't stand to be touching me for a second longer.

His striking features have always looked chiseled, but right now they might as well have been carved out of marble. He jerks a hand toward Zian.

"Stay by her. Watch that she doesn't make a run for it."

I stare at him and then at each of the other guys as Zian moves to stand sentinel over me, holding up the highest point of our makeshift tent. A strange energy crackles through the air between us, suffocating even now that my airway is open.

I'm surrounded by the guys I've spent more than four

years dreaming of saving, all of us tucked into this cramped space little more than an arm's reach away. The awareness of their presence sends a giddy shiver over my skin even as I grapple with my confusion.

When I try to speak, my throat throbs. I swallow and cough and swallow again, and then manage to say hoarsely, "Why would I want to run? I—I came for *you*. Of course I figured we'd stick together. That's how it was always supposed to—"

Jacob steps toward me as if he's considering strangling me after all. "Shut *up*."

How can he be the same guy who once grinned so fiercely at me as we planned our winning tactics for a game of capture the flag? Who'd watch me spar with eyes alight with appreciation and call me "Wildcat" when he applauded a win?

Have the guardians done something I can't even comprehend to the boys who were once mine?

My bewilderment brings heat to the back of my eyes, but I clench my jaw against it. Breaking down in tears isn't going to help anything.

I need to stay calm and focused, and we'll get through this.

We have to get through it.

The guys have simply been watching my reactions. Andreas rakes his fingers back through his tight curls. His copper-brown skin has grayed, and I don't think it's just because of the dimness beneath the tarp.

"We know, Riva," he says. "Did you think they wouldn't tell us? That we'd just assume you were dead or something?"

I honestly had no idea what the guys would know about my whereabouts, but no matter what they believed, I expected them to be just as happy to see me as I was to get back to them.

I peer up at him, meeting the dark gray eyes that always used to shine with amusement or friendly warmth. "I don't know what you mean. The guardians took me away after— I guess they figured we were less likely to attempt another escape if we were apart."

It was a mistake to include a female.

Jacob lets out a scoff so ragged it's almost a snarl.

Dominic eases closer, hunched beneath the tarp even though he's the shortest of the guys, the plastic a few inches above his head. His dark hair hangs loose from its usual ponytail, but his pale greenish-hazel gaze is as pensive as it always was.

"There's no point in lying," he says in the same softly measured voice as before, bobbing a little with the vibration of the truck. "We heard about the deal—and everything."

My hands ball at my sides, but I will my frustration down. "It sounds like the *guardians* were lying. What deal? What 'everything'? I just broke you out of that torture building—"

Jacob snorts and can't seem to restrain his caustic remarks any longer. "*You?* When we found you, you were manning the control room, probably trying to figure out how to put the building in lockdown so we'd never make it out."

"Why would I be— I went in there to let you out, because I had no idea you'd already managed it."

"You had the door barricaded," Zian puts in, his words coming out in a low growl. "It seemed like you were trying to save yourself."

"Yeah, from the guardians." I gesture vaguely. "I'd already taken down one just getting into the building. I didn't know how many more were still inside who'd interfere."

Andreas cocks his head. "I don't remember seeing any bodies lying around when we left."

"I shoved her into a storage room so the body wouldn't tip off anyone else!"

"So there's also no proving it now—very convenient," Jacob sneers.

Why are they finding this so hard to understand?

I just barely keep my voice steady, my throat getting ever tighter with an ache that digs way deeper than any of the pain Jacob inflicted with his physical attack. "Why do you think the guardians went rushing out of the facility in the first place? How do you think you got your opening to break out of your cells? Why the hell would I have been doing *anything* other than trying to help you?"

Have you all gone fucking insane? I restrain myself from adding.

What did the guardians do to them? How have they warped the guys I loved so horribly that they don't even *know* me, not properly, anymore?

Jacob glowers at me, his expression so stark with loathing it cuts me right to the core. "I don't know what enemies those assholes have made who might have decided to mess with them. I *do* know that you bargained with the pricks for better treatment, gave up my brother as a fucking blood sacrifice, and then waltzed off to enjoy your cushy new privileges someplace you never had to see us again."

I'm shaking my head before I'm even consciously aware of the movement. Is that what they really think?

"I'd never have done that. How can you even believe— They caught us. Right outside the facility while we were waiting for you. We'd done everything according to plan, but they must have known and been prepared…"

"Why don't you tell us what exactly *you* claim happened that night?" Andreas says, still unusually terse.

I drag in a breath. Are we going to get somewhere now?

"Griffin used his ability to make one of the guardians want to open his door and then mine, just like we discussed. I knocked the guy out, but he didn't have keycards for the other floors. So we went up to the control room and opened all of your cells."

Zian nods slowly. "They opened."

Jacob flicks his glare toward the other guy before aiming it back at me. "And then?"

"Then we headed out to make sure the front yard was clear. We thought it was at first. Griffin couldn't sense anyone nearby, and I didn't see or hear anyone. It must have been a sniper who shot him."

A lump of grief blocks off my voice for a second before I recover it. "And then a bunch of guardians all rushed in, and they shot me too, and zapped me with tasers so I couldn't move…"

One of my hands lifts to my shoulder instinctively, but I know before I say anything more that they won't find my scar convincing—not if they're doubting everything else I said.

The guardians patched me up well before delivering me to the boss of the arena as merchandise. The remnant of the bullet wound looks more like it was a shallow stab mark, not a shot.

"That's all that happened?" Dominic asks.

My mind flits momentarily to the kiss—that giddy, glorious, *stupid* act that might have cost us everything. Every nerve in my body balks against admitting that one factor in my carelessness.

It doesn't make a difference… other than making me look pathetic.

"That's all," I say. "Obviously I wasn't alert enough— you have no idea how much I wish I'd picked up on the threat in time—"

Jacob folds his arms over his chest. "And where did you supposedly go that's kept you away for four years?"

I grit my teeth at the "supposedly" and force them to relax. "The guardians sold me to some crime boss who ran underground cage matches. I became his star fighter. It was either fight or they'd kill me, and if I was dead I wouldn't have been able to come back for you. He kept me under tight security. I never left my room there except for the weekly fights."

A ragged laugh sputters out of Jacob. "Such a fantastic sob story—and how perfect that you did it all for *our* benefit. How long did it take you to come up with that script? What a load of absolute bullshit."

I stiffen against a flinch. "It's not bullshit. It's what happened."

There's a stretch of stony silence between the guys. I can't tell if any of them are even really considering that I might be telling the truth.

Whatever story the guardians beat into their brains, they must have framed it awfully well. But still.

These were my guys. We were all each other had—we were in it together until the end.

We are blood.

They should know I'd never have turned on them.

Zian glances at Andreas, the tarp warbling against his hands as the truck sways around a curve in the highway. "Can you check her memories? That'd give us a quick answer about what really happened after."

Andreas grimaces. "Not particularly quick. There isn't much science to it, remember. I don't have much to narrow it down."

He lifts his chin toward me. "Do you have the name of anyone who was at this cage-fighting place—this crime boss and his goons who made you fight?"

I wince inwardly. "No. They barely talked to me, and I didn't get much chance to overhear anything."

Jacob shifts his weight with a shudder of the truck bed. "Isn't that convenient too?"

"Not really," I retort. "Since I'd *like* to be able to prove to you that I'm not some kind of murdering traitor."

Andreas's mouth has remained twisted. He clasps his lean hands together in front of him. "I'll try. Maybe I'll find something."

He doesn't ask my permission, just fixes his gaze on me.

The Andreas I knew would never have invaded my

head without making sure I was okay with the intrusion. But when I look up, the ruddy glow of his power is already flickering in his eyes, as if the process of delving inside my head requires some part of him to burn.

I can't feel him inside my skull, but my skin itches with the knowledge that he's shuffling through fragments of images and conversations. But if it means he stumbles on the truth about that night, then it's worth it.

We hold there in silence through a few more jostles of the truck and the brightening of the daylight seeping through the tarp. Sweat beads on Andreas's forehead. His eyes jitter, and he yanks his attention away from me with a swipe of his sleeve across his hairline.

"I didn't come across anything definitive," he says to the other guys, his voice gone rough. "I got one glimpse of a cage fight, but no way to tell how often they were or whether she volunteered for it."

"Then we stick with what we know." Jacob scowls down at me. "And what we know is this bitch is a manipulative schemer who'd stab us in the back too the second she gets the chance. So why the hell don't you let me finish what I started?"

"Jake," Zian says, and then doesn't seem to know how to continue.

Andreas speaks up again, sounding weary but firm. "It's a sorry state of the world when *I'm* the voice of reason around here, but like I said before, we need her. If she's been working with the guardians right there in the facility, she must know things about their plans and how they'll operate."

Dominic inclines his head slowly. "She could know

what steps they'll take trying to track us down, so we can evade them better."

"Exactly. And who knows what she's seen or heard that could help us with the next phase?"

"What next phase?" I demand. "And I don't know anything about what the guardians are doing, because I haven't even been in the facility or seen any of them for four years until last night."

The guys all ignore me. "Then we hold on to her until we figure out what we can get out of her," Zian suggests.

I want to believe there's a tiny bit of hesitance in his voice, but at this point I'm not convinced that's more than wishful thinking.

Jacob's lips curl as if the idea of keeping me around disgusts him, but he sighs. "Fine. But she is going to get what's coming to her one way or another."

He swivels on his heel and stalks to the edge of the tarp. Lifting it, he gazes out over the brightening landscape beyond the truck.

"Traffic's starting to pick up," he says. "And the guardians will probably be able to guess we ended up on a vehicle going one way or the other along this highway. We should get off while we can without being noticed and continue the conversation far away from here."

Six

Zian

Less than a minute after we've leapt off the truck, Jacob looks over at Riva where we're tramping through a sparse stretch of forest and holds out his hand. "Your bag. Let's see what you're carrying."

Riva's hand tightens around the strap for a second before she tugs it up over her head and hands it over. "It's just things I thought might help with the escape. Some of which I actually used. You can see one of the guns is empty."

It's an odd bag for her to be carrying to a fight, some kind of leather purse with a decorative fringe along the side. But she speaks with the same firm tone she's answered all our questions with so far.

"Weapons," Jacob mutters, and shoots me a look. He already told me to stick close to her, without needing to point out that I'm the only one in our group who can match Riva in strength and speed.

If she takes off on us, it's going to be up to me to catch her. The idea makes my stomach flip over, but it's already balled tight.

Where has she really been all this time? What was she doing when I stumbled on her in the control room?

She isn't *acting* like a person horrified that her closest friends think she betrayed them. Barely any emotion has flickered across her face, and most of what I have seen I recognize as anger.

If even part of her story is true—if she's been through hell for the past four years and came for us expecting a joyful reunion—wouldn't more of that show?

My mind darts back to the first moment when I saw her in the control room. I was so shocked the memory is blurry. Did her face light up right then, seeing me—more like she was happy than concerned that I'd broken in?

But even if it did, she could already have been putting on an act, realizing she was caught.

"Fuckload of guns and knives, wallets, jewelry…" Jacob fixes his gaze on Riva. "Did you just come back from a day trip robbing a bank?"

She glowers at him. "I had a chance to grab some stuff that seemed like it might be useful when I got away from the cage match place."

"Right, right." He paws deeper and lifts out a crystalline bottle of perfume. "And you figured smelling nice would help with our escape?" He tosses that back in and pulls out a ticket stub. "And going to concerts too. Busy woman."

Riva's jaw twitches, but her voice stays only terse. "I didn't bother to empty the purse when I grabbed it. I was in kind of a hurry, which shouldn't be a surprise. That stuff isn't mine."

"Uh huh. Looks more to me like you'd just come back from one of their stupid missions, with the benefit of a little R&R time." Jacob slings the purse strap over his own shoulder. "Zee, check her over and make sure she's not carrying more than what's in the bag."

Riva's shoulders tense, but she doesn't shy away from me when I step closer. Her fitted tank top and sweatpants don't leave much room for hiding weaponry. I can see with my regular vision that she doesn't have a pistol shoved in her waistband or a sheathed knife at her hip.

But because he asked, and because any tiny miscalculation could screw us all over, I stare a little harder, letting the tingling of my talent form in the back of my eyes.

I skim my gaze over her hips and back, jerking it away quickly from the curve of her small but sculpted ass with a flush of heat through my skin that I hope the other guys can't see. Then I move up beside her so I can give her front a quick scan, darting over her breasts with similar speed.

More heat trickles up the back of my neck and singes my cheeks. As I yank my focus back into regular sight, for a moment I simply watch her marching along next to me.

She looks so much like the Riva I knew. The same delicate features. The same odd hair, dark gray beneath and silver on top, pulled back in a typical if loosening braid.

The same deceptively slim frame that you'd think would snap in a swift breeze, when actually you're lucky if she doesn't snap *you* in half.

Still just as pretty—maybe even more so with the sharpening of her face with adulthood and the slight filling out of her modest curves. Still leaving me with the same urge to scoop her up and shield her by tucking her close against my much broader body.

I used to imagine holding her in other ways too, but my mind freezes up against those memories.

I thought I knew her. I believed the affection for me that I saw shining in her eyes, her determined commitment to all of us.

How could the girl I knew back then have turned on all of us—on *Griffin*, of all people—like that?

What kind of a woman is she now?

My temper stirs and simmers, but I hold back a full-out flare of rage. Wolfing out isn't going to help any of us.

And how can I feel angry and still have to hold my fingers back from brushing over her hair, her bare shoulder, as if I can reconnect with her that literally?

As if someone like me has any business touching *anyone* that way.

I wrench my mind away from those images—and a different thought hits me like a smack of frigid water.

"The trackers!"

The others all jerk to a halt, Riva last.

Jacob spits out a curse and jabs his finger at her. "Aren't you so glad your distraction made us forget?"

Riva blinks at him. "Forget *what*? What are you talking about?"

"We don't have time to argue about it," Andreas breaks in. "We have to get them out *now*."

Dominic clears his throat with an uncomfortable expression. "Riva might have one too."

She almost definitely does.

I step in front of her. "Open your mouth."

It'll be easier that way.

She knits her brow. "What—"

"The guardians put tracking devices in our teeth," I blurt out. I should have remembered it sooner—I'm the one who found them in the first place. "We figured it out after—after some things happened. Unless we pull the right tooth out, it'll be a homing beacon straight to us."

Something wavers in Riva's expression. Horror at the thought of yanking a tooth right out of her jaw or at losing some level of protection she thought she had thanks to the guardians she sold us out to?

It doesn't matter as long as we get this done.

Her lips part, and she opens wide. One of her front teeth is chipped, and another farther back looks like it's missing a chunk.

I don't think about that, only delve my gaze inside each of them searching for that bundle of metal.

There. "First molar on the top left, same as the rest of us," I announce, and hesitate. "I'm the one who needs to—"

"She's got the strength to do it too," Jacob snaps. "Let her deal with her own mouth. You can do mine first."

He steps forward, his stance rigid, and drops his jaw as far as it'll go. I tear my gaze away from Riva, revulsion coiling in my gut as I prepare to get down to work.

We talked about this part of the plan, and I pictured the process to try to prepare myself, but none of that could have matched the awfulness of actually having to reach into my friend's mouth, grip a tooth, and rip it out of his gums root and all.

As I pinch my thumb and forefinger around the right one, even more nausea fills in my stomach. "Sorry," I can't help rasping.

Then I wrench the molar out with a heave of my arm, as fast as I can manage.

Jacob is the most impervious of us all, but even he gives a ragged groan as blood spurts over his lips along with a puff of dark mist. Dominic is at his side in an instant, placing his palm against Jake's jaw by the wound. Dom's mouth presses flat, and Jacob's shoulders sag with released tension.

The sprig of wildflowers Dominic plucked up withers and disintegrates in his hand.

I want to apologize to him too, but none of this can be helped. All we can do is get it over with as quickly as possible.

"Break the tooth," Andreas reminds me in an urgent tone.

I set Jacob's molar on a flat stone and stomp my foot on it with my full inhuman strength. It shatters with a crackling of circuitry.

If the guardians were tracing us using that, the signal just went dead. But there are four more devices beaming out their radio waves.

Andreas is waiting when I raise my head. My stomach keeps churning as I perform the second extraction. He buckles over with a gagging sound, and then Dominic is there by his side.

A leafy twig crinkles away into dust from Dominic's hand. Then he faces me. "My turn."

I hate doing this one the most. Dom has been through all the same training as us, and I know his slender frame has plenty of muscle packed on it, but he's the smallest of us four. The least overt in how he's feeling.

I never know how he's really doing behind his quiet demeanor, but we all know he's got at least a few things haunting him.

Clenching my jaw, I tear out his tooth even faster than the others. As his hand shoots right into his mouth to heal the wound, I crush yet another tracker under my heel.

When I step back, Riva lets out a faint strangled sound. Shuddering, she grips the side of her face and drops the tooth she must have just dragged from her own jaw onto the stone. It smashes under the slam of her foot.

Blood dribbles over her chin, and her shoulders quiver. My gaze leaps to Dominic, but Jacob pushes between him and Riva.

"She waits," he says in a steely tone. "If she can deal out pain, she can endure a little. Take care of yourself, Zee, and Dom'll make sure you're okay first."

Riva's head droops. She doesn't protest, but something twists in my chest.

I hate what she did and everything that came after, but the viciousness of Jacob's rage is unsettling even me. And I'm normally the brute around here.

To get it over with as quickly as possible, I brace myself and catch hold of my molar. My muscles balk in the first instant against damaging my own body, but I push through the resistance and haul the tooth out.

Pain screams through my face. I sputter with it, and Dominic is by my side, palm against my cheek.

Soothing warmth blooms through my gums. When he pulls back, a dull ache remains, but the gaping hole is sealed.

We agreed beforehand that he'd only put in as much energy as it took to remove the possibility of infection.

He moves to Riva next, and Jacob doesn't argue. She holds perfectly still as Dominic works his healing power on her. Then she wipes the bloody spittle from her mouth with the back of her hand and stares at all of us with her bright brown eyes smoldering like coals.

I have to look away.

Andreas kicks dirt and fallen leaves over the crumbled remains of our teeth and the devices they contained. "We're going to want to hitch another ride as soon as we can, to get more distance between here and the last place they could have located us, yeah?"

Jacob nods. "We were heading toward another highway, weren't we?"

"It's at least a few more miles, but that's the idea."

"Then let's get going."

By the time the sun is well up in the sky, we're holed up in the back of a freight truck we spotted at a truck-stop diner.

Andreas grabs some apples out of one of the produce crates and tosses us each one—even Riva, after a momentary pause.

"Thank you," she says quietly.

I dig into mine, both savoring the tart flesh and wishing it was even half enough to settle the grumbling of my empty belly. I could really go for about five steaks and a side of bacon right now.

Jacob shifts where he's been sitting with his back against the wall near the door. "When we hop off of this ride, we're going to need to get more strategic. Focus on our goal."

My heart thumps a little faster. "Ursula."

We haven't been able to talk in much detail about any part of our plans while we were in the facility. We only sketched out the basics.

Now, the possibilities for our next steps seem to spill out endlessly in front of us.

"That one guardian suggested she might go 'back to Pennsylvania,'" Andreas points out, hunkering down against the crate. "It would make sense to start the search there."

I frown. "*How* are we going to search? All we've got is a first name and a few vague details. There won't be an official employee registry for the facility or anything like that."

Drey chuckles. "No, definitely not."

"What about a university?" Dominic says, pitching his soft voice just a little louder than usual to be heard over the rumble of the engine. "We're the right age—we'd fit in pretty well. We'd have lots of other people around to blend in with. And there'd be libraries and computer rooms and all that, right?"

Other than one mission I've run, my experience with

the American college system is restricted to TV show and movie portrayals. But his suggestion at least sounds reasonable.

"Who's Ursula?" Riva pipes up abruptly. "Shouldn't we just find someplace to settle in where no one at all can notice us?"

Jacob snorts. "Not if we want answers, but then, you'd probably rather we didn't get more of those."

I hesitate, not sure how much we even want to tell her, but Andreas shrugs. "We picked up enough info from the guardians to find out about someone important who worked at the facility in the past but then left—or got shut out. If we're going to figure out what exactly they did to us and what we can do about that, she seems like our best bet unless we figure we can take on the entire facility at once."

I can't help letting out a snort of my own at that suggestion, but a bittersweet pang shoots through my chest at the same time.

Is this actually going to work? Is it really possible we could learn something that could *fix* all the things that are wrong inside us?

Riva's forehead furrows. "Isn't chasing after anyone associated with the facility only going to make us more likely to get caught? What does it even *matter*?"

Jacob shoots her a cold look. "It matters to us. And if you were one of us, it'd matter to you too. But you're not going anywhere."

"I don't *want* to leave. I was just saying… Fine. Whatever the rest of you think you need to do, we'll do. I *am* one of you, and I'll be right there with you."

Jacob eyes her for a long moment. Then he glances at

the rest of us. A hint of a smile touches his lips, one that chills more than warms me.

"We can't have Zian playing guard dog with her twenty-four seven," he says. "So we're going to need some other way of ensuring she stays true to her word. And I just thought of the perfect solution."

SEVEN

Riva

The second the words *perfect solution* leave Jacob's mouth, I can tell that I'm not going to like his proposal. Even so, I'm not prepared for his next move.

He extends his muscular arm, almost impressive enough to rival Zian's brawn, and squeezes his fingers into a fist. And a row of purple spikes shoot from his skin from the side of his wrist to just before his elbow.

My pulse stutters, my body tensing with the instinctive sense that whatever those are, they're a threat. They look like the spines on some exotic reptile.

Jacob never showed anything like that in the time I knew him before.

He stares at me with his ice-hard eyes as if daring me to comment.

Andreas clears his throat. "Jake, man, I'm not sure—"

"It's simple," Jacob interrupts. "I give her a mild dose

of the poison. Then she'll have to stick with us so Dom can heal the damage regularly enough to keep her alive."

His lips curve into a tight smile, his gaze boring into mine. "I developed some new abilities while you were enjoying the high life. If I don't jab you much, it'll take a while before the toxin builds up enough to be fatal. But there isn't any regular cure—the guardians tested *that* very thoroughly. You take off on us, you're dead."

Zian's dark eyebrows have drawn together. I think he might protest this torturous suggestion, but instead he glances at Dominic. "But if Dom has to keep healing her…"

Jacob looks over his shoulder at Dominic, his face softening just slightly for the first time since we've reunited. Because he still cares about the other guys, just not about me.

"Only if you're okay with it," he says. "It shouldn't take *too* much, just once or twice a day, to keep her functioning. And hopefully we won't need her for too many days."

Like the boy I remember, Dominic takes a moment to think. I don't totally get why they're especially worried about him—will it really take that much energy to offset the effects of the poison?

He didn't seem all that fazed by healing our gums after we extracted our treacherous teeth. My tongue flicks over the new gap at the back of my mouth automatically, the tissue there still tender.

Dominic's stance looks a bit stiff, but before too long, he answers in his low, measured voice. "It's all right. I can do it."

Nausea unfurls up through my chest as I remember Jacob's phrasing. *Keep her functioning.*

"I might not *die*, but your poison is going to mess with my body, isn't it?" I say to him. "If the guardians catch up with us, I won't be able to help you fight them off very well if I'm physically sick."

Jacob turns to face me again, nothing but disdain in his expression now. How can he look so gorgeous and so cold at the same time?

"That's asking us to believe you'd be fighting against the guardians instead of with them."

I can't suppress the edge that creeps into my voice. "Yes, that *is* what you should believe, because that's what's fucking true."

At least the layer of frustration helps tamp down the anguish that's roiling through me underneath. Every quiver of that fraught emotion rippling through my chest makes me feel as weak as if I've already been poisoned.

It doesn't matter what the guys think right now. I have to prove to them that I'm the same Riva I always was, that I'll put all my strength toward defending them and keeping us together.

I can't do that if I'm falling apart.

"And yet somehow I'm still not seeing it," Jacob snarks back, and rolls his shoulders. "Of course, I still see just offing you as a viable solution too, if you're so upset about this option."

My mouth tightens into a flat line. None of the other guys speak up against his very explicit threat.

Memories flood the back of my mind: my dizziness last night, the shakiness of my muscles. He's asking to do the same thing to me that the boss did—the way the boss tried to murder me.

He wants to put me in a different kind of cage, with my own body trapping me.

A prickle creeps into my lungs—a tiny oscillation like something sharp-edged starting to vibrate within my ribcage.

Like a vicious, angry sound that wants to break free?

I stiffen up, clamping down on the impression and taking a deep breath to clear my lungs. That—that wasn't me. I won't let it be me.

There's no need to get angry about it anyway. Jacob is asking rather than ordering, at least.

He's telling me how this will go and waiting for my response. If I accept, if I show I'm willing to trust that they won't take it too far, that'll be one step toward convincing them that they can trust me too, won't it?

I'm not really sure what else I *can* do at this point.

I scoot across the floor of the cargo hold toward him. "Fine. Just remember that if I stumble when we need to move quickly or defend ourselves, it's not because I want to."

Jacob lets out a derisive sound. He grasps my hand, and in spite of everything, a tingle shoots straight through my nerves at the contact. My breath catches.

How can he not feel that we're all meant to be together, me included? That we really are blood in all the ways that matter?

We're connected in ways no other people on this planet are.

He'll have to realize it. I just need to keep trying.

Andreas steps closer, wobbling with the movement of the truck. "Are you sure you can control the dosing well enough right now? With our talents dulled…"

Jacob cuts a sharp glance toward the other guy. "You don't need to bring that up in front of her."

Andreas simply shrugs. "It's not going to matter by the end of the day anyway." He catches my eyes. "After you left, the guardians started drugging us somehow or other so we couldn't use our powers at full strength. Protective measures." His mouth twists into something halfway between a grimace and a smirk.

"It's already wearing off," Jacob says. "I know what I'm doing."

He tugs my arm straight in front of him and twists his arm so he can bring the purple spines protruding from it to my flesh. He lets just two of them rest against the skin and then presses them harder.

A stinging sensation like the needles the guardians sometimes injected us with shoots through my forearm and radiates into my hand and shoulder. Unlike with the needles, the sensation lingers, prickling in my veins even after Jacob has pulled his spines away.

That's the only effect of the toxin that I can feel so far. If that's all it is, I won't do too badly.

But that's probably too much to hope for.

Jacob is still holding out my arm as if he's forgotten that he no longer needs it. Because his attention has homed in on the front of my shirt.

I glance down at myself, wondering if I've gotten something on the tank top, just as his hand shoots out. He yanks on the chain around my neck to pull the cat-and-yarn charm out from its safe spot beneath the fabric.

A jolt of panic shoots through me with the thought that he's going to rip it right off my neck. My body reacts on instinct, my hand smacking away his before he can get a real hold on the necklace, my feet shoving me out of reach.

My back jars against the side of the cargo hold. Jacob takes a step toward me, chilling fury blazing in his eyes.

"They let you keep it. That was my brother's, and they let you— And you want us to believe you didn't win yourself special treatment?"

"I—" My fingers close around the charm protectively. My gaze darts from him to each of the other guys, and for the first time it sinks in that none of them are wearing their old necklaces. "What happened to yours?"

Zian's lips have pulled back with a growl. "The guardians took them from us as part of our punishment for trying to run."

They took even that from the guys—from Jacob? The one thing of his twin's he should have been able to hold on to?

My heart aches, but I don't know what to say. "I have no idea why they let me keep it. It wasn't part of any deal."

Jacob looms over me, his eyes narrowing. I brace myself for some kind of attack, but he just shakes his head with a derisive curl of his lips.

"Whatever. If you get totally out of it with the poison, say something, and Dom will balance you out. Until then, keep your mouth shut unless you're finally going to cough up some inside info about the guardians."

I frown at him. "I've told you already, I don't know any more about them than you do."

"Then you're basically useless, aren't you?" he retorts, and shifts his attention to the other guys as if I don't even exist.

〇

My introduction to the state of Pennsylvania is a dingy clothing outlet store standing between two other big, boxy outlet stores just off the highway we've been driving down. Between the guys' talents, they were able to commandeer a seven-seater SUV in a mundane shade of tan from, as Andreas described it, "the kind of people who aren't going to be reporting their car stolen."

He's behind the wheel now as he pulls into the parking lot outside the store, a little more confident after his stint in the driver's seat earlier today. Have they managed to practice their driving skills since I've been gone, maybe as a little detour on missions?

I want to ask but I have the uncomfortable suspicion that any questions about their activities will come across as digging for info for my supposed guardian allies.

"Okay," Jacob says as Andreas parks at the far end of the mostly empty lot. "The three of us will go in and grab a few sets of low-profile clothes for all of us. Dom, you stay here with Riva."

I raise my chin from where I'm tucked away in the back seat. "Why can't I pick out my own clothes? I'm the one who brought the money you're using."

Jacob twists to shoot a glare at me. "You shouldn't look

strange with that hair on a university campus, but out here in the boonies? We're trying to avoid getting noticed—at least, the four of us are."

I make a face at him, but he does have a point. My gaze slides to Dominic in the middle row, to the left of my seat.

I don't need to ask why the quietest of the guys is being left behind with me. Now that I've seen him by full daylight, I've realized that his posture isn't perpetually hunched after all.

He's got a small but noticeable lumpy area on his upper back, covered by the thin trench coat I haven't seen him take off once. Did the guardians perform experiments on him that left him disfigured?

Another question I already know will only make them more pissed off with me. But it makes sense that they wouldn't want bystanders noticing.

The other guys push open the car doors, letting a rush of cool fresh air waft over us. It's early fall, the leaves on some of the trees we've raced by already sharpening to reds and oranges with the crisp weather.

Then the doors thump shut again, and Dominic and I are alone.

I squirm in my seat, my nerves twitching with restless exhaustion and overall discomfort. I ended up dozing off for a little while on the truck and again here in the backseat after we found the car, but not nearly enough to make up for the fact that I've been on the run all night and the better part of the day after.

And Jacob's poison is gnawing away at me, setting off

little aches in my joints and flashes of queasiness in my gut.

His strategy is so stupid. If we're attacked—if I need my strength—

I close my eyes for a moment, gathering my focus. Freaking out won't get me anywhere.

And the last thing I want is to provoke that sharp prickle in my chest again.

When I feel steady, I focus on Dominic, the sliver of his profile I can see from my current angle.

He's pulled his shoulder-length waves back into his usual ponytail, the auburn strands dark against his light brown skin. In the past four years, the line of his jaw has broadened a little, but other than that and the bulges on his back, he looks the same as the unassumingly handsome guy I knew then.

Dom was always the most thoughtful of the six of us: taking his time to consider every angle, stating his opinions carefully and waiting for our feedback. He wouldn't have jumped to conclusions or gotten caught up in righteous rage.

All the others had their silly nicknames for me, but he always called me exactly who I was.

I pull my legs up on the seat in front of me, hugging my knees. "You know this is ridiculous, right?"

His head turns a little, but he's looking toward the store rather than at me. "Getting new clothes? You've got blood on yours."

I wrinkle my nose at the stains not totally invisible in the black fabric and try again. "No. Treating me like I'm allied with the guardians. *You* realize I'd never screw the rest of you over, don't you?"

There's a moment of silence before he speaks again. "I don't think we should talk about this."

"I just need to know that someone here hasn't gone totally crazy. We're *blood*. I—"

Dominic swivels to meet my gaze then, the abruptness of the gesture cutting me off. His hazel eyes aren't as cold as Jacob's, but I don't see any friendliness in them either.

"You have no idea about anything," he says, quiet but terse. "You don't even know what I'm already giving up just keeping you around. So don't tell me I'm not doing enough."

I blink at him—at the back of his head, which is all I have a moment later. "What do you mean? What are you giving up?"

Before he can answer, if he even would have, the other guys are hopping back into the SUV.

Jacob tosses a plastic bag at me. "Get changed."

By the next morning when we arrive at the college campus the guys picked out, all of us look suitably student-ish, at least in attire. I've pulled on a black tee, a pair of dark gray cargo pants with a wonderfully excessive number of pockets, and a navy hoodie that I'm using to cover my silvery hair.

The guys have picked out a range of clothes from Zian's super casual sports tank and sweats to Jacob's dressier fitted button-up and slacks. Only Dominic has left on what he was already wearing.

I suspect he's not going to take off that trench coat in front of me any time soon. Maybe he never takes it off in front of *anyone*.

But from what I know from my limited and admittedly mostly fictional experience with college life, he'll still fit in well enough as some kind of alternative punk type.

We cruise down a street lined with narrow three-story townhouses attached in sets of two. Zian went ahead of the rest of us earlier and used his penetrating sight to find one building no one's occupied.

Since it's a couple of weeks into the typical semester now, we're hoping no one with more claim is going to try to move in while we're squatting there.

Jacob parks the SUV out front, and we clamber out. Zian hangs back by the door so he can walk over to the townhouse behind me, as if I need that much of an escort.

Uneasiness jitters through my body as I scan our surroundings. Students are ambling around or hanging out on their front landings all up and down the street.

I haven't been surrounded by this many people since my last cage match. I haven't been surrounded by this many *normal* people—who expect me to be normal too—in more than four years.

It doesn't help that the twinges of nausea I felt yesterday have expanded overnight into a ball of queasiness that fills my stomach. I only managed to swallow a few bites of the fast-food breakfast we nabbed at a drive-through—and then regretted even that for the rest of the drive.

Sweat trickles down the back of my neck, adding to the clammy sensation creeping over my skin. I have to tense the muscles in my legs to make sure I'm keeping my steps steady.

But I will not complain. I won't give Jacob one more opportunity to accuse me of trying to weasel out of his security measures.

By design, Jacob reaches the door first. He lifts a fake key toward the knob, but we all know he's going to use his powers to actually open the lock.

A couple of girls are hanging out on the landing across from ours. One of the girls, a statuesque redhead with freckles scattered across her high cheekbones, glances across the lane at us and smiles. "Hey! New neighbors?"

"Yep," Andreas says in a carefully warm voice—friendly but not too encouraging. "We turned up a little late, but what can you do?"

"These places are great. So much better than the regular dorms. I'm Brooke, by the way. Let me know if you need any help figuring stuff out."

"Will do."

Jacob offers a brisk nod. Our neighbor's gaze travels over the bunch of us, locking with mine just for a second before moving on. Her brow furrows.

Do we look strange after all? Maybe she thinks it's odd for a girl to be living with four guys? Or are we giving off a vibe that says we don't actually belong here?

Before I can worry much about that, Zian is nudging me to follow the others inside.

The townhouses come pre-furnished with basic birch furniture and a sofa covered in a denim-like fabric. We find ourselves in a living room that's merged with a small dining room, an open-concept kitchen off to the side.

"There should be four bedrooms," Andreas says. "Two on the second floor and two on the third. I can take the sofa."

I'm getting my own space, then? Lucky me.

I take a step toward the stairs, wanting to find whatever bed will be mine and crash onto it. But I'm not concentrating enough, and weakness flares in my calves.

I stumble, knocking my hip against a side table when I catch myself. As I push myself upright again, my legs tremble under me. The ball of nausea swells into a boulder.

I might need the bathroom before I get to that bed.

The guys have gone silent, watching me. Jacob flicks his hand toward Dominic.

"I think she needs your first dose of healing. Don't patch her up *too* well."

Dominic nods and walks over to me. I try to catch his gaze, to search his eyes for any hint of understanding or a clue about what he suggested earlier, but he only looks at my forearm where he's resting his hand.

A soft warmth flows through my body, melting the nausea and the clamminess. My muscles relax, able to hold me up without extra focus.

A pinch of queasiness remains in my stomach, and I still don't feel quite like myself, but it's a lot better. Well enough for a flicker of heat to stir beneath my skin at

Dominic's continued touch—and a pang of loss to hit me when he drops his hand.

"Thank you," I say to Dominic as he steps away.

He simply tips his head, still not meeting my eyes.

"Upstairs," Jacob orders with a snap of his fingers, and I find myself tramping with him up two flights to the highest bedrooms. He glances into both and points to the one he's decided should be mine.

"You'll stay in here unless we need you," he tells me. He hovers his hand over the inner doorknob, and the button that should allow me to lock and unlock it twists and crackles.

He's going to trap me inside with his powers. I swallow thickly. "You really don't need to—"

"Just a little extra protection for the rest of us," Jacob says coolly. "I'm sure you get it."

He stalks out, shutting the door behind him. There's a rasp, and I know he's engaged the lock.

Of course, I'm more than strong enough to break a regular dorm room lock if I need to. That wouldn't do much to prove my trustworthiness to the guys, though.

I glance around the bedroom. At least it's nicer than my last two jail cells.

A double-sized bed with a forest-green bedspread fills a third of the space, next to glossy birch bookshelves and a desk. The shag rug looks soft enough that I'd like to dig my toes into it.

And I have a window—the greatest of luxuries.

I walk closer to it and take in the view: the building across the lane. A figure turns by the window directly across from mine with a flash of red hair.

It's Brooke. She must have gone inside after we did—her bedroom matches mine.

I should yank myself back, but right then she glances out and notices me. A smile crosses her lips, and she raises her hand in greeting.

I don't know what to do other than wave back with an answering smile I hope isn't too tight. Then I back away.

Everything is okay. I'm okay. The guys are okay.

We got away from the facility like we always wanted. The rest we can figure out as we go.

I just have to stay strong.

EIGHT

Riva

I wake up to a brisk knocking on my bedroom door and roll over, rubbing my bleary eyes.

Evening has descended beyond the window, the world now painted in shades of blue and gray. My head feels muggy despite the sleep, but I'm not sure how much of that is natural fatigue and how much it's the toxin coursing through my veins.

The knocking comes again.

"What?" I say in a thick voice.

It's Zian who answers, a little gruffly. "Dinner. Come down."

The guys are letting me eat with them instead of merely bringing up a plate? I *have* stepped up in prisoner status.

I set that bitterly wry thought aside and pull myself out of bed. There's a clacking sound as Zian disengages the lock.

Whatever Jacob did to it, he's left it so the other guys can turn it from the outside too.

When I push the door open, Zian is waiting for me, all six-foot-five of him looming over my much smaller frame. When I slip onto the small landing, there's only a few feet of space between us.

I used to take comfort in his impressive size, but that was when I knew he'd only use it to protect me.

Not so much now, even if the sight of his massive body still sends a tingle through me that I can't explain. His expression looks strained, the normally warm peachy undertones to his brown skin dulled.

Because he isn't happy about how the others are treating me or because he isn't happy they're keeping me around at all?

Not the kind of question you can ask and expect a useful answer. I stretch my arms and glance toward the door between the two bedrooms with a twinge in my bladder.

"I need to use the bathroom."

Zian nods awkwardly and steps to the top of the stairs. "Just be fast."

The bathroom smells like artificial lemon from whatever the staff used when they cleaned it after the last occupants. I use the toilet and then splash water on my face, peering at myself in the mirror.

I'm not looking so great myself, my pale skin even ashier than usual other than the dark smudges forming beneath my eyes. I pat some water on the wisps of hair that are coming loose from my braid.

My hand rises to the lump of my cat-and-yarn

pendant that's back under my shirt. I run my fingers over it, and a lump fills my throat.

None of this is going the way I pictured. None of this feels good.

But maybe I deserve it, even if not for the reasons the guys think.

I let them down. I was in the lead, clearing the way, and I got caught up in a silly impulse rather than keeping all my attention on making sure we were safe.

Griffin *died* because of me. I've never forgiven myself for that, so why should they?

Which means it doesn't matter what they think or say. All that matters is that I have to stick to the mission now —and do whatever it takes to keep these four men safe, because even after the hell they've been putting me through, I can't stand the thought of losing another of them.

With a renewed sense of resolve, I leave the bathroom and march stoically down the stairs ahead of Zian.

I don't like how sluggish my limbs feel, but at least the nausea hasn't expanded too much yet. When a whiff of greasy cheese and tomato sauce reaches my nose, my stomach gurgles with hunger rather than queasiness. By the time I reach the dining room, my mouth is watering.

The other three guys are already sitting around the table with a couple of pizza boxes popped open in between them. There are only four chairs, but they've pulled over one of the armchairs from the living room, which Andreas has sprawled in with one lanky leg over the arm and his plate balanced on his belly.

He looks perfectly at home with that jaunty pose in

his casual Henley and jeans—and as delicious as the damned pizza.

Not that it seems like he'd appreciate my thoughts on the matter at the moment. I tear my gaze away.

Jacob catches my eyes and jerks his hand toward the chair across from him. "Eat. No hunger strikes."

"I wouldn't want to starve," I inform him calmly, and pull off a slice of pepperoni and peppers.

Zian lets out a discontented rumble, looking over the offerings. "No meat lovers?"

Andreas arches his eyebrows teasingly at the bigger guy. "Take what you get, Zee. When was the last time you had the chance to eat *any* kind of pizza? It's not like we don't all know you'd rather be chowing down half a cow anyway."

Zian scowls at him without any real hostility. His love of every sort of meat—and knack for inhaling vast quantities of it—has been legendary among us since we were kids.

A trace of a smile touches my lips. At least a few things haven't changed.

I haven't eaten fresh pizza since one of my last missions years ago. Occasionally, my meals in the arena building included a slice or two, but always cold and a little stale, like they were leftovers from someone else's dinner a couple of nights before.

The first bite of this slice fills my mouth with the perfect blend of tart tomato, salty cheese, and spicy pepperoni. I can't restrain an eager hum of satisfaction.

Four gazes snap to my face. My skin heats five degrees in an instant.

For just that moment, the connection I always believed in between us thrums to life—but not quite the way I'm used to.

Then Jacob tears his attention away with a sneer and taps a few glossy brochures stacked on the table next to him. "I got a campus map, and I think I've worked out the best computer lab to do our research under the radar. We can get started tonight."

I take another bite, but this one slides down my throat with much less pleasure than the first. I still don't understand why we're risking staying here.

As if to punctuate my worry, exuberant voices filter in through the townhouse's front window as students meander by on the sidewalk outside. When I perk my ears, I catch the faint thump of bass reverberating through the wall between our side and the townhouse attached.

We're surrounded here—surrounded by people whose intentions and allegiances we don't know.

"Shouldn't we keep moving?" I say, tensing instinctively for Jacob's response. "Or totally lay low for at least a little while, until the guardians' initial search for us is waning?"

He aims his gaze at me again, but it's only chilly now. "And where do *you* suggest we go?"

I shrug, attempting a casual air. "There've got to be lots of places we could disappear to. Someplace in the wilderness where there'd be no one around to notice us. That's what we always talked about—"

"Before," he breaks in, his voice sharpening. "Things are different now."

"We need to find this person," Dominic puts in. "And the longer we wait, the colder the trail will get."

Zian grunts. "She might hear that we got out and decide to disappear herself."

"But what can anyone tell us that matters anyway?" I asked. "We are what we are. We should put everything about the facility and the guardians behind us and make our own—"

"*You* don't get to decide what we 'should' do." Jacob's voice is pure ice now. "No surprise that you wouldn't want us hassling anyone associated with the facility, though."

I grimace. "That's not what I'm saying. I don't see how it's going to help anything. And the more people see us, the more we're risking getting caught, no matter how much we try to blend in."

Andreas scoots a little higher in his armchair. "We need answers. Don't you trust us that we wouldn't be digging for them without a very good reason?"

When he puts it like that, I don't know how to argue. My teeth set on edge for a second before I will myself to relax.

"Who *is* this Ursula woman anyway? She worked in the facility? Why would she be able to tell you more than any other guardian?"

Jacob narrows his eyes at me. "Maybe you could tell us a little about that."

I frown back at him. "I've never heard her name before in my life."

Jacob considers me and then glances at Andreas. "You could confirm that, couldn't you? Search her memories for anything related to Ursula."

Andreas sits all the way up with a twist of his mouth. "Since I only have a very vague sense of who Ursula is, it might not get us anywhere, but I can try."

I go rigid in my chair, but don't protest when he fixes his gaze on me. What he sees should only prove my innocence in this one small way.

The shimmer of ruddy light comes into his eyes. He holds his stare for a full minute, not even blinking, the lines of his stunning face softening as he's absorbed by the search.

Then he drops his gaze. "As far as I can tell, Riva's never met anyone named Ursula. If she met her without knowing her name, I'm not sure I have a clear enough grasp to pinpoint that."

He drags in a breath and meets my eyes properly, something like an apology in his tone. "We think Ursula was someone high up in the facility, maybe even at the top at some point. Zian overheard a couple of the guardians who work in the testing area arguing about a change in policies—one of them saying she wouldn't have approved and the other pointing out that she wasn't in charge anymore."

"You don't need to tell her all that," Jacob snaps.

"Why not?" Andreas asks. "Even if she somehow went back to the guardians and told them, they already know a hell of a lot more about it than we do. We wouldn't be revealing anything new."

Zian looks uncertain. "The less she knows about what we're doing, the better, don't you think?"

"How else is she going to pitch in with the investigation?"

Jacob snorts. "You think we're letting her get involved with our mission? Did you get hit on the head on the way out of the facility?"

Andreas glowers at him. "What else are we going to do? Leave her locked up in her room here with someone always needing to play babysitter? If she says she wants to help us, we might as well give her a chance to prove it."

My spirits rise with a rush of hope, so swift it's giddying. Andreas believes me—enough to give me a chance, anyway.

I still don't think we're really safe sticking around here, but I'd rather be with the guys helping us get what they think they need than holed up in the bedroom twiddling my thumbs.

"I'll do whatever I can," I say quickly. "I'll be a little rusty on the computers, but I can handle the basics."

Jacob scowls at me and turns his attention back on Andreas. "If she wanted to be helpful, she'd own up to the truth about what she's been doing the last four years."

Andreas cocks his head. "Does that really matter as much as what she does *now*?"

Dominic clears his throat, and the others glance at him, recognizing that he's got something to say. He isn't the type to interrupt.

He glances at me and then the others. "The more she's around the other people on campus, there is more chance she could get across some kind of signal. If that's what she'd want to do."

"It's not," I mutter.

Andreas waves off Dominic's concern. "Isn't that already covered by the whole poison precaution? If she screws us over and loses your help, she's signed her own death sentence. Nothing to worry about."

Dominic hesitates. "I suppose we can cover more ground if she comes with us. All four of us can be working at the same time."

Jacob can't argue away the logic they've presented. He doesn't look happy about it, though.

He turns to Zian. "Are you okay with her running around on the loose?"

"No," Zian says, and my heart lurches. "Not when we can't be sure what she'll do."

"It won't really be on the loose," Andreas says in an exasperated tone. "We wouldn't let her go off on her own. One of us would always be with her."

Zian nods slowly. "Okay, that doesn't sound so bad."

"There you go." Andreas smiles at me—is that the first time *any* of the guys have aimed a friendly expression at me since I made it back to them?

I can't tell how much it's the novelty or relief or the way the smile turns his face twice as gorgeous, but a flutter of warmth fills my chest.

"It'll look better to the other students if we're all coming and going—like we really are attending classes," Andreas adds.

Dominic rubs his mouth, his expression turning even more pensive. "We should probably sit in on some lectures here and there too, just to keep up appearances so no one starts to wonder."

Jacob sighs and studies me again with his hardened eyes.

"You tell me what you need me to do to help out, and

I'll do it," I say. "If this Ursula woman is so important, I'll dig up everything I can."

"Fine," he bites out, and grabs another slice of pizza with a hostile gesture as if it's offended him too. "But we're not letting you get anywhere near the computers. You can be on cover-story duty."

Nine

Riva

Before we arrive at the room for Introduction to Sociology, my nerves are jumping at the thought of crashing a class where we don't belong. Just how badly are we going to stick out?

Then I step through the doorway and jolt to a halt before the annoyed murmurs of the students behind me propel me onward.

The lecture hall is massive, practically a coliseum. There must be a thousand people packed into the folding chairs in the graduated rows that end maybe fifty feet above the level of the central stage.

Zian and I are both minor blips in the huge crowd—which would reassure me more if we weren't also surrounded by a swarm of unknowns.

I keep my hood up, even though I can spot girls with stranger hair colors than mine in a brief glance around the hall. All my senses are on the alert.

I'm no longer worried that we'll stick out in this crowd, but my instincts are screaming at me that there's no way I can keep track of every potential threat.

Zian drops into a seat at the top next to an aisle—easy to escape from as need be. In my apprehension, I approve of his choice.

As I sink into the padded seat next to him, he yanks up the little wooden desk surface that's attached to the chair and sets his notebook on it. I've got one of those too, and a couple of pens—all part of keeping up our front.

If anyone *does* wonder about the new arrivals in the townhouse residences, we want to give every appearance of being totally normal students. Definitely no freaks on the run from sadistic experimenters here.

The twitching of my skin gradually ebbs as the relaxed murmurs of the other students flow around me. How are the other guys faring in the computer lab?

My mind slips back to the memory of them leaving the townhouse, Jacob and Andreas looking like normal if breathtakingly handsome students but Dominic a little awkward in the padded parka he swapped his usual trench coat for. It obscured the lumps on his back completely, but he must be hot in it even keeping the front wide open.

But I doubt he wants to be trapped in the townhouse any more than I do.

My hand slips my pendant out from under my shirt. I click the pieces apart and snap them back together, willing myself even calmer, even more focused.

If a threat happens to come from anywhere in this horde, I'll be ready for it.

After the third *click-snap*, Zian glances over at me. My

hand freezes, and then I stuff the pendant back out of sight, remembering Jacob's vicious response when he first saw it.

Maybe it's better not to remind the men of what I'm still holding onto from the guy we lost.

The professor walks onto the stage below, looking more like a doll than a person from way up here. He swipes his graying hair to the side of his forehead, takes his spot behind the podium, and activates his microphone with a brief fizzle of static.

"Good afternoon, everyone," he says in a drawling sort of voice. "Let's get started."

I didn't expect to pay all that much attention to the content of the lecture. My pen moves over the page, but I'm making notes about the kinds of clothes the other students are wearing, doodling their poses in their chairs.

I don't need to study Sociology. I need How To Appear To Be A Regular Human Being 101.

The short missions we went on under the guardians' instructions never lasted more than a day. We were never prepared to fully integrate.

Or at least I wasn't.

A fresh prickle of annoyance tingles through me. Why are we trying to blend in at all? It would be so much easier if we just vanished to someplace we could live off the land and avoided making the slightest ripple in anyone else's life.

Other people do that. And then I wouldn't have to be stressing about whether I'm making my ripples in just the right shape.

The professor's voice drones on with a flicker of bullet

points changing on the projection screen. I study Zian from the edge of my vision, deliberating the best strategy to get through to him.

"Listening to an old dude talk for hours on end isn't what I pictured freedom looking like," I mutter under my breath in a dry tone.

Zian's eyebrow twitches, but he keeps his gaze on whatever he's jotting down in his notebook.

Still keeping my voice low so only he can hear with his keen ears, I tap my pen against my scrawled-on paper. "I wonder if we couldn't just grab a few computers and set up our own workstation someplace out of the way."

"We don't just need computers," he replies brusquely. "Once we figure out who she is, we need to find *her*. We can't just hide."

And what kind of a mess are we going to end up in if the guys insist on confronting this woman who at least used to work with the exact same people we're running from?

I scowl at my paper, but this isn't exactly an ideal setting for getting into an extended debate. And Zian isn't really the debating type—or he never was before, anyway.

There's so much I still don't know about the guys I used to be so in sync with.

But I have him to myself for just the next two hours. There's got to be some way I can start to convince him that their crazy plan is too dangerous.

As I stew over the problem, the professor's voice filters through my thoughts. "That brings us to the concept of tribalism. Now, obviously forming bonds with our fellow human beings is an important factor in our survival as a species. But our tendency to create 'packs' of sorts can also have major negative consequences."

I cock my head, intrigued despite myself—because my guys and I are basically our own little pack, aren't we? Does this bigwig think there's something wrong with that?

He rambles on for a little while about how human brains aren't capable of comprehending huge populations as a cohesive unit and the good that can come from collaborating with like-minded peers before getting to the points I'm more interested in.

"Once we connect with people we consider our tribe, though, there's frequently an impulse to view anyone *outside* that tribe with suspicion. At its worst, we see certain groups completely dehumanizing other people, thinking of them as if they aren't even the same species— and treating them as if they don't deserve the same kindness and respect. Slavery, genocide, and other atrocities can stem from that skewed perspective."

My fingers tighten around my pen. Unwanted images trickle up from the back of my mind of the guardians' demanding voices and harsh grasps. Always pushing us to perform for them and then shutting us in a cage when they didn't have a current use for us.

Because we were different from them. Strange. Freaks.

But they *made* us that way.

Anger stirs in my gut with a pinching sensation that brings me back to other memories. The fighting ring. The boss's smirk.

All those twisted bodies.

I close my eyes for a second and swallow down the uncomfortable emotions that've started to rise up. Then I forge my voice into an arch but light-hearted tone. "Sounds awfully familiar, doesn't it? Maybe the guardians should have taken this class."

Zian doesn't answer me, but the corners of his lips curve upward with a hint of amusement.

The tiny victory gives me a surge of exhilaration, washing away the last traces of my uneasiness. I press my advantage.

"But then, maybe *they* weren't really human. With that metal getup, they could have been secret robots for all we know."

Zian shakes his head at the absurd suggestion, but his smile grows.

"They definitely treated us like they didn't have any concept of humanity," I go on. "Like we were circus animals for their entertainment."

I pause and reach toward his arm to try to solidify the connection we do share, whether the guys have been willing to admit it or not. "And I don't know if they'll ever let us go, not—"

My fingertips graze Zian's smooth skin just above his wrist. In the very first instant, a jolt of warmth flows up my arm, catching hold of my heart and tugging me closer.

The very next instant, Zian is wrenching away from me, jerking around in his seat with a flash of bared teeth. A whiff of pheromones gusts off him that's stress and also something like… fear?

"*Don't touch me*," he snarls, low but so fierce several heads around us swivel our way.

I plaster a mild expression on my face and lean back over my notebook, pretending nothing's wrong for the benefit of our audience. Underneath, my insides are a shaky jumble.

Does he really hate me that much? What would he be *afraid* of?

I don't understand any of this.

It isn't fucking fair.

But nothing in our lives has ever been fair, has it?

From beneath my pained bewilderment, a surge of unnervingly volatile frustration rises up. It sends a prickling vibration through my lungs that chills me to the bone.

No. I don't want to feel that way. I don't want to feel *anything* that could lead me back to the horror show in the arena.

So I blank my mind and go through the motions of attentively scrawling out notes until the projection screen goes dark and the students stand up from their seats.

Oh. It's over.

I shake myself out of the sort-of trance I'd fallen into and get to my feet alongside the others. As we tramp out of the lecture hall, Zian doesn't speak to me, doesn't even look at me.

What would he do if I veered off in a different direction like I was going to explore the campus on my own instead of heading back to the townhouse like a good little girl?

After hearing the hatred ringing through his voice over a much smaller transgression, I'm not sure I'd want to find out.

I'm supposed to be showing I'm still a full, loyal member of our "tribe." That I'm willing to play along because it matters so much to me to re-earn the guys' trust. It'd be stupid to jeopardize that out of some momentary pique anyway.

Zian walks a little ahead of me all the way back to the townhouse, but I can tell from the tension in his muscles that he's tracking every move I make. As he strides up the three steps to the front door, a voice calls out to us.

"Hey, neighbors!"

It's the tall, redheaded girl from next door: Brooke. She's sitting at the patio table set up in the lane between our townhouse and hers, a textbook open in front of her, but at the sight of us, she gets up, flashing a bright smile.

As she ambles over, I freeze in place and then propel myself on up to the door, taking the steps at a pace I hope looks casual. I push my mouth into my best distantly friendly smile. "Hi."

Brooke comes to a stop beside our steps and sets her hands on her hips. "I realized I never got your names."

Her gaze flicks to Zian but quickly comes back to me, as if it was mine she was most interested in.

My smile starts to feel stiff, but I hold it up anyway. One of the names I memorized to toss out easily, similar to my own but common enough not to make me stand out, tumbles automatically from my mouth. "Rita. Sorry."

She laughs, but her attention still lingers on me. "It's okay. You were busy moving in yesterday."

"I'm Zack," Zian says gruffly, giving his own alias.

"Nice to meet you both. Are you getting settled in all right?"

"Yep!" I say in an attempt at sounding cheerful. "Just had our first class."

Brooke grins. "Looks like the prof didn't go too hard on you. What's your major?"

"Sociology." It's the only answer that makes sense, although I don't know what other classes we might end up sitting in on.

Then it occurs to me that I should probably return the question, since that's how small talk works. I'm so out of practice after getting nothing but grunts from my keepers at the fighting arena for four years. "How about you?"

"Double-major in History and Economics. You probably have some overlap! It's pretty amazing looking at society as a whole and all the crazy things we get up to, huh?"

"Yeah," I say, and wince inwardly with the suspicion that my agreement came out sounding weak. "It is," I add with a little more oomph.

She'd probably have enjoyed that sociology lecture. Suddenly I find myself wondering what it'd have been like to be sitting next to her, sharing observations about the professor's remarks.

Not that I *could* have shared with her even half of the things I'd have thought about.

Brooke tips her head to the side. "You know, Rita, a bunch of us are having a bit of a girl's night at my place tonight if you want to stop by and get to know some more people on campus. It'll be fun, nothing too crazy."

My brain stalls for a second. I've never been in a position before where I had people giving me personal invitations—people I expected to see again after I talked to them now.

I don't want to give any of the students here more

chance to realize there's something off about me. But will it look suspicious if I say no?

My mouth opens and closes as I grope for my answer —and then the door to our townhouse whips open.

Jacob stands on the threshold, his bright blue eyes searing into me. "Let's get going," he says to both me and Zian in a sharp voice. "We've got work to do. You're holding us up."

I restrain a flinch at his tone, but he's given me the perfect exit. "Thanks, but sorry," I say to Brooke. "I've got a bunch of catching up to get through, but maybe another time."

I catch a glimpse of her brow knitting before I follow Zian inside.

The second the door thumps shut behind me, Jacob snatches my arm, his fingers digging in. "Don't even fucking try it," he snaps.

I stare at him. "What are you talking about? You asked me to come in, so I did."

He jerks his hand toward the front steps. "That whole weirdo routine with the girl next door. I guess you're trying to make her suspicious to sabotage our plans?"

I sputter a guffaw. "Are you fucking kidding me? I was trying *not* to make her suspicious. College students talk to each other."

At least, they have in all the shows I've seen. Brooke seemed to think it's normal.

Jacob scowls. "Not the talking. The awkward answers, the pointed hesitations."

I grimace right back at him. "I'm doing my best.

Forgive me for not having socialized with anyone in four years. It wasn't by choice."

"If you go on about that sob story with the—"

"People!" Andreas breaks into our conversation with a brisk voice and a clap of his hands. When Jacob shuts up, he smiles and slings his arm around my shoulders.

It's the first gesture of physical comradery the guys have offered me since I broke them out of the facility. The first time *anyone* has touched me in an affectionate way since Griffin, right before…

I tense up instinctively, even as the rush of heat through my body sends my thoughts into disarray. I almost miss the rest of Andreas's comment.

"I'm glad you two enjoyed your class, but you haven't even heard the good news yet."

He lets go of me, just a brief, casual embrace, and I don't have time to miss it anyway. My stomach is sinking.

Somehow I don't think I'm necessarily going to agree about the "good" part of his news.

But Zian perks up. "What's up?"

Dominic steps into view from the living room, his parka exchanged for his lighter trench coat. "We found out who Ursula is."

Jacob nods, still scowling. "Ursula Engel. But we don't know for sure. She just seems to be the most likely person."

"There was a picture," Andreas puts in. "Not the best quality and from twenty-five years ago, but she matched the impression of her I got from the few memories of her I nabbed from the guardians."

"And she's a biochemist who did a bunch of work in

this state up until around the time the facility must have been founded," Jacob continues. "Some of it for private security companies—the kinds of people who'd know how to set up a facility like that. But we couldn't find anything more specific than that."

"So, now what?" I ask, resisting the urge to hug myself.

Andreas aims his warm smile at me. "While those two were busy putting those pieces together, I tracked down someone who can help us find out all the details that aren't public on the internet." He pauses. "But of course, that help comes at a price…"

TEN

Riva

I stare through the moonlight at the waterfall tumbling fifty feet down the narrow cliff in front of me. "Oh, hell, no."

Jacob folds his arms over his chest, fixing me with a hard look. "Backing down already?"

I sigh. "No." Just extremely displeased with where my life has taken me.

Thankfully, Andreas insisted on coming along for the drive out into the wilderness too, and he balances out Jacob's harshness a little. He steps closer and gives the tip of my braid a gentle tug.

"I know you don't love the water, Tink, but you've got this. You'll be in and out in no time."

The warm confidence in his voice along with the old nickname—and the fact that he's showing any faith in me at all after the way the past few days have gone—steadies my nerves.

I don't actually mind water in general. Showers are fine. I can enjoy a quick dip in a warm swimming pool.

But immersing myself in the stuff sets my nerves on edge... possibly because of the same part of me that produces the claws from my fingertips and the pointed tufts of fur on my ears when I really give myself over to my animalistic side.

There's a reason Jacob used to call me "Wildcat."

And the faint spray lacing the air has already told me that this water is going to be cold. My skin is recoiling from it as if it thinks it can peel right off my body and avoid the whole production.

I square my shoulders and flex my fingers, feeling my strength. There's no running away from this expedition. It's the one thing Andreas's hacker wanted in return for his help—because there isn't much a hacker that good can't get on his own.

Right before we drove out here, Jacob let Dominic heal me. I can only feel the slightest prickles of the poison still coursing through my veins. But now he's watching me with a hint of a sneer.

I think he *wants* me to refuse so he'll have even more reason to question my loyalty.

No fucking way.

I point my index finger at him with a claw already extended. "I'm doing this even though I don't even think we should be bothering with this Ursula woman, because I know she's important to you and the other guys. And the four of you are important to me. That's the *only* reason I'm doing it. So keep that in mind instead of whatever snarky thoughts you'd usually be thinking while I'm getting myself chilled to the bone going up there."

Jacob blinks with a twitch of his eyelids as if he's trying to hide that he's startled. Then his mouth presses into a flat line.

Before he can let out yet another of those snarky thoughts, I stalk away from him toward the cliff.

Standing on the rocky bank several feet from where the water hits the shallow pond beneath, I study my target. It's a pretty ridiculous setup all around.

Some rich asshole our new hacker associate has a problem with built an off-the-grid cottage at the very top of this tall, slim plateau. I hate to think how much energy the prick is wasting pumping water the fifty feet up to the top only to have it spill back down again all around the house.

Apparently the only regular way in and out of the residence is by helicopter—if you can call that "regular." But he's never met a gal with superhuman strength and steely claws before.

The lights are off in the cottage. The hacker was able to tell us that his nemesis had a business trip keeping him away all night.

I don't need to see where I'm going, though. It's a simple matter of climbing straight up—and not falling.

Easy peasy.

I tug on the water shoes that are one piece of special equipment we bought for this endeavor and wade through the waist-deep pond in my leggings and long-sleeved tee, both black to blend into the night. The liquid chill bites into my legs.

The faster I pull this off, the sooner I can get out of it.

As I push right under the waterfall, I can't restrain a cringe at the tumbling water pummeling my hair. But there's a small gap between the flow of the falls and the rocky wall of the cliff, at least this far down.

I press myself into that water-free gap, swipe strands of drenched hair back from my face, reach up to hook my clawed fingers into the highest crevices I can reach, and haul myself upward.

The first half of the climb isn't so bad, as horrible pastimes go. My shoulders start to ache with the strain of hauling my weight upward, but I'm catching on enough nooks and crannies with my toes in their flexible footwear that I can propel myself up quickly and not rely on my arms for everything.

But the gap between the cliff and the waterfall narrows. First, it's just little streams hitting the back of my head here and there. Then, a continuous current gushes over my hair and down the back of my shirt.

I can't even shiver with the cold, or I might lose my grasp on the slick stone.

Gritting my teeth, I heave myself upward as quickly as I can without getting careless. Stretch a little farther. Reach a little higher.

Silently cuss out Jacob for deciding *I* should do this when Zian probably could have made the climb just as easily. More easily, really, since he's got no poison at all nibbling away at his muscles.

I'm one hundred percent sure Jacob's choice wasn't only because I might have an easier time sneaking into the actual building with my smaller frame.

Eventually, he's going to have to see that I'm completely on their side. There won't be any way he can deny it with that logical brain of his.

The worst section is the last ten or so feet right beneath the plateau. I have to grip the rocky ridges so tightly my fingers throb, digging my claws right into the limestone. My head stays bowed to the full deluge of water rushing over me.

Just a little farther. Just keep moving…

With my next reach, my hand finds no more stone surface above me. I grope forward and touch the flat plane where the waterfall originates. With a gasp of relief in my throat, I throw myself through the roaring current, clambering all the way to a wooden deck that juts from the building ahead of me.

I haul myself out of the water and lie there on the buffed boards for a couple of minutes, catching my breath and letting my muscles recover. And also shedding the buckets of water that soaked into my hair and clothes. Then I stand up and wring even more moisture out of my shirt and leggings.

I slip off my water shoes and leave them on the deck. The "cottage" looms over me, a two-story structure that appears to be almost entirely glossy windows, framed here and there by dark wood.

How much money would you need in your accounts to feel comfortable throwing however many tens of millions it took to build and maintain this place?

But that's not my business. I'm just here to grab what I came for and go.

I slip around the house, searching for the entrance.

The owner values his privacy—the only security cameras I spot are set up around the helipad at the far end of the deck area.

An alarm system wouldn't do him any good when he's disconnected this estate from the rest of society.

His mistake was assuming no one could possibly reach the place except by air.

The door isn't even locked. I stifle a laugh at the arrogance of that decision and ease inside.

Mr. Rich Dude also keeps the heat running even when he's not home. But I won't mock him too much for that, even in my head, because I appreciate the warmer air closing in around me and taking the edge off the clamminess of my damp clothes.

I take in the huge modern living room with its vaulted ceiling and leather furniture, every surface gleaming in the moonlight that seeps through the windows like it's all been recently polished—including the leather. A faintly smoky herbal scent lingers in the air, suggesting that the guy's been burning incense to set the mood.

Forget hackers and former facility bosses and all that. Why couldn't the five of us have a place like this away from the rest of the world?

Other than the fact that we don't have a billion dollars lying around, I mean. But I'd be happy with something several steps down on the fancy scale.

There's no way to argue with the guys about that right now, so I slink on through the expansive, airy rooms until I find the office.

At least, I assume it's the owner's office because there's a glass desk with two computer monitors and various other technological paraphernalia set up at one end. The rest of the space looks like a toy museum.

This is the only room I've encountered with no windows other than a couple of large skylights overhead. In the moonlight that seeps through the glass, dolls, action figures, and character statues stand poised along the built-in shelves that fill three of the four walls. Behind the desk, the one shelf-less wall holds several framed cards from what I assume must be specialized games, colorful art on the upper half and playing instructions on the lower.

This is where I need to be. But I'm looking for one item in particular…

I step closer to scan the shelves in the dim light. My gaze snags on a figure about eight inches tall, dressed in a purple suit with a black cape and gold detailing, still in its retail box.

Apparently this toy is super rare. Our hacker and Mr. Rich Dude used to be roommates once upon a time, and Rich Dude stole the collectable when he moved out.

And our hacker decided it was perfectly reasonable to send a bunch of strangers on a nearly impossible stealth mission to retrieve it.

I roll my eyes at the absurdity of the situation and pull out the watertight bags I kept under my shirt for the climb up. The action figure box slides into one well enough that I can seal the opening without a problem.

I tuck it inside the second bag for good measure, and then jam all that into a nylon backpack that's probably not at all waterproof. All it needs to do is make sure my cargo comes with me down the cliff.

Once I've slung the backpack over my shoulders, I tug

the straps tight and secure the clip between them over my chest to make it extra secure. Then I hustle back to the front door, soaking up a little more warmth before I have to face the unpleasant scramble down.

I open the door—and halt in my tracks at the growl of an engine that's suddenly audible from overhead.

A helicopter is descending fast, the rhythmic whir of its blades already reaching my ears. Its lights cast thin but widening streaks across the landing platform just a few steps from where I'm frozen.

Fucking rich pricks and their way-too-insulated walls. Fucking hacker who was way too confident about the rich prick's schedule.

Every second I hesitate is another second closer to getting caught. I don't think I want to find out how Mr. Rich Dude would handle an intruder.

Hugging the outer walls, I dash around the house until I'm on the opposite side from the helicopter. I plunge into the rushing water beneath the deck and rush with it to the edge of the cliff.

Eleven

Riva

The current catches me and hurries me toward the waterfall—a little too fast. A twinge of Jacob's poison rattles my muscles at just the wrong moment, and my foot stumbles.

I careen forward, arms wheeling, and nearly tumble right down to the pond in a fatal swan dive.

My heart lurches. I try to throw myself backwards, teeter in the rushing water, and feel my shoes lose their grip.

As they slip right over the edge, I whip around and snatch out with my hands.

My arms smack into the water elbows first. One scrapes across a jagged piece of stone with a flare of pain through my forearm.

I gasp, and my other hand manages to snag on a knob of rock. My shoulder jars, the flow of the waterfall still battering me, but my body jolts to a stop.

Pain is splintering through both of my arms now, but I can't afford to hang out here in the middle of the deluge. The helicopter might already have landed.

I gulp air and ease down the cliff as fast as I can manage. Brace my feet, slide my hands down to the next holds, then clutch them for dear life as my feet skid farther below. Press my face close to the rough, slimy rock so I can suck in little puffs of breath.

I will the throbbing in my arms and shoulders as far back as I can. Clench my jaw until it's aching too.

Gravity is working with me rather than against me now, but a little too enthusiastically. It takes all my strength not to tumble with the falls into the shallow pool below.

By the time I'm close enough that I dare to jump the last several feet, tears burn in the backs of my eyes. Thankfully, the spray of the waterfall disguises any that have crept out.

I slog back to the bank on wobbly legs. The guys are gone—retreated to the car when they saw the helicopter coming, I assume. I'm too exhausted to even worry that they've abandoned me.

Regardless of how they feel about *me*, they really wanted the plastic superhero I'm carrying on my back.

The stretch of wilderness before I reach the overgrown track where we parked the car is totally black. I make my way more by sound and feel than sight. Finally, I catch the glint of moonlight off the windshield beyond the trees up ahead.

The moment I emerge, the engine rumbles to life. It

must be Andreas behind the wheel, because Jacob leans out the passenger-side window to snap at me. "Let's go!"

As if I've been dawdling.

I stomp over to the passenger door, passing through the glow of the running lights. When I open the door to hop into the SUV's middle seat, Andreas has twisted in his spot up front.

"Are you bleeding?" he asks, his forehead furrowed with concern.

I glance down at my injured arm. The rock split the fabric, and blood streaks across the sliver of bare skin around the scrape, trickling down to the back of my hand. Somehow it hurts worse now that I can see how bad it looks.

"Just a little," I say nonchalantly.

Andreas lets out a rough noise and reaches for the key, but Jacob snatches his wrist before he can.

"I know how to bandage a cut too. We need to get out of here *now*."

Oh, joy. As Andreas reverses down the bumpy track, Jacob squeezes between the front seats to join me behind, bringing a first aid kit one of the guys had the foresight to stash in the glove compartment.

"I can do it," I inform him, not super keen on the idea of the guy who sent me cliff-climbing in the first place handling my damaged flesh.

"It's easier if it's someone else," he says curtly. Like he's annoyed that I'm inconveniencing him even while he's insisting on being inconvenienced.

I sigh and roll up my sleeve, biting my lip against a wince as the wet fabric rubs over the scrape. Jacob grasps my hand with the bare minimum of care and dabs the moisture from my arm with a folded piece of gauze.

Then he pauses. "You did get it, didn't you?"

I wrinkle my nose at him. "I know better than to come back without your prize. It's in the backpack, exactly as planned."

He lets out a huff as if even that fact doesn't please him and dabs antiseptic gel on my arm. As the stinging radiates through the muscle, he wraps some fresh gauze around my forearm.

Annoyingly, even while he's been such a jerk, other parts of my body have woken up with little tingles at his closeness. Someone should really give me a good shake.

And I shouldn't want it to be him.

"There, all patched up," Jacob says briskly, and pushes to the other side of the seat to get as much possible distance from me. You'd think I'm the one who goes around poisoning people with a touch.

"You okay, Riva?" Andreas asks.

Is he worried about the cut still or what fresh hell his friend might have wreaked on me?

I decide to assume the former. "It was pretty shallow. More an irritation than a real danger. Better I lost some skin than my whole skull going over the falls."

Jacob frowns, but just this once, his bad mood isn't directed at me. "That computer punk shouldn't have said the guy would be gone all night if he wasn't sure."

"Maybe plans changed at the last minute," Andreas says. "But you can lay into him when we get to the meetup if you want. Just don't wreck his doll." He pauses and then speaks again in an eager tone so familiar in my memory that it brings a fresh burn of tears to my eyes. "Did I ever tell you guys about the man I saw on the subway who used to work at a toy shop?"

"Probably," Jacob mutters, but he can't totally disguise the note of curiosity in his voice.

The guardians never let us hold on to much in the way of physical possessions, but Andreas built up a collection of a different type. Every time he'd go off on a mission, he'd delve into the memories of any person he saw who caught his interest and come back with the most interesting stories he was able to dig up.

He falls into that yarn-spinning cadence now as he turns the SUV off the track onto a proper road. "It seemed like he hadn't ever really wanted to run a store—especially one full of toys. He'd inherited it from an uncle, and when he first found out, he was outright pissed off. But then…"

As Andreas unravels his tale, I curl up against my window and let my eyes drift closed. It feels almost like old times, if I let myself focus on nothing but his voice.

By the time he's switched on the radio instead, I'm drifting off to sleep, exhausted enough that even my damp clothes can't keep me awake. It's a long drive back to the city. When I wake up with the cutting of the engine, the fabric is pretty much dry.

The hacker is waiting in the back room of a foreclosed arcade. When the three of us come in, his head jerks up with an eager flash of his pale eyes.

Zian and Dominic, who've been waiting with him and sort of standing guard, straighten up with pinched expressions like they've had a little too much caffeine to stay awake this long.

"You—" Jacob starts to vent, but I don't have the patience to listen to him harangue the guy. The expedition is finished now. We all survived.

I wave him quiet. "Let's just get this over with."

I unzip the backpack, meeting the hacker's gaze. "We got what you wanted."

When I pull out the action figure, still encased in its translucent watertight bags, the guy's face lights up as if I've brought him the elixir of life. He reaches for it automatically, but Andreas steps in.

"You know we got it. Now you need to dig up the information we need. Then we pay."

"Yes, of course." The hacker grins at me. "You have no idea how much this means to me. They only ever made a hundred with that specific detailing, and most of those have ended up in the trash over the years. That one—my dad helped me buy it, just a couple of months before cancer finally got him."

Oh. Maybe it's a little more than just a silly toy after all.

I offer an awkward smile and tuck the box under my arm. "We'll take good care of it until it's time to hand it over."

He chuckles, and his smile turns slyer. "I bet you will, if you had the skills to get it in the first place. I'd have liked to see you in action."

I don't know how to respond to that. His tone sounds oddly flirty, not that I'd be a good judge of that.

He can't really think I've come back from his death-defying mission looking for a hookup, right?

"There wasn't much to see," I reply. "It was very dark."

"Hmm." The hacker sidles close enough that he can trace his fingers over my forearm—the unwounded one. "But so many fun things can happen in the dark, especially with a girl as—"

"Get away from her," Zian snarls, shoving between us so abruptly that I stumble backward. Before I can even catch my balance, another hand grabs me by the elbow and yanks me farther away from the overly optimistic hacker.

I glance around and find Jacob gripping me, his eyes searing cold as he glares at the other guy with just as much hostility as Zian is giving off. "She isn't on the menu."

"Whoa, whoa," the hacker says, holding up his hands and backing up a few paces. "No offense meant. Just like to take my shots when they present themselves. I didn't realize you were together like that."

"She's with us," Zian says with a growl, and even though I know he doesn't mean like that, that he might mean simply as a prisoner, something low in my belly wobbles giddily at the sight of his protective stance.

"Sure, no problem. Here, initial gesture of good-will— I have the fake IDs you wanted too."

He hands Andreas the counterfeit driver's licenses with our photos and birthdates that make us all drinking age— which we might actually be, not that we plan on drowning ourselves in alcohol. We never celebrated birthdays in the facility, and the best we can figure is we're around twenty or twenty-one.

The hacker takes another step back and gives us a flippant salute. "I'll get on with your search... and maybe with fielding a phone call from one very pissed off trust-fund kid too."

A smile touches his face as he says those words, but it tightens almost as soon as it's formed. A shadow passes over his expression. He tramps out the door without another word.

I watch him go, a strange pang echoing through me. His happiness about getting his toy back didn't last very long, even if the figure had a special meaning to him.

How much did his former friendship mean to him? Getting this one thing back might not be enough to heal all the wounds dealt when it was stolen.

I look around at the guys I've reunited with and somehow found myself so much farther apart from at the same time, and suddenly all I want to do is burrow under the covers on my bed and imagine we could start this whole situation over from the beginning. And that it'd turn out better this time.

TWELVE

Andreas

Riva doesn't act all that different even when she thinks she's alone. At least, I assume she believes she's alone.

It was more than a year after she disappeared that I stumbled onto one of the new extremes of my talent—in front of a couple of the guardians, just my luck. I was in the middle of a testing session, trawling for memories in the mind of some random woman they'd pulled in from who knows where and pretending I couldn't find half of what they asked for, when I started thinking about how nice it would be if I could just erase *myself* from all their minds.

Technically, I could have. Or, it'd have been possible if my talents hadn't been blunted by the drugs they kept us on. I could right now if I really wanted to—simply wipe all memory of my existence from every mind in the world but my own.

It wouldn't be the first time I've essentially erased someone.

But my skill with memory doesn't come with that many gradients. I could destroy one set of memories at a time, person by person, or I could sear away all impressions in a massive wave.

I'd be screwed if even my friends couldn't remember me. And it wouldn't have gotten me very far with the guardians anyway, since they'd still see me right in front of them and know something was up. The digital records of me wouldn't disappear.

All those thoughts passed through my head in a meandering sort of way, with the wish to vanish getting increasingly strong—and then I glanced down at my hand and realized I could see right through it to the chair arm I was resting it on.

Invisibility should have been a super useful skill, but all the accidental discovery accomplished was giving the guardians even more to prod and question me about. The few times they tapered off the drugs enough that I could pull off a full disappearing act, they had me in an ultra-secure exam room I couldn't escape from anyway.

Most of the time, when I tested myself in the semi-privacy of my regular room, the best I could manage was to hide a limb or two. Not enough to factor into our plans in any significant way.

But the drugs wore off completely a few days ago, and I feel like I'm breathing unclouded air for the first time in years. When Jacob suggested I follow him and Riva up to her room invisibly and keep an eye on her for a couple hours, it was a piece of cake to come along.

I slipped into the room after her while he held the door open and propped my transparent body in the corner away from anywhere she might walk, since she could still bump into me. And since then, I've been watching.

But really, there hasn't been much to see.

She sits on her bed for a little while with the same serious expression that's been alternating with annoyance on her face since we found her, pulling out her necklace and clicking it around. Then she hunkers down on the floor and runs through a series of exercises—pushups and crunches before getting back up for some squats and lunges.

It's impossible not to appreciate the strength that flows through her deceptively delicate-looking frame. As her face flushes with the exertion, tingles of heat course through my own body.

I'm not any kind of peeping Tom, though. When she moves to swap her now-sweaty tank top for a clean one, I turn toward the wall until I'm sure she's done.

It's not my fault images of what her slender curves might look like play out in my mind anyway. Riva was the only girl I ever really wanted, even after I had a chance to meet others—if briefly—on my missions into the wider world.

No matter what else has happened since, some feelings don't just vanish, even if you'd like them to. As I'm pretty sure Jacob could attest to if he was willing to own up to it.

When the rustling of fabric fades, I let myself look again. Riva walks over to the window and pushes it open a few inches so a waft of cool autumn breeze can seep in.

Good. I think we'll both benefit from that.

There's a digital clock on the dresser. I've been in here a little more than an hour. I flex my muscles, checking for any sign of flagging energy, but there's no indication that maintaining my invisibility is wearing me down.

At least not that way. I've gone as long as several hours in the facility's exam room, with none of the aches that creep in if I've been poking around in people's memories for too long. But the sensation always rises up after a while that I'm permanently fading—that if I wish my body out of view for too long, I'll never be able to bring it back.

It's probably just paranoia, but I don't plan on pushing myself to the limit just to test that assumption.

Riva sits back down on the bed and flips idly through a magazine she grabbed on our foray into the campus convenience store. It doesn't appear to be doing much to captivate her.

Jacob is going to be disappointed that I can't report back some vast conspiracy that she's been conducting behind her closed door.

Boredom itches at me. I could slip into her memories again, but so many of them I'm already familiar with because I was there too—and I'm not totally sure how well I'll hold my invisibility if I divert my concentration that much.

I fish in my pocket for the smooth shoelace I picked up a pair of along with our new clothes and twist it between my fingers. One knot, another knot, another knot, until I can't tie any more and I need to pick them all apart again.

The shoelace isn't as good for my fidgety habit as the length of woven cord I kept in my room at the facility, not quite slick enough to unravel quickly, but it keeps the restless itch at bay.

Soft strains of music start to filter through the open window. Someone in one of the townhouses nearby is blaring an upbeat pop song, like they're trying to pep up the neighborhood.

And Riva begins to sway.

At first, I can't say it's a definite motion and not just my imagination as I tune into the beat. But the gentle rocking of her torso becomes a little more pronounced, so it's obvious she's absorbing the music.

I can't tell whether *she* realizes she's moving with it. Her gaze is still focused on the glossy magazine pages.

Then her head tips a little to one side and the other, forming a more complex rhythm separate from her shoulders. Her chin bobs a little with the beat.

All at once, her eyes leap to the window. She stiffens abruptly, as if she's worried some horrible backlash is about to descend on her.

She gets up and shuts the window. When she flops on the bed again, she holds herself perfectly, rigidly still.

My gut twists. I remember now—catching glimpses of her here and there when we'd have a TV show or a movie on with a prominent soundtrack, or when the guardians pumped music into the training room while we exercised. Little moments when she'd slip into the melody with a few graceful motions.

Her momentary lapse with the music is the only thing I've seen during this stint of spying that's at all different from how she's been behaving around the rest of us. The only time she hasn't seemed totally self-aware and controlled.

I'm still turning that fact over in my mind when the lock rasps in the door and Zian calls in to Riva that it's dinner time. He pulls the door wide, as planned, and I hustle out ahead of her.

By the time she makes it down to the first floor, I'm helping dish out the pasta the others managed to cook, every part of me as opaque as it's meant to be.

I glance over my shoulder at her with a grin to cover a twinge of guilt. "How hungry are you, Tink?"

It's like an unexpected gift, the way her expression softens just slightly when I use her old nickname, taking her from pretty to ethereal. My heart skips a beat.

I have to be careful I don't start expecting that gift—or enjoying it too much. It's when you assume you know how things are going to go that everything turns upside down.

"Just a little," she says, sinking into the chair that's become hers. "But it smells good."

She offers me a quick smile in return, because she's assuming *I* cooked it rather than spending the last two hours studying her in secret.

"I think Dominic deserves most of the credit for that," I admit, and bump the other guy lightly with my elbow as he grabs his plate. I get a small smile out of him too, so that's a double victory for the meal.

The fact that *I* can still smile as much as I do shows the difference in how the past few years have hit us. It's hardly been a laugh riot for me, and I've felt Griffin's absence every single day, but I know nothing I've been through compares to the worst of what the other guys have faced.

If I can distract them a little from the burdens they're carrying, at least I'm helping in some small way.

Zian needs it too. He digs into his pasta enthusiastically enough, but when Riva leans past him to grab the salt, her arm almost brushing his knuckles, I catch the slight tensing of his shoulders. The tick in his jaw before he starts chewing again.

The flicker of uneasiness in his eyes.

No, I'm definitely not the only one feeling the draw of Riva's presence—but I can't even begin to imagine all the turmoil it'll have stirred up in him, after… everything.

"I told Dom to fry an extra package of ground beef for the sauce just for you, Zee!" I call over to him from my armchair perch.

He rolls his eyes at me, but his expression softens with resigned amusement. The teeniest of tiny victories.

Maybe if I keep trying, I'll eventually stumble on a larger one.

We're just finishing eating when there's a knock on the door. All five of us stiffen, our heads jerking toward the front of the townhouse.

When no armed guardians follow up the knock by bashing the door right off its hinges or smashing through the windows, I chuckle and get up, setting my mostly empty plate on the table. It isn't as if an enemy would knock first anyway.

I open the door to find the girl from the next building over—Brooke, that's her name—waiting on the front steps. She offers me a sunny smile, but her gaze flicks past me toward the room beyond as if she's searching for something.

"Is Rita here?" she asks. "A bunch of us are going out —I thought she might like to come with."

There's no way in hell Jacob is going to okay Riva going off for a romp with a bunch of strangers.

"She's deep in a study session," I say. "Hates to be interrupted."

Brooke's eyes narrow—only for a moment but enough to set me immediately on guard.

"You boys keep her on a pretty tight leash, huh?" she says in a casual tone that I suspect isn't casual at all.

Apprehension prickles over me. If she gets convinced that something unpleasant is going on, she could raise a fuss with the campus authorities, draw attention to us that we don't want.

I prop myself against the door frame, offering my best charming grin. "Nah, she just takes the school stuff very seriously. I keep telling her she should lighten up. Where are you off to? Maybe I can persuade her to take the evening off."

I'm convincing enough that confusion flashes across Brooke's face before she catches her reaction and gives a friendly laugh. "Oh, we're heading to our favorite club downtown. It's kind of a Friday night ritual."

"And what's so special about this particular club?" I ask with a playful arch of my eyebrows.

"Just that we love the DJ who's up on Fridays. And there are four-dollar drinks until ten."

"Well, now *I'm* tempted, anyway." I shoot her another grin, and a hint of pink colors her freckled cheeks.

I've spent enough time in the wider world to determine that if I hit the right notes, very few women are totally impervious to my friendly facade. But that doesn't stop a greasy sensation from creeping over my skin, knowing I'm using it to distract her from her concern for Riva.

Riva doesn't need her concern. I'm looking after her.

This college girl has no idea what any of us have been through, what we even *are*. She'd only make things worse.

But her mention of the DJ brings my mind back to seeing Riva sway with the distant music upstairs. Encouraging her to let loose a little doesn't sound like such a bad idea.

She should have the chance to really breathe too.

"Let me know the name of the place, and I'll see what I can do," I tell Brooke. "If I can work a little magic, we'll see you there."

After she tells me and leaves, I shut the door and walk back to the dining area where the other four are waiting with wary expressions.

"At least she went away," Zian says.

"For now," I say, clapping my hands together. "I wasn't lying. I think we should all go dancing."

I notice Riva goes even more rigid in her chair.

So does Jacob. "Are you fucking kidding me?"

I give him a pointed look. "I think we *all* could benefit from a chance to blow off some steam. Let down our guards a bit and show how we can fit in."

His mouth twists, but he doesn't argue further.

"That doesn't sound like my kind of thing," Riva starts to say, her fingers curling tightly around her fork.

But Zian has perked up, getting into the spirit of the thing. "No, it is a good idea. We don't have much else to do while we're waiting on that hacker guy anyway."

I aim a softer but still bright smile at Riva. "Come on, Tink. We've got our freedom. Don't you want to live a little?"

"Your new best friend isn't going to let up until she convinces you to hang out with her somewhere," Jacob adds in a mutter.

Riva hesitates and then lets out a halting laugh. "Fine. Let's hit the club—but only for an hour or two."

Thirteen

Riva

I tug at the sides of my hoodie as we walk up to the dance club's entrance. It's the only piece of clothing I'm currently wearing that I actually feel comfortable in.

I swear Jacob must have been cackling evilly to himself when he grabbed this sparkly halter top and jeans so tight they're practically painted on. But I couldn't even argue that my comfy tank tops and sweats make appropriate clubwear.

How the hell did I let the guys talk me into this? Oh, yeah, because it's the first time they've asked me to do *anything* that actual friends would do.

Even if it's hard to imagine from Jacob's current sour expression that I've made any progress at all with him.

The pulsing bass emanating from the club makes me uncomfortable too, in a different way. The beat is already resonating through to my bones, tugging at my limbs.

But I've never danced in front of anyone before. Now I'm going to be surrounded by both strangers and three of the four guys I was most nervous of showing my few secrets to.

I can't be glad that it's only three out of four, because Dominic is the one I'd worry least about judging me for my physical grace. But he wasn't going to get away with a parka or even a trench coat in a dance club, and the other guys accepted him begging off without argument.

They know why he keeps himself so covered up—I'm sure of it. One more way I've found myself outside of the circle of trust that was once so solid between all of us.

Well, I don't have to let myself really tear up the dance floor. For all anyone here knows, the most I'd ever want to do under the flashing club lights is bob a little with the rhythm.

The bouncer waves us in, and warm air rushes over us with a tang of alcohol. It's still pretty early in the night, but a lot of people must agree with Brooke's assessment of the DJ or have a craving for cheap drinks, because figures are swaying and laughing all across the long but narrow room.

The space is painted all dark purple except for splotches of white that give off an unearthly sheen under periodic sweeps of black lights. The bar counter that stretches along the side wall gleams glossy white too, making the drinks set on its surface glow like some alien tonic when the black lights wash over them.

A tremor runs up my legs, prickling through my flesh with the toxin that's nibbling away at my insides. Ignoring it, I hold my head high and walk farther in as I scan the space for Brooke's bright red hair.

It was her idea that I come, so I'd better make sure she knows I did. Maybe now that I've accepted one invite, she won't feel the need to keep extending more.

Our neighbor spots me first—she emerges from the crowd at my right and taps my arm, grinning widely.

"You made it!" she hollers over the thumping music. "It's good to see you here."

"I'm not much of a dancer," I say in a pre-emptive apology.

She makes a dismissive gesture and motions me over to the bar. "Get a couple drinks in you, and you won't worry about that. They make the best cosmos here."

The idea of gulping down the fermented liquid I can taste in air sets all my nerves on edge. The guardians had us try alcohol a few times, just to ensure we'd be prepared for it if we encountered a situation where we needed to drink—or decided to give it a try out of curiosity's sake—on one of our outside missions. But I never enjoyed the impression of my senses going fuzzy.

I'll feel better if I can stay fully alert.

"Not right now," I tell Brooke hastily, buying myself a little time before I have to get into any questions of why I wouldn't drink at all, and fumble for an easy excuse. "I already had something before we left. Don't want to go too fast."

I think that's the sort of excuse I've heard people offer in made-up stories, and it appears to work well enough in real life.

"Oh, for sure," Brooke says without any sign of

concern, and grabs me by the wrist to drag me over to where her friends are dancing.

The other girls all offer tentative smiles and then go back to shimmying with the music. Thankfully, this isn't the kind of place where anyone would expect a proper getting-to-know-you conversation.

Maybe Andreas was actually brilliant suggesting that we take Brooke up on her invite. Not only are we putting on a better show of being regular college students, I'm getting in some normal socializing without actually needing to be all that social.

And soon we'll be moving on from the campus and we won't need to pretend anymore. I hope.

I shuffle from side to side and wiggle my arms with the beat, feeling incredibly dorky but at least in control. One of Brooke's friends catches another's hand and spins her around. Another throws back a shot and weaves away from us to order another.

Brooke giggles with them and bops along with the music, doing nothing more elaborate than I am but somehow looking like she fits in here perfectly. I guess most people around us aren't pulling off fancy moves anyway.

My gaze travels over the crowd—and snags on Jacob about ten feet away. He's turned with his profile to me, but there's no mistaking the breathtakingly chiseled planes of his face, turned even more ethereal when the black lights hit his blond hair and pale skin.

I'm not the only one who notices that either.

A couple of women in club gear skimpier than mine, strapless corset tops and pleated skirts, are fawning over him. As I watch, one trails her hand down his arm from shoulder to elbow. Another leans close to murmur something in his ear, a sly smile curving her darkly stained lips.

My fingers flex automatically, my claws itching at the tips. I squeeze my hands into balls and yank my gaze away.

Going feral cat in the middle of a dance club will not help our cover one bit. And who am I to get possessive over Jacob?

He's made it one hundred percent clear that he has warmer feelings for a piece of used gum stuck to his shoe than for me.

But the next place my gaze lands is on Zian, standing a couple inches taller than even the biggest of the other guys around, and the ring of girls clustered around him, twirling their hair with their fingers and peering at him coyly through their eyelashes.

My stomach lurches, and I rip my eyes away again—only to find myself watching Andreas aiming a flirty smirk at a dark-haired woman in a skintight dress as they move with the beat together.

Is *that* why he wanted to come—why the other guys agreed? So they could find a pretty girl or two for a quick hookup?

It shouldn't bother me. We were never together that way, no matter how much I craved an even deeper connection before. But a now-unsettlingly familiar vibration resonates through my chest, scraping against my insides.

The guys are all rubbing it in my face: how much they prefer the company even of strangers over mine.

I close my eyes for a moment, willing the thrum of anger down. The bitterness keeps creeping up my throat.

At a gentle nudge of my shoulder, I glance up and find Brooke studying me. "Are you okay, Rita?"

"Yeah—yeah, I'm good," I mumble, and focus abruptly on the fresh drink in her friend's hand.

Maybe having my senses a little muddled would be helpful for getting through tonight. Just one cocktail shouldn't affect me very much.

It'll simply dull the sharp edges of that awful feeling inside me.

"I think I'm ready for a cosmo now," I add, not entirely sure what a cosmo even is. If Brooke likes them, they're probably okay.

She grins and comes with me over to the bar, where she orders one for herself too. The pink concoction arrives in a wide-mouthed, narrow-stemmed glass that I raise cautiously to my lips, half afraid I'm going to snap the stem by accident.

The cool liquid slides down my throat, both tart and citrusy sweet, with a sour tang potent enough to make me shudder. I only take a few small swallows, and then I follow Brooke back into the crowd.

I go back to my bobbing and swaying, taking sips in between to drain the glass. By the time I set it on the tray of a passing staff person handing out shots, there's nothing left in my chest but a soft fizzing sensation.

There, that's better. Now I might as well enjoy myself.

It feels perfectly natural to meld into the bass, to let

the melody flow through my limbs and direct my muscles. A sense of elation washes over me.

I swivel and dip, sidling one way and twisting another, and the music holds me in its grasp like the perfect partner. It always tells me exactly where to go to match it.

As one song fades into another, Brooke gives a little cheer. "You've got some moves!"

One of her friends shoots me a thumbs up, and I grin hazily at her.

Was I worried about this before? Everything's good.

I'm getting hot, though, sweat trickling down my back under my hoodie. Everyone else is wearing short sleeves or none at all. Even having it unzipped isn't giving me enough air.

I tug the hoodie right off. It slips from my fingers and gets tugged away under nearby dancing feet, but I find I don't really care.

My hands soar toward the ceiling, and I undulate beneath them. I can really move without the extra fabric holding me back. Now I'm soaring.

When I notice Brooke again, her gaze is fixed on my arms. I glance at one as the black light sweeps over the dance floor. The scars that mark my flesh, just a little paler than the rest of my skin, flare with a momentary glow.

Brooke is frowning now. "What happened to you?"

I consider my arms, still swaying the rest of my body with the rhythm of the song. I don't have *that* many scars, do I? A few here and a few there. The cluster of tiny ones under my right arm are too small to show at all in this atmosphere.

"I got into lots of fights," I say, pleased that I can tell her this, and it's true, and it doesn't really reveal anything.

Brooke's frown doesn't go away. "Fights about what?"

I shrug. "Who would win. Don't worry. It was always me!"

I whirl around and laugh at the exhilaration of the movement. Brooke scoots over so we're facing each other again.

"Are you in any kind of trouble, Rita?" she asks with that serious expression.

I don't want her to look like that. Brooke is nice—Brooke should be happy. It was her idea for me to come here, and I'm having such a good time.

"No trouble," I assure her with a broad grin. "I left all the trouble behind."

"If there's anything—"

Fingers close around my elbow from behind. I turn to see Andreas standing over me, his usual warm smile looking a tad tense.

Is he getting serious too? What is up with people tonight? I thought we all came here to have some fun.

"Hey," he says, and directs his smile at Brooke for just a second before returning his attention to me. "You lost your hoodie."

"It was too hot," I inform him.

A little furrow forms in his forehead. "Well, I think you're going to want it later. Let's have a look and see if we can rescue it."

I pump my fist in the air. "It's a mission!"

Andreas tugs me away from Brooke and her friends, but instead of prowling through the mass of dancers searching for my wayward hoodie, he pulls me right over to the far wall where the whoops and chatter of the other dancers don't drown out our voices quite so much.

"How much have you had to drink?" he asks me, looking me up and down.

I do a little shimmy, wondering if I can get him to point the same flirty grin at me that he did for the other woman. "Just one. It was good!"

Andreas's expression only gets more serious, which is absolutely the wrong direction. "Maybe we should head home."

"What?" I protest. "No. We just got here, like, five seconds ago. I'm having fun."

He quirks an eyebrow at me, which at least brings back a bit of his normal easygoing vibe. "Are you really?"

I plant my hands on my hips. "Yes. Tons. I haven't been able to dance since—even when I was alone in my new room, there were the shackles, and I didn't like thinking about the boss watching—but now I don't care! I didn't realize it could be this much fun to dance *with* other people."

I don't know how to describe Andreas's expression anymore. He looks kind of like he isn't any more sure what he's doing with his face than I am.

With a surge of boldness, I tap him right on his toned chest. "Why don't *you* dance with me?"

"I'm not sure that's a good idea," he says dryly.

I grimace at him. "Why not? We could have fun together. We used to."

A sudden melancholy sweeps over me, dragging my spirits down into the toilet. I glance at my arm again, at the scars Brooke noticed and the smaller ones near my armpit.

"I always needed to be sure, you know," I say, running my fingers over the lines carved by my claws. "Bring out a little puff of the smoky stuff to make sure it still pointed toward the rest of you. That you were still out there somewhere."

Andreas's throat bobs with a thick swallow, and I'm abruptly captivated by that motion, my previous thoughts flitting away. I step closer to him and touch his neck.

"Riva," he says roughly.

"I really am so glad I found you," I tell him, and tip my head so it rests on his shoulder.

Some distant part of me expects him to shove me away, but the rest of me doesn't care. And that isn't what happens anyway.

Andreas's arms come up to wrap around me. He hugs me to his lean frame so tight that tears I can't explain spring into my eyes.

He smells just like he should, like sunshine and warm amber. I want to sink right into him.

Then he's detached himself after all—not shoving but pulling himself away, backing up a step as my head comes up to look at him. He opens his mouth and closes it again, and his gaze veers to someone beyond my shoulder.

I pivot and wobble on my feet with a wave of dizziness. Jacob's come up behind me—he catches my arm to steady me, his face set in that stupid scowl I'd like to punch right off it.

I yank my arm away. "I don't want to dance with *you*. You've been so mean to me over things I never even did."

Jacob blinks at me, startled enough for his stern expression to break, and glances at Andreas. "What the hell happened to her?"

Andreas's mouth twists. "She says she had a drink. Just one, and with that girl from the residences hovering over her I don't think anyone could have slipped something in it, but the alcohol could be interacting oddly with the poison."

"That's right!" I say triumphantly, as if Andreas has given me a trump card. I jab my index finger at Jacob, who is continuing to be way too gorgeous even when he's annoying. "You poisoned me too. Definitely no dancing."

My legs quiver under me again, even though I haven't moved them this time. I list to the side before catching my balance against the wall. "The floor's getting tippy."

Jacob swears under his breath. "We don't want her collapsing in here, for fuck's sake."

"Nope," I agree. "Then everyone would know just how big a jerk you are."

He glowers at me, which really isn't helping his case.

I glance away from him and notice Zian making his way over. One of the corset-top girls is trotting along behind him, pawing at his arm. And just like that, I'm sad again.

"He doesn't want me touching him, but these girls he doesn't even know…"

Andreas grips my shoulder. "It's okay, Riva. But we'd better head home. You've gotten kind of… sick."

I do feel that way now—all topsy turvy, like my stomach is flipping in somersaults.

I pivot, and Brooke is there, her big kind eyes even wider than usual with worry. "Is everything all right?"

My good mood returns in a flash. I snatch at her hand.

"Yes! Let's dance some more. It's definitely not time to go home yet." A whoop careens up my throat, loud enough that several nearby dancers glance our way. "Let's paaar-ty!"

Andreas keeps his grasp on my shoulder, the spoilsport. "We think she's been roofied," he says to Brooke. "She… doesn't normally act like this, even when she goes out."

Brooke's eyebrows draw together. "I can't believe someone—we've never had any problems here before. I can help get her back to the campus. It was my idea."

"It's fine," Jacob says, coolly and smoothly. "We all came together. No need for you to interrupt your night."

"I want to do *something*."

"You could keep an eye out for her hoodie," Andreas suggests. "We still haven't figured out where that got to."

Brooke doesn't look convinced, but I'm dizzy again, my thoughts too muddled to come up with an argument in my favor.

Zian reaches Jacob's side, his fawning fan gone off someplace else finally, and studies me with a flex of his arms. "Is something wrong?"

"She's out of it," Jacob says. "We need to get her home so she can sleep it off."

"Not sleepy," I mumble in an ineffective protest.

In the face of all their concern, Brooke eases back. "All right. If I find her hoodie, I'll drop it off in your mailbox."

"Thank you," Andreas says, flashing a smile, and then they're ushering me out of the club.

I grumble my displeasure as they stuff me into the back seat again, but relaxing into the pliant leather comes as an unexpected relief. My head lolls to the side when the car takes a corner, and my stomach churns.

I bring my hands up to cover my face. "I want to go to bed," I say, my voice muffled against my palms.

"That's what we're working on," Andreas says. He's stayed in the back with me, rubbing my shoulder reassuringly.

At the townhouse, I stagger up to my bedroom between Jacob and Andreas and crash onto my bed. Dominic is there, still in his trench coat costume, his face tight.

Is he angry with me? I don't know what I did wrong. There's so much I don't understand.

A little moan slips out of me, and he rests his hand tentatively on my belly. "You'll feel better soon, Riva."

Everyone else is gone. The room is dark. The tingling energy flows out from his hand and melts away my nausea and the shakiness in my limbs, but my mind still feels like it's floating someplace far above us.

He's mad at me, but he's here helping me anyway. That's what Dominic is like.

I want him even closer. I want him—

He stands up, and all at once I can't bear for him to simply walk away. The words tumble out.

"I missed you, you know. All of you. But especially…"

Dominic stops near the door. He watches me, a shadowy figure in the darkened space.

"Especially what?" he asks in a low voice.

I grope for the words to capture the memories trickling through my head. "When you weren't there, I'd sometimes still imagine the four of you. And *you*, you always had the right thing to say, like you'd thought it all out and gotten to the best answer like you always did."

I pause, and one more swell of grief rolls over me. "I wish I knew the right thing to say to you to fix whatever I broke."

Dominic is quiet for long enough that I almost forget he's in the room. Exhaustion drags my eyelids down.

Then his voice reaches my ears, steady but a little gruff. "Don't worry about it. It was already broken a long time before anything you did."

The comment makes me frown. The door clicks shut behind him, and I sink down into a hazy sleep.

Fourteen

Dominic

The marigolds give off a pungent scent, as bright and bold as their orange petals. I pour the last of the liquid from the small watering can over the raised garden bed and then sit down on the back step next to it.

Something that's balled tight and hard in my chest relaxes just a little as I take in the vibrant colors and the life the flowers exude. I don't know whether past student residents planted them or if the garden is something the campus staff normally maintain, but I'll take the little fragment of peace I get out of looking after them.

The only plants I ever got to handle in the facility were the ones the guardians expected me to kill. And then when that wasn't enough—

I shut those memories out of my mind and lean against the steps as well as I can without provoking a jab of discomfort at my back.

There are a lot of things going on in the house behind me that I can't really take care of, but then, it's been clear for a while that my talents are a lot more superficial than any of us would like to think. The damage we're dealing with has roots that run far deeper than our physical bodies.

And Riva…

Before my mind can stray very far in that direction, the sound of ragged panting has my head jerking up. As I get to my feet, Jacob jogs into view from the alley that runs behind the townhouses.

Well, kind of jogging. He's limping as much as he's running, his face gone waxy sallow.

I catch my lips before they can pull into a full grimace. The worst damage might be way down deep, but Jake does like pushing it as close to the surface as he can get.

"I'm okay, I'm okay," he mutters in a rasp as he makes it to the back steps, as if he doesn't look like he's just risen from the grave. He staggers on his way up the stairs, and I catch his arm.

He shoots me a glare that's plenty sharp despite how badly he's exhausted himself. "I'm *fine*."

Sure, he is. Just like he was fine all the days he collapsed at the side of the track in the training room, hair and clothes drenched with sweat, chest stuttering with strained breaths.

Back there, the guardians hauled him off and forced hydration into him—and whatever else he needed. Here, it's only me.

But he didn't think about that before he drove his body past every conceivable limit again, did he?

The moment the flash of resentment passes through me, shame burns it up. I know why he punishes himself like this—and what he's running away from while he does.

As if any part of it is his fault. The only person here who could possibly have saved Griffin is me.

And I didn't. I didn't even get close enough to try.

So I hook Jacob's arm around my neck, ignoring the pinch at the back of my shoulders, and support him on his stumbling feet into the living room. The other guys are somewhere else in the house, which is probably for the best.

Jacob has set himself up as de facto leader of our troop. It wouldn't be good for morale if they saw him half-dead.

Jacob grunts with annoyance, but he lets me lower him onto the sofa. "I just need some water," he grumbles.

I pour him a glass and sit next to him as he gulps it. He hasn't actually burned out *all* of his strength like he has in the past, but from the way he's set his legs, that one calf is still bothering him.

"You sprained something," I say.

He waves me off with an uncomfortably weak gesture. "It's not a big deal."

It will be if the guardians track us down here. If he's torn the muscle, it could take weeks to fully heal.

If we leave it to mend itself naturally.

There isn't a question in my mind about whether I'll do this—I can, and Jake needs me, so that's all there is to it. But there's nothing alive in the room around us.

I think about the marigolds outside. Picture snapping a couple of their stalks, and wince inwardly.

No, I can do this one all by myself.

As I bend over to set my hand against Jacob's lower leg, he sets down his glass. "Dom, you *really* don't need to—"

"I do," I interrupt in as firm a voice as I'd ever use with him. "If you don't want me needing to heal you, then don't go breaking your body."

I'm ashamed all over again at the trace of resentment that creeps into my tone, but Jake simply lets out a resigned sigh, accepting the criticism. And then, as I will a little of the energy inside me through his pantleg into his flesh, he says in a low voice, "I'm sorry."

I find a real smile somewhere inside myself. Even with the frustrations bubbling under the surface, I *am* glad I can help him this way.

"Don't worry about it. Like you said, no big deal."

Through the pressure of my hand, I sense the muscle and the fibers of tissue that've frayed. Closing my eyes, I will them to bind back together, to smooth out and strengthen.

My power flows out of me in a stream of warmth— and tugs at my gut at the same time. A prickling sensation ripples through my own limbs, little nips of discomfort here and there, spread out over my entire frame.

No big deal.

"Okay," Jacob says after several seconds. "It's good enough now. You don't need to do more."

The concern that leaks into his voice makes my gut twist in a different way.

Does he have any idea how much I worry about *him*?

Every time he wears himself to the bone like this, he's risking toppling over some edge he can't come back from.

And I'm not totally sure he isn't looking forward to the day when that happens.

But I don't know what to say to him. Riva claimed last night that I always had the right advice, but she hasn't been with us to see the wreckage she left us in.

I can't tell whether any of the comments that flit through my mind would make Jacob feel better or worse, so I keep my mouth shut.

He's just slumping into the sofa in a more relaxed pose when Andreas comes thundering down the stairs with Zian at his heels.

"Our hacker came through," Andreas announces, waving his phone. "He's got something big on Ursula Engel. We can meet up with him tonight to hand off his collectable for all the details."

Jacob sits up a little straighter, still wan but mildly re-energized by the prospect of making progress with our search. He flicks his damp hair away from his eyes. "All right. Now we're getting somewhere."

Zian frowns. "Will Riva be okay to come after last night? I guess one of us could stay back here with her…"

Jacob shakes his head, his lips curling into a sneer. "If he doesn't see all of us, he'll wonder what's up—and he particularly noticed her."

I'm not sure whether the edge that's crept into his voice is directed more at the woman upstairs or the hacker.

"I couldn't sense any lingering effects from the alcohol that wouldn't have cleared up by now," I put in.

"And if she wanted to be at the top of her game, she shouldn't have been hitting the booze to begin with."

I stiffen at Jacob's tone. I might be pissed off about the past, but even I can see he's not being fair—how could Riva have known that a single drink would interact badly with the poison he insisted on infecting her with?

But I can't see how pointing that out will do any good. Or how wondering aloud whether the information this hacker dug up is really going to help us will either.

Maybe this opportunity won't get us where we need to go, but we have to put ourselves out there if we want to make any progress at all. If we're not even going to try to find answers, what's the point of even continuing the lives the guardians inflicted on us?

I push myself to my feet. "I'll make sure she's in decent shape before we head out. What time do we need to leave?"

It only takes a few seconds after we've gotten out of the car before I'm wishing I just stayed home. The night air has cooled enough that my parka isn't totally uncomfortable while unzipped, but it's still a heavy weight I'd rather not be lugging around.

I veer closer to the closed buildings along the shabby commercial strip near the industrial district where the hacker asked to meet us. Having the thicker shadows draping over me settles my nerves a little.

If no one can see me, then no one can speculate. No

one can even notice the things I wish weren't strange about me.

Not that there's anyone much around here to notice regardless. Voices travel down the street from a few women wobbling out of a bar behind us, but they're the only people out and about nearby.

Zian scans the road and the darkened buildings along it warily. "We couldn't have parked right by the meetup place?"

Andreas runs his hand over his head, scattering his tight curls. "He gave specific instructions about parking at least two blocks away. I think he's a little paranoid."

Riva lets out a short huff of amusement that draws my attention to her. She's walking surrounded by us as usual, behind Andreas and Jacob and ahead of me and Zian—as if at this point we really have any reason to suspect that she's going to bolt on us.

It doesn't take much for her to catch my gaze. Honestly, when she's nearby, it takes a conscious effort *not* to be tracking every movement she makes.

Even her slightest gesture seems to reverberate through the air into my skin as if she's touched me.

Sometimes the sensation brings out the impulse to touch her in return, to pull her as close to me as I possibly can. But whenever that happens, other images dart through my mind: of how her expression would change if she saw all of me now, or of that scene from four years ago while Griffin lay dying…

My heart hardens up and my ribs seem to lock tight around it.

She said last night that she wishes she could fix what

was broken, but some things aren't fixable. No, she isn't to blame for plenty of our problems, but for her to talk like that when *she's* the one who smashed our tight-knit group to pieces—the memory makes my hands clench.

How can I feel that way but not be able to shake the certainty tugging at me that she belongs with our broken shards?

I'm lost in those thoughts rather than paying attention to the world around us, so the man who lurches out of the shadows next to another bar we're passing takes me by surprise.

From the sour smell wafting from the alley and his jerk of his jeans, he was just pissing on the ground. That's all I have time to register before he's letting out a whistle and making a grab at Riva's ass.

Rage flares through my body. Even though there are three guys around me who are all more skilled at fighting than I am—not to mention Riva herself—my fist is flying before I've realized what I'm doing.

I punch the guy right in the face, catching his cheek and the side of his nose. An ache radiates through my knuckles, and his head snaps to the side with a pained *woof* of air escaping his mouth.

Zian has leapt to join me a second later, but the jerk is shuffling off, swearing under his breath and cradling his bruising face.

I lower my hand, staring at it for a second as if it could tell me where that split-second reaction came from. A faint hum of fury is still humming through my gut.

Riva has turned to peer at me. When I hesitantly meet her bright brown eyes, she offers me a slanted smile. "I could have walloped him myself and saved your hand. But thank you for defending my honor."

Jacob snorts at the second comment, and I feel twice as awkward about my reaction.

"Yeah," I mutter, ducking my head.

But I remember how Jake reacted when the hacker guy started putting the moves on Riva. I wouldn't be surprised if he'd have punched this jackass if he'd seen him first.

She belongs with us. She left us behind, but now she's back, and she is *ours.*

Even if I don't like thinking that way, the understanding is here, simmering away in the back of my skull.

No one speaks again the rest of the short walk to the out-of-business restaurant where we're meeting the hacker. The back door is unlocked, as promised.

We step into a room quite smaller than the one before, empty other than a couple of bare shelves and the smell of stale bread. Zian stays poised near the exit, and Jacob immediately moves to the inner door to check it as an escape route.

As he rattles the doorknob, it jerks in his grasp. He backs up a step so the hacker can step into the room with us.

The beady-eyed man looks us all over, his arms crossed over his chest. His attention narrows in on the bag Zian has slung over his shoulder.

"Where's my payment?" he asks.

Zian pulls out the action figure in its box but keeps it close.

Andreas cocks his head. "Where's our information?"

The hacker turns to him. "Your target was difficult to trace. Someone's done a lot of covering of her tracks. She must be important. But they weren't quite good enough to completely throw me off."

"So, what do you have, then?" Jacob says sharply.

The hacker shrugs as if our impatience means nothing to him. "I was able to confirm that she worked in a very hush-hush branch of a specific security company starting about thirty years ago, for several years after that. I have the address for the office where she was located. I can't tell you what happened to her after that, but the people there might have more answers for you."

After that, she probably moved on to the facility. It's the right timeframe.

My heart beats faster. Jacob motions for Zian to come closer, and the bigger guy does, carrying the action figure.

The hacker pulls a folded piece of paper from his pocket. "Full directions and coordinates," he says. "I didn't slack off on you."

"I should hope not," Jacob grumbles.

Andreas holds out his hand. As the hacker extends the paper to him with one arm, he reaches the other toward the box. The exchange happens perfectly simultaneously.

The hacker shoots us all a broad grin. "A pleasure doing business with you." Then he vanishes into the front of the derelict restaurant again.

While Andreas unfolds the paper, my breath catches in my throat.

"All right," he says. "Let's see where we're heading tomorrow."

FIFTEEN

Riva

With every passing minute of the drive, watching the terrain that reminds me of the forests around the facility, my skin creeps more. It's like we're going backward, heading closer to the people we should be running away from.

The information Andreas got from the hacker didn't show any reason to believe the company that owns this property is associated with the guardians or the facility we broke out of. Ursula Engel was only employed there until twenty-four years ago, definitely at least a couple of years before we could have been conceived.

But that doesn't mean there is no connection, or that the guardians are unaware of their former colleague's past work and that we might seek her out. We have no idea how much they know or don't.

Just this once, I wish Jacob was right that I was privy to a whole bunch of their inside info.

Andreas is driving while Jacob consults the GPS on the phone they've been sharing. In a particularly dense section of forest, he holds up his hand. "We're almost there. A couple of miles northeast of here."

Zian leans forward from the middle seat. "We should go through the brush, right? We don't know how closely they're monitoring the area."

Jacob nods. "Let's find a good spot to pull over, and we'll cover the rest of the distance on foot. Stay alert for any sign of guards."

He glances back at me pointedly, although in the middle of the woods, Zian's ears are going to pick up anyone patrolling faster than my enhanced senses. Especially since as far as we know, anyone patrolling around this building has no reason to be stressed out just yet.

I can't help thinking it's an understated jab about my becoming the opposite to alert the other night in the club. It's all a blur in my mind, nothing horrendously shameful sticking out, but he's made it clear that I both embarrassed myself and nearly jeopardized our mission.

Willing back a blush at the memory, I tip my head in acknowledgment. I'm here—he should know I'm going to help any way I can.

Even if I don't really think we should be sticking our necks out like this at all.

About a minute later, the shoulder widens enough that Andreas can pull the SUV all the way off the road. We ease out of the car, shutting the doors as softly as we can, and set off through the forest with Jacob and his phone map in the lead.

All of us know how to move quietly across any kind of terrain when we're not running for our lives. The faint rustling of our clothes and rasps of our footfalls blend into the wild sounds of the forest.

The fresh pine scent carrying on the lightly cool breeze puts me a little more at ease. We're not under the guardians' thumbs anymore; we're walking free.

I just hope that we're not currently walking straight back into our cages.

As we come up on the coordinates, Jacob slows even more, and the rest of us follow suit. We slink between the trees until we come within view of a cleared area up ahead.

It isn't like the facility, not really. There's no fence at all, let alone one beefed up with electricity and barbed wire. The structure standing in the middle of the grassy clearing is plain brown brick with a slanted roof, looking more like a bungalow than a place of industry. It's maybe twice the size of a typical single-story house, although for all we know there's more underneath.

A man in a gray uniform stands near the edge of the clearing toward the front of the structure, a few paces from where a narrow driveway leads into a small parking lot that holds two vehicles: a sedan and a jeep. He has his hands slung in his pockets in a casual pose, although I bet he knows how to use the gun holstered at his hip just fine.

No metal helmet or armor. Nothing on him that reminds me of how the guardians dressed. I relax a little more.

These people could still be dangerous, but at least they're not the exact same kind of people we fled from.

At Jacob's gesture, we prowl farther around the

clearing until we determine that there's only one other guard on duty, strolling back and forth behind the building. From his bored expression, I don't think he's anticipating any significant trouble either.

Somehow I can't find it in me to feel particularly sorry for him. This company may not be affiliated with our facility, but if they employed someone who ended up helping run that facility, I doubt they're the most wonderful folks in the universe either.

We pull back deeper into the woods to confer.

"Since we have time and they're stationed where they can't see each other, I can knock the guards out one after the other," Jacob murmurs. "Then we tie them up and gag them so they can't get in our way once they come to."

He glances at Zian, who's got a bag with the lengths of cord we brought along as well as other equipment the guys felt was necessary. Andreas has already stolen one of the cords, twisting it around his hands with a knot tied in the middle.

We return to the edge of the clearing, standing in the shadows out of view. I'm not totally sure what Jacob means about knocking the guards out, figuring he's going to hurl a rock at their heads with his telekinesis or something, until his face goes rigid with concentration.

The guard's mouth clamps shut. As his lips twitch with a muffled grunt of surprise, his eyes widen.

His hands jerk to his throat. He gropes at his neck, the suppressed sounds he's making turning thinner, his cheeks turning bluish… like he's being strangled.

I can't see any marks against his throat, but understanding jolts through me. Jacob is using his talent in a much more subtle way. He's either compressing the man's airway right inside his body or willing the air not to move in and out of his lungs.

Both will have the same effect.

The guard tries to run for help, but his legs wobble. He sways and staggers toward the windowless back of the building.

My pulse lurches with sudden recognition. He's trying to throw himself against the wall so he can make a loud enough sound to alert the other guard—or whoever's inside—that way.

The threat of being discovered propels me into action without another thought. I hurl myself forward, racing across the short span of grass and yanking the man away from the building just as his legs give completely.

Zian catches the guard with me as the man slumps down unconscious, not that I need the help supporting a single ordinary person's weight. We lay him down on the grass carefully, and Zian fixes the cords in place. Then we carry the man into the shelter of the trees.

Jacob watches us return, his expression unreadable. His gaze lingers on me for a second. He dips his head, just for an instant, and stalks on around the clearing toward the other guard.

Well, I guess that's better than him spitting venom at me as if I sabotaged him rather than saving his ass.

With the other guard, Jacob nudges him toward the edge of the forest while he cuts off the guy's air, so we have no repeat of the last potential disaster. We leave that man hidden among the trees and walk over to the building's front door.

Zian peers at it with a momentary distant expression. "There's no one right on the other side," he says quietly.

"Be ready just in case." Jacob twists his hand by the door handle, and the lock disengages.

We brace ourselves. We discussed during the long drive out here that we wanted to question the people working here, which means we need them alive. But I know all of us are prepared to kill if it comes down to us or them.

An image of twisted bodies and splatters of blood flashes through my mind, and my stomach clenches.

Jacob eases the door open. The hall beyond with its light gray walls is empty, as Zian said, no one rushing out to confront us. A faint clicking sound carries from farther within, like someone tapping on a computer mouse.

We creep inside: Jacob and Zian in the lead, me in the middle, Andreas and Dominic behind me. The guys never leave *me* unobserved even when we've got much bigger fish to fry.

Zian stares at each of the doors we pass before giving an all-clear motion. The first rooms we peek into aren't even locked. They open to what look like studio apartments with a twin bed, a love seat facing a TV, and a kitchenette with a tiny table, all close to identical except for a few personal belongings and decorations scattered around.

"The employees must live here at least part of the time," Dominic says under his breath.

The work rooms appear to be at the windowless back of the building. We pass a storage room full of boxes of test tubes and latex gloves and reach the doorway the clicks are emanating from.

Zian scans the wall and holds up his hand with two fingers raised. "Scientists," he murmurs, so low the word is barely more than a breath.

Probably not also fighters, then.

Jacob glances at all of us as if to check that we're ready. He hovers his hand over the door handle, but it must be unlocked too, because I don't hear any sound before he's shoving it open.

We barge into a lab room with sleek black countertops set up with microscopes and other scientific equipment I don't recognize. Two figures in lab coats and protective goggles freeze at their workstations—and then an instant later, both whip their hands toward their pockets.

The gesture sets off an alarm inside me before I even see the shape of pistols emerging. Zian springs at the man who's a little farther away, and I leap right over the protruding counter to pounce on the woman who's closer.

She hits the floor with a soft grunt and a wince when I smack the pistol away. Andreas is already there, snatching the weapon up as well as the one Zian freed from his scientist. He hands one gun to Dominic and then peers down at our captives.

The woman beneath me is giving off whiffs of fear. "Who the hell are you—what are you doing here?"

She sounds young. I jerk up her goggles to properly see her face beneath her short brown hair and find myself staring at a woman who couldn't be more than a few years older than most of the college students we've been hiding among.

Andreas grimaces. "She isn't going to know much about anyone who worked here two decades ago." He stalks closer to the man Zian has pinned and shakes his head. "Neither of them would have been around at the right time."

"Check them anyway," Jacob says.

"Check us for what?" the guy demands. "We're just following orders here—we don't—"

Zian clamps his hand over his captive's mouth. When the woman starts to sputter, I do the same to her. Zian and I exchange a look, a hint of exasperation crossing his face, and a weird but welcome sense of comradery stirs in my chest.

This is how it's meant to be—all of us working together toward the same goals.

Andreas kneels down next to the woman. His eyes flare with a ruddy sheen, and I know he's searching her memories for any interactions with Ursula Engel.

His grimace makes it clear that he got nothing, as expected. He moves on to the man, studies him for a few beats, and then straightens up.

"They never met her."

Jacob's eyes narrow. "Is it just the two of you working here?"

The woman nods beneath my grasp, and the man does the same a moment later.

Dominic frowns. "There was a family photo in one of the apartments—everyone in it Asian. Neither of these two would fit, and the guards wouldn't either."

Trust him to have paid that much attention to the

details. We all pause, listening for any sign of another presence in the building.

Our captives stay silent, but mine's stress spiked at Dominic's comment. It's possible that whoever that photo belonged to isn't here at the moment, but I'm willing to bet they are.

"We should search the other rooms," I say.

Jacob scowls at me, but it's the obvious next step. He motions to Zian.

"Let's get them tied up and gagged, and then we can move on. Make sure they don't have any other weapons— or phones—on them. We can always question them more later if nothing else pans out."

I suppose we could at least find out what they're working on here—although whether it'll have much to do with what Ursula Engel would have been working on nearly two and a half decades ago, there's no way to know.

Once the scientists are bound, we venture on down the hallway. There are just a few more doors.

The first leads to a records room with shelves stuffed with textbooks, binders, and storage boxes. The next is merely a washroom.

Zian gazes through the doorway and shakes his head with a frown. The door swings open to reveal another lab room with a single counter and then two desks with computer equipment, and no one in view.

I step inside, my nerves prickling uneasily. The woman I caught was worried about us finding *something*. What are we missing?

A faint tang in the air interrupts my thoughts. It's a trace of nervous adrenaline—fresh, tainting the air.

Someone *was* in here, recently, and now they're not.

Or at least they're not anywhere we can see.

The guys have started to pull back, but I wave at them to catch their attention. They watch me as I slink farther into the room, Jacob with unrestrained skepticism, the others curiously.

I make a circuit of the room, taking several breaths, and stop where the scent is strongest. Where a tiny, renewed whiff reaches my nose.

I point at the wall behind the desk and turn to mouth the words to the guys: "There's someone in there."

Zian hustles over. His eyes widen as his penetrating vision must confirm my suspicions. He beckons Jacob over and points to where I suppose the opening mechanism for the safe room must be.

The people who run this place weren't prepared for anyone like us. Jacob focuses on the wall, flicks his fingers, and a hidden panel detaches itself from the edge it sat flush against, whirring open.

Zian didn't just see the woman who's hunched in a corner of the narrow room on the other side. The second the panel glides open, he lunges at her and snatches the rifle she was lifting out of her hands.

As he snaps it over his knee, she flinches and cowers back against the wall.

She must be the one who stays in the room with the photo Dominic saw. She looks Chinese or maybe Vietnamese, her smooth skin beige in contrast with Zian's peachy brown but her rounded features reminding me of his.

Her black hair is streaked with gray, and tiny lines

have formed at the corners of her eyes and mouth. *She's definitely old enough to have known Engel, if she's been working here that long.*

Zian grasps her wrists to hold her in place. There's no need to gag her when there's no one left for her to call out to.

"We're not here to hurt you," he tells her gruffly. "We've just got some questions."

"I don't bargain with terrorists," she snaps.

Andreas laughs. "It's a good thing that's not what we are, then. We're looking to tone down the terror, not increase it."

He ambles over and crouches down next to Zian. "I don't suppose you ever worked alongside a woman named Ursula Engel?"

The flicker of surprise the woman can't suppress sends a surge of triumph through me. *We're going to get some real answers after all.*

Andreas doesn't ask anything else out loud. He stares into the woman's eyes, already rummaging through all her memories of the woman in question.

Our captive flinches and twists away as well as she can, but Andreas doesn't need the eye contact. Zian keeps his hand clamped around her wrists. "You're not going anywhere."

Andreas starts to speak, his voice distant as if he's in a trance. Which I guess he sort of is, still riffling through her mind.

"It seems like they worked together a little more than two years. Dr. Gao here mentioned it when Engel was getting ready to leave. From the discussions they had, they were working on 'compounds' and 'chemical enhancements' for improving the focus of soldiers in the field—strength and sensory acuity and things like that."

Dr. Gao squirms in Zian's hold but doesn't get anywhere. She hisses through her teeth in panicked frustration. "What are you *doing*? How can you—"

Zian shuts her up with his other hand. Andreas keeps watching her, delving through her skull with his gaze.

"She saw a paper Ursula tried to hide—a deed to some land. Someplace out in Kansas. She bought property out there, not long before she quit, and she was being cagey about it, which caught Dr. Gao's attention. I think I can make out the coordinates if I focus—someone get me a piece of paper!"

Dominic dashes off and returns with a notepad and a pen. Andreas moves the nib over the paper without breaking his gaze, pausing a few times with a furrowing of his forehead.

He's silent for another few minutes. A sheen of sweat has broken out on his brow. I bite my lip, hoping he isn't pushing himself too hard.

"Engel left behind some bits and pieces in her office," he says finally. "Nothing anyone figured was important, but they stuffed it all in a box that they put in the records room just in case they wanted to go through it later if something came up. It might still be there. That's the only other useful thing I'm seeing."

"That's great," Jacob says, his voice unusually soft. "You got plenty, Drey."

He must be able to tell the strain Andreas has put

himself through. A tremor runs through the leaner guy's legs as he stands up.

But he isn't done yet. He focuses on the scientist again and gives her a thin smile. "Don't worry. You won't remember any of this—or any of us—after we're gone."

Zian starts tying her up. Andreas waits there to complete his work and sear away the newest of her memories—all of those we feature in.

When Jacob prods me toward the door, I tear my gaze away. He, Dominic, and I hurry back to the records room.

Dominic spots the right box first. A peeling, yellowed label on the side has ENGEL written in small caps. He pulls it off the shelf and sets it in the middle of the floor so the three of us can sit around it.

A sour smell rises up out of the box the moment Dominic lifts the lid. I wrinkle my nose and start digging out the various bits of paper and other odds and ends alongside the others.

It quickly becomes clear why Engel wasn't worried about leaving any of this stuff behind. The highlights include a post-it note that simply says, *More coffee!!* and an empty chip bag. I don't understand why they didn't just throw this stuff in the garbage.

But down near the bottom of the mess, I unearth a magazine clipping. Unlike the rest of the contents, it hasn't been affected by age quite as much, because it's encased in a sealed plastic sleeve. The photo that fills the clipping is still glossy, the colors sharp.

I stare at it, tightening my grasp as a wave of emotion sweeps through me.

It's a snowy forest scene, but not like this place or the

facility. There's a log cabin nestled between the trees, amber light glowing through its windows in welcome.

I can almost taste what it would be like to step through the doorway into the warmth and peace, so far away from the rest of the world.

Jacob knits his brow. "Is that another property she bought?"

Dominic leans closer to examine it. "I don't think so. Look at bits of text where it was cut out—I'm pretty sure that was from a magazine, not a real estate listing."

I finger the plastic covering. "It was something that mattered to her, though. She wouldn't have sealed it so carefully otherwise."

"Yeah." Dominic nods slowly. "And look, there are tack marks on the corners of the plastic. She had it hanging up somewhere—so she could see it regularly, I'd guess. Maybe it's someplace she *wanted* to have or go to?"

I swallow thickly. Is it possible that Ursula Engel dreamed about the same kind of escape and peaceful isolation that I do?

How absurd is that?

I want to tuck the picture into my pocket, but I'd have to fold it to fit, and that seems wrong. Zian and Andreas join us a minute later, and I slide the clipping into Zian's now mostly empty bag.

We've pawed through the rest of the box's contents, and nothing else has jumped out. We all stand up, clustered in the records room.

"All right," Jacob says. "We got everything these people can offer that might be useful. Andreas will wipe all memory of us from their minds, and I'll untie one of them before we go so they can all get free. No point in killing them. They don't seem to have had anything to do with the facility anyway."

Zian cracks his knuckles. "And then what?"

Andreas is looking at the phone. "I guess we head out to Kansas? It'll take a couple days, but if we leave right now—"

I blink at him. "You want us to head straight to this other spot from here?"

Jacob scowls at me. "Why not? Do you have a better idea?"

"I just…" Every inch of my body balks at the idea of charging off on a quest into some new unknown when we've only just survived this venture.

Do we really have to race straight into sticking our necks out all over again?

With each step we take, we're getting closer to Ursula Engel's connections to the facility. Closer to the enemy. Why can't they see how dangerous that is?

I drag in a breath and speak before Jacob can sneer at me again. "We pushed ourselves pretty hard here. Wouldn't it be smarter to go back to the townhouse and take a day or two to go over everything we've learned and rest up? We're tracing what this woman did more than twenty years ago—it's not like a couple of days is going to make a lot of difference to that."

Andreas rubs his head. I suspect from the flattening of his lips that he's fighting off a headache.

"She does have a point," he says. "I'm not sure I can even drive right now."

Jacob raises his eyebrows. "So you're going to trust *her* judgment?"

Andreas shrugs. "She did help us here a lot. She stepped up every time we could have expected her to, even when she didn't need to."

He smiles at me, and I smile back through a rush of warmth. Maybe a couple more days will be enough to convince them to see this situation completely my way.

Jacob scoffs. "We don't know if the guardians might catch on and start covering their tracks—or Engel's. Every minute could count."

A spark of inspiration hits me. "But shouldn't we scour the townhouse to make sure we're not leaving anything that could be used against us? It'd be careless to leave it without making sure we've totally covered *our* tracks. We didn't expect to be abandoning it when we left this morning."

Dominic's mouth twists. "That's a good point."

Zian rubs his hand over his thick black hair, his forehead furrowing. "Should we come up with some kind of story too, to explain why we're leaving all of a sudden? So that our neighbors don't ask too many questions?"

Jacob glares at him as if annoyed that even the guy whose main focus is brawn is coming up with solid reasons to go along with my suggestion. But now it's four against one, and while he's pissed off at me, he isn't so spiteful he's going to screw his own mission over just to stick it to me.

"Fine," he bites out. "We'll go back for *one* night and tie up loose ends. But we don't want to waste any more time than that. We could be risking the entire mission."

Andreas hesitates, and for a second I think he might change his mind. The others would probably follow.

He glances at me, and I let my smile slant wryly as if to say, *There he goes, being a grumpy jerk again.*

Drey's expression relaxes. "Until tomorrow," he says.

I can't deny that there's a flutter of hope in my chest that maybe Ursula Engel's tracks *will* be covered before we can follow them any further.

If there's no trail to follow, then the guys will have to stop chasing her down this reckless path.

SIXTEEN

Riva

By the time we make it back to the townhouse, night has draped itself over the sky, blotting out all the light except a speckling of stars and the artificial glow in the windows along the street.

Jacob parks out front in the usual spot. As the guys open the doors, laughter drifts out through the living room window of the townhouse next door, which they've left partly open to enjoy the warm early autumn air.

I scoot along the back seat and clamber out, discovering when I set down my feet that the poison in my system has been gnawing its way deeper again. A prickling jolt races up the legs I haven't used in a few hours, and I lurch to the side.

My hand slams against the side of the car to catch my balance. I take a breath and steady my body before starting forward again.

The prickles pinch at my muscles all the way up to my

hips and dig into my gut. I don't like asking him, because there's something about the process he obviously doesn't like, but I think I'm going to need to get Dominic to work his healing skill on me again sometime tonight.

I roll my shoulders and walk a little stiffly to the front steps, uncomfortably aware of how Zian has hung back near me and the other guys are waiting for me rather than going on in. Not because they're concerned about my well-being, but because they still see me as a potential threat to be monitored.

Well, Andreas is actually concerned. He catches my gaze and offers a sympathetic grimace.

I've just gripped the railing next to the stairs when the door on the other side of the lane opens, letting the buoyant voices spill out louder. Brooke emerges. She trots down the steps with a little wave and strides right over to us.

"Hey!" she says, taking all five of us in with a glance, and then focuses on me. "I'm glad I caught you, Rita. I was really hoping I could talk with you for a sec."

I push my lips into a smile as I pray to whatever higher powers might or might not exist that I can improv my way through the unexpected conversation. "Sure. What's up?"

That's what college-student-type people say to their friends, right?

With a flick of her gaze toward the guys poised around me, she purses her lips and tilts her head toward the lane. "Just the two of us, away from the street? It's kind of… private. Girl stuff."

She shoots another, more pointed look at the guys.

Jacob frowns, but he knows how weird it'd look if my

supposed roommates start dictating whether I can even talk to another person without their presence.

Andreas speaks up for all of them, with a casual motion of his hand toward the back of the buildings. "Go have your girl talk."

The guys troop inside as if it's no big deal, but my nerves creep as I follow Brooke down the lane to the small patios that border the alley behind the townhouses. I have no doubt at all that Zian is following my movements through the wall. Most likely Jacob will keep watch surreptitiously from one of the back windows as well.

As if I'm going to be plotting their downfall with a history student who's probably never encountered anything more dangerous than an A minus.

Brooke stops by the patios and leans against the wooden fence that borders her townhouse's. It's even darker back here beyond the reach of the streetlamps, just a couple of dim security lights illuminating the alley.

She pushes her hair back behind her ears and studies me. "I get that you might not be ready to talk about this yet. It might be hard to even think about it. But I want you to know that if you decide you need help, you can reach out to me, and I'll do whatever I can."

I stare at her, too bewildered to gather my words for a moment. She *can't* be referring to any of the things I'd actually need help with, so what the hell is she talking about?

"I don't know what you mean," I manage after an awkwardly long silence.

Brooke's mouth tightens. "Look, I've been there before. This guy I dated for a year in high school—I know what it looks like. How it feels. You might not want to believe it, but the way they're treating you isn't okay."

She's talking about my guys—what exactly has she noticed? A chill tickles through me.

"I'm not dating any of them. And nothing's wrong."

Brooke drops her voice. "It is, though. They don't ever seem to let you out of their sight. They didn't even want you to come talk to me—I could tell. They expect you to do whatever they say, I bet."

"It's not like that," I say quickly. "We're just—we're all new here. We rely on each other."

She knits her brow. "And what happens when you don't go along with what they expect? Sometimes it looks like you're trying not to limp, and those scars on your arms… I don't want to get you in trouble with them, but you've got to realize that's not normal. That's not how anyone who cares about you should act."

As she's spoken, my stomach's gotten so twisted up it probably looks like a pretzel now. *She* cares, clearly. Way more than someone who's only had a few brief occasions to get to know me really should.

But she's obviously more compassionate than the average person—and sharper-eyed. I don't know how to explain the things she's observed in any way that could make sense given what she'd be willing to believe.

I have to try anyway. I don't want her stressing out over my situation when she doesn't need to—and it's better for us if she thinks everything's fine over here.

I tug my hoodie closer around me. "I told you—I've gotten into fights. And not with those guys. I go to martial arts classes. Sometimes things get kind of rough in the sparring."

That seems like a reasonable explanation, but Brooke's expression stays skeptical. "Like I said, I understand if you don't want to talk about it. As long as you remember I'm here if you change your mind."

I wet my lips and stiffen against a wave of dizziness. Shit.

I wish I'd gotten Dominic to heal me up during the drive. She's really going to freak out if I start swaying around like I did at the club.

"I swear," I say, "I can see how it might look bad, but it's really—"

My deflection is cut off by the bang of the back door slamming open and a flurry of bodies springing out of the shadows from all around us.

I yelp and instinctively dive for cover behind our patio's planter. All four of my guys are barging out of the house—and at least a dozen black-clothed figures have burst from the darkness down the alley and between the other buildings.

In the first couple of seconds as my pulse stutters and my mind scrambles to make sense of the scene, I register the black helmets that cover all but the intruders' eyes and a slat around their jaws. Just like the helmets the guardians wore in the facility, only painted for stealth.

Our jailers have found us.

A startled gasp bursts from Brooke's lips, and one of the armored figures lunges straight at her.

Panic flashes through me. I leap back over the planter,

hurling myself between my unexpected friend and her attacker with my claws flicking from my fingers—

But my weakened muscles react too sluggishly. I lash out a foot shy of the incoming guardian, who barrels straight into Brooke before she can emit a full-out scream and stabs a curved blade into her neck.

Her voice cuts out with a gurgle. Blood gushes down her fuzzy sweater and splatters the ground I've just fallen to.

A cry of protest tears up my throat.

No. No. She didn't do anything—she was just standing there—she barely had anything to do with us.

The guardian shoves Brooke's body away, and it topples over like a puppet cut off its strings. Every nerve in my body clamors to snatch her up, to drag her away from these menaces as if there's any way to keep her safe now, but her attacker is already spinning toward me.

I spring backward, falling into a defensive crouch. My heartbeat thunders behind my ears, but not loud enough to drown out the smacks and grunts careening from the patio.

The man whips up an odd-looking gun. I hurl myself to the side just in time to avoid a dart that clatters off the brick wall behind me.

They're trying to tranquilize us. Of course.

The bastards don't want *us* dead, only back under their control.

I can't let the brute I'm facing off with get another shot at me—I have no idea how badly the drugs in those darts will react with the toxin already in my veins. I roll to the side, leap off the wall, and ricochet straight toward him.

As I crash into him, an electric crackle sounds from where he's tried to pull some kind of taser-like device from his pocket. But it's his own thigh that spasms with the electric jolt, and then I'm gouging out his throat like he did to Brooke, the closest thing I can get to poetic payback.

Fury sears through my chest. He won't hurt anyone else who didn't deserve it now.

My gaze passes over her slumped, bloody form, and anguish floods me in turn.

Fucking damn it. If I'd just made it to him faster...

Another figure sprints toward me. I jerk around to defend myself, but before I need to, an invisible force wrenches him off his feet. It smashes his helmet against the corner of the neighboring townhouse, the metal denting right into the man's skull.

Jacob is standing by the planters, his face rigid with concentration, his hands slashing through the air as he directs his talent. He flings another guardian against an electrical post hard enough that the crack of a spine echoes through the air. Then he yanks another that's gotten too close right toward him—impaling him on the purple spines now jutting from his forearms.

The victim of his full dose of poison twitches like a fish flopping on a dock, spittle spewing from her lips before she collapses.

A massive form charges forward, so familiar and alien at the same time that my mind jars as it tries to process what I'm seeing.

It's Zian, and yet it's not—not any version of him I've ever seen before. Coarse, dark fur has sprouted from his peachy golden skin all across his shoulders and down his arms to where his own vicious claws protrude from his fingertips. His face is partly human but partly beastly, a stunted, wrinkled snout protruding where his nose and mouth used to be, huge fangs protruding over his wolfish jowls.

He slams straight into two attackers one after the other, bashing one's head around so far the neck snaps, driving his claws into the other's gut and ripping out a heap of intestines.

I catch a glimpse of Dominic farther away by the other end of the patio, silhouetted against the dim glow of the distant alley light. He's pulled off his trench coat, and *something* long and sinewy is lashing out from his upper back toward the incoming attackers.

One of those snake-like tendrils stretches out and yanks a man toward him, close enough for him to wrench off the guy's helmet and pummel him unconscious.

Andreas appears beside me out of thin air, panting. His voice comes out in a rasp. "Are you okay, Riva?"

Because I've been frozen in shock for the last several seconds. I heave myself out of my daze, toward the fray, making my actions an answer to his question.

The guys are fighting off a bunch of the guardians, but even more are converging on us. They knew this was going to be a tough fight.

Even as I throw myself at the nearest figure with my claws extended, I see another beyond her aiming a tranquilizer gun at Jacob.

"Jake!" I shout, tackling my target to the ground. The

next second, Andreas is blinking into view behind the shooter and plunging a knife into the side of her neck.

He vanishes again an instant later like he was never there. I don't know how to wrap my head around that, but there isn't time to.

More footsteps are thumping toward us. More triggers are clicking with launched darts.

They aren't going to be happy until they have us caged and ready for their tests and torture all over again.

The fury that sparked when I watched Brooke fall blazes through my body. The pressure of it reverberates through my chest and sears the base of my throat.

Something is swelling inside me, something that wants to burst free through my mouth. Something that wants to rend every asshole around me limb from limb and make them *pay*.

A chilling certainty grips me: I could demolish them all, wrench them apart until they're made of nothing but pain—and then death. I could make them all fall.

They'd deserve it.

The vibration heightens to a caustic thrum resonating all through my body, condensing in my lungs. Fuck them. Fuck them all.

My lips part, but in the same instant, my gaze catches on Jacob. A fresh flare of anger rushes through me with the memories of all the shit he's hurled at me, followed by an icy splash of fear.

The scene from the arena rushes through my mind. All that carnage, all that savage destruction.

Like some creature way more monstrous than Zian

looks right now rampaged through. Do I want to find out if I'll become that brutal beast?

I clamp my jaw shut. I can't—I don't know what I'd even do. I don't know how much I can control it.

There are so many things and so many people that've infuriated me in the past several days. So much emotion churning inside me, more than I can grasp hold of.

I don't know that my frustration wouldn't get away from me and ruin the people I want to save too.

I suck in a breath, forcing down the rage resonating inside me, and dizziness whirls through my head. I push myself forward regardless.

Slash. Shred. Smash. Stop every one of the pricks who're gunning for us until there's no one left—in my usual way.

The safe way that doesn't make my nerves wobble and my throat ache with a disturbingly potent hunger.

Bodies hurtle through the air. Flesh rips. Bones crack. My guys are a blur of motion around me.

The urge prickles up from my lungs again and again, and I shove it down harder each time.

And then there's no one left in front of me.

I sway to a stop, my legs trembling, my gut knotted with queasiness and exhaustion. The alley and the patios are painted with blood and draped with bodies.

Far off, a siren is wailing.

"Come on!" Dominic hisses, yanking his trench coat back over his slim form before I get a closer look at the shapes protruding from his back. He pushes Jacob toward the lane, spurring the other guy into motion.

I stagger after them, and Zian catches me up like he

did at the facility. His face has morphed back to normal now other than a hint of fangs curling over his lower lips; the fur has vanished. As he heaves me over his shoulder, I spot Andreas wavering in and out of sight, each time a few steps closer to the sidewalk.

Without another word to each other, we dive into the SUV. Zian looks at Jacob and then jumps into the driver's seat. He starts the ignition with a roar of the engine.

We tear off into the cover of the night.

SEVENTEEN

Riva

The guys mentioned before they were getting Zian and Dominic up to speed on the basics of driving so the responsibility didn't all fall on Jacob's and Andreas's shoulders. Zian must have caught on quickly, because he steers the SUV out of the campus without running us into any lampposts or trash bins, although a few times it's a near miss.

The vehicle sways with another sharp turn, and the engine roars as he presses on the gas again. I bump against Andreas's shoulder where he's thrown himself into the back seat with me and realize that shoulder doesn't look totally… right.

I blink, doing my best to focus through the muddle in my head, and my stomach lurches. He's technically visible now, but I can make out the seams in the seat and the edge of the window through his translucent body.

His hands have clenched on his lap. When a shudder runs through his lanky frame, my gaze shoots to his face.

His eyes are wide, gleaming with fear.

"Drey?" I say, my throat tightening with the same emotion.

His voice comes out in a strained rasp. "I'm trying. I can't quite…"

His body wavers, becoming closer to opaque and then more translucent again.

I don't know how to help him—I don't even understand what exactly is happening—but I can't just sit here and watch him struggle. My hands shoot out to grasp one of his, squeezing it tight between my fingers as if I can hold him fully in this world.

"You're here," I say, more babbling than with any clear strategy. "You're here with me. I can see you. You're going to stay right here with us."

Andreas stares down at my hands clamped around his. His breath evens out a little.

I give him another squeeze. "Don't you dare go anywhere. This is where you belong."

A shaky laugh spills out of him, and then he inhales deeply. With a couple more heaves of his chest, he's fully solid again.

His gaze lifts to meet mine, so fraught I don't know what to say but can't tear my eyes away either. "Thanks," he says roughly.

I swallow and force myself to loosen my grip on his hand, my fingers sliding away from his. "What was that? Are you okay?"

"Seems like it, now." He sags back against the seat with a humorless chuckle. "Every new talent has to come with its fun side effects, huh?"

His body was acting up like that because he was turning himself invisible earlier? I haven't seen him do that before—but then, I guess I wouldn't necessarily know about all his abilities.

He couldn't do that back when I was in the facility with him, though. How often has he practiced using the skill? It sounds like he didn't realize it could mess him up that badly.

Zian's panicked voice draws my attention to the rest of the vehicle. "Uh, where exactly am I going from here? What's the plan, Jake?"

It's Dominic who answers, from the middle seat where he's kneeling next to Jacob. "Get on a highway. The first one you find. We want to get away from this city fast. The rest we can figure out later."

He's clutching Jacob's shoulder. As I look at them, he gives the other guy a shake.

Jacob barely moves, sitting so rigid he might as well be a mannequin.

My pulse stutters. Something's gone wrong with him too.

I scramble past Andreas to the middle seat, falling back against the door when Zian swerves again. My head knocks into the edge of the window, and a hiss of pain escapes me with the spinning of my thoughts.

Andreas is grabbing my arm to steady me a second later. "Dom, you've got to heal her. The poison was getting to her even before the fight."

Dominic's gaze darts from me to Jacob—who remains totally motionless other than a brief blink of his staring eyes—and back again. He must decide my situation is more critical, because he reaches over the arm of the seat to press his hand against my sternum. "Try to stay still."

"Easier said than done," I mumble, but I let myself lean against the door, hoping the manufacturers didn't cut any corners with the lock mechanism on this thing.

Between that and Andreas's supportive grasp, I manage to only jostle a little while Dominic's warmly soothing power flows through me. My strength solidifies in my muscles; my stomach and my thoughts settle.

When I feel like I'm stable enough that I won't be causing more problems than I'm fixing, I pat Dominic's arm to indicate that he can stop. As he draws back, I hold on to the back of his seat and peer at Jacob.

From this angle, I can see that Jacob's fingers are flexing where his hands are braced rigidly against his thighs. A tendon tics in his jaw, every plane of his chiseled face pulled taut.

An uneasy shiver ripples through me. "Is *he* going to be all right?"

Andreas frowns. "He pushes himself too hard sometimes—just keeps going and going until he bottoms out."

Dominic's forehead furrows as he studies his seatmate. "He isn't normally quite like this. It's nothing physical— nothing I can tackle. It's like his mind is stuck in one place."

He touches Jacob's arm again, trying to jostle him out of it, but at the same moment, Jacob's hand outright clenches. And the front passenger seat starts to crumple over.

The steel frame inside the padding groans as the fabric frays. Zian flinches, the SUV jerking to the side before he recovers his grip on the wheel. "What the fuck?"

"Jake!" Dominic says, pitching his voice loud even though he's right next to the other guy's ear. "The fight's over. Snap out of it!"

His yank of Jacob's arm and the wave of his hand in front of Jacob's face don't interrupt whatever the other guy is caught up in. With a creaking sound, the headrest pops right off the seat back and smacks into the glove compartment hard enough to dent it.

What's Jacob going to aim his powers at next—the doors? The engine?

He could have shattered the windshield just now if the headrest had shot off sooner.

The urgency of the situation propels me forward. I scramble past Dominic and plant myself right in front of Jacob, sitting on his knees and gripping his face between my palms.

"Wake up, Jacob! We're getting away. You don't want to hurt—" Well, maybe he does want to hurt me, but not the others. "You're making it harder for Zian to drive. You're freaking out Dominic and Andreas. And me. Stop it!"

The twisting metal shifts from groaning to shrieking. Jake's eyes don't even flicker.

Wincing, I extend my claws from my fingers and take a quick swipe across his jaw.

Four thin lines of blood spring up in his pale skin, and

Jacob's muscles jump. The metallic screeching halts. His eyes sharpen into focus—and fix right on me.

In that first second while I'm poised over him, our gazes locked and our faces just a couple of feet from each other, my emotions scramble like someone's taken a beater to them.

The last time I was this close to someone who looked like him, it ended with a kiss and then catastrophe. My body is caught between the conflicting urges to lean closer and wrench myself away.

But only for a second, because then Jacob moves— slamming his hand into my throat to heave me against the back of the driver's seat. He pins me there, his eyes flaring with icy rage. "You fucking traitor!"

Some distant part of my mind asks, *Haven't we already been through this?* I smack at his arm and squirm against his hold, not wanting to do any more physical damage than I already have.

Dominic and Andreas dive in, and between the two of them they dislodge Jacob's arm enough that I can flounder to the side and push myself away.

"She was helping you—helping us," Andreas is snapping. "For fuck's sake, dude, you almost wrecked the goddamned car."

"I—" Jacob's gaze shoots to the deformed passenger seat, and the harshness of his expression falters with a rush of bewilderment. He looks at his hands and then at me again.

"How do you think they found us?" he demands. "She must have alerted them somehow."

"What?" I burst out. "*You're* the ones who've been

putting us out there, interrogating people and stealing stuff. I've spent this entire time trying to convince you to lay low!"

"She didn't exactly have much of a chance to send any messages either," Dominic reminds him in a steadier, quieter voice. "She hasn't been alone except in that one room, and Zian checked her carefully for any kind of devices."

At the mention of the fifth member of our group, my attention jerks to the driver's seat. Zian's fingers are clutched around the steering wheel, his knuckles pale with tension. Through the windshield, the wide stretch of shadowy road ahead suggests he found his way onto a highway, at least.

But just minutes ago in the fight, he wasn't himself any more than Jake or Drey were just now.

"Are you all right, Zian?" I ask quickly. "You didn't get hurt in the fight or—or anything?"

I don't know how else to ask about lingering effects of his transformation, but his grimace suggests he can guess what I'm getting at.

"The monster's back inside," he says with a trace of a growl. "Nothing to be afraid of right now."

Even though "monster" is exactly the word I'd normally have used to describe how he looked in his beastly state, my mind balks at accepting it—or the bitterness in his tone.

"You're not a monster," I say automatically.

All Zian responds with is a dismissive snort.

Jacob slumps in his seat, looking exhausted, but he still

manages to aim one more glare my way along with a caustic mutter. "Still not convinced I shouldn't have killed you when we first caught you."

I wish those words didn't sting as much as they do.

Andreas scowls at him and tugs me back to our original seats. He tucks his arm around me, but I'm too twisted up inside to let myself relax into his offer of comfort.

Jacob isn't totally wrong to be angry. I might not have called the guardians down on us, but if we'd gone with his approach and headed straight to Kansas, we'd never have been back at the townhouse to begin with.

I was the one who argued that we should stick around the campus for another day or two. If I'd given in, we wouldn't have faced that attack.

And neither would Brooke. She'd still be alive, smiling and hanging out with her friends, studying for her double major and going out dancing…

The memory of her bloody body rises up in the back of my mind, and queasiness that has nothing to do with any poison bubbles in my stomach.

One more death of someone I should have protected that's now on my shoulders. One more stupid mistake.

There's a stretch of uncomfortable silence, and then Dominic speaks up, his voice low. "I suppose we should drive toward Kansas now, since we're already on the road."

Jacob lets out a huff. "As long as the traitor didn't tell the guardians all about that too."

I resist the impulse to kick the back of his seat. It's not that hard when I'm weighed down by guilt.

My other impulse is to argue against the plan, to point out all the reasons we'd be safer staying away from anything to do with Ursula Engel. But after the battle I was just part of, can I really say that's even true?

Somehow, the guardians tracked us down to that townhouse on a university campus where we hadn't gotten into trouble with anyone. We'd only been living there for a week.

Who's to say there's anywhere they couldn't trace us to?

Even that rich prick with his off-the-grid, waterfall-top cottage wasn't impervious to intruders, so how the hell could anyplace we hole up ever be totally safe?

But it's not just that. I think I understand now why getting answers is more important to the guys than staying out of danger.

I already knew they'd changed since I last saw them, but I hadn't realized how much. Their powers have expanded and shifted… and so have the consequences of those powers.

How much more are they struggling beyond what I've even seen so far? What have they done or think they might do that they want so desperately to find a solution to?

Because that's what this is all about, isn't it? Find Engel, get her to explain what she and the other experimenters did to make us what we are… and hope that somewhere in that explanation, there'll be a way to fix us too.

To make us something better. Less erratic. Less monstrous.

Is it possible she'd know how to turn off the thing

inside me too? The brutality that wants to claw its way out and…

All those bodies around the arena. The sickening angles they were broken and contorted into. Like someone had taken *joy* in mutilating them…

I rub my eyes, willing down another wave of nausea.

It wasn't me. I didn't *want* to do that. I can't even say for sure I did.

But the knowledge pricks at the back of my mind: If I ever let that rage loose again, it will be my fault.

My guys have changed, and so have I, so maybe we're not so different from each other after all.

I don't want them seeing the thing inside me; I don't want it ever coming out. But it's possible I should have let them see more of *me* if I wanted them to trust me, instead of trying to prove myself with strength and stubbornness.

At the very least, I can admit that I've been wrong and that their quest matters to me too.

"I'm not a traitor, but I am sorry," I say into the silence that's fallen in the car, the words coming hesitantly. "I've been arguing with you all about going on this search for answers the whole time instead of just believing you that it was important."

"No kidding," Jacob grumbles.

I ignore his remark. "I can see—I can see why it *is* important. For you and for me. I'm not going to try to convince you against it anymore. I say we get to Ursula Engel and take back all the things people like her stole from us."

"There," Andreas says, his arm tightening around me.

His light tone sounds a little forced. "Destination settled. Now, have I told you all about the woman I met who…"

As he spins his story to diffuse the tension hanging in the air, I close my eyes, and picture a future where this mess could all be just a memory too.

EIGHTEEN

Jacob

The new car is the best we could nab in the short timeframe we were working with, but I don't like it. The engine makes a periodic coughing sound, we need a whole minute to bring it up to full freeway speed, and one of the back doors nearly falls off its hinges every time we open it.

We also realize as soon as we set off in it that it's only got about an eighth of a tank of gas, but at least that's something we can fix.

I stand in the early morning darkness next to the pickup truck I found parked by a farmhouse, about a mile down the road from where we parked. At the tug of my mental energy, a steady current of gasoline flows past the open fuel cap into the large jug I'm filling for the third time.

My nose wrinkles at the cloying chemical smell. I breathe shallowly through my mouth until the jug is full, replace both its cap and the one on the truck, and set off toward our sort-of camp, lugging the sloshing weight.

Part of the reason we stopped was to crash for the night and catch up on our rest. I've only slept a couple of hours, but that's okay. Keeping busy stops me from thinking about anything but the task at hand.

We're not doing so badly. We destroyed the guardians who came after us. We ditched our former SUV in a lake where it vanished well beneath the surface, leaving no sign of us behind.

Now we're another fifty miles farther away, down a winding path of several obscure country roads the guardians have no way of tracing us down.

At least, they shouldn't.

The thought of how they found us at all is an uncomfortable niggling in the back of my skull. I scowl as I march through the grove of trees that shelters our camp from the road.

There's nothing down the overgrown lane but a small, rusty storage shed that's missing its door, but we didn't need much.

Zian is keeping watch at the moment, leaning against the shed next to the doorway. He gives me a nod when I emerge from the trees.

Andreas is dozing in the back seat of the car. Dominic sprawls in the tipped-back passenger seat, the collar of his trench coat pulled up so it'll shade his eyes when the sun peeks over the horizon.

I told Riva to take the shed. It's the only spot with just one exit for Zian to monitor.

I ease open the fuel cap on our new junker and propel

the current batch of gas into the tank by sheer force of will.

We should almost be full up after this. I'm hoping we can cross a couple more state lines before we have to do anything as blatant as stopping at an actual gas station.

The process only takes a couple of minutes. I tuck the jug into the trunk in case we need it again and step away from the car.

A light breeze washes over me and rustles through the leaves of the poplar trees looming over us. I amble a short distance away, drinking in the fresh air and the silence of the night.

It got this dark in my cell in the facility, but that darkness was tight, controlled, suffocating. Standing here, I can feel the entire world stretching out around me with no walls holding me back.

There's only one path I want to take, but there's still a relief in the freedom. I close my eyes, absorbing the quiet and the openness and letting it carry all my thoughts away so I'm nothing but an empty vessel.

The scuff of footsteps breaks my reverie. I turn to see Riva emerging from the shed in the hint of a dawn glow that's just starting to touch the landscape.

As I watch, she nods to Zian with a quick smile. "Thanks for keeping watch," she murmurs, as if she doesn't know he was guarding *against* her as much as for her. "Are you going to be able to get some more sleep too?"

I don't like how his posture turns a bit awkward as if he's concerned about how she'll feel about his answer. She shouldn't matter to any of the others any more than she does to me.

She cut herself off from us the second she decided getting a few privileges was worth more than Griffin's life. But apparently the others are soft enough to be willing to forgive the past.

They never did see things as clearly as I did—and it wasn't *their* brother she sentenced to death.

I step closer before Zian has to answer and motion him toward the shed. "You should rest a little more. I can keep an eye on things."

On her.

A frown crosses Zian's face, maybe as he tries to calculate how much rest *I've* gotten, but he's never been the type to enter a debate voluntarily. He pushes himself off the shed wall and ducks inside.

Riva stalks toward me.

She stops a few feet away from me with a hesitant expression that irritates me even more. If she doesn't like how she knows I'm going to respond to her, maybe she should leave me the hell alone.

I fold my arms over my chest and keep my voice low so I don't disturb my sleeping friends. "Do you need something?"

Her shoulders come up for a second at my purposefully cold tone, but she appears to force them to relax a moment later. The movement of her body makes me annoyingly aware of the wiry grace with which she holds herself—and the rise and fall of her breasts behind the fabric of her hoodie.

Her presence stirs up all kinds of sensations in me, but most of them I choose to ignore. They don't matter either.

Her voice comes out soft but steady. "I just wanted to say that I understand why you're upset with me. I was right there, and I didn't— You have no idea how much I've beat myself up for not realizing something was wrong sooner—" She shakes her head. "I still think about Griffin every day."

My spine stiffens at her last comment, a sharper anger flaring inside me. "Keep his name out of your mouth. You don't deserve to even talk about him."

Riva's head droops for a second before she catches my gaze again. "I'm sorry. I hate what happened, and I know it must have been harder for you than anyone. I thought I should say that. Before, I was so focused on getting us away and keeping us all alive—I didn't show how much I cared."

And I'm supposed to believe she does now? This is obviously all part of the sob story she keeps trotting out to try to wear down our defenses and steal our trust.

But I never would have believed the girl I knew four years ago, the girl I—

I never would have believed that girl could have turned on us as viciously as we all know she did. I'd hurl a derisive laugh in her face if I wasn't still trying to stay quiet.

"Sure," I say instead. "You care so very much—about making sure *you* stay alive to get whatever the hell it is you're after now."

Riva's face twitches with a flash of emotion. It isn't right that she still looks as pretty as she always did—more so, even, with the last hints of childhood faded from her features, all striking, powerful woman now.

But not as powerful as she used to be. I've clipped her wings so she can't pull another sudden flight.

She wets her lips, and I don't let myself track the movement of her tongue, focusing on the burn of anger in my chest. Her voice comes out even quieter than before.

"Is there *anything* I can say or do that would make it easier for you to believe me?"

She's even worked a hint of desperation into her voice. I start to glower at her, and a flicker of inspiration shoots up inside me.

The other guys wouldn't let me destroy her, and maybe they were right, but I still intend to pay back all the pain she dealt out. And if she's going to offer herself up so willingly in her charade of innocence, why shouldn't I take her up on it?

There is a chance that I'm protecting all of us at the same time.

"Come here," I say with a jerk of my hand toward the trees.

Without questioning, Riva follows me into the grove. Leaves rustle under our feet. The faint beams of dawn light seeping through the branches catch on her silvery hair.

I don't want to do this where the other guys could see if they got up. They'd probably interrupt.

When the tree trunks block clear view of the shed and car, I stop and turn to fully face her. She stands stiff and ready, her chin raised.

Even that annoys me.

I let my gaze trail over her body with a detached expression. "It's possible you led the guardians to us without even knowing."

Riva knits her brow. "What do you mean?"

"There could be another tracker on you that we didn't find."

"But Zian scanned me—he would have—"

I shake my head. "Zian can only *see*. They could have implanted a device that would blend in with whatever it's up against. But I can test you with my power, make sure nothing moves that shouldn't or in ways it shouldn't."

It's unlikely she has any kind of tracker on her, really. It wouldn't have taken the guardians a week to find us on that campus if they'd had a signal pointing straight to us.

But it isn't impossible. It could have been something that needed specific circumstances to activate.

It could be something *she* needed to activate and couldn't right away. So even making the request is a test in itself.

Riva simply shrugs with no sign of concern. "Then you should definitely check. If there's anything like that in me, I want it out right away."

I fix her with a hard gaze so she knows I mean what I'm saying. "It's going to hurt. Your joints and veins aren't going to like me prodding them."

Her jaw clenches slightly as if she's bracing herself. "That's fine."

So fucking stoic. Part of me wants to *admire* her response the way I used to get a rush of elation watching her race through a brutal training course, throwing herself over every obstacle, and then circling back to help Dominic or Griffin if they needed it.

The rest of me wants to strangle that first part.

"Good," I say. "We'll start at the bottom."

I aim my attention at her feet, encased in the black sneakers we picked out for her. Reaching out with the force of my talent, I can trace the lines of bone and sinew, tendons and cartilage, all through those delicate appendages.

Then I start to twist them.

A little here and a little there. Nudging and tweaking every surface and strand of flesh. Watching for something that feels a little too hard or that shifts amid the rest in a way no part of the human body is supposed to.

Riva's breath gives a slight hitch. That's the only sign she reveals of her discomfort.

So far.

I work my way up, from her ankles to her calves to her knees. Her legs tremble, and I glance up at her face just for a second, taking in the flat line of her mouth with a jolt of satisfaction.

Griffin must have suffered so much—the agony when he realized she'd betrayed him, the blast of the gunshots ripping through him. She's still only gotten a small taste of payback, but it's a start.

"You could sit down if you want," I say.

She squares her shoulders. "No. I can handle it."

"If you insist."

I continue my upward journey, clamping down on the flush of heat that ripples through me around her groin. I can't ignore it, because if the guardians were going to trick us, that's exactly the sort of tactic they'd use, but I move over it quickly and efficiently, no lingering.

This won't be a very good test if it compromises *me* too.

Onward and upward; organs, ribs, arms. When I tug at her spine near the base of her skull, she sucks in a little gasp she couldn't quite suppress.

I restrain a smile.

But I reach the top of her head without any sign of a hidden piece masquerading as bone or tissue. Releasing my focus, I shake the tension out of my own body from the intense concentration of the last several minutes.

Riva's shoulders slump a little, but she isn't shy with her smile. "There's nothing? They couldn't have traced me?"

The brief satisfaction I got out of this ordeal vanishes in a snap. "Not like *that*," I retort, and my gaze homes in on the chain around her neck. "There is one more thing."

My hand shoots out faster than she could have been prepared for, but Riva's reflexes are sharper than mine even in a weakened state. She jerks backward, her own hand whipping up to cover the lump of the pendant under her shirt.

"What are you doing?" she asks with a flash of teeth.

This is what gets her upset? Not all the jabs of physical pain I just sent through her body—the thought of me so much as touching the necklace that my brother bought?

My teeth grit with the impulse to bare them in return —like Zian would, as if I've got an animal lurking inside me, mutating my body, too.

"They could have hidden a tracker in there," I snap. "Give it to me."

It's not as if she deserves that piece of him anyway, not when the rest of us had our last connection to Griffin stolen from us.

Riva pulls the cat pendant out but keeps her fingers closed around it. "You don't need to take it. You tested everything else without even touching me."

She's right, but that doesn't mean I have to like it. "It should be mine. He was my brother."

Something both fierce and haunted flares in her bright eyes. "It's the only thing I have left. We—we can look for the other ones—we'll get them back someday. But he gave this one to *me*."

Her voice turns ragged with the last few words, anguished enough that I find myself hesitating despite my best intentions. And that pisses me off more than anything.

"Fine." I glare at her hand, which she unfolds tentatively so I can at least see the little silver sculpture, and press my talent against every nook and joint to confirm it doesn't contain hidden circuitry.

I could break it so easily. One swift twist, and the cat and yarn would crack apart for good. But I'm not quite angry enough to do that.

It isn't just hers. It was Griffin's too.

When I sigh with the release of my attention, Riva tucks the pendant away. "Nothing there either?" she checks eagerly.

My teeth set on edge. I aim the full force of my glare straight into her eyes.

The other guys might be starting to forget who she's proven herself to be, but I *never* will, and I won't let her forget either.

"No," I say, flattening my voice so it's hard as steel. "But it doesn't make a difference. It doesn't matter even if you really are trying to help us now. There's nothing in this hellhole of a world that you can do to make up for what you've already done. You killed *all* of us that day, one way or another."

Riva flinches. "Jake—"

"Don't you *dare* talk to me like I'm still your friend." I take a step forward, looming on her tiny frame. "The only reason I've hung in here is so I can annihilate everyone who had a part in destroying my brother, and that is always going to include you."

My anger doesn't feel hot anymore. My veins might as well be full of ice.

I whip around before Riva can try to respond and stride back to the car, lifting my voice to wake the others.

"Let's go! The sun's coming up, and we have gas— we've got to get moving before those pricks find us again."

NINETEEN

Riva

Given that the town we've stopped in is about the size of a postage stamp, it shouldn't surprise me that the local version of a supermarket is all of three aisles and a single dingy wall freezer. I peer through the smudged glass at the offerings, feeling strangely adrift.

I've shopped for food before, but only to grab a quick meal during a mission. The idea of building up a stash of groceries to last across multiple days, even weeks… and there are so many different options I've never tried…

I guess regular people have their whole lives to figure out what they like and don't, so they can casually stroll through a place like this and chuck stuff in their basket without even thinking about it.

Staying away from the frozen stuff seems like a good idea right now, considering we don't even have a fridge. I pull myself away from the tubs of ice cream and meander to the pre-prepared food section, where at least everything is already organized into a full meal instead of separate ingredients.

Jacob stalks by and pulls a loaf of bread off the shelf behind me. My skin tingles with his passing, the sensation sharpening into prickles that dig deeper inside.

My limbs have felt shakier ever since he checked me over for hidden devices. Little aches have formed in my joints and in the back of my skull, not quite the same as the pangs and twinges set off by his poison.

But I'm not going to act like a liability. I won't go begging Dominic to heal me up yet.

For however much longer Jacob keeps his stick up his ass when it comes to trusting me, I need to be more prepared. I need to adjust to this new normal of physical discomforts so they don't slow me down if we end up in another fight.

So I'm never again tempted to let out that shrieking, vicious thing inside me.

If I had, even if I managed to focus it completely on our attackers, what would the guys have thought of me after? Once I started to wonder that, I couldn't shake the question.

None of them are happy with their own talents. I don't think they'd appreciate an even more horrible one from the girl they already see as a traitor.

Please, let this Ursula Engel woman know something that will help us turn back to normal. Or at least closer to normal. I can live with retractable cat claws and a sensitivity to bodily chemicals.

I pick up some premade sandwiches that look vaguely

appealing, a smile crossing my face when I catch sight of one stuffed almost to bursting with three different kinds of deli meat. I wave it in Zian's direction where he's just come around the aisle toward me. "This one's obviously for you."

His gaze latches onto it, and an answering smile springs to his lips for just a second before his mouth flattens again. He pushes on past me without a word.

My heart sinks. Okay, after last night's battle, maybe reminding him of his carnivorous tastes wasn't the best call.

Naturally, I turn around and catch Jacob glaring at me as if he thinks I was rubbing the subject in Zian's face on purpose.

I resist the urge to grimace back at him and meander farther down the aisle to the snacks and desserts.

Memories of past group meals flit through my head. A little of my good mood returns as I snatch up a box of chocolate fudge brownies and a bag of coconut macarons.

We meet up near the counter, and Jacob looks over my selections with a scowl but no complaints. I hope he remembers that I'm the one who provided the money so we can do this shopping at all.

Back at the car, we drop the bags in the trunk. Andreas hits the gas the second we're all inside, me crammed to one side next to Dominic and Jacob. It'd make more sense for me to take the middle seat given how much smaller I am than even slender Dom, but apparently Jacob can't stand the thought of so much as brushing up against me.

About a half hour outside the little town, Andreas veers down a scruffy lane and parks on the shoulder. We pile out to eat picnic-style in a secluded overgrown field.

Zian does take the particularly meaty sandwich, I notice with a flicker of triumph.

I grab the two desserts and carry them over to our circle too, with a gesture toward Dominic. "Since you've got the real sweet tooth, I figured you should get to pick which we have today and which we save."

Dominic glances up at me, startled in a way that's mostly gratifying.

The other guys haven't bothered with desserts when we were eating at the townhouse, probably because Jacob was in charge of the shopping and focused on practicalities. But I haven't forgotten how Dom's face used to light up when the guardians would include cookies or chocolates with our shared lunches.

Now, he hesitates and seems to draw into himself a little more, like he can merge with the parka he's switched back to wearing despite the warming weather as we veer south.

"Thanks," he says without meeting my eyes again, as if it costs him something to accept.

I set my offerings down in the grass in the middle of our circle and sit down to take a bite of my ham and cheese sandwich, but my stomach has condensed into a solid lump.

Maybe I was too distant with them before, too cool and stubborn. Too focused on my own sense of practicalities and not considering the turmoil they're obviously dealing with.

But I'm trying every way I can think of to show them that the friendship we shared hasn't died, and nothing I do seems to be going right.

It shouldn't be this hard. We're blood; we have each other's backs. We always did.

How the hell did Brooke manage to hit it off with all those friends just by hanging out and talking with them?

My frustration awakens a shiver of that caustic vibration in my chest. I close my eyes and then stand up to walk back to the car.

Maybe they need me to give them a little space—and maybe I could use some too.

I slide into the back seat, leaving the door open so the mildly warm air can flow through, and peel off my hoodie since I'm starting to sweat in it. I'm about halfway through my sandwich when Andreas ambles over, a couple of macaroons in his hand.

"Mind if I join you?"

The tightness inside me eases. I have made progress with *one* of my guys.

"Of course not," I say, offering him a smile I don't need to force at all.

He drops into the seat by the open door and holds out one of the macaroons. "I thought you might like one too. We can't let Dom eat *all* of them. It'd be unhealthy or something. We're saving him from himself."

I laugh and take the lumpy cookie. My first bite dissolves on my tongue with a mix of sticky sugar and creamy coconut, and just for a moment, everything feels like it could be okay after all.

Andreas considers me as I alternate between the cookie and the rest of my sandwich, his own dessert polished off in a matter of seconds.

"Are you nervous about what's up ahead?" he asks

when I'm licking the last crumbs of coconut off my fingers.

Is that why he thinks I went off to eat on my own?

I swallow thickly, the sweetness that lingered on my tongue turning sour. I'm not sure I want to have this conversation.

But if I can't talk to even him, then what am I doing here?

"A little," I say. "But I know we can handle a lot. We'll figure out what we have to do when we get there."

"You just seem kind of tense."

I look down at my hands and then at him. Andreas gazes back at me with his usual warm, open expression.

Just the sight of that handsome face with his dark eyes so focused on me makes my pulse flutter, but *that's* not what my issue is really about either.

I wet my lips and make myself say it. "Everything's all messed up. Between the five of us, I mean. Between you guys and me."

Andreas's smile falters with concern. "Riva, it's not— it's complicated. And you can't let Jake get you down. He's got his own stuff that he's working through."

I duck my head again. "It's not just Jacob, and you know that. And I could tell things were wrong when I first got you guys out, I saw that you didn't trust me, I just— I didn't know it would last this long." The last words catch at the back of my mouth, but I push them out. "I miss you."

I missed them so much, for all those years, and now they feel farther away than ever. But saying that much only feels pathetic.

Andreas reaches over to grasp my hand. "I'm here. The others will come around."

I clutch his fingers and speak past the lump in my throat. "I just thought you all knew *me*, that you would know I'd never have done anything I thought would hurt Griffin on purpose. It was a stupid mistake."

I stop there with a flush of shame and embarrassment. I hadn't meant to say that part.

Andreas studies me. "What mistake?"

Every particle in my body recoils from the idea of telling him about the silly, careless kiss. "Not paying enough attention to what was going on around us," I say vaguely. "Not catching on that we were in trouble soon enough to prevent it."

Andreas frowns as if he can tell I meant more than that, but I *really* don't want to continue the conversation in that direction.

I grope for a change of subject, lifting my gaze to fully meet his eyes again. "That thing last night where you were… fading—has that happened before?"

It's Andreas's turn to hesitate. His gaze drops to our linked hands.

"Not like that. Sometimes using the power makes me feel a little strange, but it hasn't had an obvious physical effect before. But then, in the past I've never gone back and forth between the two states so many times that close together either."

"I guess that could do it."

He manages a crooked smile. "Hopefully I won't have to pull any more stunts like that again."

Picturing him fading away sends a jolt of fear through

my chest. I can't imagine how *he* feels about the possibility.

I squeeze his hand tight, seeking out his gaze. "If you need to use that tactic again, I'll do whatever I can to keep you with us afterward. I always will."

My voice gets a bit rough with those words. Andreas blinks at me, emotion shimmering in his eyes, and then he's scooting closer to me so he can wrap me up in his arms.

His warm, summery scent fills my nose. As my head tips against his shoulder, sudden tears prick at the backs of my eyes.

It's like our embrace in the club—except my memory of that earlier moment is blurred by the alcohol, and I initiated it. This hug is all him.

He pulls me even closer, tucking my head right under his chin, one hand stroking over my braided hair and the other resting against my side. His thumb sweeps up and down over the thin fabric of my tank top.

With each movement of his fingers, a starker heat sparks beneath my skin. It flows over my limbs and through my veins, as potent as Jacob's poison but exhilarating instead of draining.

I draw in a breath, and even more of Andreas's scent floods my lungs. A hot, heady pressure forms low in my belly.

I think the hug was only meant to be friendly, but my body clearly has other ideas. With these guys, it always has, but the flare of attraction has never swept through me quite as strongly as now.

I haven't been quite this close to any of the guys, not

like this, since I found them again. And we're nothing like kids anymore.

It isn't just me, either. A new tang reaches my nose alongside the delicious smell of Andreas's skin: a waft of pheromones that's not stress but desire.

Of their own accord, my fingers curl into Drey's shirt where they were resting against his chest.

Andreas's hand dips a little lower to where my top has ridden up from my cargo pants. His thumb hooks under the fabric and glides over my waist skin to skin.

My breath catches. That simple motion lights flames across my torso.

I want him to tease his touch higher—lower— everywhere. I want everything.

If I tipped my head just a little back, I could brush my lips against his neck, flick my tongue across his throat. Taste his scent as well as breathe it in.

The rush of need blots out the rest of my thoughts for only a second before a chilling wave crashes over me.

What's wrong with me? I can't let myself get wrapped up in this crazed impulse that's sending all my thoughts spinning.

The last time I got distracted like that, it ruined everything.

The image of Griffin's slackening face and sagging body flashes through my mind, and I jerk out of Andreas's arms. My hand fumbles for the door handle behind me.

Andreas stares at me as if he's just woken up from a daze. "Tink?"

Somehow the old nickname makes the guilt punch

even deeper. I shove open the door and scramble out into the sunlight.

"We should—we should probably get on the road again," I say, as if that makes any sense when I'm getting *out* of the car while I'm saying it.

But the other guys are already heading over to us. I should be thanking the stars above that Jacob didn't see Andreas and I before I broke our embrace.

Instead, my gaze snags on Drey's uncertain expression, and a twinge of regret shoots through me.

He's the only one who's been here for me, and I just pushed him away.

TWENTY

Riva

As far as I can tell, Kansas is basically one really big grassy field. With some extra grass on the side.

The lonely road we're cruising along winds through those stretches of grass, up and down and around low hills, and past the occasional more cultivated stretch of fading corn or other crops I can't identify. We haven't seen a building up close in over an hour.

Jacob is driving now, with Dominic studying the specifications Andreas wrote down from Dr. Gao's memory of Ursula Engel's land purchase. His head dips and rises as he shifts his attention between the notepaper and the GPS map on the guys' joint phone.

"We should be just about there, from what I can tell. But I don't know what the property will look like."

He glances over his shoulder at Andreas, who's sitting in the middle now, squished between me and Zian. "You didn't see any mention of the usage of the property or buildings on it?"

Drey shakes his head, the slight motion sending a ripple of heat through my body that only amplifies my regrets about how I responded to his touch yesterday.

"It was definitely listed as a land purchase, not a house sale or something like that," he says. "But that was more than twenty years ago. Who knows what she did with it?"

Zian gazes out the window with a frown. "At least if there are guardians around, we should be able to spot them way in advance."

He's right, but there doesn't appear to be anyone at all around. I haven't even spotted a tractor in the last thirty miles.

Something makes Dominic lean forward in his seat. "There's a fence up ahead. That could be the boundary of the property."

My expectations have clearly become skewed by life in the facility, because when he says "fence," I immediately anticipate a ten-foot-tall monstrosity topped with spikes of barbed wire. What actually appears on the other side of the shallow ditch is a weathered wooden fence that'd only come up to my chest.

Here and there, boards are sagging or have fallen right off it. I crane my neck to get a better look past the guys. "I don't think anyone's been maintaining this place for a while."

"Or they just want it to look that way," Jacob mutters.

"We have no idea if it was ever connected to the facility," Andreas points out. "Who knows how many projects Engel might have had going on?"

Jacob lets out a brusque huff. "We go forward assuming they're here. That's a hell of a lot safer than assuming they're not."

For once, I agree with him.

Dominic points at the windshield. "There's a gate up there, so probably some kind of driveway. Should we head up that way in the car or on foot?"

Jacob slows the car as we come up on the gate. We all peer at the landscape around it.

There *is* a dirt lane, so overgrown with tufts of grass that it's barely visible amid the larger field around it. No recent tire marks have crushed the blades or dug into the soil. The padlock securing the gate is blotchy with rust.

Beyond the gate, the field stretches out perfectly flat as far as my eyes can see. There's no sign of any people, not a single building. Not even a freaking bush.

"Maybe she never actually used the property?" Zian ventures. "Or she tore down whatever she built here before she left?"

Dominic rubs his mouth thoughtfully. "If it's the latter, we should still check it out. There could be remains that'll give us an idea of what she was doing here."

Jacob scans our entire surroundings and makes the final call. "We'll drive up. It'll look stranger for there to be a car stalled here on the side of the road. Let me get the gate."

Not bothering to turn off the engine, he tenses his shoulders and makes a brisk motion with his hand.

The padlock clicks open. It floats through the air to hang on one of the fence boards.

With another shove of his power, Jacob pushes the

gate wide. Its hinges let out an ear-splitting creak that has us all wincing.

He drives us through with a brief pause to heave the gate shut again. The flattened grass from our tires would give our arrival away, but only if someone looks closely.

The car creeps onward slowly as both Jacob and Dominic crane their necks to trace the faint path of the overgrown lane through the field. The bumps in the road jostle us, and my stomach starts to churn.

The effects of the poison have been sinking deeper into me throughout our drive here, but I've mostly been able to tune them out. I grit my teeth and focus on the terrain outside.

When Jacob hits the brakes, we've traveled far enough that I can't see the road or the gate anymore when I check the rear windshield. "I think the lane ended here," he says.

Dominic tips his head in agreement, and we all get out to scope out the area. The grass is noticeably thicker beyond the front bumper, supporting Jacob's theory.

But there's still nothing useful around us. Just grass, grass, and more grass.

We spread out through it, our eyes fixed to the ground for clues. The tall blades rustle against my calves. I walk slowly so that I don't miss anything—and so that the tremors shooting through the muscles in my legs don't have the chance to trip me up.

Every now and then, Dominic bends down and yanks a slightly taller plant out of the ground by the roots. Without comment, I watch him tuck the weeds and wildflowers into the pockets of his parka.

Someday he'll tell me what's going on with him.
Pushing the guys to open up hasn't gotten me anywhere.

I don't want him to have to do anything for me that he
isn't happy about.

We've been scouring the area for at least ten minutes
when Zian gives a little shout. He's staring at the ground
just in front of his feet, but when we all hustle over, I can't
see anything there at all.

I mean, other than grass.

He motions toward the ground. "I've been trying
looking *through* the soil as far as I can. A couple of feet down
right here, there's more than just dirt. I think it's cement."

My heart skips a beat. "There's an underground
building. Like the facility."

Andreas glances across the field again. "Except it's
either a hell of a lot bigger or they didn't bother with the
aboveground part."

Jacob's brow furrows. "Whoever was using it must
have had some way to get in."

You'd think so, but another half hour of searching,
with Zian guiding us as he traces the outline of the
building through the earth, turns up nothing remotely
resembling an entrance. Or any other sign that anyone at
all has come out this way in the last couple of decades.

It's Dominic who calls out to us next. While we rush
to join him, he kneels down in the grass.

He's crouched by a small metal grate, a circle no wider
than his shoulders. "Any underground structure would
need ventilation."

Jacob claps his hands together. "That's our way in."

Andreas cocks his head skeptically. "I don't think we're going to fit. How big is the vent under it?"

"Only one way to find out."

Jacob untwists the bolts holding the grate in place, and Zian heaves it up with a rasp of degrading metal. He leans down to poke his head inside, but *his* broad shoulders won't even make it through the opening.

"It looks even tighter in there," he announces with a faint echo.

Jacob's attention fixes on me. The other guys' gazes follow him.

My skin tightens up, but it's the obvious answer. I'm by far the smallest of us.

"Sure," I say before Jacob even needs to volunteer me. I'm part of the team; I won't shy away from doing my bit. "You want me to just crawl in there and…"

"Look for a way into the building, and then find a better way to get *us* in," Jacob says in a tone like I'm dim for not realizing that right off the bat.

Maybe it should have been obvious. My brain has started to feel kind of wobbly too, like little bursts of static electricity are crackling through my thoughts.

"Right." I peek down into the dark passage. "Anyone have a light?"

When Jacob hesitates, I let myself glower at him. "I know you don't want me armed, but what do you think I'm going to do with a flashlight that I couldn't with my fists? There obviously aren't any windows down there. I'm not finding any entrances if I can't even *see*."

He grumbles something under his breath and jogs

back to the car. When he returns, he passes a keychain-sized LED light to me. "Get on with it."

"Happy to." I give him a mocking salute and bend down to squirm into the vent.

I have to go head-first, because there's no room to turn around once I'm inside. My gut twists and shudders as I squeeze into the space that's tight even for me.

The smell of aged metal clogs my nose, like long-dried blood. I swallow down the acid that creeps up my throat, switch on the light, and army-crawl forward.

The vent stretches out into hazy darkness ahead of me, all smooth metal with no markings to tell me anything about where I am. The tremors from my legs quickly migrate to my arms and shoulders, nibbling away at my muscles while I propel myself along.

Just keep moving. I can do this. I'm stronger than Jacob's stupid poison.

My back starts to ache too. The narrow space presses in on me, and my breaths become increasingly shallow.

Is there even enough air down here now?

A wave of dizziness sweeps over me. I pause, bracing my head against one hand.

I can't stop now. What am I going to do—just die here in this underground tunnel like a sniveling kid?

The guys wouldn't even know what happened to me.

Somehow, that last thought is the most terrifying of all. They'd probably assume I've abandoned them purposefully.

Fuck that.

I shove myself onward, my teeth clenching so tight my jaw throbs, which at least distracts me from the expanding aches and queasiness everywhere else in my body. The tunnel veers to the right, and I contort myself to follow it, the corner jabbing my belly.

A new addition to my collection of bruises. Hurray!

A couple of body-lengths after the bend, the vent slopes sharply downward. I hesitate at the top of the incline, clutching the tiny flashlight.

But where is there to go other than forward?

Elbow by elbow, I haul myself forward and down. When my thighs slide over the edge of the slope, gravity yanks me forward with more force than I can brace against.

I skid the rest of the way down at a freefall, bumps in the metal scraping against my stomach while my shoulders and hips bang against the metal sides. I try to shove my arms forward to shield my head, but the surface drags at them in the opposite direction.

The next thing I know, the top of my skull is slamming into a wall.

The impact radiates through my mind. My ears ring, and more bile creeps up my throat.

I hold still until the splintering pain eases off enough that I don't feel like my head's going to fall right off my neck when I move it. No sound reaches my ears.

If my thump was heard by someone down below, there's no sign of it.

Cautiously, I peer around me. I've come to a stop at the bottom of the incline, where the vent branches out in two directions like the head of a T.

Left or right? In the glow of the flashlight, both directions look almost the same. But I think I spot a slight ridge on the floor of the passage to the left, like there might be an opening there.

I heave myself around the corner and drag my body over to it.

There *is* an opening, a square a little smaller than the grate on the surface, with slats to let the air flow through. The space beneath it is pitch black.

I hold perfectly still and listen for several minutes. There's nothing but silence down below. Not the faintest flicker of light either.

As far as I can tell, if anyone is still using this place, they're nowhere nearby.

Tensed to jerk it away at the first sign of trouble, I aim the flashlight downward so I have some idea what I'd be dropping into. The glow catches on a tiled floor, a cupboard off to the side, and the edge of what I think is a desk.

Okay. Time to get out of this torture chamber.

I flick out my claws and dig at the edge of the grate. To my relief, a few sharp tugs are enough to dislodge it. I drag it out and push it down the passage across from me.

The real problem is compressing myself enough to fit through the hole. I hunch my shoulders together and wriggle, dropping an inch at a time until they pop through—and my hips catch me in mid-fall. Dangling upside down, my head whirls.

Just a little farther. I tug at my body with little hitches that send my gut roiling again and finally plummet to the floor.

I manage to roll in mid-air to land on my hands and

knees, if not my feet. The thud when I hit the floor makes my whole body stiffen in alarm.

No footsteps come thundering over to investigate. And when I lift my hands, I find my fingers are smeared with grainy dust.

It's been a long time since anyone came into this specific room.

Grimacing, I wield my flashlight and stagger out through the doorway. My entire body is throbbing now, and I think my stomach may have permanently flipped upside down, but I haven't completed my mission yet.

My sneakers leave a trail through the dust coating the floor, down the hall and to the doorways of a couple more rooms that hold nothing but bare furniture and walls. Then I push open a door and find myself gaping at a smaller replica of a very familiar control room.

The screens mounted on the wall are thicker and outdated, the consoles beneath them similarly old-fashioned-looking, like something out of an old sci-fi movie trying to imagine the future within the current style. I run my light over the rows of buttons and switches.

There. A small cluster of controls off to one side has the label BACKUP GENERATOR overtop. I punch the ACTIVATE button with my thumb.

Thankfully, that particular control doesn't require any special identification. A whirring sound emanates through the room, and the overhead lights flicker on.

Hallelujah. It's a fucking miracle.

I scan the rest of the controls faster in the clearer illumination—as fast as I can through the pulsing headache that's emerged in the back of my skull. Where the hell is the FRONT DOOR control?

Finally I spot a lever and a couple of buttons that say ENTRY. I jab at them and yank the lever.

Something I did works, because a low mechanical groan reverberates from the hall outside.

I stumble to the doorway and stare with bleary eyes as the ceiling at what appeared to be a dead end in the hall unfolds. While part yawns upward, steps unfurl down to the floor.

A sliver of sky emerges above, expanding into a huge square at the top of the new staircase that appears to go up at least a couple of floors in height. No wonder Zian couldn't spot this entrance from up there.

I clutch onto the doorframe for balance, thinking I should yell just in case the guys somehow missed the giant trap door opening in the middle of the field, afraid that something much more solid than words might come out of my mouth if I dare to open it. The headache bangs on my skull like a toddler with a xylophone.

It's only a minute before the guys' voices become audible. They ease down the stairs, Jacob and Zian in the lead, walking a little faster once they've spotted me waiting.

"Wow," Andreas says, peering around him as they reach the hallway, and shoots me a grin. "Nice work."

I attempt to smile in response and promptly vomit all over the floor.

TWENTY-ONE

Riva

I'm lucky that Zian can move as fast as he does, because he catches me right before I crumple into the puddle of grossness I just spat up. There's a flurry of motion around me: Zee tugging me off to the side and resting me against the wall, Andreas rushing over with frantic questions about how I'm feeling, Dominic coming to stand over me with one hand deep in his pocket.

And Jacob, of course, walking up behind Dom and sneering down at me like *I'm* the one who poisoned me. "This isn't really the time for dramatics."

I'd give him the middle finger, but my limbs appear to have transformed into lead, too heavy to lift. Andreas pats my cheek firmly, and I blink at him.

His face doubles before my eyes, and I sputter a choked giggle.

He glances up at Dominic. "When was the last time you healed her?"

I can't focus on Dom's face—my head won't lift either
—but his voice comes out tight. "Yesterday afternoon. It
has been a while—but she didn't say anything. She seemed
fine."

"Maybe if she couldn't tell you hate doing it, she
wouldn't pretend she's fine until she's literally falling over."

"I haven't been refusing. I can't help it if I'm not
jumping for joy—I'm doing as much as I can."

"Well, if you wiped the poison completely from her
system this time, we could all stop worrying about it."

Jacob cuts in. "And then we'd have to worry about her
taking off on us instead."

"You can't really think—"

"Guys!" Zian breaks into the conversation in an urgent
tone. "Look at her. I think Dom had better heal her
somehow right now."

My chin has come to rest against my chest. A weird
shudder is running through my body. I'm sinking and
drifting away at the same time—and then a hand rests
against my sternum just below my face.

The warmth that flows from Dominic's touch brings
me back to earth and my body back into focus. My heart
thumps steadily; my breath flows in and out.

There's a floor beneath me. A wall against my back.
I'm still here. I haven't gone anywhere.

Dominic rasps something to the other guys about
getting him "more," which doesn't totally make sense to
me, but my mind is still too hazy to follow what's going
on. Footsteps stomp one way and another.

A second rush of warmth washes over me, and my
vision clears. Yes, I'm sitting on the floor, in the hall under

the wavering lights powered by the backup generator. A sour smell laces the air—oh, right, because I puked.

I make a face and manage to push myself upright and away from the puddle in the same motion. Dominic straightens up too, brushing what looks like more dust off his hand against his parka.

He doesn't meet my gaze. Andreas said he *hates* doing this—hates having to heal me.

I tried. I tried so fucking hard not to need him, but it didn't work.

Andreas touches my arm tentatively. "Are you doing okay now?"

My face flushes with shame. I *was* doing just fine until… until I wasn't.

"Yeah," I say roughly. "Sorry. It caught up with me too fast. I'm fine."

My gaze flicks back to Dom. "Thank you."

He gives a slight nod in acknowledgment. I can't read his expression to tell whether he's pissed off or just tired.

Jacob strides past us. "Let's see what the hell we've stumbled on here."

As the rest of us follow him down the hall, I tuck the no-longer-necessary flashlight into my pocket. "There's a control room that looks a lot like the one in the facility— both of the facilities I've seen."

Andreas's mouth is still slanted at a worried angle, but he perks up with curiosity. "Are there stairs going farther down?"

"I haven't seen any, but I wasn't specifically looking for them. I wanted to let you all in first." I kick at the dust on the floor, sending a few fluffy bunnies floating into the air.

"I don't think we have to be on guard for anyone still working here, though."

Zian snorts. "Not unless they float and are really bad at cleaning."

We pass the room where I dropped out of the ceiling and continue to where it branches out much like the ventilation system did. Down the passage to the left, we come across several rooms with thick control panels that send a shiver of recognition through me.

They look like the locks we had on our cell doors.

The rooms aren't locked, though. The doors stand slightly ajar. Peeking into one, I find myself staring at a low table, a plain dresser, and a crib.

Everything's covered in the same thick layer of dust we've encountered in the rest of the underground building. The furniture is as barren as in every other room —nothing hanging on the walls, no trinkets on the desk or dresser, no blanket in the crib.

There are marks of life, though. A shallow dent in a wall as if a toy were flung at it with greater than expected strength. Notches in the finish on the crib's slats as if the wood was tested with budding teeth… or claws.

I tear my eyes away and move to tug open the dresser drawers. Those are empty too, just a faint plasticky scent drifting up from them.

"They stripped the place down but must have decided it'd be easier just leaving the larger pieces behind," Jacob says from the doorway. As he takes in the room, his face remains a rigid mask, betraying no emotion.

Six of the locked rooms have the same layout. Exactly

six. A queasy sensation unfurls in my gut that I don't think Dominic could heal.

A couple more doors down, we arrive at an office that's more compact than the larger meeting-style rooms near the entrance. The furniture is nicer, though: an old oak desk that actually smells like wood rather than plastic or metal, a heavy leather rolling chair, a couple of tall bookcases that match the desk.

The bookcases have a little motif carved into the upper section of the frame, like a forested skyline rippling with the points of evergreen trees. It reminds me of the preserved clipping of the cabin in the woods that we found in Ursula Engel's things at her former workplace.

A sense of certainty settles over me. "This was *her* office. Engel's."

Andreas runs his fingers through the dust on the desk. "She owned the property, and this is the nicest workroom we've seen so far. She must have run this place."

"It sounded like she was pretty important to the facility, right? Or at least she used to be? She made a lot of the decisions?"

"Something like that," Zian says in a low voice, shifting his weight from one foot to the other. "It was hard to tell from the snippets I heard. You don't think…"

"This is where we started," Dominic fills in when the larger guy doesn't go on. "This was the first facility, from when we were too young to remember. We must have moved when we were still really small."

An uneasy silence settles over us all. What are the chances that his explanation *isn't* accurate? The guardians up and moved once before, after our escape attempt.

There's no reason they couldn't have other times in the past.

Once upon a time, a woman named Ursula Engel bought this property, had this structure built, and held the nicest office. This was *her* project.

And she raised six very unusual babies within these walls. Why? Where did we come from?

What did she want from us?

"Did she leave anything at all behind that's useful?" Jacob asks, pushing into the room. "Zee, check for any compartments in the walls."

Jacob starts testing the bookshelves for moveable panels. I peek behind the bookcases and then crouch down to peer beneath and behind the desk before checking inside the drawers.

In one of the lower drawers, my groping fingers catch on a small paper wedged right at the back. It tears a little as I tug it free, but when I smooth it out on my lap, it's still perfectly readable if faded.

My pulse stutters.

"What's that?" Jacob demands, turning toward me, but my throat has constricted too much for me to immediately answer.

It's only the size of a post-it note, but I recognize the handwriting from the box of Ursula's things, a distinctive mix of curly and spiky. And that handwriting has formed my name at the top of the note.

Riva

54 days – 9.5lb – 20.7"

First smile today. Like she was so pleased to see me. Lots of cooing. Lovely to hear.

My fingers tighten around the scrap. Am I imagining the affection in those words?

It sounds like… like she actually cared about me. About how I responded to her.

About whether I was happy enough to smile and coo.

Who was this woman, really? And if she raised us from when we were infants, if we mattered to her… why can't I remember her?

TWENTY-TWO

Zian

Andreas sighs and frowns down at the console he'd been prodding. "I still can't even get the screens to turn on. Any luck over there?"

On the other side of the room, I shake my head and glower at the buttons in front of me as if I can intimidate them into functioning. "The power's on from the generator. The door opened. There's got to be some way to get the rest of the system going."

My gaze slides down from the waist-height controls area across the smooth base of the console that stands it on the floor, where most of the electronic workings must be hidden. "Maybe there's something inside that needs to be fiddled with. I'll check if I can make out the problem."

As I plant myself on the floor so I don't have to crane my neck, Dominic peeks into the room.

"Still nothing," Andreas tells him before he has to ask, and lets out a rough breath. "Man. How long do you figure they kept us in this building before we moved to the first one we remember?"

"It couldn't have been many years," Dominic points out in his typical contemplative way. "If we were here when we were much older than three, we'd definitely remember the move."

"I wonder *why* they moved us," I murmur, as much to myself as to the other guys. It's hard to pay attention to their conversation while I focus in on the console wall in front of me.

With a faint fizzing sensation in my eye sockets, I direct my vision through the thin plastic surface to the nest of cables and circuit boards I find behind it. Sliding my gaze across those features feels like dragging my eyes through mud rather than air.

My eyeballs are already kind of tired from scanning so much of the ground overhead. Hopefully I can figure this problem out fast.

My attention homes in on a cluster of cables off to one side. The coating around the wires has melted together into a lump.

The connection there must be broken. Maybe if I cut out the melted part and twist the wires back together, that will get the juice flowing through the system properly.

It can't be that hard, right? Just match up the wires by the color of their coatings. A toddler could handle that.

"I think I might see how to fix it," I say, glancing up for a second, and realize I'm alone in the room. The other guys must have gone off to investigate more of the building.

They probably either told me they were leaving and I

was too zoned out to hear, or they didn't want to interrupt my concentration. No big deal. I'll patch things up and call them back in once I've saved the day.

Or the computer system, or whatever.

I can't see any proper way to open up the base of the console, but I can take care of that easily enough. With a few well-placed smacks of the side of my hand, I create a rectangle of cracks in the plastic and then snap out the chunk I've outlined.

The fused ball of wiring is right in front of me. Scissors would be nice, but my hands will work just fine for that too.

It doesn't even take that much of my strength to snap the cables at either end of the mess. I chuck the melted ball into the far corner of the room and get to work peeling back the coating so I can twist the wire ends together.

A couple of sparks shoot from one of the wires and zap my fingers.

"Shit," I sputter, smacking them against my thigh to stop the stinging.

"Are you okay?"

My head jerks around. Riva's standing in the doorway, the color back in her cheeks—a welcome sight after she got so sickly pale for a minute when we first trooped in here.

I don't welcome an audience now, though, especially when the first part of the show was me looking like an idiot.

"I'm good," I mutter. "It'd take more than a little wire to hurt me."

Riva walks over and crouches a few feet away from where I'm sitting to consider the severed cables. "I could probably hook them up faster." She waggles her slim fingers. "One of the few benefits of being tiny."

She's poised that close to me, her coolly sweet scent wafting into my nose. All at once, a whole lot of me wants to tell her that even if it would still make total sense for me to call her "Shrimp" like I always used to, she's absolutely perfect exactly the way she is.

The perfect size for tucking into my arms and carrying to safety. The perfect size for shielding if danger descends on us.

But I'm not supposed to be worrying about *her* safety. We still don't know for sure that she isn't going to put the rest of us in danger.

The guys are the ones who stuck with me. She's the one who left.

My irrational impulses need to remember that.

"It means there's less of you to spread out a zap, so you might get totally fried," I retort. "I'm managing."

She doesn't argue, just watches as I attach a couple more wires. "You figure getting those connected will be enough to get the full console running?"

"Not sure yet, but it seemed worth a try."

Riva hums in apparent agreement. "It'd be pretty amazing to get into the records they'll have stored in that thing. If they didn't wipe the hard drive before they left."

Somehow I hadn't even considered that possibility, I was so intent on simply getting the damn thing up and running. I scowl more at myself than her and push onward, grasping the next cable.

I've come this far, and there are only a couple of wires left. We have to at least check.

Who knows how many answers could be hiding behind those blank screens?

The last cable gives me another zap as I connect it, hard enough that I shake my hand and let out a few more curses. So I'm already irritable when I stand up and poke at the controls on the console.

Nothing happens. The screens stay dark, taunting me for my useless work.

I glare at them, a growl slipping from my lips. The skin along my neck and shoulders prickles with fur itching to spring free.

This whole thing is garbage. I might as well smash the console all for the good it'll do us.

Riva's even voice breaks through my rush of frustration. "Technology never works the way you want it to when you want it to, does it?" She wrinkles her nose at the controls. "I think artificial intelligence already exists, and it thinks it's fun to mock us."

Hearing her echo my annoyance takes the wind out of my own anger. I swipe my hand across my mouth. "Yeah."

Bashing it up would only be satisfying for a few moments while I'm letting out the rage. After, I'd feel rotten about it.

It'd make me even more like the monster the guardians turned me into.

Did this Engel woman intend for my weird powers to emerge so blatantly and physically once I got older? Did she have any idea how I'd turn out?

What was the point of any of this?

I hunker back down on the floor, gritting my teeth against the turmoil inside me. I know I'm more than a monster.

I *have* to be more than that.

"There could be something else I missed," I say, peering at the other cables and the panels of circuits.

A couple of the panels look scorched to my untrained eyes, the green surface marred with black and grey smudges like miniature storm clouds. Is that normal wear and tear or a sign that *they've* been fried beyond functioning.

I scoot over to gaze through the unbroken side of the console to get a different example for comparison. The circuit boards on that side look pretty similar, which isn't helpful.

Which part of the console do we know for sure is working? Whatever connects to the backup generator and the controls for the entrance to the facility.

I move even farther to crouch by the area beneath the spot labeled for the backup generator. There is some circuitry there too, and a cluster of cables that aren't at all melted.

I stare hard at the circuit boards through the shell enclosing them, but it's too hard to make out the details when it's all so dark. Grimacing, I crack open that part of the console as well and let the light spill in.

There. Glancing back and forth between that panel and the other ones I've exposed, I can see that the scorched-looking marks aren't necessarily normal after all. The circuits for the backup generator don't appear to have them. And the details of the little bits and pieces look...

sharper somehow, like the other panels have melted a tiny bit too.

Did the people who worked here fry the rest on purpose to make the system inoperable? Why would they have bothered if there was nothing to see if we got in anyway?

It seems too strange that *everything* would be significantly damaged except for a couple of key controls that have stayed pristine. They must have been worried there was some kind of data still retrievable inside this thing.

But I don't think I can unmelt circuits. I sure as hell don't know how to unscorch them.

I frown at the messed-up panels. "If we could find enough functional circuit boards, ones that look the same, maybe we could swap the panels out…"

"We can't take anything that's working with the generator," Riva reminds me. "Nothing will work if it shuts off."

Right, of course. I eye the area of the console near the entrance controls, but I don't think it's wise to fiddle with those either.

What if the door closes and then we can't get the circuits hooked up properly to re-open it? Riva can scramble out through the vents, but the rest of us would be stuck.

I suck in a breath, grappling with a fresh surge of frustration.

Okay, so I don't have the materials here. Think it through, Zee. You have a brain in the middle of all those muscles somewhere, right?

I'm not just the freak that sprouts fangs and fur and hurtles into a fight. I'm *not*.

I could take the messed-up boards… and bring them to some kind of electronics store. See if they could make a functional copy of them.

A smile darts across my lips. That's an actual plan. It'd mean having to leave and come back, but totally worth it if we can get access to the computer systems afterward.

We could find out exactly what the guardians did to us when we were just babies. How it all began.

And if we can see how the freakishness started… that might also tell us how we can end it.

High on hope, I reach for the nearest panel without giving myself a chance to second-guess my idea. My fingers grasp around it, feeling for the connection points where it can snap free—

And another electric jolt, twice as potent as the last one that shocked me, crackles up both my arms simultaneously.

The bolt of electricity sears through my nerves and stabs pain all the way to the roots of my teeth. My body rears back defensively.

In all of a second, fur ripples across my back, fangs gnash in my extending muzzle, and I slam my fist into the circuit board.

It sputters and sizzles, and I roar at it. Only as I catch a shaky breath do I come back to myself, staring at the bashed panel that's now way more of a mess than when I found it.

The metal bits have fractured. Most of the green board

is cracked into little shards. A few of them patter to the floor as I watch.

There's no way any tech expert is piecing *that* disaster back together.

My face snaps back into human shape. I stare at the damage I did, panting, my fingers opening and closing at my sides.

Fucking hell. Of all the times to lose my grip on my temper…

But that grip is tenuous even at the best of times. I shouldn't have even tried.

"It's okay," Riva says softly. "Even if we could fix it, they must have wiped all the data too. There might be people like that hacker guy who could dig something out if they got the power on, but none of us know how. And we can't lug this whole console to a computer expert to ask for help."

I know that's all true. And when I glance over at her, braced for her expression, I don't see the slightest hint of horror in it.

She just saw me partly transform—right in front of her under the beaming lights, not at a distance in the dark like during the fight at the college—and she didn't cringe away. She's looking at me like I'm the exact same person I always was.

Fuck, how much do I wish I was that person.

My body starts to lean toward her as if drawn by a magnetic pull. She always understood better than the others, with all that savage strength in her own tiny frame—

My gaze drops to my hand lifting as if to touch her

arm, and an image blazes up through my memory. This hand, clawed and bloodied. A scream ringing in my ears. Blood, so much fucking blood, on me and around me…

I jerk myself away, shoving to my feet in the same motion. "You don't know anything!"

Riva blinks at me, her body tensing exactly the way I expected it to before. "Zian? I was just trying—"

My voice tumbles out with a growl woven through it. "Don't *try* anything. Just get out of my way. You have no idea what I'm dealing with. All *you* ever do is grow pretty little claws and pointed ears."

"I—"

I don't want to hear a single thing she has to say. "You have no fucking clue how bad—You don't know anything. So just stay the fuck away from me."

Because I hurt people, and even after everything, I don't want to hurt you.

I don't say that last part out loud. It sticks in the bottom of my throat, but maybe it wouldn't make any difference anyway.

Riva's expression twitches. Then she scrambles up and darts out of the room, giving me the space I demanded.

And leaving me feeling like even more of a monster than I did before.

It's better this way, I tell myself as I slump back to the floor. We're safer this way.

Both of us.

Twenty-Three

Riva

I t's on my fifth pass through the halls that my gaze slides along the wall outside the crib rooms at just the right angle, and I notice the tiniest of seams in the otherwise smooth surface.

I stop and back up a couple of steps to confirm what it took my mind a second or two to process. There *is* a nearly indecipherable line of shadow down the wall, like the edge of a partition.

"Guys!" I call out, moving toward it and pressing my hand against the surface right by the seam. "I found something else."

My prodding doesn't shift the partition at all. Jacob and Andreas come jogging over first—Jacob frowning, naturally.

"You found the wall?" he asks with an edge of sarcasm.

I roll my eyes. "I think there's a hidden doorway here like there was in the lab where Engel used to work. If you look at the right angle from the right spot, you can *just* see the edge."

Andreas has already stepped closer, cocking his head. He lets out an awed chuckle.

"There it is. Zian must have missed that."

"Too busy trying to play engineer," Jacob mutters, but there's a note of fondness alongside the exasperation that I've never heard when he mutters about me. "He was mostly looking in the actual rooms, not the halls."

He lifts his voice so it'll carry farther. "Zee, get your ass over here. We need those X-ray eyes of yours."

His call brings not just Zian but Dominic, who wanders over from the rooms he was searching.

As Jacob motions to the area of the wall, I step farther to the side, giving Zian as much space as I can. His tirade from earlier rings in my ears.

You don't know anything. Stay the fuck away from me.

Even the memory brings a burn into the back of my eyes. I inhale slowly and deeply in an effort to even out my emotions.

Zee has always had a volatile temper, one he has trouble keeping on a leash. He probably didn't mean all of what he said as harshly as it sounded.

But he's never spoken to me like that before, not even in the past week while Jacob's been laying into me. Is he *more* upset with me now than he was before?

How the hell did that happen? How am I still screwing this up?

I don't have the answers to those questions, so I do my best to focus on the conversation about the wall.

Zian must have spotted the internal mechanism to

open the partition, because he's motioning to a specific spot farther over from the seam, around chest height. Jacob positions himself there and rests his hands against the wall to help guide his talent through.

He closes his eyes. The chiseled planes of his face tighten with concentration, turning him even more starkly gorgeous than usual.

We all wait, breaths held. There's a stretch of silence, and then a mechanical rasp within the wall.

The seam widens, pulling back to reveal not an opening but an actual door: solid, natural wood unlike the painted steel ones that fill the rest of this place. It even has a bronze doorknob.

We stare at the thing for a second as if afraid it's going to launch some kind of killer door attack. Then Andreas shakes his head with a self-deprecating guffaw and reaches for the knob.

It turns in his grasp, this part of the entrance unlocked. As he pushes it inward, lights flicker on automatically with the movement.

We slink into the hidden room one by one. Andreas lets out a low whistle. The rest of us just gape.

Like every other room we've entered in the old facility, a layer of pale dust coats every surface, dulling the colors with a grayish sheen. But even so, it's immediately obvious that this space isn't at all like the others.

As with the door, the walls are paneled with natural wood, slightly curved as if to mimic the undulations of stacked logs. Vividly grained boards show when I swipe my foot over the dusty floor too.

The room's been stripped down, leaving only the largest furnishings—the items I guess it'd have been most difficult to quickly and discreetly remove—but even those are totally different from anything else we've seen in the place.

A suede sofa, so plump my limbs twinge with the urge to sink down into it and discover how comfy it'd be, stands along one wall. It faces a stone-lined fireplace that's empty other than streaks of black that confirm it was used at some time. Or maybe those were painted on for aesthetic effect.

Built-in bookcases line the wall to one side of the sofa. Next to us, near the door, stands a wooden chest large enough that Zian could have curled up inside and the lid would still have shut.

A strange sense of recognition quivers through my mind. I sink down in front of the chest, getting a whiff of its dry but sweet cedar scent, and brace my hands against the lid to lift it.

There's an image in the back of my head, a sense of what I *should* see when I push it open. I can't quite get a firm grasp on the impression, but when I shove upward and reveal only an empty hollow inside, inexplicable disappointment sweeps through me.

No. There was, before—

"We've been in here," I say slowly, testing out the words to make sure I agree with them before I continue. "There used to be—I feel like this chest should have something in it."

"That's what chests are usually for," Jacob snarks. "Holding things." But his tone is milder than usual, a hint of uncertainty and confusion touching his face as he scans the room.

"That's not what I mean. Something specific."

I shut the lid and stand up, gesturing for the guys to come over. Only Dominic responds.

He gazes down at the chest with an oddly dreamy expression and kneels down in front of it like I did. As he pushes the lid up with a squeak of its hinges, his eyes flicker.

"Yeah," he says, almost a whisper. "I can almost see—I think there were toys in here."

The second he says the word, the impressions floating in my mind sharpen. "Yes! A stuffed blue bear. And a wooden helicopter with a metal propeller that spun."

Dom runs his hands over the rim of the chest, his gaze going even more distant. "A set of puzzle blocks you could fit together into different shapes."

The other guys have gathered around us. "You remember all that?" Andreas asks.

I bite my lip. "It's not like remembering. I don't have a clear image of it. Just kind of a hazy sense of what's missing."

I turn and walk deeper into the room. Other tingles of recognition and dissonance ripple through me.

The sensations guide me to the dusty floor near the fireplace. I sit down and rest my hands on either side of me, opening myself to the fragments of memory tickling at the edges of my awareness.

"I think there used to be a fur rug here. I can almost *feel* it, coarse but soft—running my fingers into it…"

Zian crouches down next to me and runs his hands tentatively over the space. "Yeah," he murmurs.

Jacob crosses his arms over his chest. "The guardians would bring us in here, then? Run some of their tests in this room?"

"Maybe." That doesn't sound quite right.

I scoot backward and lean against the sofa, still trying to sort through the jumble of hazy impressions. "I don't get the sense that we did anything I didn't like in here. It was somewhere just to relax. I looked forward to those times."

Dominic nods. "It was just us. Us and… her, I think. Like it was a special thing when she'd bring us in here to play."

Andreas's eyes light up. "Yeah. I can almost catch that feeling. Holy shit."

Looking around the space, I realize that while it's furnished very differently from most of the facility, there is one room it resembles a little. "She had wooden and leather furniture like this in her personal office. And she had that picture of the cabin in the woods at her old office. Maybe this is what makes her feel at home."

"And she wanted to share that with us," Dominic says softly.

I ignore Jacob's light scoff. Dom is right. She brought us in here, her little charges, and watched us simply play and soak up the warmer atmosphere.

It's hard for me to wrap my head around that kind of motherliness compared to all the interactions with the guardians I recall so much more clearly.

Where did Engel go afterward? Why did she step back

from our lives and let them transform into all cool detachment and rigid schedules?

I frown at the room around me. "Do you think she *wanted* to leave the facility, or did the others force her out?"

"From the things I heard, it didn't sound like her time with them ended well there," Zian offers.

Andreas nods. "Yeah, there was a lot of tension in the few memories I caught."

And part of the path to those answers could be right here in front of us.

I glance back at the guys. "If these are the sort of surroundings she liked most, where she felt most at home, then if she left the guardians and went off someplace even the hacker couldn't track her down... maybe she got herself a cabin in the woods just like that picture."

Andreas hums to himself. "I wouldn't be surprised."

Jacob's mouth twists. "There are a lot of woods with a lot of cabins in them all over the world," he says. "Even if you're right, that information doesn't get us very far."

Dominic gets up and treads lightly in a circuit around the room. "It's a start, something to narrow things down."

"Maybe we could find another, *better* hacker—" Zian begins, and halts with a stiffening of his stance. His head jerks to the side, tipping one ear toward the ceiling. "I think I hear a car. Coming close."

We all tense up. Jacob moves first, waving us toward the door. "Come on. We'd better see what we're dealing with."

Twenty-Four

Riva

The five of us hustle together through the halls of the old facility to the massive staircase that leads to the outside world. By the time we've reached it, I can hear the car too—or cars, more like it. At least two different growls of engines hitch as they travel along the uneven lane.

It would probably make the most sense for me to sneak up and take a peek, since I'm the smallest, but Jacob must figure I might actually flag our pursuers down or something. He marches up ahead of everyone else, slowing cautiously as he reaches ground level.

After a moment, he returns to us. "Only two vehicles: a van and a normal-sized car. They're definitely heading this way—they just came past the gate."

Zian's forehead furrows. "Only two? Even with the van, those can't hold anywhere near as many guardians as they sent after us back at the college."

I swipe my hand across my mouth, my body still braced for battle. "They might not realize it's us. We have no idea if they figured out we went to Engel's old workplace."

"That's true," Dominic says. "They found us on the campus, not there. There's a decent possibility they have no idea what trail we're on."

Jacob glances toward the control room, his expression dark and pensive. "It'd make sense for the organization to have some kind of alert connected to the opening of the door, even after all this time. I should have thought of that. We should have moved faster."

"They're here now." Zian grimaces. "And I guess we'd better not let any of them leave to tell everyone else what we were doing."

Jacob cracks his knuckles. "Absolutely. Even if Drey could wipe us from their memories, these people must be affiliated with the current facility. Whoever questions them about what they encountered here will know what the gaps mean."

Andreas raises his head, looking haunted for a moment before his eyes narrow. "We need to keep at least a couple of them alive for a little while—so I can search their memories about Engel. We need to know more."

"Right. We can try to question them about what went on in this place too." Jacob glances around at the rest of us. "Target the oldest ones for that, as well as you can tell. They're the ones most likely to have worked with her and to know about the facility's history. Everyone else, we take out as quickly as we can."

"We should stay down here," I say, letting my back rest

against the wall. "Out there in the open, it'll be too easy for them to get shots at us."

"Of course. Spread out and get ready to pick them off."

Jacob shoots a final look at Zian, who responds by moving with me when I back up to the entrance to one of the offices. He's still playing babysitter, even after everything.

I bite back a caustic remark and prepare myself, extending my claws from my fingers. We fended off the last bunch of guardians, even though there were more of them then and they took us by surprise. There's nothing to worry about here.

Other than the fact that they've gotten so close to us twice in just a few days.

The rest of the guys duck into other doorways where they can watch the hall without being seen. Zian's lips pull back from his teeth in a silent snarl, but he stays in completely human form.

From the way he's talked, I suspect he prefers to remain that way when he can keep control over himself. I can't blame him, not when I'm keeping my own most destructive inclinations locked up.

The way he looked when I got a clear glimpse of his transformation in the control room—his face twisted into a distorted fusion of animal and man. Not an actual wolf so much as the kind of wolf-man you might see in a horror movie, a deformity more than an enhancement.

But he was still Zian, no matter how much fur leapt from his skin or how his face contorted.

I hope he knows that too.

Low voices carry from outside, too quiet for me to make out the words. If they say anything that Zian picks up with his keener ears and finds concerning, he gives no indication.

Footsteps travel down the steps with a faint rasp. They know *someone's* down here, and they're trying to catch those intruders unawares.

That's another sign that they don't know who they're dealing with. The guardians are aware of Zian's sharp hearing—I think they'd expect him to have already noticed their arrival if they knew he was here.

They aren't prepared for his supernaturally penetrating sight either. He taps my shoulder and flashes seven fingers at me. That's how many people he can see have entered the building so far.

The footsteps tread lightly toward us. My muscles tighten in anticipation.

The muzzle of a gun comes into view beyond the edge of the doorframe.

Zian and I spring out simultaneously. We leap at the closest of the figures, him instinctively letting me take the closer one with my shorter reach.

I slam the rifle against my thigh to bend it beyond use and haul the man who was holding it into the office room. He crashes to the floor with a clang of his helmet and vest.

They might not have realized who was in this place, but they pulled on their usual guardian gear regardless.

The man swings a fist at me and pulls a knife from a sheath at his waist. I kick the weapon away with a snap of breaking bone and yank up his helmet to get a look at his face.

He's young, not much older than my guys—not a good choice for Andreas's memory interrogation. I hesitate for just a second, but then the man rams his knee toward my belly while groping toward a holstered pistol at his hip, and I slash out with my claws.

His head lolls as blood gurgles from his throat. I shove myself away.

Bangs and thumps are echoing through the building all around me. Zian has already bashed his first target against the wall and left the woman in a crumpled heap. He has a man pinned under his immense frame now, one who looks closer to middle-aged.

"Did you know Ursula Engel?" he growls at the guy while restraining his struggling limbs.

"Let Andreas figure that out," I tell him, and dash back to the doorway.

Three more bodies litter the hallway outside, two with the bashed in helmets I know were Jacob's doing and another with a couple of bullet wounds to the chest that could have been dealt by any of the guys. In the room across from ours, Jacob has another man glued to the wall with his telekinetic force, the strands of gray in his hair suggesting he's the oldest of those we've seen so far.

"Get what you need," Jake snaps at Andreas.

Andreas stands rigidly next to him, staring at the guy with the ruddy gleam shimmering in his eyes. "I'm trying. He's—he's doing something that's muddling things whenever I try to focus in."

The man manages a sickly smile of triumph that makes my blood run cold.

What new techniques have the guardians figured out that are messing up Drey's talent?

Before I can worry much about that, more footsteps pound down the steps as a few guardians who initially hung back charge in to defend their companions. Too late.

I dart back out at the same time as Dominic emerges from the control room, a gun in his hand. With his brisk motion to the right, we understand each other.

I hurtle at the two figures on the left, my feet pushing off the ground so swiftly the soles of my shoes barely brush the floor. Dominic fires off several shots in quick succession at the two on the right.

As his targets crumple, I slam into a woman who's just aiming her rifle, too sluggish to match my unearthly speed. Even as I snap her neck, I'm already spinning my torso around to kick the man behind her in the face.

His helmet dents inward, puncturing his skull with a fleshy cracking sound like Jacob's preferred tactic. I land on the floor surrounded by the four limp bodies.

The scene brings back a flicker of the arena. My stomach lurches, and I yank my attention away, toward the entrance.

I'm okay now. We're all okay. We dealt with them all without needing any extra brutality… didn't we?

No other voices or footfalls carry from outside. I sprint up the steps to peek out into the cooling air of what's now evening.

Nothing stirs around the van or the car that've parked a short distance from our vehicle.

I race back down to the hall. "That's all of them!"

But we don't know how many reinforcements could be

on the way. Will the last of this bunch have called for backup before they descended?

They might not have been able to say *who* they were fighting, but they'd have realized the situation was bad.

When I reach the room where Jacob and Andreas were working on the one man, I find Zian has dragged his captive over there too, restraining him in the corner several feet from the first.

Andreas is frowning, sweat beading on his forehead as his eyes flare and dim.

"Fucking hell," he snaps, and glares at the man pinned to the wall. "If you don't let me in, we'll just have to kill you."

He glances at the other guy too, who I guess he also tried. "That goes for both of you."

The man Zian is holding sputters a little bloody spittle over his lips. "You're going to do that anyway. I'm not giving you a thing."

Dominic has come in beside me. We exchange a glance, neither of us knowing how to help.

"I can make the killing a whole lot more painful," Jacob warns, and twists his hand to the side. The man he's pressed against the wall lets out a grunt of agony, his features spasming.

Andreas elbows Jake. "That doesn't help," he says under his breath. "If their brain is fried with pain, I can't get much out of it then either."

Jacob scowls but eases up on the pressure.

I hug myself, uneasiness wobbling through my chest. If we can't get any answers from them, then where do we go from here?

Jacob was right that there are millions of places Engel could have set up her cabin, if she even did that.

The hovering man's gaze catches on me for a moment, and I catch the slightest softening in his defiant expression. It's there and then gone, but for a second I thought I saw a hint of... concern?

My first response is a jolt of anger. Who the hell is he to feel sorry for me?

Then understanding clicks in my head.

The hostile words Zian threw at me less than an hour ago. All Jacob's sneering comments about my "sob story." The reason I was so popular in the arena for all those years.

I don't look like a threat. I'm a short, skinny girl you'd think you could snap in two. My only outwardly unnerving feature is my claws, and I've retracted those back into my fingertips.

I hate it when people see me as someone weak and fragile... but maybe that's what we need right now. Maybe I can use the illusion of vulnerability to distract this guy from whatever technique he's using to close off his mind.

Stir up sympathy to rattle his emotions and his concentration in a totally different way from pain.

Even though it's my idea, my body balks for a few seconds before I can propel it forward. My skin prickles with discomfort as I place myself within clear view of both of our captives. Might as well see if the gambit will work on both of them.

"What the hell are you doing?" Jacob snaps at me, giving me the perfect opening.

I hunch my shoulders and let my voice come out quavering. "I'm just trying to help. Please don't yell at me."

Jacob's expression contorts with so much surprise I'd laugh if I wasn't aiming to give off the complete opposite impression. I turn back toward the captives, brushing my hands past my eyes as if swiping away tears.

I've got tears in me somewhere, the burn of grief and frustration I've felt more times than I can count since I reunited with my guys. Since all the way back to watching Griffin collapse in front of me and knowing I'd failed us all.

Blinking hard, I open up a channel inside me to bring those feelings to the surface rather than stuffing them as far down as they'll go like usual. Heat builds behind my eyes.

I don't want to risk faking it. If this is going to work, the deluge of vulnerability needs to come as fast and effective as possible.

So I open my mouth and let all my weakest thoughts tumble out, gazing vaguely at the floor, pretending I'm speaking to my guys rather than putting on a performance for our hostages.

"I always just want to help, but you never believe me. You've made me weak and sick and then you get mad at me because I can't do enough. I'm *trying*. I'm trying so hard to make things right, to be what you want, but that's never enough either."

A lump I don't have to force rises in my throat. A couple of very real tears slip down my cheeks. I take a ragged breath, leaning into the display of patheticness and ignoring the screaming of my dignity.

The guys are silent around me, but I don't dare look at them or our captives. I can't tell whether they're shocked or skeptical or if they've figured out what I'm trying to accomplish here.

I squeeze my eyes shut for a second, and more tears trickle out. "You want me dead too. I've spent the last four years thinking about nothing but getting back to you and getting you free, and all you seem to think about when you see me is how much pain you want to put me through. How horrible it is that I'm around. How much of a burden I am. I don't know what else you want from me."

My voice breaks on the last word of its own accord. I can't stop myself from sniffling, but maybe that's a good thing.

I hug myself tighter, hoping I look as frail as I feel right now with all my emotions stretched to fraying.

"You can all hate me as much as you want, but you know what? You can't hate me more than *I* already do. The mistakes I've made, the disasters I couldn't control… But I have never wanted to hurt any of you—not Griffin, not the rest of you—and every second of my life when I had the choice, I did whatever I could to protect you. If you can't ever believe that, then… I don't know."

My legs tremble beneath me, and I let them give. I slump down on the floor as if I'm totally defeated—and in that moment, I kind of am.

What if even this doesn't work? What if I've just made a fool of myself and still gotten us nowhere?

I can already hear the caustic insults that Jacob is probably forming in his head right now. A sob I can't contain hitches out of me.

I drop my head into my hands. I want to curl up in a

ball so they can't see me, so I have some kind of shell against the world again, but that would defeat the point of this demonstration.

Just hold on. Just stay here in this awful stew of emotions for as long as I can...

"I've got it," Andreas says in a low rasp. "I got everything."

As I raise my head, a strange ache spreading through my chest, Jacob sucks a breath through his teeth—and two spines crack simultaneously, our captives' heads going slack.

TWENTY-FIVE

Andreas

"We shouldn't stay in this junk heap of a car any longer than we have to," Jacob announces as he marches us out of the underground building. "We don't know if these guardians radioed details about it back to wherever they came from."

He glances over at me. "Where exactly are we going?"

"I'm figuring that out," I say without looking up from the phone I've taken control over. It'd be a hell of a lot easier to do this search on a computer with a big screen and proper keyboard, but I'm making do with my thumbs because I don't have a choice.

The conversation I plucked out of the one guardian's memories replays through my head. I've been concentrating on nothing but that since I recognized it was our best shot at finding Engel.

She's going all the way up to Glen Lily?
And a stretch farther north, it sounds like.

Must be fucking cold up there.

It was obviously a place, not a person named Glen. I squint through the reflected sunlight at the search results that pop up on the screen.

"Sometime when she was packing up to leave the facility—at least, I think that was what was happening— that one guy we caught was monitoring things from outside her office with another guardian. They made a few comments to each other about where she was going." I frown. "The main thing popping up is someplace in Kentucky—I can't tell whether it's an actual town or just, like, a landfill site or a road name."

Zian perks up. "Kentucky isn't too far from Kansas."

"Yeah, but... it doesn't really make sense with the other things they said. They were talking about her going 'all the way up' there. Kentucky isn't 'up' from any of the facilities we know about."

"Keep digging and see if you can find anything else," Jake orders.

As we reach the car, the other guys yank open the doors. I lower the phone for a moment to glance at Riva.

She hasn't said anything since her breakdown in front of the guardians—however much it was actually breaking down and not a sort of performance. But her silence now makes me even more certain that even if she released all that emotion on purpose, there was nothing fake about the anguish in her voice.

The tears that streaked down her cheeks have already dried, but there's still a hint of redness along the rims of her eyes. Her gaze has gone distant as if she's pulled back inside to collect herself.

To rebuild the dam that kept the torrent of grief and despair shut away before.

If the outburst hadn't really taken anything out of her, if it'd only been an act, it wouldn't still be affecting her now. And I didn't really think it was an act even in the moment.

I had to focus on our targets, on watching for their mental defenses against my talent to weaken, but the pain in her voice matched the brief comments she made to me in the car yesterday.

I move to get into the back with her, wanting her to know I'm still with her even if she pushed away from me before. I don't know what's going through her head, but it's a hell of a lot more than we've acknowledged.

Before I reach the door, Jacob gives me a sharp look and motions me to the front passenger seat as he gets in behind the wheel. My jaw clenches, but we don't have time to argue about this.

If I'm going to end up navigating, it does make more sense for me to be up front. He might not even be trying to separate me from Riva.

Given how he's treated her since the first moment we crossed paths with her, though, I'm pretty sure that's at least an equal part of his motivation.

The second all the doors are closed, Jacob hits the gas. I dive back into my search results.

I dig deeper and try a few different added words, and then sigh. "Nothing looks quite right."

"Are we sure that going after Engel is still our best option?" Zian asks from the back seat in an impatient tone. "I mean, we could just stick around here and more guardians will show up… If we're prepared for them, we could pick off a few to question."

Jacob shakes his head. "Those are grunt workers—expendable people. No one who's in charge with a real understanding of the big picture would be running into a fight. Anyone else who has an in-depth understanding of what they did to us will be behind all the facility's security."

"And it seems like Engel's the one who painted the big picture to begin with," I say as I continue skimming the internet. "She'd know more than anyone."

"Do you think they'll take her into protection after they realize we broke into that place?" Dominic asks.

We all sit in momentary silence as his question sinks in.

Jacob grimaces. "It's possible. But they shouldn't have any idea how we ended up at the old facility or why. Engel wasn't around us enough when we were older for us to have any memories of her—there's no reason for them to assume we were focused on her."

I nod. "As far as they know, we shouldn't even be aware she exists. And they don't seem to *want* her around the facility anymore. The guardians I just checked had no memories of her that seemed at all recent. Nothing where they talked to her about us escaping, for sure."

It's Riva's voice that pipes up next, low but clear. "That's why she's the best option. We were her project first, and the others shut her out somehow. The guardians are willing to die to keep their secrets. We could interrogate dozens of them and not get anywhere. But Engel… she might even think we deserve to know. Maybe that's why they kicked her out."

"Right," Jacob says, sounding a little annoyed to be supporting her point even as he agrees with her. "So, we track her down and see where that gets us. And if it turns out the guardians have brought her back under their wing to shield her, then we're in the exact same scenario we'd face if we never go looking for her."

Zian sinks deeper into his seat. "So… where exactly are we going, then?"

"I'm still working on that." I jab at the screen, flick through another list of results and another. "I guess it's possible I misunder—oh, wait!"

Jake glances over. "What have you got?"

"There's a town called Glenlily in British Columbia —Canada. That's definitely up north." With excitement bubbling up inside me, I flick through to the photos that come with the search and smile. "Jackpot. That looks like snowy cottage country to me, don't you agree, Tink?"

I hold the phone so Riva can see it from the back seat.

She sucks in a breath. "That's exactly the right kind of place."

Dominic lets out a hitch of a chuckle. "British Columbia's quite a hike from here."

"Maybe we should check Kentucky first, just in case?" Zian suggests.

I balk at the suggestion. "That's in the opposite direction. We'd lose days. The longer we wait, the more chance there is that the guardians will catch on."

Twisting in my seat, I catch Riva's gaze. She nods,

understanding the question I'm asking without needing words.

I turn to Jacob. "I say we go straight to BC. It's our best shot by far."

Jake hesitates for a second and then waves his hand toward me. "Let's do it. Give me our route and see where we can look for a new ride along the way."

With a few beats of my thumb, I bring up the map for our location. I meant to focus on the roads streaking across the state around us, but as I study the landscape, another detail catches my eye.

I zoom in and trace the markings crisscrossing the map. "What if we didn't get a new car right away?"

Jake's gaze flicks toward me as he propels our current vehicle down the bumpy country road that brought us here. "The guardians could already be on the lookout for this one. We don't want—"

I hold up my hand. "That's not what I meant. They'll be looking for us in cars in general. We've got a long way to go—it wouldn't be a bad thing if we could get some rest while traveling too. There are a bunch of freight train lines through Kansas. We could hitch a ride like we did with the truck before."

Dom speaks up from the back. "Would we be able to catch one that goes all the way up to Canada?"

I tilt my head, studying the screen. "I don't know what the typical routes are, but there's a network with tracks that go northwest all the way up to the border. It looks like… we could pass through Nebraska, then Wyoming, and then Montana, and cross into BC there. We'd have to check the GPS periodically, and I suspect we'd need to switch trains at least a couple of places, but they could get us most of the way there."

Jacob's expression turns pensive. "That method could be faster or slower depending on how consistently the trains are running. But we can always hop off once we've gotten some distance from this place and grab a car somewhere there's less heat on us."

I nod. "Yeah, exactly. The more we mix things up, the harder it'll be for the guardians to predict what we're doing or where we're going."

"All right. Figure out the best place for us to catch a ride nearby—and where we could ditch the car easily too."

I shoot Jake a tight smile in return. "Already on it."

The light in the train car gradually fades with the sinking of the sun. We eat the rest of our stash of food, making plans to pick up more wherever we get off this first train, and sway with the jostling of the car on the tracks.

Every half hour, I check the phone to confirm our progress on the line this freight train is traveling along. When I curl up on a musty canvas sheet next to the stacks of wooden crates to try to get a little rest, Jacob takes over.

I'm not sure he's been sleeping at all. He always pushes himself to his limit, even when he doesn't have to, but how the hell any of us could convince him to take a break, I don't know.

I wake up to a soft creaking and the sight of Jake and Zian peering at the phone with the electronic glow splashed across their faces. Dominic is lying against a different stack of crates, the hood of his parka pulled up to cushion his head, but when I move to join the others, he stirs and sits up.

All I can make out of Riva is her sneakered feet poking out from the thicker shadows where she's tucked herself in an alcove between more of the boxes.

"Don't leave it on too much," I say in a hushed voice, sinking down next to Jacob. "We don't know when we'll be able to recharge the battery."

"We got that extra battery pack," he mutters.

"Yeah, and eventually that needs to be recharged too."

He sighs, but he turns off the phone. "We're coming up on an interchange. Based on how fast this thing has been moving, I'd say we'll get there in twenty minutes or so. Then we'll have to see whether it keeps going the way we want, stops to unload, or veers off in the wrong direction."

We might have to get off, he means. I nod and glance toward Riva. "Should we wake her up?"

"No point until we know for sure, right?" Zian says before Jacob can answer.

Jacob grimaces. "If she is even sleeping and not pretending so she can listen in."

Listen in to what? What secret plans are we making that he thinks she'd want to spy on?

I fight down the urge to shake the guy. I know I don't understand how it's been for him in the past four years, but at some point, he needs to open his eyes and see that he's imagining a monster that isn't here.

Dominic moves closer to Riva with quiet steps and rests his hand gently on her calf. "She's definitely asleep," he murmurs a moment later. "Pretty deeply too. I don't know how much rest she's gotten in the last few days."

If she can't hear us, then Jake can't object to me bringing up the specific issue that's been niggling at me more and more during those few days. I turn to him, making my voice as firm as I can manage.

"I think it's time we got rid of the poison."

Jacob snorts. "So, you've totally fallen for her fragile victim act, huh?"

I glower at him. "She *hasn't* been acting like a victim, and the only times she's gotten fragile are when the toxin has worn her down. She's *killed* for us in at least two different fights with the guardians, even if you don't believe she hurt any of them when we first escaped. Whatever happened in the past, she's obviously on our side now."

"For how long?" Jacob demands, his voice harsh even as he keeps it low to avoid waking her. "You saw her back there, getting all weepy and whiny. Either that was a fantastic show of acting, which means we can't trust anything still, or she thinks she shouldn't have to prove herself after everything she did before."

"Is that what you got out of the things she said?" I shake my head. "We've been beating her down this entire time, and she's been taking it. Do you really think she's *enjoyed* it? If she cares at all about us, which she clearly does, then of course the way we've treated her would be hard for her. But she didn't say a word about it until she realized even that could help us."

"And when she was drunk."

"That wasn't her fault either," Dominic says. "The

alcohol mixed with the poison really messed things up."

She's shown a little of the pain inside her only to me, too, but I'm not going to mention our conversation in the car. I encouraged her to see me as the one person among us she could open up to, and I'm not bringing up what she said then when all it'll get me is more snarky remarks from Jake.

"She's doing what she needs to do to survive," Zian says abruptly. "If something happens to us, she knows the poison would kill her. We can't be sure if she cares for any reason other than that."

Okay, now I want to shake him too. Why does he have to bring out his bull-headed stubbornness now?

"There's too much on the line," Jacob says before I can keep arguing. "If she tips off the guardians somehow at this point, we'll lose all the progress we've made, and we might never be able to find Engel again. We'll have nothing."

He meets my gaze steadily. "Once we've found out everything we can from the scientist, then we can talk about fully healing her."

Jake is always way too good at making his perspective sound like the most reasonable one. My jaw clenches, but I don't actually have a counterargument that I can imagine him accepting.

And Dom, the only one of us who could override Jacob's decision on the matter if he wanted to, has gone back to his typical silence.

I feel the need to try one more time anyway. "Even if back then she got caught up in some promise the guardians made or—"

Jacob doesn't even let me get to my point. He jerks forward, even the little warmth he'd shown me a moment ago vanishing behind the ice of his eyes.

"*If?* We *know* what she did. Don't try to wave it away now. Griffin deserves a hell of a lot better than that."

My mouth clamps shut. There's nothing I can say when the guy who's no longer with us is invoked. Even if inside, there's a question that's started tugging at me and won't go away.

Do we really know even that much?

The train car jostles with a metallic squeal, and Riva flinches where she was sleeping. She shoves herself upright looking both panicked and bleary-eyed, strands of her rumpled hair that've come free from her braid floating around her face.

"We must be at the interchange," Jacob says, ignoring her and pulling out the phone. "Let's see where our ride is going to take us from here."

As he studies the screen and the car shudders again, Riva slinks closer. She sits cross-legged a few feet from any of us, clearly not feeling comfortable outright joining our circle. In the thin light, the weariness etched on her pretty face makes my gut tighten up.

I want to pull her into my arms and hug her tight like I did before, but I'm not sure how much she'd welcome the gesture. It wouldn't actually do her much good anyway.

Instead, I motion to Dominic. "You should heal Riva up in case we need to make a run for it."

Dom moves to her side despite his tight expression, because that's an explanation they'll all accept—not to cure her completely, but to make sure she doesn't become a liability. Because apparently that's what we're now reducing this girl to.

The girl who was once just as vital to our group as Griffin was.

A memory rises up in my head of some afternoon not that long before our escape attempt, when Riva and Griffin were standing near each other in the training room, and he leaned over to say something by her ear. She laughed with that secretive little smile that made her whole face shine…

Only he could ever make her light up quite like that.

I also remember the jab of jealousy that ran through me even as I basked in the sight. I could make her laugh, sure, but not quite like that. There was always something a little more with him.

The one thing I've never understood, no matter what we've seen, was how she could have given up that light. Not just given it up—destroyed it and the guy who sparked it.

But what if she didn't? What if we've been completely wrong all this time?

If anyone's going to figure it out, it's got to be me— both because she *has* started opening up to me, and because none of the other guys are willing to even consider the possibility.

And if I'm going to figure it out, then for all our sakes, I'd better do it soon.

The train jolts and rattles, and Jacob looks up from the phone. "It's taking the southwest route. This one isn't good anymore." He gets to his feet. "Everybody ready to jump?"

TWENTY-SIX

Riva

Stones rattle under my feet along the side of the train tracks. The occasional kicked pebble patters off into the brush where it's too dark for me to follow its path.

Enough moonlight streams down over the tracks as they cut through the sparse woodland for me to make out the two guys ahead of me, though they aren't much more than silhouettes. Jacob marches forward with purposeful strides like he could keep going all night—and maybe he could. Dominic looks like he's drooping a little, though.

It's hard to judge how Andreas and Zian are doing from the crunch of their footsteps behind me, but they don't sound particularly energetic. No one's spoken in ages.

My muscles could keep going for hours longer, but my eyes are starting to get heavy. I only managed to get an hour or two of sleep on the train.

I suppress a yawn and peer through the scattered trees alongside the tracks. We're following the route that should take us closer to our intended destination, but since we set out, no trains have come rushing by. We haven't spotted any ideal place to steal a vehicle of our own either, although I'm not totally sure what criteria Jacob is going by to make that decision.

After several more minutes of trudging, the tree line peters out at our left. Fields sprawl out for miles, leading to low hills faintly outlined against the night sky.

Dominic's head turns to gaze out over the same landscape. I sense his pause before he speaks.

"There's a house down there. No lights, and the garage roof looks damaged. I don't see any vehicles in the driveway. Maybe we should scope it out and if it's abandoned, use it to crash for the rest of the night?"

Jacob lets out a disgruntled sound, but he seems to consider the possibility before he answers. "That might not be the worst idea. We're not making a lot of progress like this, and who knows when the next train will be by."

"We might be able to scrounge up something useful in the house," Zian adds.

Andreas comes up beside me, stretching his arms. "I could use a longer rest on a floor that's not shaking me around."

No one asks my opinion, but I'm perfectly happy to tramp with the others down through the weedy grass and across the field toward the house. Imagine if the place still has *beds*.

Such luxury.

As we get closer, I make out a sign on a post out front.

By the time we reach it, I can read the thicker letters even in the darkness.

"The place is for sale," Zian says in a low voice, frowning at it.

Dominic motions to the smears of dirt on the sign and the crumbling edges. "That's been here for a long time. Doesn't look like anyone's been trying to show off the property lately."

Jacob squints at the garage roof, half of which appears to have caved in. "Could be once the roof went, they gave up, or at least couldn't be bothered to get it fixed right away."

We poke around the edges of the property, confirming there are no vehicles squeezed into the still-roofed side of the garage or parked elsewhere out of view. No one else stirs in or around the house.

Zian scans the walls with the tensed expression that comes over him when he's peering through things. "I don't see anyone inside. It's pretty empty—like they left some basic furniture for buyers to see but that's it."

Jacob walks up to the front door. "All right. Might as well make use of what we've been given."

I can't tell whether the door is already unlocked or if he uses his talent. Either way, we're walking into the front hall moments later.

The place is still and silent other than the creak of the floorboards under our shoes.

Like Zian suggested, the furnishings are totally spartan. The living room holds only a futon sofa and a plain coffee table.

There's a dining room with only the table and four chairs, nothing along the walls. All the kitchen appliances are on hand, but the fridge and the cupboards are bare.

"I guess room *and* board would have been a little much to ask for," Andreas says dryly, and then tries the tap. The faucet sputters and then expels a stream of water into the sink.

His eyebrows shoot up, and a smile crosses his face. "I, for one, could go for a shower before I get back to snoozing."

My skin itches with the grime I'm abruptly aware of coating it. "Me too."

Jacob gives me a pointed look. "You can have your turn last." Then he glances at Andreas. "Go ahead, but don't take too long. We have no idea how much hot water we might get, if any."

Andreas nods and jogs upstairs. He's already ducking into the bathroom when the rest of us follow.

There are only two other rooms up there, a larger bedroom and a smaller one, both with double mattresses on blocky wooden frames and no other furniture. Jacob considers them and then heads back downstairs.

I figure he'll tell me I need to sleep on the floor while he and the other guys share the beds, and at this point I don't even care. I rub my hand over my mouth to suppress another yawn and wait for my chance at the shower.

The guys are at least considerate enough to heed Jacob's instructions and keep their time short, although that's probably more for each other's benefit than for me. I don't think Jacob considered that by having me go last, I can take as long as I want, since there's no one left to delay or stiff on the hot water.

I strip off all my clothes except my necklace, with a faint twinge of uneasiness like Jacob might try to steal it if I remove it from my neck even for a second. Then I start the shower running.

The tub area doesn't come with any toiletries, but there's a pump bottle of liquid hand soap on the sink that's damp from earlier usage. I bring it right into the tub with me.

Luke-warm water pelts me, but it's better than the nothing-at-all I've had for days before. I rub the pearly white soap all over my skin.

My fingers graze the moon-and-droplet tattoo on my thigh. I glance at it, blinking through the spray, abruptly choking up.

One more sign that I belong with the guys I came here with. One more fact they've somehow decided doesn't matter.

I yank my gaze away and finish scrubbing myself down.

My hair's been tied in the same braid since the last time I showered, which was enough days ago that I've lost track. I pull off the elastic, but the strands catch on each other, refusing to fully unwind. So I work the soap into my scalp as well as I can and rinse it off, figuring that's good enough.

As I'm shutting off the water, the door squeaks open, and there's a soft thump on the floor. "We found some clothes in a box in the basement," Andreas says. "And a washer-dryer set. Figured you might like the chance to wear something clean too, even if it's a bit big. I'll grab your old clothes to take them down, if that's okay?"

"Thanks," I call out, feeling weirdly exposed even with the opaque curtain between us.

When he's gone, I ease out to find he's left me with a simple cotton dress that's only a little loose around the waist but falls to my calves when I think it was meant to be knee-length. And it's not exactly my usual style. But I'll take it if it means I can have my hoodie, tank top, and cargo pants back clean in a few hours.

He took *all* my clothes, including my panties and sports bra. Which I'll be glad to have clean too, but I feel oddly exposed even with the dress draped over me like a curtain.

Girding myself, I pull on my sneakers and head out.

Jacob is waiting by the top of the stairs dressed in a tee that's stretched on his muscular physique and a pair of gym shorts, both obviously borrowed like my dress.

"I'm escorting you to your room so the rest of us can get our sleep," he says.

I blink at him. "My room?"

He gives me a chilly smile and gestures for me to follow him.

We walk downstairs and through the kitchen to another, dingier flight of steps that leads to the basement. A damp, mildewy smell tickles my nose as we descend into the depths, but the guys have risked turning on the light down there where there are no windows, so at least it's not pitch black.

On one side, there's a laundry room where the washing machine is rumbling away. On the other side is what I guess is meant to pass for a guestroom to potential buyers, with a steel-framed twin bed and a tiny side table that holds the lamp responsible for the room's light.

It doesn't seem like such a bad deal until Jacob starts back toward the stairs with a caustic remark tossed over his shoulder. "The basement is the only part of the house we can lock from outside the room. You can stay down here until we come for you."

Oh. I'm not being given the gift of privacy but the punishment of a prison. I really shouldn't have expected better, should I?

I sink down onto the edge of the bed and wait for the sound of the door thudding shut at the top of the stairs. Instead, there's a murmured conversation I can't decipher until the end.

"Fine," Jacob mutters. "But you should get some rest too."

It's Andreas's voice that answers. "I will. I need to wind down a bit first anyway."

His lanky form appears, ambling down the steps. He's swapped clothes too, though the new tee hangs more loosely on his leaner frame and he found a pair of jeans that seem to fit him pretty well.

I peer at him. "Adding to the laundry?"

Andreas stops near the foot of the bed and offers me a smile that looks oddly hesitant. "No, I just thought… you might appreciate a little company, without Jake hovering around like a thundercloud. Unless you wanted to go right to sleep?"

My pulse skips a beat, both startled and happy. "No, I'm kind of wound up still too."

And I'll soak up every bit of friendship my guys are willing to offer while I can get it.

There's nothing to sit on down here other than the bed. I debate for a second and then scoot all the way over to the head where the limp pillow is lying. Then I pat the blanket a few feet away in offering.

As Andreas lowers himself onto the edge of the bed at the opposite end from me, giving me plenty of space, my mouth dries up. I haven't really talked to him—to any of the guys—since I let myself break down in front of them in the old facility.

Stalling, I reach back to try to work at the knots in my hair again. Drey watches me for a moment, taking in my wince as I yank on a few strands harder than I meant to.

"It's tangled up pretty bad, huh?"

"That's what happens when it's left braided for days on end." I let out a sigh and dig my fingers between two twisted locks. "It'll be even worse if I sleep on it like this." Maybe I'll have to cut the whole rat's nest off.

A twinge runs over my neck at the thought of leaving it bare, as if my hair is really any protection.

Andreas sets his hands on the mattress and then ventures, "Do you want help? At least I'll be able to see what I'm doing."

My body seems to sway toward him and recoil simultaneously, wanting him close but afraid of wanting too much. I wet my lips, and the trace of disappointment that crosses his gorgeous face at my hesitation defeats my doubts.

"Sure. I'm obviously not getting very far on my own."

I twist on the mattress so that my back is partly to him, and he eases close enough to reach my hair. His knee comes to rest against the small of my back through the thin fabric of the borrowed dress.

Suddenly I'm twice as aware of the fact that I have nothing at all on under that thin layer.

But Andreas simply lifts the tangled locks and starts loosening one knot carefully. Of course, his hands brush my bare neck with his movements.

Each brief contact sends a flash of heat over my skin. It's pooling in my face—and lower down, where at least he won't be able to see it.

Then his next words douse me in cold. "Do you think about Griffin a lot?"

"I—" My voice catches in my throat. I have to swallow before I can continue, wishing I could see his expression now. "Of course. Every day."

"I don't think *he* would like the way Jake is trying to 'avenge' him."

The comment relaxes some of the tension inside me. Drey isn't leading up to an accusation.

A pang of guilt radiates through my chest anyway. "I guess that's hard to know."

While the agony of the bullet tore through him, in the moment when he must have realized he was dying, did some part of Griffin curse me for making such a stupid move? Would he agree with his twin that it was all my fault?

Andreas wiggles a few strands free and lets them drift

down across my shoulder. I have to hold myself back from leaning into his gentle touch.

"Do you remember that time with the cookies when we were really little?" he asks.

"The cookies…" I repeat, combing back through my recollections.

Andreas hums to himself, his knuckles gliding across my neck. "We were sitting around the table in the training room having lunch, and right after Griffin asked to use the bathroom, the guardians on duty brought out a plate of chocolate cookies. It was the first time they'd given us any dessert in weeks. We each downed ours like we were sugar-deficient, and Griffin still hadn't gotten back—"

The moment flickers up from the depths of my mind, provoking a twitch of my lips. "And Dominic took his."

Andreas chuckles. "Right. Dom snuck that last one and inhaled it, and then Jake noticed Griffin's was gone and demanded to know who'd stolen his brother's cookie. He was kind of a self-righteous dick even back then, wasn't he?"

I'm outright smiling now. "I think I'd better plead the fifth, or next time he'll have me sleeping in the garage."

Andreas's hands falter for just a moment before they resume their work on my hair. "Zian got all flustered and guilty-looking even though he hadn't done anything, because he was *usually* the one who'd eat the most, so he figured he'd get blamed. But Jake pointed out the extra crumbs by Dom's spot and started glaring at him."

"I thought Dom was going to faint, he looked so agonized." The image swims up through my mind of the much younger version of the man I know now.

"No kidding. So Griffin finally gets back and Jake wastes no time calling Dom out, Dom sits there all horrified with his eyes starting to well up with tears, but just before he can babble a gazillion apologies, Griffin just smiles at him. And says if Dom took it, he must have wanted it a lot, so it's okay."

My throat constricts. "Yeah. That was just… how he was." Griffin would have been able to sense how awful Dominic felt about his petty crime without the other guy needing to say anything.

Andreas shakes his head in bemusement. "Funny how that guy was more mature at five or six than the rest of us are even now."

I arched an eyebrow on the side he'd be able to see. "Speak for yourself." But an unexpected sense of peace has settled over me, as momentary as it might be.

I haven't let myself think about Griffin *that* far back in a long time. Mostly I've just beaten myself up with images from our last night together.

Twisting my head as far as I dare without disrupting the detangling session, I peek at Andreas's face. "You've always been our memory-keeper as well as the memory-reader, haven't you? Keeping track of all our history."

He smiles at me. "I like my collection of stories."

Yes, all the stories he's compiled from the people he saw on missions whose minds he dipped into. The remark sparks another jolt of curiosity. "Did the guardians still have you all go on missions after—after we tried to escape."

"Yeah," Andreas says, casually enough that my anxiety around asking fades away. "Not as often as before, and they'd still have us on a low dose of whatever drug they kept us doped on so we couldn't do anything too crazy. And the same old threat hanging over us that if we acted out, the others would pay for it."

His smile twists. "After they saw how we reacted to losing Griffin, they must have been even more sure of how effective that warning would be."

Losing Griffin, he says. Not losing both of us.

Because they didn't think of *me* as being lost—because they assumed I'd left them behind on purpose, for reasons I still don't totally understand.

But I don't want to bring that up again now, not when it's gotten me nowhere before and we're having this moment where things feel almost okay.

I gaze across the room toward the washing machine. "Any good stories I missed?"

Andreas clicks his tongue against his teeth. "Let's see. What would the best ones have been…?"

He lowers what must have been an entire section of the braid, now knot-free, and moves to a matted area closer to the middle. His fingers graze my spine.

"There was this woman I noticed in a park in Seattle one time," he says. "She looked like a very bookish, cautious type—hair in a tight bun, cardigan buttoned all the way up, plaid skirt down to her ankles. Sitting there with a book on her lap and a notebook she was writing in propped against it. I figured she had to be a super-committed student studying for exams."

I inhale slowly, resisting the urge to sink back and take in even more of his warmly musky scent. "But I'm guessing that's not what you found in her head."

"Nope. I got all kinds of memories of going out scuba-diving. Cruising around in this boat with fancy radar-checking maps. Swimming way down to find ruins of sunken ships, showing off artifacts she'd found online." He laughs. "An underwater Indiana Jones. I bet she was actually taking notes on what her next dive site could be."

"I bet she'd have lots of interesting stories too."

"Looking for my replacement already?" Drey gives my hair a playful tug. "I've got a whole library in this head. You don't need anyone else."

"Fine," I say, wishing it could be like this with him—with all of the guys—always. "Tell me another one then."

He's silent for a moment, thinking and unwinding my hair. Then he starts to speak in a softer voice than before.

"The last mission I did, I saw an elderly couple in a coffee shop. I noticed them because the woman was gazing around all dreamily while the man looked just… beaten. Sad and weary. I couldn't help wondering how they'd ended up like that—why he'd stayed."

My stomach clenches in anticipation of an awful explanation. "What was it?"

"Well, I searched his head for memories about her. And there were tons of them, going back decades to when they must have been only in their twenties. And in most of the memories, they were so happy, having a blast, building their life together… But then the ones from recently, when they looked a lot older, she was forgetting things, getting cranky, often not even recognizing him…"

An ache squeezes my heart. "She had Alzheimer's."

"Or something like that," Andreas agrees. "But it was hard to say it was a sad story, you know? Because they'd had so many years together before things got bad. And even the way they were right then—while I was watching, there was a moment when she turned to him and said his name and just beamed at him, and all his sadness disappeared. He looked like he figured he was the luckiest guy alive."

The ache expands into something brighter and bittersweet. The words just tumble out. "Griffin would have loved that story."

"Yeah, I bet he would have."

Andreas rests his hand against the back of my shoulder, not quite an embrace but like an offering of one. When I hold still, he moves it to finish teasing apart the last tangled bits of my hair, and I wince inwardly against the pang of my regret.

"He was the heart of our group," Drey goes on. "I mean, it was obvious even when he was there, but it got *really* fucking obvious when he was gone. I've tried to fill that gap, because the other guys sure as hell don't know how to, but I'm not sure I've done all that great a job."

His voice has gone raw. The sound cracks something inside me.

I reach back and grasp his forearm. His hands go still.

"You've been here for me," I say. "You have no idea how much that matters to me."

Andreas swallows audibly. He tips his head forward so I can feel his breath tickle over my hair. My whole body wakes up to tingling alertness and a starker craving I can't pretend away.

But how can I even be thinking about him like that when—

As if he's followed my train of thought, Andreas's voice comes out halting but gentle.

"Tink, there's something you haven't told us about what happened when you and Griffin were getting out of the facility, isn't there?"

TWENTY-SEVEN

Riva

The instant Andreas's question hits me, I choke up. "I—"

No other sound will emerge.

There are things I haven't told them about our failed escape attempt, yes—and reasons I haven't, too.

Andreas combs his fingers through my unknotted hair before trailing them down my arm from shoulder to elbow. His other hand shifts to grip mine where I reached for him.

"Maybe if you explain it to me, I can make the other guys understand. *I* know you wouldn't have hurt any of us on purpose."

Tears well up behind my eyes. For a second, I can't even breathe. I grapple with the impulse to wrench myself away from him—because I'm not really sure I deserve the compassion he's offering.

But he just admitted his own worries to me. He told me stories when I asked.

How can I shut him out when he's the only one who's even tried to let *me* in?

I want someone to know. My mind balks against the admission, but at the same time I have the sense of relief just beyond my fingertips.

I start slowly, my body braced to jerk myself back if the territory starts to feel too treacherous. "It all happened the way I already told you. Until—we got outside, and we were waiting for the rest of you, and it *seemed* like no one was anywhere nearby. And I just—it was so stupid, doing it right then—but I'd wanted to for so long, and it felt so good being so close to getting free—"

My voice fades out. Andreas waits, a patience to his silence that doesn't feel like pressure.

"I kissed him," I whisper, and suddenly I'm blinking back tears that have overflowed. "I kissed Griffin instead of keeping watch or checking the surroundings, and the second we stopped kissing, they shot him, just like that, he was just *gone*, and I— I couldn't even stay with him or say anything to him while he died because they tackled me and dragged me away."

A sob cuts off anything else I would have said. My head droops.

Both of Andreas's arms come around me. He hugs me close like he did in the car before, but an incredulous note colors his tone when he speaks. "Is *that* the big mistake you've been feeling so guilty about?"

"I screwed up," I mumble between hitches of breath as I fight to regain control over my emotions. "What kind of idiot goes for a kiss when we were in the middle of the most dangerous mission we could possibly attempt—when everyone's lives were on the line— I wanted all of us out there more than anything, and I gambled it all away for a few seconds of… of *that*."

"You said you'd wanted to for a long time," Andreas says hoarsely.

"Yeah." My voice drops even lower. "I loved him. So fucking much. But it didn't do him any good in the end, did it?"

I pause, and then raise my head to meet Andreas's gaze.

He looks strangely stricken in that first moment despite his reassuring words, but he appears to yank his reaction under control. "Of course you did. And it makes sense. You thought you were safe. If you cared about him that much—"

All at once, it feels incredibly important to make one thing crystal clear. Griffin took my secret to his grave, but maybe it never should have been a secret to begin with.

Maybe if my guys had known all along how much my world revolved around them, they never could have believed I'd have betrayed them.

"I loved all of you," I interrupt, with enough force that Andreas's mouth snaps shut. I rub my hand over my face, wiping away the dampness on my cheeks. "I wanted to kiss all of you. I wanted to have what that old man you saw had with his wife—with all of you, for just as many decades or even more. But nothing could happen while we were in the facility anyway, and I had no idea how you'd all react. Griffin knew, because he always knew how everyone was feeling, but I couldn't figure out what to say to the rest of you."

Andreas's eyes have widened. Whatever discomfort he was struggling with before, I can't see any trace of it now.

He raises his hand to the side of my face and strokes his thumb over my cheekbone. A little of his usual good humor dances like a spark in his eyes.

"I can't help noticing you're using the past tense," he says. "I guess we haven't been so loveable lately, huh?"

His tone isn't exactly playful. There's too much pain mixed into it too.

I tip my head into his touch, still holding his gaze. "Things have gotten pretty messed up. But I still think we all belong together. We just have to make it back to where we were before—or maybe it's that we need to figure out something new that works with who we are now. But we're blood. That'll always be true. I've loved you basically my whole life, Drey. A couple of weeks isn't going to erase that."

The relief I tasted before floods me, sweeping through my nerves and washing away the weight I've been carrying as if now I could float right into the air.

This is freedom. This is escape. Part of the answer was inside me all along.

Andreas's jaw works, a less familiar emotion shimmering in his eyes. Then he slides his fingers down to my chin and draws my mouth to his.

I'm not prepared for the maelstrom that hits me with the meeting of our lips. Heat flares between us, and my fingers clutch at the front of his borrowed shirt like I'm holding on to him for dear life.

All the hunger that's simmered up inside me every time we've touched fills my body. It propels me closer, pressing my mouth harder against his with an urgency that burns right down the center of me.

But that heat isn't enough to sear away the icy jolt of panic that hits me at the same time. Even as I cling on to Andreas, my spine stiffens.

I want to fall right into him, and I want to wrench myself away before some horrific catastrophe crashes down on us.

Andreas tips his head to break the kiss with his forehead resting against mine. He caresses my jaw like he did my cheek moments ago, over and over in a gentle motion as my pulse races with the spike of frantic adrenaline.

"It's okay," he says softly. "See? Nothing horrible is happening. You can't ruin anything with a kiss. It wasn't your fault then, and you aren't screwing things up now either. I promise."

My breath hitches with a strange mix of anguish and affection. He understands, and... he's right. There's no blast of gunshots or thunder of footsteps barging into the house.

Nothing about this moment feels like a mistake.

My fingers tighten in his shirt, and I'm yanking him back to me before I have a chance to hesitate in doubt. And if any doubts *had* been rising up about whether he only kissed me to prove a point, the rough sound that escapes him and urgency with which his mouth claims mine erase them in an instant.

Once we've started again, we can't seem to stop. Our

lips collide over and over, every kiss even more addictive than the last. I'm inhaling him, downing him like the sweetest of cocktails, and I can't get enough.

A heady energy flows through my limbs, as if the smoky stuff that trails out of us when we bleed is reaching from my veins to pull him even closer. As if it's seeping out of our skin and melding us together, breath to breath and blood to blood, in a way no normal human beings could experience.

Andreas's fingers delve into the strands of my hair he so recently untangled. His other hand slides down the side of my body, marking a scorching trail all the way to my hip.

Then he lifts me right onto his lap, grasping the skirt of the dress as it pools around my thighs so I can straddle him. He sucks my lower lip between his teeth with the slightest prick of pain that sparks into something so much more delicious.

He could eat me whole, and I wouldn't mind one bit. I want to be lost in him, completely intermeshed.

"Riva," he murmurs between kisses. "Wanted you for so long. *Loved* you for so long. You're ours—and mine. All mine."

I let out a whimper of agreement that he drinks straight from my mouth. His hand glides up beneath my dress to cup my bare breast.

The swipe of his thumb over my nipple has me gasping and rocking in his lap. Andreas groans, his other hand dropping to push me closer against him—against the bulge that meets my pussy through our clothes.

The press of him against me sets off a jolt of pleasure

so intense it sweeps through my mind. I'm barely thinking any more, barely aware of anything except the roar of unfulfilled need. The tendrils of smoke in my blood writhe as they reach out toward him.

I didn't know that it could feel like this—that I could ache for someone so badly I'm almost sobbing with the sensation. The desperate impulse to sate my hunger has me pushing even closer against him.

"Riva," Andreas mutters again, followed by a series of muffled swear words as he tips us over on the bed. His mouth brands my neck, my shoulder, and my collarbone before he yanks my dress up high enough to close his lips over the peak of my breast.

I cry out, my pussy outright throbbing now. My fingers rake down his chest and up under his shirt, claiming the lean planes of muscle as he devours me.

"Drey, please," I gasp out.

"Fuck," he rasps again with a blissful wash of breath over my nipple, and shoves his hand down between us. At the first stroke of his thumb over my clit, I jerk against his touch.

Bliss sings through my core and amplifies the siren call within me that's wailing for more.

It isn't enough—we could be even closer—every particle of my body is quivering with need and wrenching at me—

I don't know exactly what I'm doing, but I've seen enough poised Hollywood versions of this moment to understand the gist of what's required. My hand gropes at the fly at the loose waist of his jeans, and I manage to pop the button.

We're meant for this. We belong together. For the longest time, I've known that down to my bones, and the anticipation of finally uniting in the most concrete possible way resonates through my soul.

Andreas strokes me more forcefully, the wetness seeping from me turning his fingers slick, his breath coming ragged. As he squirms out of his jeans and boxers with my fumbling assistance, my hand grazes the rigid shaft between his legs.

So hard and so hot, because of me.

At that point, I'm not sure there's anything that could have interrupted our passionate collision. Andreas braces himself over me with just a second's tensing of his arms, his chest heaving, his lips parting as if he means to say something but can't quite find the words.

I wrap my hand around his cock and lift my hips to meet him, and all that escapes him is another groan as he plunges into me.

Being filled is a different kind of burn, giddying and searing and sending a fresh ache of need radiating through my body. I cry out, and Andreas bows his head over me, touching my face even as he drives into me again.

"Don't want to hurt you," he says with the same edge of desperation that's gripping me.

I sway to meet him, clutching at his back, his shoulder. "It's not—it's good. Don't stop."

If we even could.

A strange ringing fills my ears, as if I'm in my head but also not. Like I'm inside Drey as much as he's inside me, breathing with him, moving with him, coasting on the bliss that's swelling wider and faster.

We're disintegrating and recombining as if we're two beings made entirely of the dark haze in our veins, merging into one. One motion, one rhythm, one ripple of pleasure echoing on and on through both of us.

My claws spring from my fingers. The flavor of desire courses into my nose and mouth until my lungs are drenched in it.

Andreas's eyes shimmer red. He lowers his head right next to mine, shaking and thrusting and mumbling words by my ear like a frantic prayer.

"Mine. Love you. Always. Need you. Riva. Stay."

As if there's anywhere I could go. As if there's any part of me that isn't fused with him, caught up in the power resonating through us in tandem.

I dig my hand into his hair, managing to curl my fingers away from his scalp. He inhales with a hiss and bucks into me faster.

And I shatter apart.

I'm a whirlwind, careening in every direction, the final surge of bliss reverberating through me like the blaze of a firework. Andreas lets out a choked sound, and I feel him explode with me, both of us spiraling up and out—

And then back down, together, entangled on the bed, still half-dressed and damp with sweat.

Andreas kisses me long and lingering, looping his arm around my back to hug me to him. Then he nestles his head next to mine while he holds me against him as if he never plans to let me go.

A shaky laugh spills out of him. "That was—that was really something."

"Yes." And somehow something in me wants even

more. My nerves quiver like there's still a fire smoldering on deep inside.

Andreas eases back and frowns, touching my collarbone with a tentative finger. "Did you have a bruise here before? I didn't mean to get rough like that."

I glance down, unable to see what he's pointing to, but my gaze catches on his chest. I reach up and brush my finger over the top of his sternum. "You got one too."

There's an imprint on his coppery skin, fingerprint-sized and round, but it doesn't exactly look like a bruise. Or maybe it does, but one formed by the smoky part of our blood rather than the red stuff. Like a dab of shadow risen to the surface of his flesh.

The sense of our beings twining and merging comes back to me with a heady shiver. I glance up at him.

"We got so close we left a mark on each other."

He studies the spot for a few beats longer before lifting his gaze to meet my eyes. A fond smile crosses his lips, the corners of his eyes crinkling with so much affection I automatically smile back.

"I hope that's what it is," he says. "I prefer that to the symbol they marked us with."

I skim my fingers down his side to the tattoo on his thigh that matches mine. His gaze follows their trail and halts on my torso.

He touches a raised ridge of scar that slices across my ribs. Another, shallower but wider, near my belly button. Another, just a thin white line cutting down toward my hip.

His voice comes out taut. "These look pretty new. You got them… from the cage fights?"

I nod, feeling abruptly, weirdly shy. "It was hard to get through them totally unscathed. I did a pretty good job."

"I'm not criticizing you." His jaw tightens, his lean muscles flexing against mine. "When we're finished with this mission, we're going to track those assholes down and obliterate them from existence in every possible way."

My stomach gives a little lurch. He has no idea how thoroughly they've already been obliterated. But that's the last thing I want to talk about—even think about—right now.

Instead, I pull him into another kiss. Our lips move together more tenderly than before, but a fresh waft of desire flares between my legs.

Andreas eases back just an inch with a shaky laugh. "It's amazing, being with you. I feel like… like every part of me is more *alive*."

My smile stretches wider, my momentary uneasiness fading away. "Yeah."

We sit up together, Andreas's arms wrapped around me, and he kisses my forehead, but a trace of tension returns to his stance.

"I want to just stay here with you," he says, "but I've got to— Jacob and the others have to pull their heads out of their asses and see what idiots they're being. You haven't deserved any of this. The bullshit has to end *now*."

Twenty-Eight

Riva

The second Andreas leaves the basement, his borrowed jeans hastily pulled back on and his tight curls still rumpled, the room feels achingly empty.

Sitting on the bed, I rub my arms, but that only rekindles the memory of his hands running over me, his body moving against mine, reminding me of what I'm now missing. I've become a live wire, my nerves risen up through my skin so that every sensation is twice as sharp.

My claws are still out; I can't quite will them to retract. The scent of our shared desire still laces the air, thickly enough that I taste it with every breath.

My blood thrums on through my veins, pulsing with an exhilarated energy I don't know where to aim.

I touch the spot on my collarbone where Andreas said I was marked. A fresh tingle ripples through my body.

I can sense him—vaguely, but with enough of his flavor that I know it's him. He's standing still, high enough above me that he must be on the second floor.

That's all I can tell, but the knowledge sends a new thrill through me. If we're separated again, I don't need to cut myself open to track him now.

Did it happen simply because we had sex, or was there something more to the heightened emotions of that collision that bound us together more tightly than before?

Can he sense me too?

A smile touches my lips, and the washing machine rumbles to a stop with a harsh beep.

Apparently I'm on laundry duty since I'm the one stuck down here. I spring off the bed and go over to move the damp clothes to the dryer.

It's a small load, so it shouldn't take long. I can't wait to get back into my regular clothes. This dress makes me feel like a dwarf.

Someday, maybe I'll have a proper wardrobe, multiple outfits to pick between… that I don't have to leave behind after just a few days because brutal guardians launch an attack. Not that I have high fashion aspirations, but a little variety would be nice.

As I set the dryer running, a whiff of a different sort of emotion reaches my nose. The tang of stress hormones unfurls through the air.

Those aren't coming from me, and there's no one else in the room. Frowning, I turn my head and prowl through the space, trying to follow the trail.

I end up underneath a vent for the furnace, which isn't

currently running. Another waft of tension prickles into my lungs from above.

The vents will run all through the house. In my overly sensitized state, a trace seeping down from the higher floors must feel like a lot.

But how upset must the guys be for even a trace to trickle all the way down here?

I push up on my toes toward the vent and realize I can make out voices too. Way too faint and muffled for me to distinguish any words, but they're obviously raised, curt and hostile.

Is Andreas arguing with the other guys—about me? I guess it would be an argument if he's trying to convince them to stop being such jerks.

I shift my weight, uneasiness coiling around my gut. I don't want him fighting my battles for me, all alone.

If he's arguing on my behalf, I should at least be there to back him up.

I don't really expect to get anywhere, but my restless feet carry me up the basement steps, my nerves outright buzzing now. My fingers clutch the knob—and it turns smoothly.

I freeze for a second before understanding hits me. Drey didn't bother to lock the basement when he left.

He didn't see any reason he needed to.

A pang of joy thrums through me alongside my apprehension. I *can* go up there and stand with him, then.

Before I can think any farther ahead than that, my body is already rushing forward. My bare feet pad across the worn floorboards to the main staircase and up it, moving swiftly but silently with the stealth that comes automatically to me.

The voices come into sharper clarity as I hurry upward. Andreas is speaking, so terse his tone alone makes my heart ache.

Then I register what he's saying.

"...the whole reason I started 'getting cozy' with her was so she'd open up about things she wouldn't have told us otherwise. I held up my end of the deal. Now you've got to listen."

What?

My legs lock at the top of the stairs. I stare through the doorway into the shadowy bedroom ahead of me where Andreas stands by the bed.

All three of the other guys are poised around him, but he's facing Jacob, whose gaze slides from Andreas to me. A glitter even chillier than usual lights in his fierce eyes.

"Yes," he says, giving Drey a smile so sharp it could flay skin. "That was the deal. And now she knows it too."

Andreas turns, his gaze snagging on mine. His mouth opens, but no sound comes out.

My feet propel me forward, one step and another, through the doorway. Then I can't bear to get any closer to him.

My own voice catches in my throat before I force out the question. "You were acting friendly just to trick me into telling you things?"

Andreas's expression goes sickly. "It wasn't like that, not exactly. And it isn't like that now."

"It was exactly like that," Jacob interjects, focusing on

me again. "We had a little conversation right after we arrived at the college, while you were locked up in your room. I wanted to keep you out of our investigations, but Andreas insisted that we should get you involved so we could see if you'd give something away in the moment. He promised he'd convince you to trust him so you wouldn't be as guarded."

Pain lances right down the middle of me. My fingers flex at my sides, the tips aching around my claws.

"You argued in front of me about whether I should come along," I say, my voice not much more than a rasp.

Jacob brings out his vicious smile again. "Yes, we did. We had to sell the idea in a way you'd believe. And it gave Drey his first chance to play your champion."

They staged the whole conversation. They *all* knew.

My gaze jerks to Zian and to Dominic, and their tensed expressions confirm it. There isn't a hint of surprise from either of them, only trepidation about how I'm going to react.

"Riva, I swear that has nothing to do with tonight or —or—" Andreas stumbles and then recovers. "I believe you. I realized we were wrong. I—"

"He's very good at it, isn't he?" Jacob interrupts. "Got you to let your hair down and everything." He glances at Andreas. "You can stop now. I can't see how you'll get anything more out of her than you already have."

"Will you shut the fuck up, Jake?" Andreas snaps, but my mind is already spinning back through our interlude in the basement.

He brought up Griffin. Told a story about guilty

secrets. He prodded me about there being something I hadn't told them about the night Griffin died.

That whole thing—the affection he offered, the supposed confessions he made—it was all to lull me into thinking I could open up.

Did he come up here and tell them just how very much I opened up to him? Jacob is talking as if he knows everything.

"Why would you— How could you—?" I don't know how to voice the question that's choking me. There's a wail lodged in the base of my throat, expanding with a dull throbbing.

I loved you. All I ever did was love you, and you all...

Jacob narrows his eyes at me. "You actually think you deserve better?"

His sneering tone sparks a spurt of anger that sears up through my chest. It rattles through my ribs and grips hold of the vibration building at the back of my mouth.

My hand shoots up to close around my pendant. My thumb clicks the cat and yarn apart and together, apart and together, but the rhythm does nothing to settle the anguished fury that's thrumming through my nerves, rising to a roar.

I could hurt them just as much as they've hurt me. I could tear them a-fucking-part.

I glance at Dominic and Zian again, my voice hoarse. "Are both of you okay with all of this? Really?"

Zian's mouth opens and closes and opens again. "We needed to know—we needed to be sure..." he says weakly.

Dominic's face has hardened with tension. "We've had to look out for ourselves."

Themselves. The four of them together and me on the outside, where they've shoved me as hard as they can.

My teeth grit. The prickling vibration jabs its way up my throat.

No. I close my eyes, willing down the vicious urge that's shaking me from the inside out. But I'm too raw, too churned up already. I can't get a grip on it.

And Jacob's voice follows me into the darkness behind my eyelids. "You don't have to play *our* friend anymore now. You're not getting anywhere with that. So let's see who you really are already."

My lungs ache to scream right back at him, to show him what he's daring me to do. To make him wish he never mocked and berated my misery.

No, no, *no*.

My thumb wrenches at my pendant again—and the joint cracks. The two pieces fall apart in my hand, the ball of yarn tumbling against my palm, the cat still dangling from the chain around my neck.

I broke it—Griffin's necklace.

Like I broke him. Like I could break *all* of them if I just let myself—

"Riva," Andreas is saying, and I get the impression he's been talking longer than I've been hearing. "He's being a fucking idiot. Listen to me. I—"

He takes a step toward me, and my body recoils. A sliver of a shriek hitches from my throat.

I clap my hand over my mouth, but I see him wince. I taste the pain that one brief smack of the power in me provoked.

The thing squirming and thrumming inside me craves

more. It's clawing its way up from my chest, on the verge of exploding.

I am going to destroy everything, and part of me is going to revel in it.

Jacob steps toward me too, his eyes glinting like ice. "That's right. Tell us how you really feel."

I yank my gaze from him to Andreas, who's frozen in his tracks. He's looking at me as if he can see the storm of emotion raging inside me—or maybe it's so close to the surface now it's written all over my face.

I back up, and the door slams shut behind me with a heave of Jacob's talent. He stalks closer with that cruel smirk I want to scratch off his face.

Break him, twist him, make him suffer. And the rest of them just standing by, watching him hurt me. Lashing out in their own ways.

Show them all what real pain is.

No.

The protest barely stems the surge of rage inside me. My vision starts to haze.

I have to get away.

My hand shoots out, snapping the chain with the movement. The necklace slips from my fingers and clinks onto the floor.

"Stay away from me," I gasp out. "I don't want to hurt you."

But I also do, I do.

And the only escape from the pressure howling through my body is to throw myself toward the window that's between me and Jacob.

My shoulder slams into the pane first. I'm hurtling fast

enough to shatter the glass and careen out into the open air.

Shards slice across my arms and calves, but I barely notice those tiny pains. For a few seconds, I'm in freefall, hurtling through the air.

My body rotates on instinct, and I hit the ground with a puff of exhaled breath and a jolt through my limbs.

Voices are already carrying from the building behind me, my name ringing out through the jumble of shouts. Panic races through me ahead of a renewed roar of anger.

They're going to come after me.

They won't let me go.

My legs propel me forward. I sprint across the grass as fast as my feet can fly, veering away from the lane and the road.

Farther down, near the train tracks, scattered saplings offer a tiny bit of cover. I race toward them automatically, my pulse thundering in my ears, my lungs shuddering with the power that wants so badly to burst out.

I'm a monster. Only a monster would want to put the men she's loved through the agony I can sense I'm capable of.

Only a monster would *enjoy* the idea.

My name pierces the air again. Someone's hollering at me to stop.

No, I can't. I can't.

They've poisoned me and beaten me down with words and lies. Maybe they're monsters too, and not because of the powers inside them.

Maybe I'd be right to destroy them.

Shut up!

I just have to get away, far away, and then…

And then what's left? My whole life has been them, us. *We are blood.*

If we aren't, if I'm nothing to them, if everything I thought we had has been washed away, how can I be anything other than a monster?

My legs pump; my feet pound against the uneven ground. A different sound emerges from up ahead: the rumble of an engine.

The train's lights flash between the trees. It's whipping toward me, just seconds away.

Tears blur my sight, and still the hunger inside me to deal out a deluge of pain screams on and on. It won't let me go either.

Not while I'm still alive.

I don't think. My body swerves of its own accord, closer to the tracks. To the one simple solution that could kill both the monster and my own agony.

It's gravel rattling under my feet now. The train roars toward me with a blare of its horn.

I fling myself onward to meet it, and one final cry penetrates the anguished haze in my head.

"Wildcat, *no!*"

Jacob's voice. Jacob's old nickname for me, that he hasn't used once since I found him again.

It hits me like a plea echoing up from the past, yanking me back to where I always thought I was meant to be.

What the hell am I doing?

I wrench myself to the side, but it's a little too late.

The full force of the speeding train catches the side of

my body. It whips me around, knocking my arm out of its socket, shattering my ribs.

Pain blazes through every particle of my being as I crash into the grass beyond the shoulder. Then my mind fizzles out.

TWENTY-NINE

Dominic

Riva looks so fragile with her small frame silhouetted by the train's headlights. I was worried before, but the image sends a bolt of pure terror through me.

She wouldn't really— She doesn't mean to—

Even as my mind makes its silent protests, I push my legs forward even faster, or at least I try to. My balance wavers on the uneven ground.

The others have all pulled ahead of me, but they're still not close enough. My arm shoots out as if I can grab her across that distance and wrench her to safety.

Jacob's voice rings through the night, raw and frantic. "Wildcat, *no!*"

At his shout, Riva appears to swing in the opposite direction. But before even a wisp of hope can rise up inside me, the side of the onrushing locomotive slams into her.

She spins into the air with a spurt of liquid blood and smoke that shocks a cry from my throat. The mutilated form that falls to the ground near a cluster of saplings barely looks human, let alone like our Riva.

"Dom!" Jacob yells in the same panicked tone as before.

It comes down to me. I don't know how we're going to fix any of the mess we found ourselves in that sent her running to begin with, but I'm the only one who can ensure she's even alive for us to try.

If there's enough left of her to save. If I can make it to her in time.

A surge of my own panic pushes my limbs beyond what I thought I was capable of. The train roars on past us, but I'm barely aware of the cars rattling along the tracks.

There's only that small, shadowed form lying motionless by the trees.

Zian gets to her first. He falls to his knees and reaches his hands out to her, clenching his fingers before he actually touches her like he's afraid he'll somehow make it worse.

He leans backward, his face contorting with his wolfish features, and tips his head toward the sky. An anguished groan reverberates through the air.

My open coat flaps against my sides. I yank at it as well as I can without slowing down, heaving it from my shoulders and letting it whip off me.

I'm going to need to bring every bit of my ability to this moment, every piece of me that can contribute. No hiding, no holding back.

Andreas stumbles to a stop by Zian. With one glance at Riva's body, his eyes widen and a mumbled curse falls from his lips.

Jacob is already there, dropping down and bringing his hands to her face with a sudden gentleness I had no idea he still had in him.

His fingers slide down to her neck. "She's still got a pulse. Not much of one but—*Dom*. She needs you."

"Coming," I gasp out, hurtling the last several paces to where she's lying.

Even in the dim moonlight, partly draped in the spindly shadows of the saplings, it's a horrifying scene. She looks like a jointed doll who's been smashed on the floor by a malicious kid.

Her one arm is drenched with blood, arching away from her body at an angle that makes me wonder how much it's even still attached to her shoulder. On the same side, her torso is crumpled in, more blood drenching the pale dress and the grass beneath her. Her motionless face looks pure white except for the speckling of blood across her lips.

Streams of dark smoky stuff gush up into the air, twining with the shadows.

I collapse to the ground next to Riva, already flinging one of my extra appendages around the nearest sapling. As the suckers dig in tight to the smooth bark of the trunk, I wrap the other around her waist and set my hand on her throat.

Jake pulls back to give me room, his whole body trembling.

"Do *something*," he says, but his voice is so hoarse I know he doesn't mean it as a criticism.

Just this once, I'm the strong one, and the rest of them can only watch helplessly.

He was right about her pulse. It stutters, faint and fading against my palm.

I focus on that, close my eyes, and haul all the energy I can from the tree I'm gripping.

The sapling is full of life—vibrant, green, growing. So much fucking potential that I can see the massive tree it'd have eventually grown into in the back of my mind.

I drag all of that out of it, quivering across my back, and pour it into Riva.

I don't know all the parts of her that might be shattered or crushed, but it doesn't matter. My power senses what to align and seal.

My own heart thuds on at a sickly frantic rhythm as I pull more life, and more, and more out of the sapling.

The tree bows, its branches sagging, its bark blackening. Beneath my touch, Riva's flesh fuses back together.

Bones snap into place and meld their broken edges. Blood vessels reattach themselves.

I will more of the vital fluid to form in her arteries and veins. The flavor of raw meat forms in the back of my mouth and my stomach roils, but I ignore both sensations.

I'm inflicting death as much as I'm giving life, but only the second part matters.

Only Riva matters.

Flashes of memory dart by behind my closed eyelids. The moments when we'd figure out the answer to a problem in the same moment, and she'd shoot a softly sly smile my way to match my own.

All the times when I'd be lost in a tangle of emotions after a session where the guardians pushed me to use my talents in ways I'd never have wanted to, and she'd come over to work patiently alongside me until I'd decided what I wanted to share.

The day when she begged one of them to put a wildflower from the outdoor training field into a pot for me so I could keep it in my room, because I'd commented on how it was going to get trampled before too long.

The time Andreas challenged me to run her all the way around the track piggyback style, and we collapsed at the end in a fit of laughter, the most ridiculous but also the most free I'd felt in ages.

And then there's the moment when I healed her after the club night, when she talked about how much she wanted to fix things. The way she's hesitated to ask for my help even when she was on the verge of collapsing, because she could tell I don't like what my power costs me.

How could we not have realized sooner that the guardians were the ones who'd deceived us? How could *I* not have realized sooner?

I was so concerned about my monstrousness, about the deformities sprouting from my back, but it wasn't my physical strangeness she ran away from. No, it was my attitude, cold and silent while Jacob laid into her, shying away from her gestures of friendship.

I can't even hate what I am right now, even if it was the guardians' awful tests that grew most of this part of me, because my strangeness is what's saving her.

The sapling dwindles completely, crumbling into deadened dust. The blood seeping from Riva's body has slowed, but I can still feel it trickling out of her as both smoke and viscous liquid.

Shifting my position, I extend my appendage to the next nearest tree. Another surge of life energy, another being I'm consigning to death.

The woman beneath my hand is breathing now, in little spurts of air. Her pulse remains sluggish, but it beats stronger against my fingers even if it's slow.

She's coming back to us, bit by bit. Please let her make it all the way.

As the worst of her injuries bind back together, I become aware of the toll the healing has taken on me, even when I'm only acting as a conduit. Pain throbs at the base of my skull; my mouth tastes like ash as well as blood.

A tremor runs through my bones, and a hand rests on my back to steady me. "You're doing good," Andreas says raggedly. "You're really doing it, Dom."

The scuff of footsteps tells me Jacob is pacing. I don't need Griffin's talent for reading emotions to sense the tension rolling off of the guy.

Zian lets out another pained grunt. "Is there anything else you need? Anything we can do?"

I open my eyes and peer down at Riva, inhaling deeply as I do. The headache splinters right through my brain, and I'm not sure I can propel any more energy into her until I've rested at least a little.

"Does anyone… have any water?" I croak. Both she and I could probably use it.

Jake stops and makes a brusque gesture toward Zian.

"You can get back to the house fastest. There are a few bottles in the bag that had the food."

Zee dashes off without hesitation, and Jake stoops over Riva, staring down at her face. From his hard expression, I'd think he's as coolly emotionless as usual if it weren't for the anxious flexing of his hands.

His gaze jerks up to meet mine. "Why hasn't she woken up? Did you fix everything inside?"

Drey frowns, his hand adding more reassuring pressure to my shoulder. "He's obviously been doing everything he can, as well as he can."

I cough and manage to speak a little clearer. I don't want to tell him that I can't say for sure whether she *will* wake up.

"I think I healed all the most important parts. She seems to be stable." Another thought jabs at me, too insistent for me to ignore. "I'm going to heal the poison out of her too."

Jacob's features twitch with what might be a suppressed flinch. "Of course," he snaps. "Heal everything. Just get on with it."

I try to swallow past the dryness of my throat. "I'll—I'll keep going, I just need a moment—"

"It's fine, Dom. That was amazing." Andreas gives my shoulder another squeeze, but when he looks down at Riva, there's no mistaking the anguish that contorts his face.

"She ran right at that train," he says in a low voice.

Jacob swipes his hand over his jaw. "She was running away from us. She wanted to get away from us *that* badly…"

His voice trails off with a rasp.

"I don't think it was only that." Andreas hesitates. "Just for a second, while you were riling her up, I felt— *We* all had new talents emerge in the past few years. We haven't seen anything like that from her. Yet."

My attention drops to the unconscious woman we've surrounded. I study the body I've been melding back together.

Does she have her own unnerving abilities that she's keeping to herself, as much as I've done the same?

I didn't sense anything physically unusual about her while I healed her, but I'm not sure if I would have.

"It doesn't matter," Jacob snarls, shoving himself to his feet. "We fucked up. I fucked up, so much—"

His voice cuts off with a strangled sound—and the tearing of roots from soil. One of the other saplings rips right out of the ground, yanked by his power, and whirls across the field.

Drey tenses. "Dom might need—"

I don't hear the rest of his sentence, because right then Riva's eyelids flutter. Flutter and open, the bright brown irises shining up at me.

THIRTY

Riva

Everything hurts.

I'm not even exaggerating. I mean, there's my chest and my ribs and my stomach and my head. My shoulder and my hip and my knee, all consumed by a deep ache that rises and ebbs with my breath.

But even my ears prickle. My big toes throb. My fucking pinky finger twinges with pins and needles.

What the hell— Where am I?

I blink and find myself staring up at Dominic, his shadowed, handsome face etched with worry and strain. Stars speckle the night sky beyond him.

I'm lying on my back. Grass tickles the backs of my bare arms. The air is cooling damp patches all across my torso and legs.

Dominic lifts his hand from where it was resting at the base of my throat. Something else shifts across my belly;

something thin and sinewy… like the things I can see sprouting over Dom's shoulders.

The shapes of them are vague in the moonlight, but I make out the curves of rows of suckers along the undersides of the things. I blink again, but the view doesn't change.

He has two *tentacles* growing out of his upper back.

The words slip from my lips before I have a chance to think about them, more a creak than a voice. "When did you become an octopus?"

Dominic's expression shutters. I can feel him closing himself off from me, and the memories from what happened right before this moment rush back to me with a jolt.

The farmhouse. Andreas, in the basement. And afterward—everything they said—all the things I hadn't realized—

I close my eyes, sinking back into the physical pain that's somehow more comforting than the swell of anguish that wants to swallow my whole mind. And Dom answers my question.

"About three and a half years now. We've all been evolving."

His voice is tight but even, no hostility in it. More pieces click together in my head.

This is what he's been hiding under his ever-present coats—what I saw him flinging at the guardians when they attacked us at the campus townhouse. What he never wanted me to see.

"Why…?" I rasp, and can't quite form the question.

Dominic's hand comes to rest on my sternum. "I'm

healing you. You—you got bashed up pretty bad. I'm patching you up as quickly as I can, but it's a work in progress."

When I open my eyes again, his are shut. A rush of warmth flows through me, some at my chest where his fingers are pressed, but mostly from the tentacle lying across my abdomen.

The sensation radiates through my flesh. If the healing energy he conjured before was a stream, this is a river, coursing through every crack and gash that needs to be knit together.

The other tentacle, the one not wrapped around my belly, veers off toward… a nearby sapling. The tip curls around the thin trunk.

Its branches are sagging, the whole tree bowing toward the ground as its bark darkens as if overtaken by rot.

Dominic must notice my gaze. "The energy has to come from somewhere. It all balances out one way or another."

Oh. The flowers and weeds I saw him picking before —he was using them for healing energy.

As I bring my attention back to him, the arc of the tentacles I can see arcing over his shoulders *expands*. Just a little, maybe half an inch, but unmistakable. Like they're pulling farther out of his skin.

"They're growing," I mumble.

Dom lets out a ragged chuckle. "They do that. When I use my power."

Understanding hits me like a smack across the face. Oh, shit. "That's why you didn't want to— You don't have to. You don't—"

His other hand closes around mine—gently so that he doesn't provoke fresh pains in the delicate joints there. "It's fine, Riva. You need this. I'm *glad* I can do it." His voice dips. "I'm glad you're still with us."

I need this... because of the train. That final memory roars up to the surface, and I wince instinctively as if I'm feeling the impact all over again.

Footsteps stomp closer. "Is she okay? Don't do anything that could hurt her."

"I know," Dominic says, almost a growl, as my gaze flicks from him to the other man now standing within my limited view.

Jacob stares down at me, his expression tense, his normally cold eyes blazing as if they've been lit with blue flames. His hands are clenched at his sides, the tendons standing out in his arms.

I jerk my gaze away with a lurch of my heart that sends a new ache through my chest. I don't want... to see him, speak to him, deal with any more of his bullshit.

Jacob lets out a grunt of frustration, and then there's a groaning sound, like a weakening branch pushed by the wind. Somewhere beyond my field of vision, Andreas swears with a rustle of footsteps over the grass.

"You can't keep doing that. Calm the fuck down."

"How am I supposed to calm down when she—"

Another set of footsteps thumps toward us farther away, bringing Zian's breathless voice with them. "I brought three water bottles—totally full." He stops with a hitch. "Is she awake?"

I'm not sure I want to see or speak to Zian either. I

close my eyes again, descending into the painful darkness of my body.

"Give one to Dom," Andreas is saying. "He's wearing himself ragged. Maybe Riva should have some too."

Dominic speaks in an uncertain tone. "I don't know if her stomach and… everything that connects to it are fully recovered. She was hit pretty hard all the way down her side."

Jacob pipes up next, with an edge that rankles me. "Then get on with healing the rest of it."

"He's doing his best," Andreas snaps. "Why don't you find something more useful to do than tearing up trees?"

At a whisper of fabric and a shift in the air, I know Andreas has knelt at my other side, across from Dominic. I *definitely* don't want to look at him—don't want to think about the vulnerability and passion I offered him when his only goal was to unravel me.

I can't do this anymore. I don't wish I'd embraced the train head on, beyond repair, but that one fact hasn't changed.

If I stay with my guys any longer, either they'll tear me apart or I'll do the same to them. Maybe both.

They don't want me. What's the point in sticking around anyway?

Dominic's hand against my sternum goes abruptly limp. The current of warmth fades away, but I realize I'm not half as achy as I was when I first woke up. I don't feel all that much worse than I have on average over the past several days, with Jacob's literal venom eating away at me.

As if he's sensed that thought, Dom brushes his fingers over my forehead, swiping stray strands of hair away from my eyes. "I drew all the poison out of you too. You won't have to deal with that anymore."

As he's probably happy about, since it means he won't have to deal with it either. Although if he's going to be mad at anyone about however much staving off the toxin's effects have expanded the tentacles he's so intent on concealing, he really needs to take that up with Jacob, not me.

Part of me wants to sink right into the earth and never return, but I'm aware that's not a viable strategy.

I force myself to open my eyes. Focusing on the shadowy landscape beyond my feet rather than any of the men around me, I flex my muscles and ease into a sitting position.

Halfway up, I sway. Dominic's hand shoots out to steady me, with a tremor that runs through it as he catches my weight.

How much did the healing process take out of him?

I lean my hands into the grass so I can hold my own balance, tensing and relaxing each section of my limbs to get a sense of how much they can endure.

I might be able to walk right now. I think running is probably out of the question. Definitely no scaling cliffsides or squeezing through ventilation shafts.

Thankfully I should never have to do either of those things again, since they weren't my idea in the first place.

There's a moment of silence, as if the men are waiting to see if I'm going to say something. Andreas clears his throat.

"Riva, I'm sorry," he says, his voice hoarse despite his efforts. "So sorry. I only wanted to make sure we could trust you—and I'd seen that we could. Tonight wasn't about trying to trick you. I really did want to just talk with you. The rest… The rest I wasn't expecting at all."

A noise comes out of me that's something like a snort. At the same time, ridiculous tears burn at the edges of my eyes.

I am not going to fucking cry over this manipulative lying asshat.

Andreas goes on, still strained but not showing any offense at my response. "I went upstairs to tell the guys that they'd been wrong—*we'd* been wrong—and that you'd been telling the truth about everything. I would have told you the whole truth once I knew they'd come around."

Easy for him to claim that now.

My hand lifts instinctively to my neck, but there's nothing for my fingers to close around. With a jab of anguish, I remember that I broke the necklace. Dropped it.

It's probably lying on the floor back there in the farmhouse. Not that it matters when it's cracked apart—

Another form crouches right in front of me, hand outstretched. I'm about to recoil from Jacob when my gaze catches on the glint of sliver resting on his fingers.

"This is yours, Wildcat," he says, his eyes piercing into mine. "I twisted the broken bit back together. It should hold until we can get it properly soldered."

I don't want to take anything from him—but it doesn't really count when the thing was already mine anyway, does it?

My hand darts out to snatch the pendant from his hand. I tug the chain around my neck to attach it in its proper place, feeling abruptly like I'm a wild animal they're all trying to coax into tameness.

I'm not the one who's been going around savaging and shunning people for no reason at all.

"Okay," I say stiffly, my voice still a little weak. "I'm healed enough that I can get by. You can all go back to your quest now."

Zian steps into view and stalls at the edge of my vision. "What are you saying?"

Do I really have to spell it out?

"You don't need me. You don't want my help. I'm finally getting the message loud and clear. You can stop jerking me around, and I'll go find something else to do with the rest of my life and you can go on with yours."

"Riva."

Andreas touches my shoulder, but I jerk away from him. I glare at him before casting my gaze around me at all four of the guys.

The tears well up again anyway. I cracked something open down in the basement with Andreas, and apparently all Dominic's work didn't stitch that part of me shut again.

My emotions bubble up to the surface faster than I can catch them. "I thought we were blood, and we'd be there for each other like we always used to be. That you'd see how much you all still meant to me and know I hadn't changed. But that was obviously stupid of me, so I'm accepting reality."

I move to get up, but Jacob catches me first. He looms over me, his knees coming to rest against mine, his hands framing my face and holding it so I have to look at him.

Unless I close my eyes.

But even though I refuse his gaze, he speaks anyway, his voice taut and emphatic. "It wasn't stupid. I have been the biggest fucking asshole and an idiot on top of that. I don't know what I'd have done if we'd lost you too, if I'd pushed you all the way to— Please don't go."

It was his voice that brought me back before I went too far; his nickname, his plea. The memory makes my skin tighten.

Even after everything, his touch and his closeness send a heated tingle over my skin. I don't *want* that. No fucking way.

I squirm backward so fast Jacob releases his hold, but I bump into Dominic. With a strangled sound, I finally push myself to my feet.

My legs wobble but hold me. The torn dress clings to my body with drying blood—*my* blood, from injuries now sealed.

"I don't know why it suddenly matters to any of you," I spit out, blinking hard against the tears I refuse to acknowledge. "You couldn't have known or liked me very much even before if you believed I turned on all of you that easily."

Zian's mouth twists. "You don't understand."

"No," I shoot back. "I don't. But I don't need to."

Andreas steps toward me again but doesn't try to touch me this time. "I can show you."

My gaze darts to him of its own accord. There's so much fraught emotion in his eyes that my throat closes up at the sight.

"I can project the memory into your mind," he goes on. "My memory of what happened that night for the four of us who never made it out of the facility. It doesn't justify anything, but it might explain a little."

My body balks, but curiosity gnaws at the back of my mind. What could possibly have happened that would make a difference?

Maybe it won't. Maybe I'll feel just as done with them as I do now.

Either way, at least I'll know.

I glance around to check if any of the other guys is going to object to his offer, but they stay quiet, braced and waiting. I turn back to Andreas.

"Fine. But make it quick."

He hesitates. "You might want to sit down."

As much as I hate to admit it, he has a point, given how shaky my muscles still are. I lower myself onto a patch of grass that isn't soaked with my blood, and Andreas kneels a few feet away from me.

He focuses on me with the ruddy sheen coming over his eyes, and the moonlit fields around me disappear.

I'm dashing out through my cell's doorway, catching Dominic's eye as he bursts from his room farther down the hall.

"They did it," I say with a grin stretching my face, but it's Andreas's voice. Because this is Andreas's memory—I'm seeing everything that went down through his eyes.

We race into the stairwell, flinging ourselves upward to reach the others as quickly as possible, and a troop of guardians barrel into view.

As if they were ready the whole time. As if they knew we'd be coming.

I hear a grunt from below, and then a tranquilizer dart

has already struck me in the neck. Another guardian leaps forward with a taser that spews electricity through my body. I stumble on the steps—

A momentary blackness. Then I'm sitting in one of the smaller training rooms with Dominic, Zian, and Jacob arranged around me. All of our hands are cuffed behind our backs.

A few guardians stand around the room with weapons braced at their sides. Another paces back and forth in front of us.

"What you tried to do tonight was highly irresponsible, ungrateful, and totally misguided. Did you really think there was some wonderful life waiting for you in the world out there, without our help?"

Andreas's jaw tightens at the suggestion that we *need* the guardians, that they're helping us rather than holding us down. We all keep quiet.

The guardian goes on. "At least one of you had the foresight to realize she was better off making her own arrangements with us than spending the rest of her existence on the run."

Andreas's head jerks up unbidden. I stare at the guardian through his eyes, the others doing the same.

There are no thoughts or emotions in the memory, only what I can interpret from the sensory details, but I think they all must have noticed that neither I—as Riva— nor Griffin were in the room. They must have been wondering what happened to us.

The guardian swipes a tablet off a desk at the side of the room and stalks back toward us. "We're all built to look out for ourselves. You're lucky we take as good care of you here as we do. Remember this the next time you have the urge to start scheming."

He spins the tablet toward us with a video playing on the screen. Surveillance footage, dark and a little grainy because of that darkness.

It's a view of the empty front yard outside the facility, lit only by the hazy glow of a few security lamps. A moment later, two figures dash into view.

Me—the actual me—and Griffin. I'm distantly aware of my real heart thumping faster in horrified anticipation of what I know is going to come.

I didn't realize—I don't really want to watch him die all over again.

But I can't close my eyes, because they're Andreas's eyes, and he took in every second of this.

The figures on the screen scan the area. The one that's a younger me pauses and then steps toward Griffin, pulling him into a kiss.

Andreas flinches.

Just as the real me lets Griffin go, the shot comes, blasting into his body. His frame jerks, his legs crumpling.

But that's not even the most horrifying thing.

The me on the screen doesn't scream out and struggle against an onslaught of attackers the way I know I did. She looks calmly down at Griffin's body and then raises her head to nod to someone outside the footage.

A small squad of guardians appears. One of them pats my shoulder in a way that looks almost friendly.

They march me over to a truck and let me hop inside. I smile at them from the window before the truck drives away.

I fucking *smile*.

Back where Andreas is, Jacob thrashes against his handcuffs, pushing himself toward the guardian. "Where is he? Where's my brother? What did you do to him?"

The guardian flicks off the tablet and gives Jacob a nonchalant look. "I'm afraid your brother didn't survive. An important reminder of the potential consequences when you step out of line."

"You fucking bastard!" Jacob snarls—and the memory falls away.

I'm sitting in my own body again, surrounded by cool fresh air and rustling grass. I gulp in a breath, my eyes burning all over again.

"It wasn't true," I burst out. "That isn't how it happened. I never—they attacked me too. I tried to fight them—I tried to get to Griffin—"

"I know," Andreas says softly. "I believe you. They must have doctored the video to splice in footage they faked."

I stare at him. "But you did believe it. You believed it this whole time."

Dominic speaks up, quiet and a little ragged. "When they showed us the footage, we were already in shock. And then seeing that Griffin had died… It messed with our heads, made it hard to know what to believe. And you never did come back."

I thump my hand against the ground. "I did. I did as soon as I fucking could."

"You did," Jacob agrees. "And we made a total mess of that too. Me more than anyone." His jaw works as he lowers his gaze.

And maybe that does make sense, considering he was the one the most messed up. It was his brother who died —his twin.

But just looking at him makes something in me cringe away with the memory of all the harsh words and vicious commands he's hurled at me since I broke them out.

I don't know what to do with any of this. I don't know where to go. Here I am in nothing but a ragged, bloody dress that doesn't even fit right, not even sure what state I'm in, no money, no food…

With a monster lurking inside me, just waiting until someone makes me angry enough.

I swipe my hand across my mouth and look at the guys again. "What do we do now? The way you're picturing it, anyway."

They hesitate, exchanging glances. Jacob speaks first.

"We keep going after Engel. Find out what we can about what we are and how to fix what they've done to us —and how we can destroy the assholes who did it to us. They're the ones who need to pay. For Griffin. For everything."

Zian hunches his shoulders in apparent discomfort. "I just want to get rid of this shitty 'talent.'"

"We are close," Andreas says. "We could reach her in just another couple of days. And after we see what answers we can get… then we could decide where we go from there."

I draw my knees up to my chest and hug them, my mind whirling with everything that's happened, everything I've learned.

I want answers too. I want to meet the woman who

was pushed out of the facility she built—who recorded my first smile like it gave her joy.

It'll be a hell of a lot easier getting to her if we're all working together. A hell of a lot easier to make sure the guardians don't recapture us if we have each other's backs.

Do I trust the guys to actually have *my* back now? I guess in a way they always did. Even when they thought I was a traitor, they stepped in every time I faced the slightest threat.

The only people they didn't protect me from was themselves.

I know what I'd prefer, and I know what makes sense, and they aren't the same thing. But if I have to choose…

I've survived more than a week of them treating me like the enemy. I can make it through a couple more days of their company while they're *not* being assholes, right?

As long as they aren't acting like jerks and pissing me off, they shouldn't incite the twisted power inside me.

And the poison is gone. If I change my mind, I can leave whenever I want.

I sway to my feet again and square my shoulders. "All right. Then let's stick to the plan."

Thirty-One

Riva

The chilly autumn breeze winding between the trees north of Glenlily licks under my braid and makes me wish I had a proper jacket instead of just this hoodie. We didn't want to risk going into anywhere as public as a store, and the old clothes we found in the farmhouse didn't include any outerwear.

At least I'm back in my comfortable shirt and cargo pants instead of that overlarge dress.

I tug the zipper right up to my chin and tramp on, aware of the guys around me at the edges of my vision. We've spread out through the hilly terrain both so that we can select paths where we'll make the least noise picking our way through the brush and so we have a wider view between us over our surroundings.

We skirted the tiny town called Glenlily about an hour ago, already having left behind the pick-up truck we commandeered after crossing the border into Canada by train. If the guardians suspect we might come this way, they'll definitely be watching the roads.

We have no idea how much farther their surveillance might reach. There might not be any of them up here at all if they haven't considered that we'd be interested in their former boss—or whatever exactly Ursula Engel was to them.

But we need to keep watch not just for possible attackers but for Engel's property itself. Andreas has only gathered that it was somewhere north of Glenlily. He has no idea exactly how far.

I'm hoping "north" was at least relatively accurate. It'd be awfully easy to walk right by a secluded home in this dense forest.

There was a single gravel road stretching north from the town for the first mile or so, which we were initially following along. But it petered out into what was more of a private lane, and then an overgrown path I'm not totally sure most vehicles could even navigate.

Zian is keeping it within range of his penetrating sight, though, since we have to assume Engel has *some* way to bring supplies up here. Somehow I doubt she's living off the land right through the Canadian winter.

Can you subsist on maple syrup and pine needles?

A stone dislodges under my foot, but I catch my balance before I even fully stumble. Two pairs of eyes immediately shoot to me—Dominic's at my left and Jacob's at my right.

But this time, neither gaze holds any hint of hostility. Dom veers a little closer with a lifting of his eyebrows that I know is a question, asking if I'm okay.

I give him a quick nod. My insides still twinge at random moments, like there are a few tiny cracks that weren't perfectly fused, but I spent most of yesterday resting in one train car or another.

Right now, I feel *better* than I have for most of the past couple of weeks.

And that's mainly because I no longer have any poison trickling through me, wearing me down bit by bit.

I ignore Jacob's gaze, even though I can feel it lingering on me as we weave onward between the trees. Something about the night when the train nearly ended me spun him around from accusing to ashamed, but I haven't totally recovered from the emotional whiplash of the switch yet.

How can I be sure he won't change his mind all over again with some other move I make?

I inhale deeply, filling my lungs with the cool piney air, and freeze at the sound of a twig snapping.

Crack, crack, crack, three times in quick succession. That's the signal Zian said he'd give if he spotted anything.

Without a word, the rest of us slink through the forest to join him. He's pulled a little ahead of the rest of us, standing now at the crest of a low, mossy cliff.

He waits until we've all gathered around him and points down the steep slope. All I can make out are more trees, but Zian must be looking right through them.

"The path branches in two directions just up there," he says under his breath, barely louder than the rustle of the wind through the leaves overhead. "There's a small hut right at the junction, and I think someone's inside it."

Andreas peers in that direction as if he thinks he might

see through solid objects too if he tries hard enough. "You figure it's a guard house?"

Zian nods. "Or something like that. I guess it could be a park ranger thing, but... if the glimpse I got is what I think it is, the guy inside is wearing a metal helmet."

A guardian. My pulse hiccups, and my muscles tense instinctively.

Jacob's mouth sets in a grim line. "We go down there and question him, but we have to be careful about it. There might be others around, and he's probably got a way to alert them if there's trouble."

Dom looks at him. "If there's no one else nearby when we get close enough to check, you could yank him right out with your powers before he even sees us."

Andreas shakes his head. "Not at first. Remember the guardians that caught us in the old facility? This one might be able to block me from getting a good look at his memories... if he knows he needs to be blocking me."

Jacob offers him a hesitant smile, as if he isn't sure how Andreas will take his interjection even if it's in agreement. "Yeah, Drey should take a peek first and find out as much as he can that way before we get into a physical altercation."

I assume we've settled it, but Dom's gaze slides to me. "What do you think, Riva?"

It's the first time any of them have asked my opinion while they're working out their strategy on this mission. For most of the past couple of weeks, they've been ignoring my opinion even when I insisted on giving it.

I hesitate, feeling the pressure of their combined attention on me. I don't really have anything to add. My skills aren't going to be especially helpful in an interrogation.

At least, not the typical ones.

"It all sounds good," I say. "But if he catches on, I guess I can bring out my sob story again to distract him from blocking Andreas."

Jacob's jaw ticks at the words "sob story"—his dismissive phrase, flung more than once in my face.

Andreas shoots me a smile even more uncertain than the one Jacob gave him. "I'll do my best to make sure you don't have to."

I shrug as if it's no big deal, but I'd really prefer to avoid baring my soul for some stranger all over again if I get a choice in the matter.

If I have to, though… I just want to find this woman and finish the mission. Then we'll know what we actually have—and whether there's been a point to any of this.

We ease down the hill, setting our feet even more carefully than before. By the time we've reached the base of the cliff, I can make out a few slivers of a structure through the trees. The hut is built out of wood to blend into the forest, but the logs have darkened with the beating of the weather over the years.

Andreas takes the lead, since it's his talent's range that matters for this first part of the plan. He walks slowly and softly through the brush, his gaze fixed straight ahead.

When he stops, we all do as well, a few steps behind him.

For several minutes, we all just wait there, making no more noise than breathing. Andreas stays still and silent too, but I can see the effort he's making in the stiffening of his stance.

His shoulders come down abruptly with a faintly ragged exhalation. He treads back toward us.

"He definitely works with Engel," he whispers, "but he's been interacting with her for a long time. I can't tell which of the memories I've seen are the most recent, and none of them showed how to get to the house from here— or even for sure that the house I saw *is* all that close to here."

"Could you tell how many other guardians there might be around?" Zian asks, scanning the forest with a worried expression.

Andreas grimaces. "He definitely had memories of talking with her while there were one or two others with him, so I don't think we should count on him being here alone."

I hug myself. "Did you see anything about him hearing that we might show up?"

"No, but I can only narrow what I see by direct interactions. He's never seen us in person. If someone talked to him about us or showed him pictures, I wouldn't necessarily find that."

Dominic frowns. "We could simply sneak past him and try one of the paths, and if that doesn't get us anywhere—"

His suggestion is cut off by a sudden blare of electronic noise that makes us all startle. As it resonates through the woods, Jacob slaps his hand to his pocket.

"The phone. What the fuck? I had it on silent."

Andreas motions at him wildly. "It's got to be some kind of emergency alert. Shut it off!"

But it's too late. Even as Jacob jabs at the screen, the door to the hut thumps open.

"Jake!" Zian growls, low and urgent, and I know he isn't hassling him about the phone now.

Jacob spins toward the guardian who's marching toward our side of the forest with gun raised and whips out his hands.

The rifle hurtles away in one direction. The man crashes to the ground in the other, letting out a startled grunt.

We rush through the trees to the weedy path where the guardian fell. He glares up at us from beneath the brim of his helmet, his hands wriggling where Jacob's power has pinned them away from his sides.

From the twitching of his lips where they're pressed tightly together, I suspect Jacob is holding his mouth shut too. Only muffled sounds of consternation seep out.

"Check him for other weapons or anything he could communicate with," Jacob orders, with just a hint of strain in his voice.

We all dash in. Andreas hauls off the man's helmet. Zian jerks open his metal vest and pats down his shirt while Dominic checks his hip pockets.

I yank off one boot and then the other, peering inside them for knives and then tossing them away into the forest. Wouldn't want to make it any easier for this asshole to run.

The guys retrieve a walkie talkie and a pistol. Zian

hands the second of those to Dominic, who needs the offensive boost the most.

As he clutches the walkie in his broad hand, Jacob glowers down at our captive. "You're going to answer our questions, or you're going to die very slowly and painfully. I think that should be an easy choice."

It wasn't for the guardians we interrogated before, though. This man doesn't look like he's going to be much more talkative. His eyes narrow, dark with anger even though I can smell his fear at the threat.

"Where would we find Ursula Engel's house?" Jacob asks.

He must have loosened his grip on the man's mouth to give him the option of speaking, but when the guardian's lips part, it's with a hasty inhalation that sets all my nerves on edge.

Only a fragment of a shout of warning slips from his mouth before Jacob has slammed his mouth shut again. The man lets out a frustrated whine and squirms as well as he can against the ground.

"Wrong answer," Jacob snaps, and swivels his fingers. The man's thumb twists with a crack of breaking bone.

A fresh whiff of stress pheromones tickle my nose—and an idea sparks in my mind. Maybe there is a way my usual talents could help get us some answers.

"Wait," I say, holding out my hand.

I expect Jacob to argue, but he goes silent, watching me. I walk up to the man and step over him so I have a foot planted on either side of his chest.

Setting my hands on my hips, I stare down at him,

getting to be the taller person in a confrontation just this once.

This man doesn't know what powers I might have. Even the guardians who were in charge of our captivity must realize by now that we've shown skills we kept hidden from them before.

So let him imagine I'm reading his mind.

I pin him with my gaze for a few thumps of my heart and then point to the left path. "We go this way."

Nothing shifts in the air. I furrow my brow as if I'm picking up something new and then let out a little chuckle. "Oh, no, you're not tricking us that easily. It's this way."

When I point to the righthand path, the spike of stress I expected wafts into my nose. A grin crosses my lips with a flicker of exhilaration.

I have him.

"Definitely that way," I say with increased confidence, and eyeball the path to the right for a moment before peering at our captive again. "Now let's see how much company we can expect to tangle with along the way, and exactly how to get the jump on them."

Another spurt of nervous pheromones. There *are* other guardians down that way, and now he's worried for their safety.

With his own animalistically heightened senses, Zian catches on to my tactic first. He steps closer to the man, looming into his view with his brawny arms flexing.

"He's trying so hard to yell. There must be someone pretty close."

"Yep," I say when I get a whiff of confirmation. "But

we just need to take care of that one and then one... no, two..." There's another surge of anxiety. "Two more. Three altogether, and we're home free."

Zian cracks his knuckles and grins at me, the admiration in his eyes warming me despite my intent to stay totally detached from these guys. "That shouldn't be too much trouble."

"I wouldn't think so. Especially since they've only got guns like this dude, and maybe a couple of tranqs."

Another flare of stress confirms my guess. He wouldn't be worried if I was underestimating his colleagues, if they had some other trick up their sleeves.

I study him for several seconds longer. "Too bad for the guardians that the ones back home didn't think there was much chance we were headed up here. They couldn't be bothered to send a whole army."

The man grimaces at me, unable to express his futile anger in any other way. My statement must at least be close to the truth, because it's pissed him off and frightened him all over again.

I shove myself away from him and glance at Jacob. "I think that's all we need to know."

Jacob gazes steadily back at me and inclines his head, a gesture of trust that sends an unexpected ache lancing through my heart. He believes me, just like that.

He turns his attention on the guardian and, without a word, snaps the man's neck.

Zian moves automatically to haul the body into the woods out of sight. Andreas catches my eyes and lets out a soft whistle.

"That was pretty badass, Tink. We'll have to remember that trick."

I look away, my nerves jumping at the compliment and the affection in his tone. "Let's hope we don't have to. Come on. We've got three more of these assholes to deal with."

And then, if I'm right, we'll come face to face with the woman who started it all.

THIRTY-TWO

Riva

The house reminds me so much of the magazine clipping from decades ago that I have to stop and stare for a moment to make sure I'm not hallucinating.

The trees surrounding it aren't draped with snow, but their needle-laden boughs swoop around the log walls in a woodsy embrace. Those walls rise two stories above the low slope where the house is perched, to a sharply peaked roof that makes me picture a vaulted ceiling beneath.

Large windows gleam darkly glossy, reflecting the forest around them. The afternoon light is too bright to allow any glimpse of what's inside.

To my eyes, anyway. Zian peers at the place and then glances at us.

"I'm going to sneak a little closer to get a better look inside. Make sure she doesn't have other guardians in there with her."

Jacob nods. "Just be careful."

As Zian treads lightly between the trees to approach the house, Andreas rubs his mouth, his expression unusually pensive. "All of the guardians we tackled on the way here—in their memories of talking to her, it seemed more like they were her jailers than her protectors. She always sounded like she was irritated that they were insisting on staking out the house."

There were three more guards stationed along the path through the woods, just as I'd thought I'd determined from the one we questioned. None of them revealed anything more useful than the first, though—other than what Andreas just said.

I think back to the other things we've learned about Ursula Engel. "They pushed her out of something she set up... They're probably worried she's going to reveal secrets they don't want getting out."

To us? Or to the general public?

What *would* ordinary people think if they found out that people like me and the men around me exist?

An image of Brooke's crumpled body flashes through my mind. That wasn't our fault—but we've dealt out plenty of violence ourselves.

Somehow I don't think we'd get a cheerful reception from the average human being. Every monster movie I've ever seen, the strange creatures, the mutants, and the freaks are greeted with screams and gunfire, not open arms.

But the woman inside that house knows what we are and cared for us almost like a parent. She had some part in *making* us, I have to assume, whether directly or just instructing others.

And maybe we're about to find out how and why.

Andreas motions toward me, his fingers skimming the air a few inches from my arm without quite touching me. "Riva, can I talk to you for a second?"

He's beckoning me away from Jacob and Dominic. As the other guys give him a curious look, my legs balk instinctively.

Andreas swallows audibly, a trace of queasiness crossing his face. "Please," he adds. "I'll give you plenty of space. I really just want to talk."

It was talking that ruined everything to begin with, but the rawness of his voice tugs at my heart against my will.

If I don't like what he has to say, it's not as if I can't march right back to the others without finishing hearing him out.

"Fine."

He leads me back through the brush in the opposite direction from the house until the others are just fragments of color between the trees. Then he stops, keeping a good five feet of distance between us as promised, and turns to face me.

Andreas has always been the most fun-loving one of us, the quickest to toss out a joke or latch on to an opportunity for amusement. But there isn't the slightest trace of humor in his expression now.

His gray eyes are shadowed, his lips pressed in a tight line. His normally rich brown skin looks tarnished even in the bright daylight, as if the base color has been leeched out of it.

In spite of everything, seeing him like this makes me want to grab him in a hug. My arms itch with the urge, but I hold them rigidly at my sides.

"I'm sorry," he says abruptly in a low voice. "I know I said that before, and I know it's not enough—I just don't know what else to do, and we're about to walk into that house, and I don't know what's going to happen."

He stops to drag in a shaky breath, and I just stand there silent, my stomach twisting itself into knots. How can I ache so much with both the agony this man inflicted on me and the pain I can hear twined all through his voice?

Andreas holds my gaze with a glint of determination lighting in his eyes. His hand twitches as if he wants to reach for me but held himself back.

I can taste his nervousness. He thinks that what I do here, what I say, could hurt him.

"I shouldn't have believed the guardians' story or that stupid video," he goes on. "I should have realized you were telling the truth from the first moment you came back to us."

My jaw clenches. "Yes, you should have."

His head droops slightly, but he doesn't break eye contact. "I was wrong and an idiot, and I'm going to do whatever it takes to make up for that, however long it takes. But I need you to know—that night in the farmhouse, I'd been trying to convince Jake that we could trust you beforehand. I *knew* you were on our side. I wanted to understand everything you'd been through, and I was hoping if I had more of the story I could make him see what I already had."

"You still…" I grope for the words through the constricting of my chest. "You nudged me in the direction you wanted. You manipulated the conversation. You told me those stories, talked like you thought *you* were failing the other guys—"

"That was all true," Andreas breaks in with a rough laugh. "Hell, I have been failing. They all fell to pieces, and I'm the only one who wasn't really shattered, and I still couldn't figure out a way to put them back together, not properly. And now I've failed you too."

"*I* can't fix that."

"I know." He drops his gaze for just a second before catching mine again. "But I meant everything I said that night. Every single thing. I love you, and I've loved you for as long as I had any idea what the word even meant. It's a fucking *honor* to be connected to you however I am."

His hand rises to his chest, to the spot where I know his skin is marked beneath his shirt. "I fucked it up, I broke the most precious thing I've ever been given, and no matter what happens, no matter what those assholes come at us with next, I'm going to be fighting to my last breath to make it right again. I just hope my last breath doesn't come in the next hour or two."

His words have sent wave after wave of churning emotion through me. The last sentence jars me out of the haze. "You think it's that dangerous, going in there?"

Andreas grimaces. "I don't know. But this is big, and

we don't have anything close to the full picture… I can't shake the feeling that we might be walking into something we can't come out of, one way or another. And I didn't want to take the chance of that being true without telling you how much you mean to me."

He touches his chest again, over his heart this time. "We are blood."

My fingers curl toward my palm of their own accord, wanting to rise to the same spot on my own chest.

"We are blood," I murmur. "I don't—I don't know how the rest will go. But I want to find out exactly what that means. And then… whatever else we do, whatever else happens, it'll begin there."

"Yeah."

Andreas searches my face for a moment, but if he was hoping for more absolution from me, I can't give it to him. Dominic did an amazing job mending the torn-up pieces of my body, but my feelings are still jagged shards scraping against each other from the base of my throat all the way down to my gut.

Drey doesn't push for the answers he wants this time. He simply dips his head and turns slowly to give me time to recognize that he's returning to the others, so we can walk together.

I keep the same definite distance the whole way back, but maybe some of those broken pieces inside me don't scrape quite as sharply as they did before.

We reach Jacob and Dom just as Zian does from the other direction.

"I couldn't see anyone else inside," he says quietly. "Engel is there—or at least a woman who looks like how

Drey described her. Sitting in the living room with a mug and a book. The rest of the place is empty."

We all exchange a glance. I raise my chin and speak before Jacob can give the final command.

"What are we waiting for, then? Let's see what she has to say."

THIRTY-THREE

Riva

Jacob uses his power to unlatch the basement window and nudge it up bit by bit with the softest of rasps. Zian's keen sight spotted an alarm system mounted near the doors on the house, but Engel hasn't protected the windows as well.

One after another, we slip into the dark space. The tang of pine sap hangs in the air, no doubt from the stacks of logs that fill most of the unfurnished room.

The chill follows us in from outside. As soon as Zian has squeezed through, the last of us, Jacob eases the pane shut again.

Who knows if Engel is sensitive enough to notice a strange draft? But then, she's going to know we're here soon enough.

We prowl between the stacks of logs to the narrow staircase that leads to the ground level. There's no door at the top of the stairs, only a rectangle of light that a current of warmth wafts through.

Andreas goes first based on prior agreement. We don't know if he'll be able to get a look at Engel and read her memories surreptitiously, but if he can get the chance to, we want him to take it.

She might be at odds with the facility we escaped, but we have no way of knowing how she'll welcome us.

Zian described the basic layout of the house to us from his observations, and what we emerge into matches what I pictured from his words. The main floor is an open-concept space with the basement doorway at the far end of the expansive kitchen. Dark wooden cabinets and black appliances gleam around us.

A matching kitchen island, several feet across, sections off the kitchen from the dining and living rooms beyond —and hides us from the rest of the building while we stay crouched. We creep across the smooth tiles toward it.

When he reaches the island ahead of the rest of us, Andreas peeks around the side. He cranes his neck for a few seconds and then glances back at us with a frown and a shake of his head.

He can't see Engel to get a lock on her mind from here. We're going to have to rely on our other skills—and her potential willingness to talk.

Jacob makes a gesture of caution, reminding me of the instructions he gave before we entered. *We approach slowly, staying alert, watching in case she has a weapon. I'll be ready to disarm her if I need to.*

We shouldn't go in too strong, Dominic put in back

then. *She might not be a real enemy. We have to give her the chance to let this be a peaceful conversation.*

Jacob made a face but nodded. That's what we're all hoping for—no more fighting, just answers.

Is it crazy for us to even hope?

I can't see Engel either, but the whisper of a turned page reaches my ears. The clink of her mug set down on a side table.

The sounds give me an impression of her in my mind's eye, off to the left side of the room where the ceiling looms highest. The second floor only fills half of the space, over the kitchen and dining room. Dark beams crisscross the far wall of the living room around towering windows, stretching so high I can see them even crouched behind the island.

This isn't how accepted guests are supposed to enter, but we can't risk slipping back out and simply knocking on the door, not knowing how she'll react. Instead, we rise cautiously to our feet.

The woman who's only been a name to me before now flinches in her armchair beneath the tall windows. Her book falls from her hand to thump on the floor.

My eyes skim over her, absorbing my first real view of the woman I've wondered about so much.

Her hair, a mix of fawn-brown and gray, curls lightly where it's tucked behind her ears. Her oval-paned, wire-rimmed glasses slide down her nose with a flinch, revealing pale eyes with crinkles of age at the corners. A cozy sweater and faded jeans clothe her softly rounded frame.

I can't help thinking she looks almost motherly, even in her startled state. Like the moms I've seen on TV screens, sending their grown kids off to college or comforting them through breakups.

It isn't hard at all to imagine her offering a warm hug or reassuring words—I mean, if she wasn't staring at us like we've nearly given her a heart attack.

Andreas has raised his hands in a gesture of surrender. "I'm sorry for sneaking up on you like this. We were hoping to speak with you—we don't mean any harm."

As long as she doesn't try to harm us, he means.

The rest of us stay perfectly still, watching. Engel nudges her glasses up her nose to study us through them. Then her hand swipes downward in an odd motion I don't totally understand.

It looks almost like she's reaching for her mug, but instead her fingers dip between the arm of the chair and the side table. Just a brief skim before she's folding her hands in her lap.

Jacob tensed beside me for a second, but once both her hands are in view and empty, he relaxes again, just a smidge.

"Do you know who we are?" he asks, managing to sound more curious than hostile, although I don't think he's capable of completely erasing the demanding note from his voice.

A hint of a smile curves the woman's lips, enough to send hope flitting through my chest.

"My shadowblood children, all grown up," she says in a crisp but gentle voice. "I haven't seen pictures in years, but you haven't changed that much since the last time."

That voice. The faintest of recollections, not even really a memory it's so vague, wisps through my head like the hazy impressions I got in the playroom at the old facility.

I've heard that voice lilting in a lullaby before—I'm sure of it.

Now that I can see the living room properly, it occurs to me that it looks an awful lot like that playroom. Log walls, suede seating, a fireplace where flames are crackling away over pine logs.

An image so familiar yet distant it sends a pang of homesickness through my chest.

If we ever had a real home, it was something like this.

As I take that in, Engel's brow knits. "It's only the five of you?"

She doesn't know about Griffin. The realization jabs me in the gut like he's dying all over again.

I swallow thickly, but Dominic speaks before I can. "He's gone. Four years ago—we tried to get out, but it didn't work."

"Ah." Engel appears to hold her emotions close, but a flicker of sadness crosses her face. "I heard about the attempt but not the entire outcome. My condolences."

She leans forward slowly, and it occurs to me that she must feel just as wary of us as we are of her. She doesn't know how much we know or what we think of her.

Picking up her mug, she gets to her feet. "I can be a proper host, even if the visit was unexpected. Before we get into the talking, how would you like some hot chocolate?"

A whisper of a memory passes through my head of buying a cup once while on an outside mission. I remember the sting of burning my tongue better than the actual flavor.

But the fact that she's offering at all sends a quiver of elation through my chest. "That would be nice," I say automatically.

Jacob casts a wary glance around at the rest of us, and I know what he's thinking. As friendly as she's being, we need to watch her—and probably we shouldn't actually consume anything she gives us even if it looks safe.

Still, I can't help relishing the idea of simply holding a mug radiating heat and breathing in the sweet steam rising off it.

As Engel approaches the kitchen, the five of us move like one being, both giving her space and keeping our own out of our honed sense of self-protection. We cluster to the right of the island as she passes by on the left and then gather around its far side, leaving it between her and us like a barricade.

I get the sense that she wouldn't mind us sinking onto the cozy seats in the living room, but none of us is ready to relax anywhere near that much.

Engel moves through the kitchen with soothing ease, pulling out a pot and setting it on the stove, grabbing a measuring cup and a box of cocoa powder from the cupboards. As she gets a carton of milk out of the fridge, she shoots a soft smile our way.

"It's impressive that you found your way here. But then you were always quick studies, the bunch of you."

I can't keep quiet any longer. "You had something to do with— You started the first facility. You were there from when we were born."

She picks up on the question I'm asking before I've figured out exactly how to ask it. "I arranged for you to be born."

"We're not just people," Zian says abruptly. "We have…" He raises his hand, extending his wolfish claws as he does. "We can do things no one else can."

"Yes. You are very special, my shadowbloods."

Something about Engel's tone itches at me, but my mind latches onto that last word—one she used before. "What does 'shadowblood' mean? What *are* we?"

"That's why we're here," Jacob adds, setting his hands on the edge of the island. "We want to understand what was going on at the facility, how we turned out like this."

Dominic speaks up, his voice quiet but steady. "And why."

"I see." Engel pours the milk from the measuring cup into the pot. "I suppose we have time to get into that story."

We all lean a little closer in anticipation. A crimson sheen glimmers in Andreas's eyes. He's searching her memories even as he listens alongside us.

Engel's lips purse, her expression momentarily tightening as she adds more milk to the pot. Then she turns to face us while she unscrews the lid on the cocoa powder.

"You know that you don't bleed exactly the way a regular human does."

I touch my arm where I scratched open my skin so many times. "There's smoky stuff that comes out too."

She inclines her head. "Like shadows. That's why I've always thought of you as 'shadowbloods' in my mind."

As she spoons some of the dark brown powder into the pot, my pulse skips a beat. "Our tattoos." A moon for night—for shadows? And a droplet... of blood?

"Yes, that was the inspiration for the design, although it wasn't my idea to imprint it on you." Her mouth tightens again. "But as for what and why... Many years ago, when I was younger than you, I found out that there are creatures that enter this world that are pure shadow. They don't bleed red at all, only that dark haze."

"Creatures?" Zian prods.

Engel swirls a whisk in the pot with a faint clinking as it taps the sides. "All the things from fairytales and folklore, all the monsters and myths we'd have liked to believe were only made up. They sneak into our world and blend in among us as well as they can, using us, preying on us..." She sucks in a sharp breath. "And barely anyone knows."

Uneasiness prickles over my skin. Monsters and myths... with powers like ours?

"But some people do know," Jacob says. "*You* know."

"Yes. And those who know push back as well as we can. My sister and I joined a group of those aware, under the name the Company of Light. Light to combat the shadows. We thought it was very clever."

Engel's expression darkens. "After some time, it became clear to me that we couldn't do enough. Even if everyone in the world knew, it might not be enough to protect humanity when the fiends we were up against had so much strength and were so difficult to destroy."

"So you made us," Andreas says with a distant quality

to his voice. My head jerks toward him, but his gaze is distant too, still with the reddish glow over his irises.

He must be talking about something he's seen in her memories.

He inhales sharply and goes on. "You thought *we* could fight them if you made us strong enough."

If it bothers Engel that Andreas has picked that information up from her mind, she doesn't show her discomfort. "Some members of the Company had been capturing the shadow creatures and running tests on them, experimenting with the essence they're constructed of, toward a goal I suspected was untenable. But I saw the possibility for taking some of what made the fiends such formidable foes and enhancing humans with it."

Jacob's mouth twists. "So, we have some of that monstrousness—that essence—mixed up in us?"

"Yes. I wanted to create humans who could match our enemies while standing alongside us." A trace of wryness colors Engel's tone. "Unfortunately that required starting from scratch at infancy, but this war has always been a long game."

A lot of things suddenly make so much more sense than they did before. "That's why we've had all that training," I burst out. "Keeping us physically strong, making sure we could fight, practicing our powers." I'm not sure what the missions were for—maybe the little tasks they sent us on worked against these shadow creatures in some way we didn't realize?

Did the guardians justify the more torturous parts of the training thinking they were preparing us to face something even worse?

Andreas frowns. "But why did the other guardians make you leave? It was your project—you set everything up... You haven't seen us since we were around ten, it looks like?"

"And we haven't seen you at all since... since as long as we can remember," Dominic adds.

Engel whisks the heating chocolate mixture some more, trickles of steam starting to rise from the pot. "Yes. Over time and with changing circumstances, I came to have different ideas about how the project should proceed than most of my colleagues did. About what our specific goals should be, about how you should be treated."

A slight edge creeps into her voice. She wasn't happy about how they treated us.

"But if you were the one who started everything, couldn't you decide for the others?" Zian says.

Engel sighs. "I didn't have all the power—I'd needed to seek funding and guidance. I was overridden, limited in my involvement and then pushed out completely, other than when they feel the need to consult me."

The bitterness in her tone sends another quiver of uneasiness through me, but I can't explain why. It sounds as if they treated her badly—why shouldn't she be upset?

The question tumbles out of my mouth. "What did you want to happen to us?"

Did she see how cruelly the others were treating us and want to set us free? Is that why she's seemed so calm about us showing up like this?

Her smile returns, appearing to confirm my guess. "I'll be able to show you. Now that you're here, I can see my intentions through."

"Is there a way to take *out* the shadow parts of us?" Dominic asks abruptly. "If we don't—if we'd rather not—"

The shoulder area of his parka shivers where his tentacles must have twitched underneath.

"I'm afraid not," Engel says, "or I'd happily do that for you. But the shadow essence is entwined with your genetic code. It would be like attempting to carve the musical talent out of a violin prodigy or the coordination out of a natural athlete."

Dominic's face falls, and Zian's expression tenses too. My gut clenches.

If there's no way to remove the thing that's been growing inside me, trying to take me over…

Jacob crosses his arms over his chest. "What do we do now? How do you see things going from here? The guardians will probably figure out we came up this way soon, and—"

Engel pauses in her stirring and cuts off his concerned statement with a dismissive wave of her hand. "You don't need to worry about *them*. When they mentioned you were roaming around, I told them I doubted you'd have any interest in me, that they shouldn't waste their resources up here. The nearest reinforcements are hours away. I knew they'd only want to recapture you."

Her comments should be reassuring, but my apprehension rises more. She hasn't actually answered the question, has she? Despite the fact that both Jacob and I have asked.

As she clicks off the burner on the stove, I take a step toward her, scanning her posture, trying to figure out what my subconscious is picking up on. "What do *you* want?"

"Give me a little more time to gather my thoughts, and we can get into that."

Engel gives me another smile, but the scent that catches in my nose at the same time makes me freeze in my tracks.

She *sounds* calm, and she's acting as if she's glad we're here, but she's giving off an unmistakable tang of stress. If she isn't worried about the guardians crashing in on us, and she isn't worried about us hurting her, then what could be wrong?

I drag in a deeper breath, and recognition sets off a spike of alarm through my nerves.

It isn't the same kind of stress I tasted from the guardians we've interrogated, sharply metallic with fear. It's closer to the pungent anticipation I breathed in so many times in the fighting arena, from opponents both worried about my reputation—and determined to crush me.

Like she sees us as enemy combatants, ones she stands a real chance against.

But she isn't fighting us—she *wouldn't* stand a chance if she tried—

Full understanding clicks in my head. She's stalling. Because she's waiting for something else.

Before my thoughts have quite caught up with me, I'm spinning around. I dart across the living room to the chair where she was sitting when we first came in.

My fingers dip between the chair arm and the table where hers did in that brief, odd gesture I couldn't make sense of and then forgot—and catch on the edge of a button hidden beneath the lip of the table.

Engel's posture stiffens. I whirl around toward the guys.

"There's a control here—it's got to activate some kind of alarm system. She's signaled for someone to come."

All of the guys immediately jerk into defensive stances. Jacob's gaze turns searingly cold.

"Who did you—"

Before he can even finish spitting out the question, a swarm of dark-clothed figures swing into view from above and smash straight through the high windows in a shower of shattered glass.

Thirty-Four

Riva

As I fling myself away from the windows, glass shards slice at my hoodie, one scraping across my jaw. Heavy feet thud onto the ground inside Engel's house with enough force that the floorboards tremble.

With the ear-splitting booming of the first shots, a broad hand snags around my arm and yanks me farther away from the intruders with supernatural strength. Zian and I tumble toward the kitchen island, propelled by his backward lunge.

He was standing ten feet away when the attackers burst in. He leapt *toward* them rather than away just to pull me to safety.

A bullet whizzes across my upper arm, clipping me and searing through my skin. As I bite back a yelp of pain, Zian grunts, flinching where he's still gripping me. My heart stutters with panic.

"Here!" Jacob's voice rings out, taut and furious. Scraping, creaking sounds surround me, mingling with the thunderous rattle of the gunfire.

I roll onto my feet and spin around, flicking my gaze over the chaos that now surrounds us.

The other guys dove down by the island too. Jacob's turned this spot in the middle of the house into a sort of triangular fort, with the sofa and the overturned dining room table yanked close by his powers to form the other two sides.

The reason we haven't leapt *behind* the island is obvious from the cacophony of sound battering my ears. Some of the shots are blaring from the kitchen. Others from the front of the house, opposite the living room.

Our attackers entered from all sides—front, back, and up from the basement. We're surrounded.

And those are actual bullets, not any kind of tranquilizer. Blood is soaking through my hoodie from the shallow gouge in my arm, and Zian—

Zian's right shoulder has completely sagged, a splotch of red blooming fast around a bullet wound right where his shoulder meets his chest. I can't tell whether the bullet is still lodged inside or tore straight through, but if it'd been even a few inches farther to the right…

He almost died, pulling me to safety.

The figures shooting at us almost *killed* him.

Something Engel said echoes up from the back of my mind with chilling clarity. The disdain in her voice when she talked about the guardians. *I knew they'd only want to recapture you.*

In the moment, I'd thought she'd meant as opposed to

letting us keep our freedom. The sickly certainty coiling in my stomach tells me it was just the opposite.

She didn't want us to even survive.

The prickling vibration resonates through my chest. I clench my jaw against it and force myself to focus on the battle.

The initial barrage of gunfire has dwindled for just an instant. One benefit to being surrounded is that our attackers can't pelt us with bullets wildly without significant risk of hitting their colleagues.

Of course, the benefit only lasts as long as they can't get close enough to shoot us like fish in a barrel.

My claws jolt from my fingers, my nerves buzzing with combat alertness. But there isn't much I can do to fend off the pricks without charging out there on a suicide mission… or letting lose the stirring power inside me that has a mind of its own. A vile, vicious mind I don't want anything to do with.

Near me, Jacob's face has gone tight with concentration, his hands jerking as he throws his telekinetic force through the room around us. Bones crack and pained groans reverberate through the air.

Andreas grimaces. "I can't project memories to distract them from down here where I can't see them. But if I—"

He cuts himself off and vanishes into thin air in the next moment.

All at once, several of the sets of footsteps around us start stumbling. Shouts of confusion echo them.

Andreas has slipped out there among the enemy combatants unseen, muddling their minds.

There are too many of them, though. Bodies thump

closer to our makeshift shelter, and Dominic bobs higher, his tan face turned greenish. Having shed his parka, he lets his tentacles whip free to smack away the gunmen attempting to get at us.

Another figure charges up to the overturned table. I spring at him before he can get in his shot and slice my claws right through his forearm.

Blood spurts and tendons sever, but the man still slams his other fist toward me.

Zian roars. The massive guy pummels my attacker in the face hard enough to bash in his skull and wrenches the rifle from his grasp in the same moment.

I spin toward my protector, my pulse stuttering at the thought of the wound he's already taken. More blood is leaking out through his shirt, but he shoves me out of the way while scanning the room beyond the table warily.

In his protective rage, his wolfish fur has sprouted from his skin all across his neck and arms. His jaw has extended with the beastly folds of flesh, widened nose, and protruding fangs.

But his dark brown eyes are still Zian's even as they flash with fury. Only a brief shudder through his massive frame reveals the pain he's in.

Even shot, he's right here with me, looking out for me like we always promised to do.

All of the guys are. We fend off the attackers in a weird sort of dance, Zian and I hurtling up to tackle anyone who gets too close, the other guys keeping most at a distance.

As I slash through the calf of a gunman who's jumped onto the island, Dominic heaves out his tentacles to bat away a second foe I hadn't seen launching herself at us.

There's a clatter and a splash as the woman must stagger into the pot of hot chocolate.

When another enemy shoves the muzzle of his rifle through a gap between the table and the sofa, I shatter his jaw with a kick moments before Jacob hurls him away.

And all the while the yells and mutters of confusion tell me that Andreas is working his powers, keeping our attackers unsteady. One of the fighters manages to snatch my arm in mid-swipe, and Drey appears for just an instant behind him, jabbing a knife between his ribs.

Even if the bonds of friendship—and whatever more we could have had—have fractured between us, we're still a team. Right now, in the midst of the fray, not one particle in my body doubts that I could trust each of these men with my life.

And I'll be here for them too, whatever it takes. We are not letting these assholes take any of us down.

If the battle weren't so fraught, maybe I'd take comfort in the thought. But just as I start to think we might be able to withstand the onslaught, they throw a new tactic in to the mix.

One of our attackers hurls an object over our barricade. I yelp out a warning.

Jacob whirls in time to heave it away before it hits the floor—but as it soars away, it explodes in mid-air.

We all fling ourselves to the floor instinctively under the hail of shrapnel. Jacob's body spasms where he's fallen next to me.

I jerk myself onto my hands and knees to see him clapping his hand to his temple. Blood streams out from under his fingers. His eyes twitch as if he can't quite focus them.

"Dominic!" I cry out. I don't give a shit about what a jerk this guy has been to me when he's fading before my eyes.

Dominic stretches a tentacle to encircle Jacob's head, but his gaze darts around us with a panicked expression. There's nothing here for him to grab onto to suck in the life energy he must need to heal a serious wound.

If he took it out of himself, would *he* be the one crumpling?

Andreas must have seen and recognized the problem, because the next second he's flitting into view near the table and flipping one of our attackers right over it, headfirst. Dominic's other tentacle lashes around the intruder's neck, tight enough to strangle, but another of our enemies shoots at Andreas in his momentary visibility.

Andreas flickers translucent and throws himself to the side, not quite quickly enough. His torso lurches with the impact as the bullet catches him in the back.

He staggers toward us with a choked gasp, snapping back into completely solid form. Zian and I lunge together to haul him into our shelter.

He collapses there, wincing as he struggles to push himself more upright. "I can't—I need to—"

Blood is pooling beneath him. Jacob is still bleeding too, as quickly as Dom is trying to stabilize him. Footsteps close in around us again.

Panic chokes me. And the vibration within me that I've been suppressing thrums up through my lungs too forcefully for me to ignore.

I can stop them. I can shred them apart and make them wish they'd never tangled with us.

My claws dig into the floorboards with the wrenching longing to do just that.

I open my mouth, and my gaze snags on the faces around me. Dominic's, tight with urgency and strain. Jacob's, fighting the slackness that's creeping over his muscles. Andreas's, his eyes glazing with pain. Zian's, his anguish showing even across his wolfish jowls.

In that instant, I can feel that I'll be able to shield them from the vicious rage. I'm not angry with them, not right now. I can aim this brutal energy beyond the boundaries of our little barricade, away from those within.

But that's not the only problem.

The growing shriek at the base of my throat makes me feel sick even as the urge clamors through my nerves to set it free.

What will the guys think of me after they see it? Once they know what I'm capable of doing—what I'm willing to do?

What some part of me will revel in?

They only just started believing that I'm the girl they always knew, and I can shatter that illusion with a single scream. Make them think they were right to distrust and shun me before.

I *am* that girl. I never asked for this power. It isn't *me*.

The wrongness of this whole situation sweeps over my body, and it's a question rather than a scream that bursts from my throat, aimed at the woman I have to assume is still somewhere in this house with us and the soldiers she summoned.

"Why? Why are you doing this? You *made* us."

Is there anything that could change her mind, make her call off the slaughter?

Ursula Engel's voice carries from somewhere behind me, crisp as before and somehow steady in spite of the battle that's being raged around her.

"I'm sorry. I didn't plan for it to end up this way when I started. But I did make you, so it's my responsibility to unmake you when no one else is willing to take that step."

"But—"

Her tone is so cool and dispassionate it lances straight through me. "I've been arguing for this since you were toddlers, when the Company of Light was destroyed by a hybrid not that different from you. I demanded it again and again when I saw how quickly your abilities were evolving and expanding, when my colleagues started pushing for you to be sent beyond the protection of the facility. But no one would listen to my warnings, and they shut me out."

"You're insane," Dom shouts at her in a ragged voice. "We're not—"

Engel cuts him off. "You're monsters of the worst kind. Abominations growing out of control, without even the few weaknesses that make the other creatures vulnerable and not enough humanity to rein your impulses in. That's not what I meant to create. So I've gathered my own guardians to my purpose, and now I can end the catastrophe I set in motion."

She must give some signal, because the booted feet thump toward our shelter again. My stomach lurches, but I know then that this is the end.

I have no other choice. I can kill the girl I wanted to be, for myself and for the guys around me, or I can watch us all die.

It isn't even really a choice.

As my lips part, it occurs to me that Engel doesn't even know. She's so confident her soldiers will be enough.

She screwed herself over by going rogue. The regular guardians haven't been filling her in on all the details. She didn't know Griffin had died; she probably wasn't aware of some of the guys' newer powers.

And she clearly has no idea about the destruction I wreaked in a cage-fighting arena two weeks ago, whether I meant to or not.

Not a single person in this building is prepared... including me.

Andreas gasps a ragged breath, and our attackers throw something that hits the dining table with a smack. The wooden surface blasts apart in a shower of splinters.

And the last of the control I was holding onto snaps.

The shriek that's been swelling in my chest claws up my throat and sears from my mouth. It screeches out of me so loud my ears ring with it.

My vision hazes. My body sways where I'm braced against the floor, the power of the scream threatening to consume my entire consciousness as it careens through the room.

I dig my claws deeper into the boards beneath me, holding on, refusing to be as overwhelmed as I was last time when it took me by surprise, when I had some toxic drug dragging me down.

If this is me, then I have to own it. I have to be awake

enough to make sure I only hurt the people who're trying to hurt us, not the men who are my blood.

Whether those men still want any kind of bond with me after this moment or not.

The piercing wail keeps pealing from my lungs and ricocheting through the room, and a sense of the figures around me ripples back into my body like some kind of echolocation. I've pinned them in place, six men still standing in the front area beyond the dining table, eight in the living room who'd been approaching the sofa, three in the kitchen behind me.

And Engel. I can feel her too: a slightly different, more familiar quiver that runs through the lancing energy I'm throwing at them.

She's tucked away at the top of the basement stairs where she must have been watching from, as paralyzed as the others.

"Riva?" I hear one of my men murmur, so distant through the scream that I can't even tell who it is.

I ignore him, plummeting deeper into the current of the scream as it radiates through every cell inside me. Hunger courses with the vicious energy, prickling all the way down to my gut.

My awareness of my captives sharpens with the heightening of the shriek. I can follow the thumping of their pulses, the trembling of their straining muscles.

All the nooks and crannies where the pieces of their bodies fit together. All the soft and tender spots filled with fragile nerve endings.

My attention homes in on the closest man. His feet.

I snap the balls up toward his shin so fast I turn the arches inside out.

The crack of the bones sets off his guttural cry, and the blaze of pain flows back into my lungs. But it doesn't hurt *me*.

No, it's like drinking the freshest lemonade on the hottest day, a balm to every place inside me that's been craving relief.

I need more. More.

They have to pay.

I close my eyes, lost in the ringing in my ears, the screech of my own voice, and the bodily reactions reverberating into me. Every sensitive spot on our attackers lights up in the picture painted by my new senses.

Crush his knee caps. Burst his balls. Crack every bone in his spine from the tailbone up—but careful not to sever the cord.

Let him feel every tremor and stab of agony I'm inflicting on him. I can only gulp it down if he tastes it too.

Pop his elbows inside out. Mash every finger from tip to knuckle. Break his ribs and shove the shards down into his kidneys.

The stream of anguish widens into a torrent. It floods me, shockingly exhilarating.

Somewhere way deep down in the back of my mind, there's a flash of horror, but not enough to distract me.

The current halts as the man blacks out, his mind short-circuiting. Nothing more to gain from him. I wrench his head around to end him completely, my awareness already leaping to the next.

One and then another and another. Faster with each iteration as I gain momentum.

Tendons rent, sinews torn, bones fractured. Organs punctured, joints unhinged.

The glorious flood of agony tingles over every inch of my skin. I'm vaguely conscious of the wound on my shoulder sealing up, the flesh smoothing out like it was never split.

The last lingering tears that even Dominic couldn't totally heal inside me meld together good as new.

I'm stronger—so strong. Stronger than I ever imagined I could be. Stronger than anyone else could have guessed.

More foes fall like dominos, and the surge of giddy elation propels me to my feet. My scream still resounds through the building.

With every thump of my pulse and heave of my lungs, I obliterate another life.

Until there's only one left, other than the four clustered around me.

One woman huddles at the far end of the kitchen, trembling with both rage and terror. Spittle flecks her lips as she tries to force out words.

I don't want to know what the experimenter who made us has to say about me now. If I'm a monster, then I learned it from her.

She made us, she raised us, and then she set us up to be slaughtered. How *dare* she expect any better in return.

My shriek hitches even higher. Bones burst into

cutting shards from Engel's toes across her feet, through her ankles and knees up her legs.

They carve waves of pain out of her to feed the fire burning inside me. It's so fucking bright now.

I could take on the whole facility. I could raze an entire fucking town.

But her torment is most satisfying of all. The closest thing we ever had to a mother—the attempted murderer of her own children.

Her spine bows back. Her ribs split from her chest.

Every horrible thing she thought about us, every vicious plan she had for our demise will disintegrate with the agony ravaging her mind.

Then I wrench her heart in two, and she collapses into a puddle of blood and urine.

The scream whips around for a new target, and I suck it in with a gasp.

No. No fucking way. We're done now.
We did what we needed to do.

The hunger clamors for more, but I tense my entire body, hauling it back. I will not let this horror take me over, not completely.

The sound peters out. My jaw swings shut.

And I find myself standing, my muscles quivering with restrained power and the flavor of blood coating my mouth, in the middle of a tableau of carnage.

Contorted bodies lie sprawled all around our shelter. The sight of them sends a jab of shame and a splash of revulsion over me, but the high of the moment is still humming through my veins.

The guys are standing too, staring at the massacre:

Jacob gripping the edge of the island, Zian's shoulders held at a lopsided angle but looking full human again, Andreas with his arm looped around Dominic's shoulder while one tentacle mends his wounded body. The guardian slumped at their feet lies still and lifeless, but nowhere near as grotesque as the deaths I wrought.

Their gazes slide from the deformed corpses to me, and the bottom of my stomach drops out.

I rescued us all. I seized our freedom.

And deep down inside, I loved every second of the butchery I carried out.

Now I get to find out whether I've lost everything after all.

What made Jacob realize he was wrong about Riva and decide to race to her rescue? Find out in a bonus scene from his POV by going to this URL or using the QR code below: https://BookHip.com/BMRWARH

About the Author

Eva Chase lives in Canada with her family. She loves stories both swoony and supernatural, and strong women and the men who appreciate them. Along with the Shadowblood Souls series, she is the author of the Heart of a Monster series, the Gang of Ghouls series, the Bound to the Fae series, the Flirting with Monsters series, the Cursed Studies trilogy, the Royals of Villain Academy series, the Moriarty's Men series, the Looking Glass Curse trilogy, the Their Dark Valkyrie series, the Witch's Consorts series, the Dragon Shifter's Mates series, the Demons of Fame series, and the Legends Reborn trilogy.

Connect with Eva online:
www.evachase.com
eva@evachase.com

Printed in Great Britain
by Amazon